Members Only

Published in the United States of America.

This is a work of fiction. Names, characters, places, and incidents either are the products of the author's imagination or are used fictitiously. Any resemblance of actual persons, living or dead, businesses, companies, events, or locales is entirely coincidental. The publisher does not have any control and does not assume any responsibility for author or third-party websites or their content.

Members Only

By: MZ. Demeanor & A Dysfunctional Mind

Chapter 1

Audrey Harris-Reynolds

Radiance Film Festival

My hands began to sweat profusely as I looked out into the crowd. I cleared my throat as my husband, Earnest, rubbed the back of my left hand for support. In my right hand was a suitcase that I clenched tightly. Even Earnest didn't know what was inside. Leaning down and placing a warm kiss on my cheek, he whispered softly in my ear, "Babe, you got this. Stop worrying. I can feel all of that nervous energy."

I couldn't help but grin from ear-to-ear as his cocoa brown eyes locked into mine. Even with the grey from his hairline slowly making its way down the lengths of his locks, and the patchy beard that he could never get just right, I still was mesmerized by Earnest Harris. Had it not been for him, I don't know that I would've even been able to go through with this ceremony. He kissed my cheek gently before turning his attention back to the stage. At 45 years old, I had just finished my most important documentary. It was grueling, emotional, crazy, but most of all...poignant. I had gotten to understand my father in a way that I never imagined possible.

"Now, if you will all join me in welcoming to the stage the daughter of Drexler Davis, the lovely Mrs. Audrey Harris," the host announced through the mic, getting the audience up on their feet.

I didn't think my feet would work as the mass of people stood to their feet, giving me a standing ovation. I sat there glued in my seat until Earnest stood up, taking my hand. My king winked his eye in that familiar way that he did whenever he was proud of me. It was the same kind of wink that daddy used to give my mother, Audra.

"You'll be just fine, baby," my husband whispered before his lips grazed my cheek with a kiss.

Earnest then led me to the stage of the United Center where I carefully gathered my mermaid gown before taking the stairs. My presenter was gracious enough to meet me at the top. Blair Underwood had never looked sexier in his life than he did tonight in his gold blazer and black slacks. I nearly swooned as he took my arm, leading me up to the podium. Cameras flashed as we walked across the stage, and I silently hoped that my husband was going live on Facebook; I needed everybody to remember this moment with me.

"Knock em' dead, my dear," Blair whispered as he reached onto the podium, handing me the crystal trophy shaped like a sunburst.

He kissed my cheek before stepping into the shadows. I rubbed it trying my best to keep from blushing which caused everyone to laugh as they took their seats.

"Y'all got to forgive me," I spoke into the microphone. "That man has been on my wish list since *L.A. Law*." I lightly chuckled.

Another wave of laughter and applause filled the arena. I think I heard a woman shout out, "I love you, Blair," as I set my suitcase on the ground next to me.

"I want to thank God first and foremost. He gave me two of the best parents that life had to offer. They were not perfect, but they were mine. They were kind, sweet, loving, and they belonged to me and me alone. I didn't have to share them with siblings, although I shared them with the world." A tear slid from my eye as I paused to catch my composure. Being the gentleman that he was, Blair stepped up, offering me his pocket square which I graciously accepted. I whispered a quick *thank you* before going on.

"When I decided to embark upon this project, I didn't know what to expect. Can you imagine dealing with five cantankerous old men with various health problems? They wore me out y'all." I glanced over at Earnest who was laughing the hardest because he knew what I was talking about.

"I took a month of my life away from my husband to do this which is why I graciously thank him. That is the longest we have ever been apart. Earnest, honey, I love you, and I thank you for your sacrifice. You slept in an empty bed, cooked your own food, and managed to keep our house from burning down. Yet, you did not complain. That means the world to me that you would be so free-hearted to allow me to follow my dreams."

The cameras panned into the audience, catching my husband as he dabbed at his light brown eyes. He looked like a handsome lion with his dreads pulled back into a French braid. He blew me a kiss as I shook away the rest of my nervousness. Looking down at the speech before me, I gathered my nerves and continued.

"Anyway, I was not really expecting any accolades. All I wanted to do was what I was asked. These men entrusted me to tell their stories, and it was not always an easy thing to do. I had to learn things about my father and uncles that was unsettling. Some were things that no child ever wants to hear about their parents. Nevertheless, I pushed on.

What you saw in the theatres was brutally honest and often required breaks for us to cry or take care of medical issues. Nothing was scripted. This was the last testament of each person that made up the group, *Members Only*. For those that will be screening it here for the first time, I hope that you all have tissues because you will need them. Thank you for choosing me to take home the innovative film award. It is my first award and hopefully not my last. Please stick around for the Q and A session after the screening because that's when I will reveal the contents of this here briefcase." I tapped it with my foot. "Other than that, God bless and thank you again."

As I spun on my heels to go backstage, Blair bent down grabbing my suitcase. It wasn't until I was out of view of the audience that I finally was able to exhale.

"You did a wonderful job. I grew up listening to their music," Blair complimented.

I looked up at the stage light above me. "You hear that daddy? I did a good job."

Chapter 2

Harmony Healthcare

Benny 'Velvet Rose' Pryor

Cough! Cough!

"Mr. Pryor, let me get you some water."

Cough! "Jumpstart, hurry yo' ass up." *Cough!* "I'mma bout to pass out and shit," I coughed into my fist, waiting for my baby momma to stop playing and give me something to drink before I puked up a lung.

"Mr. Pryor, I'm not Jumpstart. I'm your nurse, Mandala," she said, wearing a sweet smile.

Cough! "I know who in the fuck you is." *Cough!* "Stop playing all the damn time," I said, snatching the water from her grasp.

"Let me help you," Mandala began, reaching her hand in.

"I said, I don't need yo' damn help." After slapping her hand away, she just glared at me. "While you standing there looking like you done sucked a bad dick," *she gasped* "Where in the hell is Razor and nem? They was supposed to be here an hour ago."

"Mr. Pryor, I don't know who you're talking about," she stated.

"Bitch, I swear you the dumbest ape in captivity. I just talked to you this morning and told you they was coming. What you done did now? Huh?"

"Mr. Pryor-"

"Mr. Pryor me again and I'mma knock yo' teeth down yo' windpipe." She jumped back and grabbed her neck. "Which one you done fucked now, Jumpstart? I know all about you and Dick'Em Down." *Cough! Cough!* "Thought I was a fool, didn't you? You thought I didn't know? Umph! I saw yo' thot ass, ain't that what the kids are calling hoes nowadays?"

She looked at me like I had just slapped her momma and fucked her sister.

"Umm, Benny?" she smiled finally.

"That's more like it. Now, what you want, Jumpstart? I ain't got no money, and I think my dick is outta commission, so I can't do shit for ya'."

She cleared her throat all the while blushing. "I have to go check on the other patients. I'll be back in a couple of hours to check on you." She patted my hand and turned to leave.

"A couple of hours? Where you think you going? You going to hang out with that damn Charlene, ain't ya'?" *Cough!* "You know she one of them thot things."

"I'll be back, Benny," she smiled, pulling the door open and leaving out.

I couldn't wait for that bitch to leave. She thought a nigga was losing his mind, but I'm *Velvet Rose,* baby. I came sliding out the pussy on August 4, 19 and 50 sumthin'. Everything about a nigga was smooth as silk. I had to play the role. It was the only way I could get the bitches to trust a nigga.

"Knock, Knock," a female voice rang out.

I turned my head to the door, and very hoarsely I said, “Come in.”

I didn’t know who was knocking, but I was playing it safe.

“Hey, Uncle Benny,” the voice said. I had to squint my eyes to make sure I ain’t went home to the Lord.

“Audra?” I asked skeptically.

“No, Uncle Benny,” she chuckled. “It’s me, Audrey. Audra was my momma,” she smiled.

I pushed my fist into the bed to sit up some. “Audrey?” I scratched my head.

Something had to be going on for Audrey to show up in Chicago. “Baby, is everything okay?” I didn’t need no bad news while I was sitting up in this hell hole.

She walked across the room, stood at my bedside, and patted my hand reassuringly. “There’s nothing wrong, Uncle Benny.”

“Well, what is it?” I scratched my head in confusion, then it hit me. “Baby, I ain’t got no money,” I voiced.

“I don’t want your money, Uncle Benny,” she responded, shaking her head. “I have a surprise for you.”

“Well, give it here, child, for that ole’ nosey ass Mandala, comes back.” She turned up her nose like my tongue was covered in shit. “Earth to Audrey,” I said, snapping my fingers. “You got something wrong wit’ you?”

She laughed and before she could open her mouth the door pushed open. "Get yo' damn hands off me. I's tied of you cracka-muthafucka's putting y'all hands on me," some nigga yelled, aggravated. "Y'all been putting y'all paws on me since 1962," he fussed.

Stifling her laughter, Mandala pushed Drexler, also known as Dick'Em Down, into the room. "Mr. Davis, will you please calm down?" she asked politely.

"I will after you suck my dick," he said, mad as hell, all the while grabbing her hand and placing it over his crotch.

Audrey gasped, and Mandala damn near pushed him on the floor trying to get her hand back.

"You two," Mandala said pointing between myself and Dick'Em Down.

"I don't know who that nigga is while you pointing fingers, but I do know," he paused, "that you can get this dick whenever you want it," he flirted while licking his lips.

"Daddy, now that's enuff," Audrey fussed, stomping her foot.

Drexler looked at her and smiled.

"Hey Audra." She shook her head at her old man and then turned to Mandala.

Audrey extended her hand, "Hello, I'm Audrey. I'm this ole' fool's daughter," she smiled, shaking Mandala's hand. "Audra was my mother," she explained.

"Nice to meet you," Mandala smiled in return. "Now, if you'll help me. I can get Mr. Davis where he needs to be." Audrey placed her things down on the chair to help the nurse with her father.

After about ten minutes, Mandala walked over to my bedside wiping sweat from her brow. "Well, Mr. Pryor, it looks as if you have a new neighbor," she beamed.

I raised my brow at her, "Did I ask for some company, Jumpstart?"

She scratched her head and blew out a breath of frustration, "One day you gon' have to tell me about this Jumpstart. She must be a hell of a lady if you keep getting us mixed up." She patted my foot and headed towards the door still laughing.

***

We waited about ten minutes before we both broke out laughing. "You gon' have that young bitch give you the wrong pills and kill yo' old ass."

Drexler sat up and laughed, "She gone get this old dick first."

Audrey shook her head and sat down exhausted. "Y'all ain't gon' never change," she voiced, turning to her father. "You and yo' mouth. You don't care what comes flying out of it."

"I'm old," he said as if that was a reasonable excuse. Dick'Em Down had been this way since we met some 50 years ago. He fanned her off, then turned and looked in my direction.

"When the rest of them fools gone show up?" I asked.

“Shit, I don’t know but while we waiting,” he reached over and pulled a cigar from his nightstand drawer, “let’s smoke something.”

“Is that weed?” Audrey asked, panic-stricken.

“Calm down, baby girl. Just stick to the story,” Dick’Em Down reasoned.

“What story?” she asked, looking from me to her dad.

“We got glaucoma,” he chuckled.

I damn near choked on the weed smoke trying to laugh. “Nigga, you trying to kill me.” *Cough! Cough!* “I ain’t trying to die in this muthafucka.”

He looked around as if there was somebody else in the room besides us before he said, “Pass me that shit, baby girl.” Audrey shook her head and reached for the blunt, passing it to her old man.

“Y’all know y’all gotta tell me why we’re all meeting in Chicago,” Audrey voiced as she observed her father inhaling the weed smoke.

“Wait until the other niggas show up and we got you, baby girl,” he said, hitting the blunt.

Audrey sat back and pulled out her phone, tuning us out.

Chapter 3

En Route to Harmony Healthcare

Ronnie 'Papa' Willow

"If y'all don't hurry up and get me out of here," I fussed. This ride had been taking longer than I wanted it to and this damn ambulance was hitting every bump in the road. "Y'all bout' to piss me off. Took my damn flask."

"Sir, you aren't allowed to drink in the back of an ambulance, it's the law," the female paramedic explained.

"Who said that, Trump's dumb ass?"

She tried her best to stifle her laugh, but she knew I was right. This had to be the longest ride of my life. It made me think about all of the times when we used to be on the road, back in the day. We had to have the raggediest bus in the world. A hard bump in the road lifted me off my bed, causing me to land with a thud. "Where that heffa get her license from?" I complained.

"Sorry. Let me make sure she isn't texting."

As soon as that white girl was out of my face, I slid my hand along the side of the bed, grabbing my flask. They had me fucked up. At 69, nobody was gonna tell me I couldn't have some Jack Daniels. I slid it under my pillow just in time for the white girl to come back in, taking a seat across from me.

"Mr. Ronnie, I don't want to alarm you, but I was told that the reason she's speeding is because there is a burgundy Cadillac fishtailing behind us."

"Damn, damn, damn! That crazy bitch done followed me to my death. A man can't even die in peace."

"Wait, you know who it is?"

"Yeah, I know. It's my crazy-ass wife, Charlene. She part of the reason I'm going to this nursing home to die. The bitch done 'bout worried me half to death," I snickered. "We used to call her ass 'Pop Rocks' when we was on tour because she always was popping up somewhere. Hell, one time she popped out from under the bed while me and the fellas was taking turns with this groupie. That crazy gal tore up that hotel room and everything in it. Cost us almost a thousand dollars in damages."

"That's quite the story," the girl remarked as she brushed a stray hair from her face.

"What your name is, baby?"

"My name is Brooke."

"I used to know a Brooke a long time ago. We should've called her fountain with all that squirting and carryin' on she used to do."

Brooke's face turned a deep crimson as her eyes bulged out of her head in surprise.

"Baby, I apologize. When you get my age, you don't know what's liable to come out ya' mouth."

"That's okay. You have more than earned the right to say what you want to say. It must have been fun being a musician."

"Fun? If you like sex, drugs, big money, and all the traveling you could handle. The shit was paradise." Sitting up in the bed, I scratched the side of my nose as I thought back. There were things I could tell this young girl that would turn her brunette curls into blonde. She looked like she was no older than 21, so I figured it was best to keep it somewhat clean. Nothing about my past was clean though.

"How much longer we got til we get to Chi-Town?"

She glanced down at that fancy contraption on her wrist that had been buzzing every five minutes. It didn't look like any watch I had ever seen. Damn thing looked like a phone strapped to her wrist.

"We have at least two more hours. Are you uncomfortable?"

"Nah, but you might be after I tell you this story. Now, what Mr. Ronnie tells you is between us. You got it?"

"Yes sir," she nodded her head as her blue eyes twinkled in anticipation with what I was about to tickle her ears with. I cleared my throat and took a quick spit in a napkin before I proceeded.

"You got to roll your hips

Then let me do my dip

Tell that man of yours

Ain't no need to trip

See, I wanna love you

Just for a night

Let that fool buy you a ring

I already know you ain't right."

She appeared disappointed as I stopped singing. My falsetto hadn't changed too much over the years despite the lung cancer they claimed I had. Stage four my ass. How you gonna be stage four and still sound like silk?

"That was wonderful, Mr. Ronnie," Brooke said, clapping.

"Thank you. That's as far as I can go with that song though. It was recorded on the worst night of my life."

"What happened?" she asked, clutching her stethoscope.

"That little ditty was called, *I Just Want the Cat.* That was the very first song me and the fellas wrote together. We started out with six members. It was me, Red Rooster, Dick 'Em Down, Po-Man, Razor Mouth Slick, and Velvet Rose. We were some knuckleheads that you couldn't tell nothing to. Well, Red Rooster was sweet on this little high-yella girl. He thought that girl's shit didn't stank."

Brooke was giving me her full attention as I paused to lick my dry lips.

"Do you need some water?"

"I need some oxygen. I can't damn breathe back here."

"How is this?" she asked as she placed the oxygen tube back into my nose.

"That's much better. Now, what was I talking about? Charlene's crazy ass, wasn't it?"

"No sir," Brooke giggled. "You were talking about Rooster."

“Oh yeah, Red Rooster. So anyway, he loved this little yella gal, but we kept telling him she was trouble. Those mulatto girls always were trouble. Well, we had been trying to get a deal. Motown closed the doors in our faces first, talking bout we sounded too much like The Temptations. I could out-sing all of them niggas any day of the week, but I let it go. Rooster had wrote this ole sappy ass ballad for that lil’ girl, talking about how he wanted to marry her. We wanted to write something more upbeat, so me and Po-Man wrote our song. We got invited to a talent show down at this lil spot in Louisville, Kentucky. Our old bus messed up on us and caused us to stay an extra night where we got picked up to do a gig at the Brown Hotel. In those days, your kind didn’t mix with my kind, so the shows were segregated.”

“I’m sorry to hear that,” Brooke interjected, patting my arm.

“That ain’t the sorry part. All of us refused to go on stage, but Red. His girl was out there in the crowd blending in with the white folks. He took it upon himself to sit down at that piano and sing by himself. We were backstage mad as a sissy in a women’s prison. Well anyway, the show was going good. He had all tho se peckerwoods passing out over him. Then he made one fatal error. He dedicated that last song to his girl, Diego. She turned about fifty shades of red as he serenaded her. We didn’t know it at the time, but her daddy was in the audience. Soon as Red exited the stage a big ass man, at least 6’7 snatched him up.”

I could feel myself getting choked up. Brooke must have noticed because she handed me a tissue. I dabbed at my eyes determined not to bawl like a baby in front of this girl.

"Everybody blamed us, but it happened so fast. The man heaved Red over his shoulder, and that was the last time we saw him. We gave chase, but they disappeared into the crowd, leaving the theatre. The next day Ole Red was found in the Ohio River with his left foot in his mouth. Them crackers ain't have to do Red like that."

It was at that point that I lost it. Suddenly, a machine behind me started beeping.

"Mr. Ronnie, you are getting yourself all worked up. I think you need to lay back and rest a while."

"Yeah, I think so too."

Every time I thought about Red Rooster, my heart couldn't take it. As my head hit the pillow, I stared up at the ceiling. Once my maker came and got me, I hoped he would forgive me for not keeping my promise.

Chapter 4

Middle of the Highway

Sharonda & Razor

"Ronda, I ain't got no time for these games. We was supposed to been in Chicago an hour ago. Something told me not to ride wit' you in the first damn place."

"What? You thought I was gone let them young bitches just do whatever?" she smacked her teeth and rolled her eyes. "You been my man for over 40 years and ain't no way in the hell, I'mma let some other woman take care of *my* man. What them young girls say nowadays? Oh yeah-," she snapped her fingers. "You got the game fucked up." She swerved into the middle lane mad about nothing.

"Ronda, we too damn old for this shit. You been on the same bullshit since 1972."

"I was fine back then, caramel skin, deep dimples, hazel eyes, pouty lips, and bowlegs. Now, all I can show for it is a dimpled ass, crow's feet, ashen skin, and a sorry ass nigga. You know back in the day you was a catch. I couldn't wait to see you prance around on that stage and sing until your heart was content. But now, I wish I could throw yo' sorry, catfish head ass back into the ocean." She swerved, yet again.

"Ronda, stop playing and drive like you got some sense. I used to be afraid to die alone, but now, not so much. I can't wait to get away from yo' nagging ass." I pulled the sweater I had on closer to my neck. I don't know why she had the damn air on. It was the last of the winter months in Chicago or wherever in the fuck we was. It was cold as shit, and she had the audacity to turn the air on.

"Why in the fuck you got the air on anyway? It's cold as shit in here."

She sucked her teeth and smacked her lips. "You should be used it. You cold-hearted bastard."

"What's yo' problem? What I do to make you hate me so much, huh?"

Ronda rolled her eyes around in her head as if she was contemplating on telling me the truth. I knew this woman all too well. "Do you remember July 16th, 1975? I was 23 years old at the time," she voiced, squinting her eyes as if that would help her remember.

"I barely remember yesterday. How in the hell do you expect me to remember 43 years ago?"

"Oh, you remember. It was the night I caught you with Sally Jensen." I smiled inwardly because I remembered ole' Sally. She had this thing she did with her tongue that made her real popular amongst the fellas.

"I'on know what you talkin' 'bout," I grunted.

"Oh, you know, it was the night that you and your friends had just signed that contract with that Struthers, nigga."

"What about it?" I asked, ready for her to get to the meat of the story. I was exhausted and tired of talking.

"You had a red-light party that night that I knew nothing about," she responded. "I got a call from this girl name Terry, and she told me to get to your house quick," she sniffled.

Now, if she started that crying shit, I was gone have her pull over and I would hitch a ride to Chicago.

“Get to the point, Ronda, and turn this fuckin air off. It feel like a morgue up in here.”

She rolled her eyes and continued, “I rushed up in that house so fast I had no idea how I even got there. I rushed through every room until I got to yours. I went to twist the knob but froze at the sounds of passion coming from the other side,” she sniffled more and more, and I wanted to comfort her, but I couldn’t. She flung her tears off her face angrily. “You fucked that girl, didn’t you?”

I gave her my truth, “You wasn’t fucking me.” Ronda took her right hand off the wheel long enough to knock me in my chest.

I gasped for air while looking at her. “I oughta smack the shit out you,” I wheezed, trying to catch my breath. This dumb heffa knew I had COPD and not to mention high blood pressure. She gone roll her eyes at me before pulling off at the nearest exit. I stared at the side of her head. “What the hell is you doing?”

“Going to grab something to snack on,” she smirked. Her big ass had been snacking since we got on the road.

“Ronda, care yo’ ass in there and get what you need, and you better not steal the shit. You too damn old to be going to jail and being pimped out for a pack of smokes.”

She shook her head at me and parked at the nearest gas pump. “I’ll be right back.” She leaned over and kissed my cheek before pulling the door open, climbing out. “Keep the motor running,” she whispered, before slamming the door closed.

I turned the heat on full blast and let my seat back some and tried to relax. What felt like ten minutes, my eyes soon shot open and out ran Sharonda with her grey tresses blowing in the wind. I leaned over the middle console and pushed her door open. She hopped in, threw her seat belt on, slammed the gear into drive and took off.

We were on the highway for about fifteen minutes before I turned to her, "What the fuck did you just do?"

She licked her lips and let the window down. "It's hot in here, Razor."

"You worried about it being hot when we finna go to jail. I'm too old and too fine for jail. You know what them young nigga's gone do to me?"

She smacked her lips, "What Razor? What they gon' do to you, huh? You ain't got shit."

I wanted to smack Ronda's dentures down her throat. She was just so damn disrespectful at times. Nothing about her had changed. I heard people mention the saying, *old dogs,* well, Ronda was an *old bitch.* She'd been the same since I met her ass standing outside the high school. Back then she wasn't even a student. She had just recently graduated so she would come up to the school and write papers for all the dumb jocks and sell em'.

When she found out that I was a part of a singing group known as *Members Only*, she wanted to be a part of the hype. So, she became my main-squeeze. Once I blessed her with this dick, she did what the fuck she had to do to get shit done. I understood her hustle. When you grew up with parents that was pretty much nonexistent, you had to do what you had to do to survive. I watched her for weeks. She was on the pickpocket shit heavy and when she wasn't pickpocketing, she would straight run up in Montgomery

Ward and clean them out, then sell the shit for profit. She was nice at what she did. I didn't approve, but it stopped us from spending unnecessary money on bullshit we couldn't afford.

"Earth to Razor," she snapped her fingers in my face. "We about 45 minutes from Chicago. Do you remember what to do?"

"Don't question me, woman. I've been running scams long before you was even thought about."

"Nigga, you only three years older than me," she huffed.

"Exactly my point. You just make sure you know what the fuck you need to do and don't be out here on no bullshit."

Ronda smiled and patted my leg, "Don't worry, I got this." I hoped she did because if this plan fell through, we might not make it up outta Chicago.

Chapter 5

Snuck Inn (Somewhere in Illinois)

Willie 'Po-Man' Jenkins & Bertha

"Oh, Willy. This is so romantical," Bertha marveled as she set her duct-taped suitcase on the bed.

"Yeah, this is kinda classy. If I could get my old tool to work, I might have to give you a lil' taste. Look at these nice sheets. They way better than anything we got at the house."

"Tell me about it," Bertha commented, taking off her wig.

I was glad, too, because the unnatural blue color was about as flattering as the blue veins in her neck. I didn't realize just how baldheaded she was until she patted the single braid on her head. Damn thing looked like a zipper.

"How long we got to stay over here?" Bertha asked before pulling out her bottom row of dentures.

"Damn. Can you at least let me be attracted to you for five minutes before you start pulling shit off?" I complained.

My baby used to be the fox out of the crew. Now, she looked more like a plucked chicken. My old girl had been with me a long time. She had been through more with me than I was probably worth, which made what I was about to do to her, so bad. By the time tomorrow evening rolled around she was gonna realize that she had been used to drive me up here. Me and the fellas had a few scores that had to be settled. With my dementia starting to take over, I had only a small window of time to get this done.

"Why you over there staring at me like that? You ain't looked at me like that in almost forty years," Bertha commented as she proceeded to stuff motel towels in her overnight bag.

All I could do was shake my head. She used to be a real class act until she got with me. I slowly lowered myself onto the bed, trying to avoid the pain in my knee that I knew was coming. I don't know what convinced my half-dead-ass to get this knee replacement. Maybe, I feared having to fully rely on her. Or maybe, it was because I didn't want to be as broke down as these sorry sons-of-bitches I was about to meet up with. I hadn't seen these bastards in years and now all of a sudden, they want to call me with this big plot. I forgot a lot of things in my life, but the day I met those niggas was one I would never forget.

"My word don't mean nothing to you? Ain't that a female dog?" Harriet sat on the porch with her head in her hands. We knew this was a bad situation, but she could have at least tried to understand my point. "You know my momma getting sick is something I can't avoid, darlin'."

"Po-Man, go head on now," Harriet said, using my nickname.

The only time I got called that was when I was in trouble. I hated it because it constantly reminded me that I was less than everyone else. Nobody wanted to believe that about themselves, even if it was true.

"I leave tomorrow. If you wanna come, you can come. You just got to have your own money because all I got is enough to get to Detroit."

"Carry your ass on then. You just gon' up and leave me after I lost our baby. Damn shame."

"You ain't got to be sassy. I'm hurting behind losing Jr. too." I took my hat off before attempting to take a seat next to her on the porch steps.

"Po-Man, you gon' get up there and forget all about a Mississippi gal like me. Now, I understand that your momma is sick and all, but my momma is raising 11 youngins by herself since my daddy died. You think I'm about to up and leave her to be with you? You must be foolin'. Anyway, I got to get to work. You know how Mrs. Capernaum carries on if I'm late."

Harriet stood to leave, dusting off the back of her checkered dress. With her Sunday-go-to-meeting- shoes on, she was a sight to see, skin the color of black ink with those honey eyes that cut right through a man's heart. Her heart-shaped lips were turned into a slight frown as I stood to join her.

"I'm gonna miss you, Po-Man. Don't forget to come down here from time to time to check on me. We always gonna mean somethin' or another to each other."

Harriet's poor attempt to hold in her emotions began to weigh on me. Maybe, momma could manage without me. I loved this girl with all of my 17-year-old heart.

"Give me a hug now. Don't be tryin' to squeeze my hind parts either. That's what got us in a mess last time."

Had I realized that would be the last time I would see her face, I would have held her longer. The moment I got to Detroit, I got the telephone call from her mother, Dorothea, explaining that Harriet had never made it to work that day. She was raped by some white boys and thrown in front of a train. I was mad at myself and mad at momma for needing me. That anger was the very way I met

Bertha and the rest of the crew. I was sitting inside of the only black-owned diner in the city when she came up, asking me for some change to catch the bus.

"Do I sleep next to you every night?" I replied without bothering to look up from my bowl of chitlins.

"You don't have to be nasty. Just was running low on bus fare. Seems like somebody up in here done took my wallet!" she yelled, looking around the crowded restaurant.

All I wanted to do was be left alone. That was the only thing that prompted me to dig two quarters out of my pocket. I sat them inside of the softest hand I had ever felt. That was when I looked up at the graham cracker-colored girl standing in front of me. The blue and white waitress uniform was tight on her plump curves. Bright red lips like the ones the street-walkers wore, adorned her face.

"Thank you. You eat in here a lot? If so, your next bowl of that nasty stuff there is on me."

"I can buy my own dinner. You can just give me my money back. I only eat here when I don't feel like cooking for me and my momma."

"Oh, you one of those. You still stay with your momma. I should've figured the way them church pants is all creased up."

"I iron my own clothes, miss, and if you must know, I take care of my momma. Her gallbladder ruptured on her, so I had to come up here and take care of her since she ain't got no husband. What you lookin' down your nose for? Look at this greasy spoon you work in."

"This greasy spoon just so happens to be my brother-in-law's restaurant. First black man round here to have a business. You wouldn't know nothing about that though, country boy."

That heffa really thought she had me told as she huffed off to finish her shift. Personally, I thought it was funny. She was too pretty to really get upset with.

"That ole girl' got a fire mouth on her. She get smart with every man come up in here."

I turned my attention to the left. A man around my age was eating a plate of meatloaf, cabbage, and cornbread. It looked much better than the dollar meal sitting in front of me. Momma had already schooled me about spending too much money up here. These city niggas would rob you blind if they thought you had a little bit of change on you.

"How she keep her job with a mouth like that?" I joked.

"The boss married to her sister. That thing is wayyyy meaner than her. Sylvia will clear out the place if you get on her bad side. I just now been allowed to come back up in here. Where you from though? I hear a lil' down South in your tone.

"I'm from Tupelo, Mississippi," I stated proudly.

"The birthplace of Elvis? No shit? My name is Raymond Hathaway. They call me Razor though. Actually, Razor-Mouth Slick. The name means just what you think it means, too. I'm from the Southside of Chicago. Just moved out here with my old lady."

"Old lady? You don't look old enough to even buy cigarettes. What you talkin' bout an old lady?" Razor appeared to be at least six feet from where he was sitting. A pencil thin mustache set over a set of wide lips that took up nearly half of his face when he smiled. The old man hat he wore looked like something that belonged to his daddy, and his pants and shirt were so wrinkled, I wondered if they had ever seen an iron. The only thing decent about him was the mass of curls on his head.

"Guess the jig is up," Razor replied, taking a napkin to wipe off the fake mustache. "Used my woman's eyebrow pencil. I told her this shit wouldn't make me look older."

"Why you in a rush to look older?"

"I don't know you good enough to go into all that. Just out here trying to get me a gig, so I ain't got to go back home. Shit is rough out my way. Course, I wouldn't be welcomed back no way. Not after what I did."

The nosiness in me wanted to ask, but the way he lowered his head made me keep my mouth shut. Something was weighing on this boy.

"Nice to meet ya." I extended my hand. "I'm Willie Jenkins, but they like to call me Po-Man' to remind me that my daddy wasn't shit. Hell, I guess I won't be neither." We laughed heartily as we shook hands.

He was the first friend I made in Detroit. That chance meeting would seal my fate in ways that I still couldn't believe."

"Willie, they got nice shower curtains in here. These ain't the plastic kind neither. Help me come get em' down so we can take em' home," Bertha said from the bathroom.

I lowered my head as I followed her inside, knowing that only one of us was going home.

Chapter 6

Harmony Healthcare

Mandala

I was hiding out in the supply closet. It was the only way that I could get some peace and quiet. Benny and Drexler had been running me ragged ever since they got here. If it wasn't one thing, it was another. Not to mention, them ole' fools was in there smoking weed like it wasn't against policy. They was gone mess around and get me fired.

My phone buzzed in my pocket, and I wiped the frown from my face before I answered. "Hello?"

"Don't hello me. Where in the hell have you been?"

"Hello, mother. I'm fine, thanks for asking," I replied sarcastically.

"Don't take that sarcastic tone with me, young lady. Where are you?"

"I'm at work, mother. Why?" I asked snidely.

"Work? When did you decide to get a job?"

"A few months ago. Why, what's wrong?"

"Ain't nothing wrong. I'm just checking on you is all. You're never home and you barely answer your phone."

"My apologies but this job is so damn demanding."

"Look, I know what I'm about to say you probably don't wanna hear it, but you don't have to work, Mandala."

I rolled my eyes so far up in my head, it's a wonder I didn't stroke out. "I need to work, mother. How do you expect me to live?"

"Your father may have been a no-call, no-show, but he made sure that you had more than enough money to live."

"Mommy, I have to go. I have to get back to work."

"Okay sweetie, call me later. I love you,"

"I love you too, old woman."

"I ain't that damn old now," she chuckled.

"Whatever you say," I laughed while disconnecting the call.

The door pushed open, and Jennifer stuck her head inside. "Umm, Mandala. You're needed in the front ASAP."

I groaned in frustration and pushed myself up from my seating position. "Which one is it this time? Benny or Drexler?"

She laughed, shaking her head, "Neither." She turned and walked away.

I walked through the hall with my shoes squeaking across the linoleum and tried to prepare myself for the next phase but nothing, and I mean nothing prepared me for these two.

"I'm telling you right nie', I was supposed to be transported and this here ole' wench wanted to do shit her way and now look."

"Keep on talking, and you gone be transported alright," the elderly lady said, mushing the side of his head.

"Don't put yo' hands on me no mo'. I done told you about that shit, Ronda. You gon' make these crackas call the laws cause you about to catch these paws," he sang.

"You don't want these problems, Razor."

"Does that include yo' ass, cause you full of problems, Ronda."

The nurse tried to defuse the situation, but she couldn't get those two ole' fools to stop if she wanted to. I cleared my throat, and they both turned in my direction. "Hi, my name is Mandala," I began. "And you are?"

"None of yo' damn business." The lady rolled her neck and gave her husband the evil eye. "The hell you smiling for, nigga? You trying to get cut? Matter fact-" she paused and grabbed the back of his wheelchair.

"What you doing, woman?" the elderly man asked as the chair began to roll.

"You been disrespecting me for 40 some odd years. I'mma 'bout to roll yo' ole broke dick ass down these damn steps. I's sick'a you." I could see the sole of his shoes scraping the linoleum trying to get her to stop before security intervened.

I took a deep breath and tried not to laugh. I've been dealing with crazy ass old people all damn day, and something told me that this man, was about to the join the *He-Man Woman-Haters Club***.**

"Get her on outta here with all that foolishness," he screamed at security.

"You ain't shit, Razor. I can't believe you gon' let these men manhandle me like this," she screamed.

"Somebody need to manhandle yo' big ass because I can't," he coughed and wheezed. He placed his handkerchief up to his mouth as he continued to cough. When he removed it, I could see the specks of blood on it.

I ran to his aid. "Can you tell me your name, sir?"

"They call me Razor-Mouth Slick sweetie," he smiled.

"Umm, Mr. Slick. I'mma need your real name in order to help you."

He chuckled, "Raymond Hathaway. The lead singer of *Members Only*."

I shook my head and read his name off to the receptionist. After a few short minutes, she gave me his room number and told me a bed was already set up and waiting for Mr. Hathaway. I guess I was right in my assumption. I was taking him to the very room that housed all the other crew members. I wondered what these old men was up to. Only time would tell, and I had all the time in the world.

Chapter 7

Drexler 'Dick' Em Down' Davis

Harmony Healthcare

I had to go take me a breather. Looking at Audrey was enough to near 'bout stop my heart. She was the splitting image of her mother, Audra, when we first met. Sweet Audra. Every time I thought about the death sentence I had imposed on her, I wanted to die myself. The hardest part about what me and the fellas had planned, was going to be looking into the face of my daughter and telling her that her momma might still be living if it wasn't for me. In those days, it was the cool thing to be loose if you were a fella. The ladies were the ones that were expected to be modest. Growing up in The Prophetic Temple of Faith, as the preacher's son meant that I was supposed to be perfect. They wanted me to get up there every Sunday and damn near walk on water like my daddy did. He was interested in saving souls, and I was interested in filling holes if you know what I mean. Plenty a girls had been bent over in the Sunday school room down in the basement. Me and the girl of my choice would hide in the bathroom until everybody else went upstairs, then we would meet back up in the room since it was the only door that wasn't liable to be open again until after service. I would bend her over the desk and bang-bang-bang that ass until we were both sweaty and satisfied. Then I would go upstairs just in time to lead the first hymn in the choir.

Who would have ever thought that women would be my downfall in a world where there was so much more to tempt me.

"Daddy, they say it's time to take your medicine," Audrey announced.

I hadn't even heard her walk up. As she rolled me back into the building, the beeping of various medical machines bothered me as we traveled down the long corridor. Velvet Rose was sitting up in his bed watching television as we passed his room.

"Where you taking me, Audra?"

"Daddy, I am not Audra. It's Audrey," she corrected, gently. "They put you down here in the last room on the left.

"Oh lawd. They put me right by the got-damn exit. When my crippled ass dies, they just gon' roll me down the stairs and burn me in the incinerator, ain't they? Fuck that, I ain't goin' without a fight."

Audra slapped at my hands as I attempted to stick them in the spokes of my wheelchair.

"You trying to rip your arms off?"

"Better than gettin' pushed on down the stairs. Bad enough you done throwed me away."

"Nobody has thrown you away, daddy," Audra reassured as she opened the door to my room.

I had to admit, the view of downtown Chicago was nice. I could see the Monadnock Building. My window appeared to be bigger than the one in Razor's room, too. Maybe this place wouldn't be a bad place to stay for the night.

"Please don't give me any trouble about taking these. I'm too tired to be arguing with you." Audra hit the brakes on my chair before going over to my bedside table where they had all of my meds set out.

It looked like a got-damn pharmacy in there. The nurses weren't too happy about my daughter dispensing my medicine until they saw that she used to be a registered nurse herself. That was before she took on caring for me full-time while going to film school. Now that I was nearing the end, she figured I was too much to handle. I told her if she was putting me in a hospice it would have to be with somebody I knew. What she didn't know was I already knew exactly where I wanted to go and why. I had to let her think this was all her idea.

"Girl, I don't need you to stand over me. You all light-bright with them, whatcha call em'.... highlights in your hair. You almost lookin' like one of them crackas."

Audrey appeared to be offended as she handed over the cup of pills. It wasn't her fault she was so high-yella. Her momma was a mulatto, and I was quite light myself. I swallowed down the pills I wanted but kept the other ones cleverly hidden under my tongue. I had been doing this so long that I didn't even need to look at them to know which ones to swallow. Audrey handed me a lukewarm bottle of water to wash it all down. As soon as she went to turn down my bed, I cuffed the other ones in my sleeve.

"Let's get you rested so I can get me a nap before I get back on that road."

My baby-girl was strong as an ox. Her small size didn't affect her strength at all. At 5'2, she was a foot shorter than me and couldn't have weighed no more than 120 pounds. She was Audra through-and-through except for that blonde mess she had put in her head.

"You comfy?" she asked once she had me settled into the bed.

"The only way I would be comfy was if I had a woman on top of me. Why you ask me is I'm comfy?"

"I see you're cranky. I can't deal with you when you're like this. I'm gonna go get me something to eat so you can get your language together. You been foul-mouthed all day."

"And I'mma keep on being foul-mouthed. I'm a grown-ass man, Audra. Why you can't understand that?"

"You know what… I can't with you right now. I'll bring you back a fish sandwich."

Audrey stomped out of the room like she used to when she was a teenager. I wasn't thinking about her attitude because I needed her gone anyway. I waited for a few minutes to make sure she was really gone before tipping over to my wheelchair. If she knew I could walk, she would've been kicked my ass. It took me a little longer to get to my destination, but I very much had the function of all of my limbs; especially the one between my legs. After lowering myself into my chair, I opened the door and rolled down to Velvet Rose's room.

"You gon' sit out there in the hallway watching me on the shitter, or you comin' in?" he asked.

"You in there layin' in the bed shittin' is just nasty. Least you can do is close the door. Got it smellin like them nasty-ass liver pudding and onion sandwiches Bertha used to make us on the road."

"If I can deal with a lifetime of your bullshit, you can deal with a few minutes of mine. Close that door behind ya," Velvet directed.

Reluctantly, I rolled inside of the room. After the door was closed, I pinched my nose to keep from inhaling the noxious fumes emanating from his rotten asshole.

"So, Papa just called me. He say they gettin' real close. Still waitin' on Razor and Po-Man," he managed before grunting.

The plop in the bedpan damn near turned my stomach as he looked over at me smilin'.

"Oh, Mandala, I got a surprise for you, baby," he sang in his deep baritone voice into the nurse call receiver.

We both had to laugh at that one. Nothing had changed. The nigga was still smooth as silk.

"I ain't got much time 'cause Audrey is getting us dinner. I just thought I would settle somethin' before the other fellas get here."

"Oh shit. You still talking 'bout the same thing from fifty years ago," Velvet waved me off. I approached the bed getting dangerously close to his stench.

"Velvet, she's dead and gone now. Just tell me the truth, and we can be done with the shit."

"You rang," Mandala said as she entered the room.

Bitch could of at least knocked before she interrupted an important conversation.

"Yeah, I need you to handle that," Velvet pointed to his bottom.

"Will you excuse us for just a moment?" she asked.

He wore a smirk on his face like he had avoided something. If he thought this conversation was over, he had another thing coming. The first score I was gonna settle was the one that had been fifty years in the making. He had better hope his answers were acceptable, or he would be meeting his heavenly father just a little bit sooner than he expected. I patted the backpack on the back of my chair for reassurance. Even though my hands trembled, I was still a good shot.

Chapter 8

Willie 'Po-Man' Jenkins

"Where are you taking me, child?" I asked the nurse as she pushed me down the long corridor.

"I'm taking you to your room, sir," she smiled and continued to push.

"Well hell, I know that," I snidely remarked.

We passed Razor out in the hallway, and he looked like he was up to something. He gave me a head nod to acknowledge me and I smirked his way. Razor had been a dirty muthafucka since we met back in the day. He was one of those types that would sleep with yo' woman behind your back and not see anything wrong wit' it. I wish he would've tried me back in the day. I wouldn't have gave a shit about the nigga always carrying a razor.

"Here we are, Mr. Jenkins," the nurse said, snapping me back to reality.

It felt like a morgue in here and believe me, I've been inside my share of morgues.

"Why is it so cold in here? I don't like the cold, sweetheart."

The nurse smiled while locking my chair. "I can turn it down if you like."

"How about turning it off. I don't like to be too hot or too cold. I guess it got something to do with what's ailing me."

The nurse stooped down in front of me and smiled with kind eyes. "I don't know if you remember, but my name is Mandala. When I'm not around to take care of you then my colleague, Jennifer, will step in. She's a very nice young lady," she spoke slowly.

"Baby, I'm sick in my bones not in my ears. You can speak to me civilly. I can understand anything you put down."

Mandala laughed, "You sound like the other patients I have on my roster." She stood to her feet and unlocked the brakes on my chair. "Let me get you settled in."

"There's no need, darling. As long as this chair won't roll from up under me, I can get around just fine." Mandala held onto the back of the chair as I pushed myself to stand.

After stretching my back, I moseyed on around the room and checked everything out. I can't believe that this it. This is the last ride before I'm called to Glory. I always thought my last days would be surrounded by my children and grandchildren, but me and Bertha were too busy for a family.

I sat down in the recliner by the window and looked out at the water. It was so peaceful that I could actually hear myself think. Taking a deep breath, the coughing started.

"Let me run down the hall and get you something to drink and while doing so, I'll grab your file and see how I can make your stay a little more than comfortable."

I nodded my head, giving her the go ahead. I didn't have much time on this earth as I looked down at the blood splattered on my ole handkerchief.

I bawled the hanky up in my fist and looked back out the window. If this was the last view God granted me, then I would appreciate it. With Bertha in the bathroom I was finally able to get some much-needed solitude.

"Uncle Willie? Is that you?" I turned around and damn near slipped into my grave.

"Audra?" I questioned, unsure if it was her or not.

"You know what, between you, daddy, and Uncle Benny, I might as well be my momma," she responded, hanging her head.

I went to stand to my feet when she started across the floor. "Don't get up, Uncle Willie. I just wanted to speak. I'm headed out to get daddy and me something to eat," she smiled softly.

"Okay, baby," was all I said because honestly, there was nothing else to do but stare.

She was the splitting image of her mother. I remember when I first met Audra, she was beyond beautiful. We all tried getting her attention, but she only had eyes for Drexler's dirty ass.

"Bye, Uncle Willie," she bent down and kissed me on the cheek.

When she turned and walked away, I allowed myself to breathe. Turning back the view before me, I left my mind to wander.

"Willie, I got something to tell you," Bertha said as she hung her head, sitting down beside me on the couch.

"What is it, Bertha?" I grumbled because for the past few days she'd been on my nerves.

"I have something to tell you and -."

I cut her off mid-sentence. "Look, I gotta get up in the morning and go down to the warehouse to see if I can get on. So, whatever you gotta tell me, make it quick."

Taking a deep breath, she blurted out the very words that I didn't wanna hear, "I'm pregnant." She twiddled her thumbs and looked up at me with tears brimming the edges of her eyes.

"What you telling me fo'?" I asked, standing to my feet.

"Because I want you to be just as excited as I am."

"You don't look excited to me."

"But I am," she finally smiled.

I hated to do this, but I had my reasoning. "Get rid of it."

"GET RID OF IT!" she screamed.

"You heard me, Bertha."

"But why?" she cried, openly.

"You know why," I said, running my hand down my face aggravated.

"It's about that Harriet girl from Mississippi, isn't it?"

"Do what the fuck I said, or you can take that little bastard and both of y'all can get in the wind, and I mean it, Bertha."

She stood to her feet and slapped me with what seemed like all 210 pounds of her weight. "I hate you, Willie," she sniffled, wiping away her tears angrily.

"I know, and you'll continue to hate me. But while you doing so, do what the fuck I asked you to do."

That was it, and that's all that needed to be said. I had to get up in the morning. I was tired of struggling. Yeah, Bertha got out there and did what she had to do, but I wanted to live better than this rat and roach infested shit we were living in.

Walking off to the small one-bedroom we rented where I had to fight with the roaches before I got in the bed, I sighed and did something I hadn't done in a long while, and that was pray. That morning when the sun caught my attention, I jumped up, handled my hygiene, and marched out the door. I was determined to be something. I just didn't know what that something was. That shit that ole' nigga I met in the diner said that day wasn't about nothing. I needed something tangible, and I was on my way to get it, or so I thought.

"Ah-em." I heard coming from behind me. I turned slowly, and it was that Mandala girl. "Are you okay, Mr. Jenkins?" she asked, passing me a big ass cup of water.

"I'm fine," I solemnly replied as I sipped from the huge cup she shoved in my hand.

"Well, I placed your things in the hall closet. If you need to get changed, let me know. I'm here to help." I shook my head no. "Well, here's a remote. It controls not only the TV, but there's also a button on here you can push in case you need me. Also-," she paused, "Mr. Jenkins are you sure you okay?"

"Yes, baby, I'm fine. Stop worrying about the old man. Now, what was you saying?"

She smacked her forehead as if she was trying to remember. "Oh yeah, your phone is over there," she pointed. "And this door," she walked over to it, "is the bathroom." I nodded my head in understanding. "Okay, if you need me, just press this here button," she smiled, then turned and walked out.

I pushed myself up from my sitting position and started towards the bathroom. First, I would handle my business, then I'll go roam the halls until I located the rest of the crew.

Chapter 9

Ronnie 'Papa' Willow

Harmony Healthcare

"Mr. Ronnie, I have to give it to you. I never had this much fun on a shift in my life," Brooke commented as she helped roll my stretcher into the building.

"This ain't nothing compared to the times we had back in the day. Of course, you couldn't have hung out with us then because of…" I pointed to the skin on the back of my hand.

"Mr. Ronnie, let me let you in on a little secret. My boyfriend is black."

"Sho' nuff? I knew you was looking at me a little bit too hard in that ambulance. You hadda' got up in that bed with me, I woulda showed you something that youngin' can't."

She burst out laughing. I was dead serious, though. Charlene hadn't been puttin' out on the regular. That woman had been crying menopause for ten years now; knowing she ain't had no eggs since 86.

"Suga', I show thank ya' for takin' good care of Papa. You was tender with me."

My bed made an abrupt stop in a narrow hallway as the fatso that was driving, checked me in. She hadn't said two words to me the whole trip. I looked up at her in disgust as she handed over the paperwork to the woman behind the counter.

"How you work with this homely broad?" I whispered.

"Mr. Ronnie, you are something else." Brooke playfully slapped my arm.

"Oh, hell no, white gal! You betta' get ya' hands up offa' that one!" Charlene's loud voice echoed in the hallway.

In the blistering cold, this woman had the nerve to be wearing a multi-colored windbreaker I bought her at least 25 years ago. Her mid-section held up the jacket, just fine, but her lack of ass had the pants sagging like a thug. Don't even get me started on that white wig that looked like a bowl of spaghetti noodles.

"Get on now. You say you hope I die and that's what I came here to do. You can take your ass on back to Ohio."

"So you can be out here carryin' on like you ain't got no wife? Nigga please." Charlene placed her tiny hands on her non-existent hips.

"You're his wife? Nice to meet you." Brooke extended her hand.

"I don't shake hands with the help. Never have, never will," Charlene asserted, crossing her arms.

"Can y'all call security and get this bitch tossed outta here? She been a thorn in my side for over 45 years."

"I done told you 'bout that name callin'. I'll drag your frail ass up out that bed, Papa."

"Is there a problem?" the woman behind the counter asked.

It was then that we realized all eyes were focused on us.

"Nothing to see here. Get on back to work wit ya' nosey asses," I answered, struggling to sit up.

I could feel myself getting worked up as that familiar dizzy sensation began to take over.

"Oh no, his oxygen level is dropping. Mr. Ronnie, lay back so I can get your oxygen please."

I followed Brooke's orders, allowing her to place the tube in my nose. I hated this thing because it dried out my nasal passages. I had to admit it was a relief to be lying back down on my back again. A soft, wrinkled, hand I recognized as Charlene's, grabbed my left hand gently. She walked along the side of the bed as they pushed me down the hallways. With all the stained-glass windows in the place, you would've thought it was a church.

"Well, here you are," Brooke announced as we came to a wooden door.

I had to hold back a laugh when I read the number 69 on the plaque. Inside it was as cozy as can be. A let-out couch sat in the corner, I had my own bathroom, and there was a nice sized television mounted on the wall. This was a far cry from the three-story home I left behind in Cleveland, but it was more practical for my needs. Me and Brooke said our goodbyes, and she went on her way. As soon as the door closed behind her, Charlene started in on my nerves.

"Whatchu' think you pullin'? I just saw Velvet and Razor."

Oh shit. She's on to me. "Woman, what are you talkin' about?"

“Papa, I will slap all four of your original teeth down your throat if you don’t quit playin’ with me. This ain’t no damn coincidence. What them fools doin’ here?”

I couldn’t pretend to be surprised because she would see right through that and send my ass flying into next week. I scrambled to think of something.

“Knock-knock,” a soft voice interrupted our argument.

“Ooh, if you ain’t every bit of your momma,” Charlene cooed as I strained my eyes.

For a moment, I saw a silver sequined gown with matching shoes and a bouffant hairdo. As Audrey got closer to my bed, I couldn’t help but smile.

“Uncle Ronnie, it’s so good to see you,” she said as she reached down, hugging me around my neck. Even her perfume was the same as Audra’s. It was like taking a glance in the past.

“Audrey, what you know about this reunion these old fools havin’?” Charlene questioned.

“Reunion? I don’t know what you mean. What reunion?” Audrey winked at me before raising up to face Charlene.

“Now, I know I done saw Velvet and Razor. I’m old, but I ain’t crazy.”

“Uncle Benny and Uncle Razor here? Where?” Audrey asked, excitedly.

“They right down the hall. Let me show you,” Charlene offered, opening the door.

As they walked out of the room, Audrey stuck her tongue out at me. She was in on our plan. I was relieved because I didn't want none of them half-dead muthafuckas driving me around.

Chapter 10

Audrey

Harmony Healthcare

"Knock, Knock. Uncle Benny, you have a visitor." I pushed the door open, sticking my head inside. He cut his eyes at me, I guess waiting to see who was standing behind me.

"Is that-," he stammered, reaching over to grab his glasses off the bedside table. "Pop Rocks?" he questioned.

"Don't start that Pop Rocks shit wit me, Benny. Or shall I say Velvet?" Aunt Charlene snapped with her neck rolling from side to side.

"You didn't mind a little Velvet that night you stumbled into my room." I snapped my head back and forth like I was at a tennis match.

"I was drunk," she reasoned.

"Yeah, let that be the reason. Anyway, why you in my room?"

"What are you old niggas up to?" she snapped.

"We ain't up to shit and if we are-," he paused for dramatic effect. "What yo' fat ass gone do about it?" he smirked.

"Fat?" she huffed, folding her arms across her chest.

"Yeah fat. You ain't Coke bottle shaped like you used to be. You more like a squeezed 2 liter."

“You know what? Fuck you, Velvet.”

“I already had that opportunity and it wasn’t shit then, and I definitely know it ain’t gone be shit now. Get yo’ ass outta my room with that bullshit, Pop Rocks. And Audrey, don’t bring her bean bag built ass back in here.”

I promise you I was trying not to laugh, all the while, grabbing Aunt Charlene by the wrist.

“Let go of me, chile. I know how to walk,” she snapped, spinning around on her worn-out Reeboks.

“Well, walk yo’ fat ass on outta here and don’t come back,” he yelled before cutting his eyes at me.

“I’m sorry, Uncle Benny,” I chuckled softly.

“Umm-hmm, don’t bring her ass back in here,” he sneered.

“Yes sir,” I giggled, turning to leave the room.

Looking up at Charlene, her pretty, caramel skin was beet red. I hated to laugh, but it was so funny, especially if she thought she was gonna get anything outta Uncle Benny.

“This way,” she pointed.

I shook my head because I just knew she just went from bad to worse when she decided to push my daddy’s door open. I wasn’t even gone follow her inside because my daddy’s mouth was the worse at times.

“You coming?” she asked, looking at me over her shoulder.

I simply shook my head no. Aunt Charlene shrugged her shoulders and pushed the door open to proceed.

"Where in the fuck did you come from? This damn place is just crawling with no good bitches."

"Don't be like that, Drexler," I heard her say before the door closed.

Fuck that, I pushed the door open just enough to be nosey but not enough to give myself away.

"Why the fuck are you here?" my dad asked.

"To see what you niggas is up to. I know y'all up to something simply because you niggas can't stand one another, but yet, y'all all piled up in the same damn facility. So, somebody gon' tell me what's going on?"

"Was you worried about what was going on when that nigga ran up in the hotel and stole all our shit? Was you worried about what was going on when yo' so-called man ended up in the hospital when them crackas beat his ass damn near senseless? Were you worried then? You was always popping up when a bitch was involved but never when we needed you the most."

"Fuck all that. What you niggas up to now?" she snapped.

"Fuck outta my room, Charlene," my dad yelled before having a coughing fit.

"I ain't getting out shit."

I pushed the door open and rushed over to my dad to get him some water. After taking a few generous sips, he looked at me with hooded eyes.

"Get this confused bitch outta my room before I stuff my dick down her throat."

I dropped the cup I was holding on the floor and water splashed everywhere.

"You would do me like that, Drexler?" she said as if her feelings were hurt, yet on the verge of tears.

"In a heartbeat," he growled. "Now get the fuck … outta my room."

I patted his hand as I rounded the bed.

"Come on, Aunt Charlene," I said, and she wiped the tears from her eyes.

"I'm sorry, Drexler."

"Then get yo' sorry ass outta my room."

Once out in the hall, I steadied my nerves and prepared myself for door number three. "You still wanna go see Uncle Willie?" I asked, trying to lighten the mood.

"Naw baby, I'mma head back to Papa."

She hung her head and turned down the hall. I don't know what ole' Charlene did to piss off the fellas, but whatever it was, she had to live with it. Taking a deep breath, I turned and headed back into my dad's room. He was looking up at the TV, watching it with no sound. I tried to get his attention but paused when I saw the tears falling from his eyes. The one thing about my dad that I knew from personal experience, crying made him feel weak and he hated feeling vulnerable. I approached his bedside and instead of asking him what was wrong. I crawled up in the bed beside him and laid my head on his chest and allowed him to cry.

“Dad?” He shushed me and patted me on the head like he used to do when I was a kid.

I closed my eyes and listened to the sound of his heartbeat. It was always so soothing.

“I need thee, oh I need thee

Every hour I need thee

Oh, bless me now my savior

I come to thee.”

Listening to him sing always took me back to when I was a little girl. I wrapped my arm around him, then closed my eyes and allowed sleep to consume me. Hopefully, all this would be over soon

Chapter 11

Sharonda & Razor

Harmony Healthcare

After a good, long piss, I was ready to get down to business. Ronda had carried her ass off somewhere, looking for something to steal. Me, I wanted to get this show on the road. I had only been here a few hours, but I was itching to get moving. Pop Rocks had just walked past my door with Audrey. I was glad that no-good bitch didn't come to my room. She knew we had some unfinished business. After all the money I had spent buying her fur coats, and jewelry, that bitch had the nerve to tell my wife we were messing around. Talkin' 'bout she thought she was gonna die after her heart attack and wanted to clear her conscience. She should've died and did all of us a favor. Hell, with all the babies she had swallowed over the years, it's a wonder she didn't choke to death. I rambled through my overnight bag looking for my phone. After locating my bifocals, I looked through it until I found the number to my bank.

"This hoe bet not have touched a dime," I said to myself as the phone rang.

After a series of them damn computers talking to me, I finally got a voice on the line.

"How you doin', suga'? This is Raymond Hathaway. I was calling to check my account."

"Good afternoon, Mr. Raymond. I can help you with that? May I have your account number or social please?" the friendly female's voice answered.

She sounded like one of those sexy ole pink-toes I used to mess with back in the day. Yes indeed. I jumped out of many windows, avoiding shotguns.

"Mr. Hathaway, are you still there?"

"Yes, ma'am. I apologize 'bout that. Let me see if I can't find my bank book."

I checked in the overnight bag, but there was no sign of it. I didn't get too nervous until I checked my suitcase. It wasn't there either. *No honor among thieves.* "Ma'am, I seemed to have misplaced it. Let me just call you back."

"No problem, Mr. Hathaway. Have a nice day." I threw that phone across the bed before checking one last time. "You fuck wit' snakes and get bit every time."

"What you talkin'?" Ronda asked, walking into the room with a McDonald's bag and cup-holder.

She wasn't gonna admit she had my bank book, so I had to play it cool.

"Just talkin' to myself. You know how I do. What you got in the bag?"

"Got us some lunch. What it look like?" she snapped, sitting the food on my bedside table.

"You couldn't go get no real food? No ribs or turkey chops?"

"You look like a damn turkey chop. Stop complainin' now and sit down to eat. Why all these clothes and thangs on the floor?"

"I was looking for something."

"Well, did you find it? Got all my bras and panties from Victoria's Secret all over the floor. How it gon' look if they come up in here and see this room trashed. I swear you ain't got no home training."

Ronda busied herself cleaning up my mess as I crept over to the chair she had set her purse in. While her back was to me, I opened it up. My bank book was on the very top. She didn't even try to hide it.

"Boy, I tell ya'... scratch a lie, find a thief. Now, just what you think you doin' with this?" Ronda spun around, laughing as I waved my book in the air.

"Bout time, nigga. I thought you had started slippin'. Used to be a time you wouldn't let me nowhere near your money. Now, you turnin' your back on me like I ain't the biggest thief on this side of the Mississippi. All I did was use your debit card to pay for our food."

"You don't be using shit without my permission." I had to laugh, though, because I met Ronda stealing and when I died, she would probably still be at it.

"Oh, I know y'all better open up these damn doors!" I tried to enjoy my lunch, but this girl had been screaming and carrying on for the last 20 minutes. As hot as it was that summer, her screaming made me want to hurry up and get back to my paper route.

"Those biscuits and gravy was mighty fine, Mrs. Dixon," I complimented the elderly black lady behind the counter.

She nodded her thanks before sliding the quarter I had laid down back over to me.

"You get my papers here bright and early every morning. This one is on the house. Go buy your momma something."

"Yes, ma'am." I stared at the brown-skinned troublemaker as I walked out of the general store.

Her long pigtails were stuck to her face where she had been crying her eyes out. The dress she wore was made out of croaker sacks, so I knew she had to have been down on her luck just like most of us was. Momma had always taught me to mind my business, but something was nagging at me when I went over to pick up my bicycle.

"Nah that ain't right." Propping my bicycle on the side of the building, I walked back inside the store where the girl was still being held captive by Charles-Lee, who was Mrs. Dixon's son.

"I don't care about you bein' mad. Shoulda' thought about that before you stole that souse meat."

"Let go of my wrist. You actin' just like white folks!" the girl yelled as she struggled to free herself.

"Aye, Charles-Lee, how much that souse meat was that she took?"

"Prolly about a dollar's worth because she had bread and hook cheese too."

Although I knew we desperately needed the money at home, I reached into my pocket and pulled out a dollar bill to give to Charles-Lee who snatched it greedily. He pushed the girl so hard that she landed at my feet. Before I could assist, she jumped up and kicked that man in the privates as hard as she could. Judging by the scream that left his throat, ole boy was hurt pretty bad. He dropped that dollar, and she snatched it up before racing out the door. Mrs. Dixon ran to the front to see what all the fuss was about, but we were outside by then.

"Get on, girl," I instructed as I grabbed my bicycle.

She hopped on the back, and we had been riding together ever since.

"Look at you drifting off to space. Eat your food before it gets cold," Ronda instructed.

I took the hamburger she was handing me. Sure enough, there was no pickles and extra onions when I removed the bun. This woman knew me like the back of her hand. I was certainly gonna miss her.

Welcome To
“Members Only”

Mz. Demeanor
&
aDysfunctional Mind

Chapter 12

The Beginning

Razor

"Hurry yo' old ass up, Dick'Em Down. Ain't nothing wrong wit' you but yo' blood cells," I yelled as I began coughing.

"See, that's what yo' ass get for talking shit," Drexler chuckled.

"I move faster than you two niggas, and I'm in a wheelchair," Po-Man stated, throwing in his two cents.

"Fuck..." *'Cough'* "Both y'all. Specially you, Po-Man, ole *which way did he go* lookin' ass."

"Come on fellas, Audrey ain't gon' be waiting all day," Papa Willow rolled up and voiced his opinion.

Me, Razor, and Po-Man waved our hands at him as if he was getting on our nerves.

Audrey came around the corner and smiled. "You fellas ready?" she asked a lil too chipper for my liking.

I raised my hand like I was in high school. "I wanna know which one of us is driving because Po-Man ain't driving me no damn where."

Audrey chuckled, "I'll be doing the driving, Uncle Razor. Now, can we go?"

We shook our heads and gathered our things. Looking around the room, I was gonna kinda miss this place. Specially, ole' thick ass Mandala. Maybe I could smack her on the ass before we left.

We all peeked our heads out the room like cartoon characters before we bolted for the door. Audrey was pushing Papa Willow, and I was pushing Po-Man.

"Where we going now, Silky?" Po-Man asked me.

I hated when he had these spurts of stupidity. I knew the nigga suffered from dementia, but it took a toll on all of us.

"We going to see a man about a horse," I replied, pushing him through the hall.

Audrey turned around and smiled at me, and I gave her one back. Probably not as bright but it was one nonetheless. We passed Mandala in the hall, and we all froze. She stood before us with her fists placed on her hips. "Going somewhere?" she asked with her eyebrows raised.

We all turned in Audrey's direction. "Well Mandala, I-."

Mandala threw her hand up to cease her lips from moving. "You don't have to explain anything to me." She stepped forward and stooped down in front of Po-Man. "I'm gonna miss you, Mr. Jenkins."

Po-Man smiled and patted her hand. "I'mma miss you too, Bertha." She kissed his cheek and stood to her feet, seemingly, wiping her tears away.

She turned towards Papa Willow and stooped down. "Hey, Papa Willow," she smiled.

"Hey, baby, what you got for the old man?"

She kissed his cheek and then looked deep into his eyes. "Don't go out there and break any more hearts you hear?" he shook his head as she patted his hand and stood to her feet.

She turned and looked in my direction. "Don't come over here with all that crying shit, Mandala."

"Between you and Dick'Em, I don't know who's worse." She started towards me, and I licked my lips.

"I'm telling you now. If you swing them wide hips over here, you might not make it back the same way you came. I might be old, but baby girl, this ain't what you want."

She chuckled and swatted at my arm. "You better take care of yourself," she sniffed and pointed her finger at me.

"Always, baby girl," I smiled genuinely.

"Now give me a hug,"

Like I said before, I was gone miss ole' Mandala. She made me feel like a young man again.

Last, but not least, she walked over to ole' Dick'Em Down. "I probably won't see you after this, but I wish you the best. Take care of yourself and can you do me a solid, playboy?"

"Anything for you, sweet-face," he licked his lips and threw on his million-dollar smile that was denture ready.

"Look out for Po-Man because Razor doesn't have the patience," she smiled.

"Me either," he grunted.

“Audrey, I’m only a phone call away if you need me.”

She gave Audrey a hug and then stood back and waved us all goodbye. As we moved down the hallway, I couldn’t help but remember the first time we all went out on stage.

Please help me welcome to the Apollo Stage ... MEMBERS ONLY!!!

I can sometimes still hear the crowd roaring. That was the best feeling ever. If I could go back in time and do it all over again. I would do it with the best five niggas to ever do it. We struggled, but we made each step our best step. Now, we was finna do this shit all over again. I heard somebody once say, until the casket drops. Well, London Bridges, nigga.

Chapter 13

Drexler 'Dick' Em Down' Davis

"When you wanna know the truth just ask me. I'll blink twice if these niggas is lying."

"Daddy, that is not how this works. Every man gets a chance to tell his own story. Nobody is going to infringe on that. You understand?"

I nearly turned my hearing aid off to that garbage. My daughter was not about to have her head filled with lies about me, especially when I had something so sensitive to tell her at the end of all this.

"Move over so I can put my oxygen tank in," Papa fussed.

"Fuck you and that tank. Y'all both full of hot air," Po-Man replied.

Audrey went over to break them up as I took one last look at Chicago. We had a lot of good times here. It was one of Audra's favorite cities. I could still see her now with her small waist sashaying to our dressing room. She always made sure she came in and fixed anything that needed fixin'. Po-Man was always in need of a good hair combing since he was too cheap to get a process. Ronda had put a million miles on that pressing comb straightening his naps.

"Aw hell naw. You 'bout to burn my scalp off! Get Audra in here!" Po-Man yelled as he snatched the cape from around his neck.

"You don't need Audra. You need a magician to tame lil' Africa on top of your head," Razor laughed as he finished shining his shoes.

"Will y'all stop foolin'? This is a big show we got here tonight. I heard Berry Gordy was gon' be in the audience with Smokey and a few others," Papa spoke up.

He had to be the most level-headed one of us.

"Smokey? Who cares about that pretty-eyed son-of-a-bitch? Man, he made me lose my girlfriend after one of his concerts. Maybelline got on that tour bus, and I never did see her again," Velvet lamented.

"Man, please. You wasn't worried about that girl. Hell, we all know you was knockin' off her older sister. What her name was, Po-Man?" I instigated.

"Hell, if I know. She sho' could make a mean pound cake though."

"You should know because yo' cheap ass ate the whole thing to avoid buying food on the road," I replied.

All of us chuckled because Po-Man was the cheapest man God had ever created. Nigga would eat the crust off your bread, the left behind meat on a chicken bone, and any swallow of pop left inside a bottle. In the few months we had been singing together, I hadn't seen him spend more than two dollars, and that was only to chip in on a hotel room.

"We laughin' now but wait til we get old and I'm sittin' on that million dollars."

"Man please," Razor interjected. "You couldn't see a million dollars if you was in a bank vault wearin' bifocals."

I laughed so hard that I almost stabbed myself with the needle I was using to repair the button on my trousers.

"Knock-knock," Audra greeted from behind the curtain that was serving as our dressing room door.

The theatre was one of the more run-down ones in town. In fact, I think that was the name of it.

"Come on in Sweet Audra," Razor flirted. I raised my fist to him. He knew that was my nickname for her.

"Hey, I was coming to see if you all needed any help. The house is packed."

"Don't you look mighty fine," I commented as I took her hand, twirling her around.

The sleeveless canary yellow dress stopped just above her knee. The floral design went perfect with the pink rose she had tucked into her thick curls. I could tell she had taken her time with the curling iron to get her look just right.

"Thank you," she flashed a deep-dimpled grin up at me. Even with her heels on, she still came up to my chest. "You look handsome yourself. Oh, let me get that for you." She took the needle from me and had me fixed up in no time. I stared down at her the whole time wondering what I'd ever done to deserve a woman so perfect.

"Audra, can you help me out when you're done with him? I can't go out there looking like this," Willie pleaded.

"Sure. Who else needs help because we got less than 20 minutes now?"

She looked at her watch. In that short time, she made sure we all went out there looking like stars. We didn't win the talent show that night, but it put us in position to get our name out there. We couldn't have done it without Sweet Audra.

"Daddy, we're waiting on you," Audrey said as she took my hand gently.

I walked back over to the van of fighting old men wondering if this was even worth it. I promised Audra I would make it right though, and nobody broke promises to Sweet Audra.

Chapter 14

Benny 'Velvet Rose' Pryor

"Hey Velvet," Dick'Em chuckled. "You remember when you and Jumpstart got into it?"

"Maaan, that shit was crazy," Papa chuckled.

"What happened, Uncle Benny?" Audrey inquired.

"Peep this. So, me and Jumpstart (Joanne) was lounging around, doing nothing. I mean the TV was on, and there was no sound coming out. She was sitting beside me filing her nails and Earth, Wind, and Fire was crooning in the background."

"Hey baby, why don't you get up and make me one of dem' turkey burgers."

Jumpstart rolled her eyes up in her head and huffed in frustration. "What's wrong wit' yo' hands?" she asked snidely.

"Ain't shit wrong wit my hands."

"Well, why can't you make yo' own damn turkey burger?"

"Because I asked you to do it, damn. What's the problem now, Joanne?"

"You're my problem, Velvet," she yelled, jumping to her feet. "Plus, you only call me Joanne when you're pissed off. I'm the one that should be pissed off."

"I'm listening," I said, putting my finger behind my ear.

"Where were you last night?" she asked, rolling her neck.

"I was out with the fellas."

"You're an I -was- out- with- the- fellas- lie. I was out with 'Pop Rocks' last night at the juke joint, and I saw yo' triflin ass."

"And I saw yo' triflin' ass. Yo' point is what?"

She threw her nail file at my head and stomped off into the kitchen. I could hear her slamming dishes around and talking shit.

"Gone have the nerve to call me triflin. I ain't triflin.' Just because he in that singing group he don't think he gotta be faithful. YOU GOT ME BENT, VELVET!!!!!"

"WELL BEND YO' DUMB ASS AROUND THAT KITCHEN AND FINISH MAKING MY DAMN FOOD!!!!" I yelled back.

Joanne came stomping out the kitchen five minutes later with a scowl on her face. "You know what, BENNY!"

"I told you about that Benny shit, Joanne." I responded, focused on the female dancer coming down the Soul Train line.

"I got yo' Joanne," she sassed, pitching my turkey burger in my lap.

The grease from the burger soaked through my linen slacks and burned my thigh. I jumped up from my seat as she started for the kitchen at full speed.

"Don't run now, bitch. You damn near burned my dick."

"It's better for me to than those triflin, loose pussy bimbos you been screwin'."

I lunged across the kitchen table, and she smacked me upside the head with the frying pan she grabbed from the stovetop. Luckily it wasn't the same one she had cooked my burger in. "Come on, Velvet. I double dog dare you. I'mma whoop yo' ass in here."

I grabbed the top of my head where a lump was starting to form. "You know what?" I pointed my finger in her direction. "I'm leaving. Don't expect me to come back to this hell hole because I'm sick'a yo' shit."

"Gone, leave nigga. I ain't keeping you here," she replied, still wielding the frying pan.

I snatched my keys up and started for the door. I could see Jumpstart smirking from where I was standing. Once I snatched the door open and stepped out in the summer's breeze, I walked to my car, yanking the door open. Once I was inside, I closed the door and placed the key in the ignition. I could see the front door of the apartment open. Joanne walked out on the porch with a cigarette hanging from her lip and her fists placed on her hips. She blew smoke in my direction with a slight smile on her face.

I shook my head and turned the key, and my car wouldn't start. After flooring the gas a few times, I tried it again and nothing happened. Leaning over, I rolled the window down manually.

"What the fuck you do to my car, Joanne?"

She laughed loudly before answering, "I took the alternator out," then slammed the door in my face.

I laid my head back on the headrest and couldn't help but to chuckle. Pushing the door open and walking about six or seven blocks, I ended up on Dick'Em's doorstep. Once I told him what happened, he would never let me live it down.

You was walking for about two weeks before Jumpstart gave you yo' alternator back." Dick'Em slapped his knee while Papa just shook his head.

"What you shakin yo' head for, nigga?" I asked him, coughing into my fist.

"I can shake my head or anything else I want to nigga," Papa answered smartly.

Chapter 15

Ronnie 'Papa' Willow

"I sho' appreciate you doin this for us, suga," I said to Audrey as I buckled my seatbelt.

"It's my pleasure, Uncle Ronnie. You all are unsung. *The Temptations, New Edition*, hell even the *Five Heartbeats*, all had movies. I feel like y'all never got your just due. I'm glad to do this for you. Where are we off to first, gentlemen?"

They all answered different cities at the same time.

"I knew this would happen. That's why I made an itinerary," Audrey said as she passed me a stack of laminated papers. I took a quick glimpse before passing them to the fellas.

"Naw, naw, naw, and hell naw," Uncle Razor exclaimed. "How this cheap bastard get to go home first?" He pointed a gnarled finger in Po-Man's face.

"Man, if you don't get that sticky digit out of my face. Wait a minute, let me count the words on my paper because that nigga will steal anything." Everyone laughed at Po-Man's joke except for Razor.

One thing I recalled from our younger days was that he hated to be laughed at.

"Like I said, why he get to go first?" Razor reiterated.

"Can you calm your nerves? You know Po-Man has the most important affairs to get in order. This is going in order of seriousness," I spoke up.

"What he got to do that's so serious? We already in my damn city. I can do my shit now and be through with all of y'all," Razor pouted.

"We are in your city, Uncle Razor, but if you recall, when we were planning this, you said that you wanted to go on the ride. If you change your mind now, you will ruin my film and all of the money and time I put into this. Matter-of-fact, Scott, cut the camera for a second." Audrey turned around in her seat and faced all of us.

I didn't know what to expect so I sat back as far as I could in my seat. The cameraman sitting between me and Dick'Em looked nervous as well as he fumbled to shut down his camera.

"Let me tell you something, and you listen good. All of you listen good. I'm a nurse by trade; that is my job. I'm good at what I do. However, my passion is film-making. I didn't wait until I was in my 40's to go to school for this, to have to deal with foolishness and unprofessional people. Now, y'all asked me to do this. We had a contract signed by everybody. Nobody's arm was twisted. I may look like Audra, but I am not her. The things she put up with from you all, I won't! Let's get that understood right now because I could be cuddling up with my husband every night instead of spending the next few months with five grouchy, old men. Anybody that wants off can go right back in that hospice and wait for their time to come, or we can move full steam ahead. What y'all wanna do?"

Audrey scanned each one of us from head-to-toe. Dick'Em had told me she was rough, but I had no idea she was this sassy.

"This nigga here," Dick'Em whispered. "Always got to be causing trouble."

"I sho' do but aye, I apologize. Now, let's get on wit' it. Y'all not about to make me the bad guy, like that time y'all voted me out the group," Razor stated, matter-of-factly.

"Here comes the bullshit," Po-Man chimed in. "We ain't put you out."

Audrey turned the ignition before putting her seat-belt back on.

"Okay, Scott, let's go," she directed.

Scott breathed a sigh of relief as he fired the camera back up.

"Now, what happened, Uncle Razor? How you get booted out?" Audrey asked as the van warmed up.

"Now, you know this nigga 'bout to lie through them false ass teeth of his," Dick'Em whispered.

I just laughed and nodded my head because I knew it too. Razor couldn't tell the truth if it was programmed in him like a computer.

"Ok, now let me start from the beginning so it all makes sense. I was the one that started *Members Only*." Razor declared.

"The only thing you started, is telling a lie," I interjected. "Baby, let me tell you what really happened."

"These cigarettes are gonna be the death of me," I said to myself before taking the last puff.

If I didn't get my ass back on the assembly line, I knew I was done for.

"Them thangs are bad, and they stink," Drexler complained.

"Looks to me like you need to go stand somewhere else," I joked.

We went through this every day. Drexler was a cool guy, but there seemed to always be a chip on his shoulder. We trudged back into the Ford plant, taking our places on the assembly line. It provided a decent living, but it wasn't what neither of us wanted to do for real.

"Davis! Willow!" Mr. Horowitz yelled as we picked up our tools.

"You know this cracka' ain't never got nothing good to say. Now what he want with us?" Drexler whispered.

"We ain't did nothin' wrong," I replied, cutting my eyes at Mr. Horowitz.

"Drexler and Ronnie. In my office now!"

The whole line paused to meddle as me and Drexler took our gloves off, placing them in our back pockets.

We followed the short, balding, Jewish man into an office the size of a janitor's closet. He flopped all 400 of his pounds into a chair that was leaning on the Lord's side. A mass of papers sat on a desk crammed in the corner.

"Have a seat, boys. This will just take a second." He gestured toward a small couch.

"Boy? Oh, you must think we some teeny-boppers. We're both grown men," I corrected.

Drexler nodded his head in agreement. Mr. Horowitz raked his hand through thinning, black hair that clung to his sweaty face before speaking.

"As long as you're working my shift, on my clock, and I gotta watch you thieving apes, then yes, you are a damn boy to me. Not even a whole boy because that would make you human," he smiled, revealing even rows of corn-colored teeth.

"Naw, a boy is what you got in your pants, Freddy," I addressed him by his first name. "If you think I'm about to sit in here and be sassed by a buttery toothed redneck, you got another thing coming. What you called us in here for anyway?"

"It's funny you should ask. I was gonna give you boys a raise. I been seeing the good job you were doing out there on the line. Now that I have you close to me, I don't think I like what I see."

"What is it you see?" Drexler asked, cracking his knuckles. Mr. Horowitz looked like he would shit himself at any moment.

"I don't want no trouble, boys. As a matter of fact, why don't you all just take the rest of the day off to cool down."

"We cool, but what about them raises though," I enquired.

"I would really rather you take the rest of the day off, so I can think about it. I don't know if we need your type working in the higher paying jobs. You might forget your place."

"Didn't I just say we ain't goin' home? You might have to call the police on us," I voiced, leaning forward in my seat.

"Ronnie, think about what you're sayin'. If dem' crackas run up in here, we gon' be the ones getting' our heads cracked. Let's just go on home for the day."

"A'ight man. Only because you said it."

I felt slightly less than a man as I followed Drexler out of the office. Back home in Alabama, I had seen my daddy beat more than his fair share of men like Horowitz. He taught me to do the same if it came down to it.

"You won't have a job to come back to, that's for sure," Horowitz mumbled as I turned to close the door.

That voice of reason that had been in my head must have gone on vacation because I ran back in that office and lunged at Horowitz with all my might. He squealed as I delivered kidney shots left and right. So much blood was flying that I didn't know if it was his or mine. It took four men to pull me off of him. The damage was looking pretty bad. My steel-toe boots had damn near killed him from my kicks to his ribs.

"Get him out of her before they call the police," an older man named Maurice demanded.

He didn't have to tell me twice. I ran my ass up out of that plant almost breaking my neck on the icy roads outside. It wasn't until I was a few blocks down that I stopped to catch my breath. Drexler was right on my heels.

"Now, you know we can't never get a job in this city again," Drexler asserted between breaths.

"Who said we got to stay here? This was just a temporary thing for me anyway. I want to go to New York."

"What a country boy like you gon' do in a big, expensive place like that?" Drexler questioned.

"I sing, dance, play the drums, and I play piano by ear. That's money all day long. What can you do?"

"You say you can play piano? My daddy been lookin' for a player. He got a storefront church over on Chene Street. We sho' could use some music."

"What it pay?"

Now he had my full attention. It didn't matter that the wind was ripping through the holes in my moth-eaten coat, or that my shoes were balder than a poor man's tires.

"Well, I don't really know about all that. I do know the last guy that played got to stay in the basement until he ran off to play at a juke joint."

That sounded like music to my ears because the rooming house I was living in had four men to a room and no indoor plumbing. I didn't want to sound too anxious, so I acted like I had to think it over. That night I went home with Drexler where his momma had a meal fit for a king ready when we walked through the door. That was the beginning of our brotherhood.

"The first Sunday I played, these fools walked in trying to impress their lady-friends, if you can call Ronda, Jump Start, and 'Pop Rocks' ladies."

"Charlene is your wife though, Uncle Ronnie. How can you keep calling her 'Pop Rocks' after all these years?"

"These fools the ones that introduced me to her. Worst mistake I ever made was getting with her."

"You done fantasizing yet, so I can tell her the real story?" Razor asked.

"Oh, that's not the real deal, Uncle Razor?" Audrey laughed.

"That's the gospel according to Papa. Let me tell you the gospel according to Razor."

Chapter 16

Raymond 'Razor Mouth Slick' Hathaway

"Now, Audrey, I want you to listen and listen well because if you don't, you might miss something."

Turning the signal on, she giggled. "I'm listening, Uncle Razor."

"Now, that whole job incident did have some truth to it, but there was at least one turning point that got us disrespected."

"You better shut yo' old ass up, Razor." Papa spun around in his seat, facing me with a scowl.

"I don't give a shit about yo' face being all balled up. This road trip is about redemption. So, let me redeem you, nigga," I lightly chuckled.

"Now, normally, I keep a level head but I'm 'bout to whoop yo' ass if you open that filthy mouth of yours."

"Whatever, it ain't my fault you slept with the man's daughter."

Papa tried to come up out his seat and forgot his seatbelt was even on. "I swore yo' raggedy ass to secrecy and you gon' sit here and do this. In front of Audrey of all people."

"It's about time she found out the truth. We been ducking and dodging for fifty years now and if you want me to enlighten you further, we ain't gotta 'nother fifty in us. So, sit back, chill and listen. It's my turn at the mic."

"Nigga, you always thought it was your turn. That's why yo' ass was always standing in the background. You always wanted to be in the spotlight even when the shit was dim," Dick'Em Down expressed.

"I'mma dim yo' damn light you keep on playing wit' me. You gon' meet yo' maker before it's time, nigga," I threatened.

"Aww, fuck you." Dick'Em spat.

"That's all yo' broke down ass better say," I huffed. "Anyway, back to what I was saying. I knew before that day that Papa was sleeping with Mary Lynn. She used to bring her flat-back ass up in the Ford plant and always flirt under the radar. When I asked him about it, he told me that it only happened once, and it wouldn't happen again, but then the broad came up pregnant and soon disappeared. I don't know what her daddy did to her, but I do know, he took that shit out on us. All of us, not just these two idiots." I pointed between Papa Willow and Drexler.

"So, Uncle Razor." Audrey cleared her throat, looking over at an angry Papa Willow.

"Back to the original question. Why do you feel as if they kicked you outta the group?"

"Ain't nobody kick him outta shit. If it wasn't for that bullshit him and Red Rooster pulled he would still be alive." Papa's voice cracked.

"What girl, Uncle Razor? What you don' did now?" Audrey asked.

"I ain't done did shit, but I will tell you what happened. Since Papa thinks this shit is all my damn fault.

"Hey Razor, bring me that notebook over there in the corner," Red Rooster yelled, tapping his pencil on the table slowly.

I didn't know what kinda music he heard in that head of his, but it was putting a buzz in his fingertips.

I located the notebook and started across the floor. "What you don' cooked up now, negro?"

He chuckled, "You know ole' girl from last night?"

"I know you ain't talking about Diego?" I asked, folding my arms across my massive chest.

"Yeah man, ain't she far out?" he asked all dreamy eyed.

"You gon' be 'far out' if these white folks catch yo' ass. You know that damn girl is mixed with the cracka' DNA."

"Well, I really don't care, man. That's gon' be my wife one day," he said, looking off into the distance.

"Man, you a damn fool." I threw the notebook down on the table and walked away.

I wasn't about to be a part of this here bullshit if I could help it. Red Rooster was playing with fire messing with the Mayor's daughter.

"I might be a fool, but she gon' be mine one day, just watch and see." Red Rooster was wishing on a star, and I was praying that the star didn't fall out the sky on his naive little head.

The motel phone rang, and I bolted across the floor to answer it. I was waiting for Beth Ann to call me, so we could meet up and play hide the banana. "Hello," I smiled, rubbing my hands together.

"Hey Razor, this Velvet."

"What's up, Velvet? Everything groovy?"

"Yeah, yeah, but umm, I need y'all to meet us down at the Brown Theatre."

"What's going on down there?" I asked because I was trying to get in the panties of some lucky lady.

"We performing tonight so be there or be square."

"A'ight, what time?"

"Meet us in a couple of hours and don't be late." I hung up the phone and walked back into the breezeway.

"Yo' we gotta gig in a few hours," I mentioned to Red Rooster.

"Alright, I'm almost done," he smiled down at his notebook.

Red Rooster was still a little wet behind the ears. He was younger than me at 16 and sometimes I felt like he just didn't get it. We were growing up in a time where free love and all that shit was dead. These crackas was still mad at the idea of a white woman hanging off the arm of a black man.

Eventually, we all met up at the theatre. We were supposed to be here for one gig at Charlie's Chicken Shack which was no more than an inner-city dive bar. Our bus had broken down, giving us an extra day in Louisville; a place none of us knew nothing about. The moment Diego walked through the doors, I could sense trouble. After we did our set and sat down to eat, Rooster slid off to talk to her. All of us were worried so we sent Audra to get the scoop on Diego. After we found out she was the Mayor's daughter, the plan was to keep Red away from her for the duration of the trip. As we got dressed for the concert I could see that Red was grinning from ear to ear about something. I didn't even want to know what it was. The plan was to just keep an eye on him until we left the city.

Since it was only a few blocks to the theatre, Red Rooster and I decided to walk.

"You really like ole girl, huh?"

"She real special," Red beamed. "She not like the girls back home."

"You damn right about that. She is the daughter of a white Mayor that would likely have you hanged for even talking to her. We got plenty more shows lined up. Plenty more women to see. Don't just settle for this one," I pleaded.

"I ain't settling. I really care about her."

"Red, it's only been one night. You ain't even sampled the sweets yet. How you know you like her?"

"Look," Red stopped and jabbed his finger into my chest. "Y'all go out here and knock off broads in every city. I don't never say nothing. Just because you ain't never loved nobody don't mean that I can't. I said what I said now just leave it be."

Even though Red was about 6'7 and outweighed me by fifty pounds, I knew I could take him in a fight.

"If that's how you wanna play it then fine. Don't say I didn't warn you."

We walked the rest of the way in angered silence. I didn't like being made to feel like I was hassling him when I was only trying to look out for his best interest.

Audra was standing front and center when we approached the service entrance to the hotel. The place was breathtaking as she led us through the kitchen and into the basement where they had a makeshift dressing room set up. She was just as nervous. It was hard performing in front of these crackas, knowing our skin color was a problem but we all needed the money.

Audra ran around making sure we were all together since she was the only one of our women who was able to make this trip. Red's face continued to sweat profusely as she powdered him down. Something had his nerves all messed up. Nobody seemed to notice but me. When we were finally dressed, Dick'Em, Papa, Po-Man, and Velvet all went outside to have a last-minute smoke session. Once the coast was clear, Red pulled me to the side and told me he wanted to sing a song to Diego. I just knew it was a bad idea, and it was gon' cause some backlash, but he didn't really care. He was in love with Diego, and he didn't care who knew, not even her white ass daddy.

We watched a few corny white groups that failed miserably at covering black music before we were announced. Papa peeped around the curtain to see what the crowd was looking like and discovered that they were segregated. We all had it with that shit at the time, so we said we weren't going out. Red was fired up because his girl was there. I tried to pull him to the back to talk some sense into him, but he snatched away from me and ran out on the stage. The announcer didn't bother to say anything, he just moved as the lights dimmed.

"This is dedicated to a special girl. I see you, baby."

I looked out into the audience and low and behold, there stood Diego with her cheeks all flushed red. The worst feeling of dread came over me as I rushed over to where the fellas stood looking pissed off.

"That nigga done lost his ever-loving mind," I said frantically.

"You got that right. Nigga ain't never gonna get no respect pulling shit like that," Velvet declared angrily.

"It's deeper than that fellas. He about to get himself killed."

"What you talkin?" Papa asked concerned.

"Just come on. He got that damn white girl here. Said he wanna sing to her."

I was just as scared of them white folks as Red Rooster should've been, but tonight he was fearless. We all rushed out to the stage causing the audience to cheer with excitement. They thought this was all in the act.

"Get him off the stage, Razor. Why you just standing there?" Papa yelled in my direction.

I was frozen in place. What the hell was I gon' do? It was about 50 angry cracka faces out in the audience as Red kneeled down at the center of the stage holding Diego's hand.

Red Rooster ended his ballad with a high note kissing her hand before he stood to his feet. Any other night, I would've been proud but tonight wasn't one of those nights. He smiled out in the audience as Diego made her way through the crowd back to her seat. He strutted off the stage and Papa being the oldest of all of us went off on him. "Why would you go out there and make a mockery of yo'self? You know what you just did was dangerous, right?"

"I don't care, Papa, I'm in love." Papa slapped the shit outta him.

"That shit will get you killed. Just like it did so many others. What has gotten into you? You don't listen," Papa yelled, all the while wagging his fingers in his face.

"Now Papa, wait a minute," Audra spoke up.

"You stay outta this, Audra. This boy has got to learn how to stay in his place," he spun around and spoke.

"I ain't gotta learn a damn thing," yelled Red as he stormed off.

"See what the fuck you don' did, nigga." I pointed as Red Rooster ran from backstage.

"The boy needs to learn, Razor."

"But why did you have to talk to him like that Papa?"

"You know what, get yo' shit and get on with that, nigga. Y'all too damn soft. You have to develop thicker skin in this industry and not only that but y'all need to stop thinking these white folks ain't gone kill you over something that they think rightfully belongs to them."

I gathered my things and headed out behind Rooster but not before Dick'Em Down rushed in, in a panic, "THEY GOT RED!" he screamed, jumping up and down like he had to pee.

"Who got Red?" we all yelled out in unison.

"Some big ass white boy."

We all ran from backstage and out into the parking lot.

"Over there," he pointed.

It seemed like the parking lot went on forever as we ran full speed ahead but before we got there, the truck spit gravel in our faces.

Audra pulled over to the nearest gas station and parked. Placing the van in its correct gear, she turned it off. Taking a deep breath, she turned in her seat and stared at Papa Willow first.

"You alright, Uncle Ronnie?"

"Yeah, baby girl, I'll be okay," he sniffled and wiped away his tears. "I just wished things could have panned out differently. You know?"

She nodded her head in acknowledgment, then turned in her seat and gave me her undivided attention. I shook my head as the memories flooded through me. I didn't wanna talk about this any further. I pulled the handle, releasing the latch and slid the door back. I needed some air.

Chapter 17

Willie 'Po Man' Jenkins

"Uncle Razor, close that door!" Audra yelled before any of us got the chance to.

She had just gassed up and was well on the highway when Razor pulled that crazy move. I knew he was feeling guilty and all, but there was no need to kill the rest of us. I had my own guilty conscience to worry about.

"Can we please stop talkin' bout Rooster for a moment?" I asked as Razor slid the door shut. "That brings back bad feelins.' Lawd knows we got enough of those floatin' around. Let me take it back to that first Sunday."

Dick'Em whipped his head around, smiling at me. He already knew what I was about to say.

"What was so special about that first Sunday?" Audrey beamed as she looked at me through the rear-view mirror.

"Tell her about that note I hit that would've made Sam Cooke jealous," Dick'Em bragged.

"He did have the church to' up. I got to give it to him," I smiled.

"You 'bout to get us in trouble," Razor laughed before Ronda jabbed him in the ribs.

He shot her a dirty look as Bertha snatched my face towards her. "Y'all betta' not start no fuss. My momma is sittin' over there with the church mothers, giving me the evil eye. If I get in trouble, I'm snitchin' on everybody."

I looked over her head to the other side of the church where her mother was sitting upright with her arms crossed. With her pointed lips and black-and-white dress, she looked just like a penguin. I gave her a toothy grin before turning my attention to the center aisle as the sound of singing filtered in from the tiny front foyer. The ushers opened both doors, allowing the preacher to walk in. I had to admit that he was sho nuff' dapper in his white robe with gold stitching.

"Sweet Georgia Brown, it's hot up in here," Bertha complained.

It was only hot because she had her arm looped through mine as we sat cheek to cheek on that wooden pew. I felt almost like a convict, the way she was keeping tabs on me. When I went to the bathroom before service, she stood outside the door waiting on me.

"Sweetie, you gotta let me breathe just a little bit," I said, sliding my arm from under hers.

My best shirt was soaking wet at the sleeve. It was too hot to put my suit jacket back on, so I fanned my sleeve attempting to dry it.

"That heffa near 'bout had you in chains over there," Razor snickered.

He wasn't doin' no better with Ronda watching his every move.

"How long is this service 'bout to be? I gotta meet this other Philly later on," Razor whispered.

"This my first time being here. I don't know."

"Y'all need to be respectful in the house of the Lord and hush," an older lady interjected.

Her hat looked like a fruit salad in a straw bowl. I could hardly contain my laughter as plastic grapes dangled from the side. Bertha cleared her throat, redirecting our attention to the front doors. The pastor reminded me of a movie star. He looked straight ahead as he walked with his Bible tucked under his arm as if he could see something we couldn't. Black waves sat on top of his head just as fine as you please. Bertha's hair wasn't even that slick. His beard glistened like he had greased it with Murray's Pomade. I was so busy taking everything in that I didn't realize I was supposed to stand up until Razor grabbed my arm. Bertha's momma, Ms. Penguin gave me a death stare from across the church. I wasn't thinking about her.

The smooth sounding falsetto and tenor blending together had captured my attention as a high-yella fella, and tall, dark-skinned brother walked down the aisle after the preacher had prayed and taken his seat.

"What a fellowship

What a joy divine

Leaning on the everlasting arms"

I naturally began to sing along since it was a familiar hymn from my church back home. I was surprised when Razor joined in because I didn't think he knew any church songs.

"Y'all always did underestimate ole' Razor," he interrupted.

"You had your chance to talk. These my memories so shut the hell up," I snapped.

Razor mouthed "asshole" to the cameraman, pointing over at me. I wasn't about to let him ruin my story though, so I ignored him.

"Anyway, before I was rudely interrupted," I continued.

"Now, them brothas can sing. They can really blow," I commented to Bertha after we had taken our seats.

The dark-skinned guy took to the organ, playing Jesus Keep Me Near the Cross, as the yella guy directed the choir. In the second verse, something went wrong with the sopranos. It was as if they had stopped singing altogether. That must have annoyed the director because he began to sing their note to them. Those girls screwed up their faces, obviously embarrassed that this man was out-singing them.

"Oh, so now y'all wanna show out?" the director asked.

The girls all looked like they wanted to cry as he signaled for the organist to stop playing.

"We rehearsed this song two hours the other night with this arrangement. Now, y'all wanna get up here and act like y'all done forgot? Y'all go on and have a seat since you wanna play with God. You won't do it on my time. Go on now."

The sopranos filed out of the choir stand looking completely shamed. Some of them sat in the congregation, but a few walked straight out the door. I had never seen nothing like it.

"Y'all correct me if I'm wrong, but we came here to serve the Lord. Am I right?" the director yelled at the

congregation. A chorus of agreement filled the room, encouraging him to go on. "That's what I thought. I don't want no rocks crying out in my place!"

"I know that's right!" Fruit Hat yelled, jumping to her feet.

The cherries decorating the lid jingled so hard I thought they would end up across the church.

"Well, let's come up in here actin' like we know who woke us up this morning!" the director continued to preach.

The organ began to play as the director grabbed the microphone. "I will go if I have to go by myself! Hit it!" The organ player swiped his hands across the keys like it was a blues concert before playing the first chords of the song.

"Now, this here is jumpin'," Razor whispered.

We all jumped to our feet. I couldn't get over how good the organist and director sounded when they sang together. It was perfect harmony.

By the time they finished that song, there were people slain in the aisles, in the pews, and in the choir stand. The ushers had to open the doors just to keep everyone from circulating hot air as they fanned the fallen.

Even 'Fruit Hat' was passed out. This was the type of thing I had only seen at a tent revival. The pastor hadn't uttered a word yet, and already the church was to' up. This was the first time since I had been in Detroit that I had been to a church that felt like back home in Mississippi. Once the service was over, I made my way through the crowd of girls to speak to the director. He was sweating so bad that his processed hair was glued to the side of his face. A pretty girl in an olive green dressed dabbed at his forehead with her handkerchief.

"I enjoyed, brotha'. Never heard no sangin' like that up this a-ways," I said. He shook my outstretched hand.

"Sho' appreciate that. My daddy gonna have a fit later on about me dismissin' his choir like that, but I'm tired of the half-singin' they wanna do. I'm tryin' to build my reputation up around the city so I can get some bigger gigs than this. I just lost my job at the car plant. I need money If I'mma try to marry this one." He hugged the woman dabbing his head.

Her hand felt soft as cotton as she shook mine.

"Now, that there is music," Razor said over my shoulder. "Y'all made me wanna actually pay attention up in here. Plus, y'all got some real deal foxes walking around through here." He looked over his shoulder as he said that, making sure Ronda wasn't behind him.

"I can't take all the credit. Before Ronnie over there on the organ, got here, it was just boring traditional stuff. My daddy ain't too keen on nothing new. Always cryin' bout something bein' too worldly. I get tired of all that noise."

"Why you ain't put ya foot down?" Razor asked.

"Hold that thought a minute," Drexler answered as his father approached us.

All of the women standing around parted like the red sea, even Drexler's woman.

"Now, you know that ain't the way that song goes. You and Ronnie think y'all runnin' the show around here now?" Me and Razor attempted to back away.

"Nah, y'all young fellas stay right here. Ya' daddies probably never taught y'all nothin' no way, the way y'all were talkin' and carryin' on during my service." Knowing that Razor had a bad temper, I silently prayed that he would keep his mouth shut.

"Now, as for you." The pastor turned back to Drexler. "I want you to know I appreciate what you've done round here. I don't even mind so much the new arrangements. You see them women over there?" He pointed to an elderly bunch of women that were talking by the front door.

"Yes sir, I see them."

"Son, those are the people keeping the lights on in this place. Without their tithing, we would be closed down like most of the other churches that used to be around here. If we run them off, then we have no future. They like the hymns, not the blues. You understand me?" He firmly placed his hand on Drexler's shoulder.

"Yes sir, I understand. The problem is, I like the blues. I like rock too. Everything that you tell me not to listen to is pretty much what I like. If you want me to come up in here and sing these old dusty hymns, then you need to find yourself another director."

"Oh shit," I thought to myself. Drexler's father was taller and bigger than him. He looked like he could punch him into another century. I didn't want to witness that, but I had to respect him for standing up for himself.

"That's how you feel? Come on in the back and let me pay you for your services and you can go on. One thing about it though, once you hit those streets, you better keep on walkin'. Can't no man live in my house that's growner than me." Drexler held a hand up, signaling for us to stay before following his father through a narrow door in the back of the church.

"Don't make no sense," the organ player said, walking up behind us. "What's up, my name is Ronnie Willow, but everybody around these parts call me Papa." I shook his hand while Razor stood there looking crazy.

"I ain't about to call no other man Papa. That's what my woman calls me."

"Fair enough," Ronnie replied, patting Razor's shoulder. "Let me go in here and make sure these niggas don't kill each other. "

"Looks like we got church and a show," Bertha remarked, circling her hands around my waist. I gently pulled her off me, not wanting to deal with her mother.

"You got to stop all that. I don't feel like hearing her mouth."

"Momma already left. She went home to get dinner started."

"Why don't you run along with her? I got some things to handle over here right quick."

"Like what? One of these hussies walking around here in their tired ass wigs?" Her voice was loud enough to turn a few heads.

"Don't you start that. I told you I got some business and then I will be over to the house."

"Take Ronda with you," Razor pleaded.

"Y'all jokas think y'all nickel slick. Let me find out you been in here courtin' with these heffas. You gone have to ask the preacher to lay hands on you before I do. Come on girl," Bertha snapped as she grabbed Ronda who was walking toward her.

"I hope that girl ain't pick-pocketed nobody up in here," Razor joked as they both stormed out of the church.

"Is she that bad?"

"Negro, please! That girl will steal the slick out of paint. She'd steal the silver off the collection plate. Hell, she'd steal the stained glass out the windows."

We were both laughing when Papa and Drexler returned from the office.

"Y'all fellas hungry?" Papa asked.

"If you payin', yeah, I'm hungry," Razor replied.

"Say no more. We goin' down to the Broadnax," Drexler announced.

I thought I had heard him wrong. "You talkin' about over in the red-light district?"

He looked over at me as if I was an idiot. "Your point is what? I'mma send my old lady to the house. We gon' go over there to the Broadnax and get us some vittles and maybe even a few other things," he winked.

Everybody else seemed comfortable with the idea, but that wasn't really my type of thing. My momma had always warned me to stay away from prostitutes since it was a prostitute that gave my daddy the syphilis that killed him. "You gon' bring ya square ass on?" Razor whispered.

Papa and Drexler stared me down.

"Yeah, I'm goin. Y'all lead the way."

We got to that motel and ate to our heart's content. They had every damn thing on that buffet. After we were good and full, we sat around in the parlor, entertaining the women with a few songs. As good as we sounded together you would think we had been performing for years. My voice was just a step under Drexler's falsetto, Razor had a raspy tenor, and Papa's tenor was a little more polished like he had been trained. We didn't miss having a bass, but that was the only thing that could have made us any better.

That night was the first time I had ever laid down with a prostitute. Wish I could say it was the last time. Black Licorice was her name. She was just as nasty too. That morning at checkout time, Drexler paid for everything. Turns out his daddy had went on and paid him out for the rest of the year. I thought it was crazy that he had spent so much money on people he didn't even know. It just showed what type of man he was. He told us we could pay him back by singing with him and Ronnie at this juke joint a few nights a week. We agreed, not thinking too much about it. That's where we met Velvet, but I will let him tell his own story.

Chapter 18

Raymond 'Razor Mouth Slick' Hathaway

"Now wait," Audrey chuckled. "I have a question before Uncle Benny gets started because his storytelling is a little eccentric for lack of a better word. Now, for the sake of the audience-."

"The audience?" Velvet interrupted, looking around. "Ain't no damn audience. It's just us five niggas and these fools you got back here with they cameras all in my damn face. Would you scoot over?" he yelled at one of the cameramen.

"Uncle Benny, don't start acting crazy. I done been through this one time too many. Now pay attention."

Velvet mumbled something under his breath, and Audrey cut her eyes into slits as she dared him to make a peep. After an intense stare down, Audrey cleared her throat and continued.

"Like I was saying," she rolled her neck. I would like for the audience to get a chance to understand the reason behind these nicknames or some po' fool is gone be confused," she reasoned. "Now, who wants to start?"

Raymond cleared his throat and turned towards the camera. He smiled, and his front teeth shined brightly being he had them outlined in gold. I don't know what possessed his ass to dip his dentures in gold, but that was neither here nor there. The cameraman sat up and tapped away on some buttons and then pointed his finger in Raymond's direction.

"Hey black people, my name is Raymond Hathaway better known to the world as Razor Mouth Slick. Now, I earned this name. This wasn't no shit that was passed down by a bunch of hard-legs. Naw, this name earned me the right to roam the streets freely with no fear." he paused and swooshed his tongue around in his mouth and pursed his lips. We all watched him as he pushed his tongue out slightly and his dentures fell out and right behind it was the razor he always kept placed under his tongue.

We all fell out laughing, even ole' Willie got him a few chuckles in. Raymond's face was so balled up it was like he swallowed too much lemon juice. I damn near pissed on myself at the look of shock on Audrey's face.

"I used to do this with ease," he said, still trying to play debonair while fixing his teeth and pressing the razor under his tongue.

"Why do you still keep a razor in your mouth, Uncle Razor? Aren't you afraid of cutting yourself?" Audrey asked.

"Naw baby, I ain't thinking 'bout nothing like that, and to answer your question, I do it outta habit. Once I learned that I could conceal a weapon in the one place they wouldn't look. I practiced at my craft. Every time one of them crackas put they lily white hands on me, I would spit my razor out and slice they asses good." He had a scowl on his face as if he remembered a bad time in his life.

Audrey nodded her head signifying that she understood where he was coming from.

"Okay daddy, I don't know if I wanna know but, what about you?"

Dick'Em rubbed his chin and sat back in his seat. All he needed was a cigar and a snifter of cognac. He looked up briefly and chuckled as if he remembered something juicy. "What's up y'all? My name is Drexler

Davis better known to the world as Dick'Em Down. Now, my name is pretty much self-explanatory. At the age of 14, I lost my virginity to my mother's best friend. I remember her well. She was about my momma's height at 5 feet and 7 inches of pretty caramel skin, a warm smile, big knockers, a small waist and an ass that put the state of Texas to shame. Umph!" He stopped to shake his head.

"Anyway, one night she calls me over and basically tells me she's gonna give me some life lessons on how to be a man. After that first night, I went back for lessons two and three. That woman sho' could swivel her hips. It was like once I got that first piece of pussy, I couldn't help myself after that," he chuckled.

"You just don't care what you say, do you?" Papa yelled out. "Yo' daughter sitting right there and you talking about yo' first piece of pussy."

"It's okay, Uncle Ronnie." Audrey waved him off. "I've been knowing this man all my life, nothing surprises me anymore."

Dick'Em being childish turned in his seat and stuck his tongue out at Papa.

"Were you done talkin', dad?" Audrey asked him, trying to give him a chance to finish.

"Yeah, I'm done man." Now, he had an attitude.

"Okay, umm, Uncle Ronnie. Why don't you elaborate on your story?"

"I don't have a story, suga. Before I was shipped off to live with my father in Alabama, I was raised in Mississippi by a single mother who had a dream she couldn't wake up from. Every morning, she would come in my room and say, *"Get up, Papa; it's time for school."* and in those days, even though school was important, I didn't wanna walk damn near three miles or more just to share a school closet with twenty or thirty other niggas that was itching to learn the white man's knowledge of how *we* the black community was *supposed* to live. We still lived in a time that if you even sneezed in a white woman's direction, you could get killed. We still lived in a time where niggas was still being hung from trees which soon earned the name *'Strange Fruit'*. I didn't earn my name like some of these fellas. My name was given to me by my momma who said that I look so much like my Papa that she felt since he wasn't shit, I wasn't gone be shit either. Well, I proved her wrong, and one day she'll understand that; whether in this lifetime or the next."

We all sat there gaping at Papa. This was the first time in a long time no one had a rebuttal. Even ole' Velvet stopped shaking for a whole minute.

We all looked at Audrey, and she was wiping her tears away. "Umm, who's next?" she cleared her throat and tried smiling. "Uncle Benny? You ready?"

That nigga nodded his head in three different directions. "Get it together nigga, damn," I mumbled.

He struggled, but he sho' in the hell just flipped me off. I'm trying to tell you, we was a bunch of old nigga's with the hearts of children.

"Fuck you, Razor," he finally said.

"Took you long enough nigga," I laughed slapping my knee.

"You better stop slapping that thing before it falls off," he chuckled, referring to my prosthetic leg.

I couldn't even be mad at the nigga as we all laughed at my expense.

"Anywho, my name is Benny Pryor, better known to the world as Velvet Rose. I know y'all wanna know if my name was given or earned. That's something you'll have to figure out on your own. I was the coldest nigga in the wind beside Razor over there. I was born and bred in Chicago, Illinois. My father was a factory worker, and my mother was a waitress down at the local diner. I had eight brothers and four sisters. I was somewhere in the middle, getting lost in the remembrance of each child. We were so poor that our hand-me-downs had hand-me-downs. My father wasn't making much, and with what my mother brought in, was only enough to cover rent and bills. We ate so many sugar sandwiches, I'm surprised I didn't get the sugar like this ole' fool," he coughed and laughed while pointing in my direction.

"You gone leave me alone, ole' shaking ass nigga," I retorted.

Velvet dismissed me with a wave of his hand and continued his story, "Like I was saying, since food was scarce, and money was leaving as fast as it arrived, I decided to get out there and see what I could do to help. There was this young cat by the name of Fletcher, he had to be about 17 or 18. He would normally get the little kids from the block together and pay them to fight. Well, I walked up to him one day and asked him if I could fight for him. He laughed me off, called me scrawny and swore up and down that I couldn't bust a grape," he paused to laugh.

"Fletcher called this boy over that was waaayyyy bigger than me. He told me if I could knock the bigger boy out before he could rip me apart he would pay me five dollars. I was too excited. Do you know how much five dollars was worth back in them days? You could probably buy a coupla' sacks of groceries." Po-Man sat up front shaking his head. That was right up his alley.

The crowd was thick, and I was terrified, but you wouldn't have known by just looking at me. I squared up. I was at least 5 inches shorter and 30 pounds lighter. Fletcher counted down from five, and before he could say one, I was on that boy's ass. I was throwing right hooks, left hooks, kidney shots, and uppercuts. Before the boy could throw a connecting punch, he was asleep on the sidewalk. Fletcher slapped five dollars in my hand.

"Here you go slick. I'mma have to come up with a name for you. You was as smooth as silk out there. That nigga didn't know what was hitting him or who for that matter," he laughed, walking off.

As I got older the more fights I got into. Being a street fighter wasn't an easy task, but it earned me more than enough money to take care of what was needed. I went from hand-me-downs to crushed velvet. I had all the ladies swarming around me. If I wasn't singing, I was kicking ass down behind the old elementary school that no one attended anymore.

Then one night, I was sitting on this crate with this old head sharing a bottle of Red Irish Rose.

"So, what you gon' do youngin'? You gon' sing or what?"

"Why you need to know old head?"

"Because you need to figure out what you want and go for it."

"Well, what if I want them both?" I asked, passing him the bottle.

"Then go out and get em' both," he advised as he took a sip of the drank.

"A'ight, old head. I need to head home before my ole' lady come lookin for me." I threw my hand up and proceeded to walk away.

"See you later, Velvet Rose." I turned and looked at him and smiled. Velvet Rose, I like that. I said to myself.

So, if you wanna know how I got my name, I got it from an old head by the name of Winston Baskar," he coughed, zoned out and began that shaking shit again.

"I guess, we'll get back to this story after we go get some grub. Y'all need to hurry up. I ain't had Golden Corral in a cool minute. My stomach is introducing itself to my backbone." I looked up and noticed Audrey staring at me. "Close yo mouth gal and come on."

"Ugh, you just rude for no reason. Get out my van, Uncle Razor," she grumbled.

"I hope you fall when you do nigga," Dick'Em threw in. I wanted to say *fuck all y'all* but I kept my mouth closed or Audrey would drive for at least three more hours while feeding us them damn cold cuts. I wasn't gone be able to do it.

"Can somebody help with getting Uncle Benny out the back?" Audrey asked, kicking her door open and placing her jacket over her shoulders.

"I'll help, as long as you hurry up," I answered.

"You ain't that damn hungry," Po-Man commented.

“I don’t know why you talking. You just gon’ wait until we all through eating before you ask for the leftovers,” I laughed.

“Nah, but for real, Po-Man, I got something to say.”

“What you want Razor? And don’t say nothing stupid or I might just jump over this here seat. I ain’t buckled in now, nigga.”

“When you get in here, pay the fifteen dollars it’ll take to buy you a real meal. You ain’t had one since Dick’Em’s momma invited us over for Sunday dinner back in 1978.” Audrey’s mouth fell open, and Dick’Em laughed so hard he nearly rolled out of his seat.

“Would y’all come on and stop?” Audrey laughed through her hand that was covering her mouth.

“Tell him to stop being a tightwad,” I pointed at Po-Man who was fire hot by this time.

“This is gone be one long ass trip,” she said, shaking her head all the while helping the cameraman Scott as he strapped Velvet into the chair lift. Nearby, you could hear Dick’Em and Po-Man arguing about something or ‘nother. Audrey was right, this was gone be one hell of a trip, and we was just getting started.

Chapter 19

Benny 'Velvet Rose' Pryor

"This here ain't goin' how I thought," I whispered to Scott, the head cameraman.

"What's the problem, Mr. Benny?" he asked as everyone else proceeded into the restaurant. Audrey gave me a look, but she wasn't my damn boss. Even her momma couldn't boss me. Here we were on Lindbergh Avenue in St. Louis.

"I told you for we started to call me Velvet." It was as if the fates had drawn me here for a reason. One of the worst things I had ever done in my life had happened in this very city. It still made my stomach rumble just thinking about it.

"Velvet, do you need a breather?" Scott asked as the other cameraman, Colin, brought up the rear.

"I just got something I gotta fess up to that's all. If I don't say it, I'mma bust open."

"I'm listening."

"It's about Carole-Anne. If I had known that she was … then I woulda' ..." I reached into my pocket fishing for the spare tissue I always kept.

"Just calm down and start from the beginning. Colin, tell Audrey we'll be along in a sec." The other camera man Colin gave me a pitied look before going inside after the others. He didn't even know what he was pitying. I never liked no man lookin' at me like that.

"All the times I done been here, I couldn't force myself to do it. Just felt that pain in my chest whenever I thought about it."

"Can you be clearer, Velvet?" I eyed that camera wanting to smack it out of his hand. "Don't nobody rush me youngin'," I smirked snidely.

"Velvet, you didn't have to do her like that," Silky said as he observed Carol-Anne leaning over the garbage can puking up the contents of her stomach.

"Silky, now look'a here, I don't tell you how to run your business, so don't tell me how to run mine. That damn girl sick as hell out here. You think I don't know she been getting' high? I know a got-damn junkie when I see one."

"Mannnnn, look'a here, the Chevettes are booked at every major club in the city right now. They even opening at a place called the Hot Fox Lounge just to showcase new singers. How we gonna tell them our lead is on junk?"

"Silky Struthers," I fixed his heavily starched lapel before pulling him close to me, "I brought you outta' the gutta' when I came out of it. You been tryin' to crawl back ever since. You go in that glorified brothel and get us a high-yella bitch to replace Carol-Anne and let me worry about the rest." Silky backed away running a comb through his signature straightened locks that signified how he got his name. The only reason he hadn't got his pretty ass kicked was because he rolled with me. At 5'3, and the color of pancakes, with a face full of freckles, nobody took him seriously. It didn't help that he always wore boots to hide the lifts in his shoes. The man looked like a woman from behind and not too much different from in front.

"You gonna regret not letting her go on," he remarked before stumbling back toward the Broadnax. We had a nice little drink that day celebrating the Chevettes getting an appointment with Motown, but now we knew those dreams were over. Carol-Anne had been the only reason they looked twice at the girls. Her voice was the least remarkable of the three, but she had an hourglass figure that made a man wish there was more than 24 hours in a day. She was also the only one that didn't have to wear a wig because she was mulatto. Her curls hung down to her shoulder blades when she wore it natural, and near 'bout to her waist when she had it straightened. Her eyes were so light they looked almost looked like stained glass. I could have choked her right then and there for costing us everything.

"Edith and Rosalyn, y'all go on. I got her," I announced, walking over towards the back door of the Broadnax. They hovered over their sister trying to protect her as usual. These wenches were the real problem because they were the ones enabling her.

"Naw, we not goin' home without Carol-Anne," Edith snapped. She moved in front of me as I tried to grab Carol-Anne around the waist to lift her up. "What I just said?" she spat from the mile-long gap in her teeth. "She sick. You tryna' kill her. All we is to you is some money."

"Money? Bitch, what money is to be made with a junkie? Y'all cruising by on her looks. Y'all ain't thinkin' bout her health. Long as you get your tar-colored ass up there and get a few catcalls and whistles, you think you done did somethin'? Me and Silky ain't fooled. We know y'all been bringin' her that junk she keep shootin' up her arm."

Edith's eyelids fluttered as she tried to avoid spilling the guilty tears that were killing her to hold in.

"She gets mad," Rosalyn spoke up in her tiny voice. "If we don't cop her nothin' she gets mad and mean. Look at this." Rosalyn stepped into the light revealing a shiner that she must have hidden earlier with makeup. Her bronze skin was beautiful except for that black ring around her left eye that threatened to close shut.

"Shut the fuck up!" Carol-Anne yelled out as she turned around. Dried pieces of vomit were crusted around her lips as she pointed a red nail in Edith's face. "You ape-lookin' bitch. All you had was one job to do. And you, you better be glad I didn't uppercut yo' ass! Told y'all to get me my shit so I could get outta here, but y'all wanna stand around courtin' these niggas that don't even want ya. I'm the reason we even sell a show, and I can't sing a lick. I got this though," she lifted her satin dress over her waist revealing a neatly trimmed bush. She wasn't lying about the gold between her legs because I had samples of it more than once myself.

"Come on, Edith. We ain't got to be talked to like this," Rosalyn piped up.

"Bitch, I will talk to y'all how I want to!" I held my hand out as Carol-Anne lunged at her sisters. As thin as she was, the girl was strong. I had to wrap my arms around her waist like a vice-grip.

"Get on out of here!" she yelled as they hightailed it down the street. "I can replace both y'all ugly whores! Fuck y'all!"

She collapsed into a fit of tears as I scooped her up into my arms, placing her on the hood of Silky's Cadillac.

"Why you startin' trouble like that?" I asked, gently grabbing her face in both hands. "We gonna lose everything because you done formed yourself a lil' habit."

She waved me off carelessly.

"Don't let them bitches fool ya'. We all getting' high. I just happen to do it more than they do." I knew she was lying, but I let her go on as the back door of the club opened.

"Aye Velvet, get in here. You gotta hear this! These fellas is somethin' else!" Silky yelled out.

"Now, you wait your ass right here and don't move." Carol-Anne looked down at her nails as if I hadn't said anything to her. "I mean it. Stay your ass right here now." I backed away from her making sure she didn't budge until I reached the door. The scent of ham hocks, greens, cabbage, fried chicken, meatloaf, and macaroni wafted around the kitchen. Ms. Katie, the head cook smiled at me as she slid a piece of chicken in my hand as we passed on by. I was gnawing on it when I heard the most angelic sound I had ever heard in my life.

Amazing Grace was a song even my heathen ass was familiar with. I followed Silky into the main lounge area where four fellas were harmonizing it to a crowd. Every John and whore in the building was sitting around listening to these guys as they crooned their hearts out. The falsetto of the yella guy knocked me out. It was as if he had swallowed an angel when he opened up his mouth. We all stood there transfixed as they sang every verse finishing with the falsetto guy going back to the top. Me and Silky exchanged looks because we suddenly had the same idea. After the applause died down, we made our way over to the table introducing ourselves. The main guy I was interested in was the falsetto singer named Drexler. He had a voice that could really go places. Surprisingly, they said they weren't a group. Said something about meeting up at church that same day. Well, Silky wasted no time lettin' em' know our connections in the music business.

Drexler was excited, but the other guys didn't seem sold on it. They mentioned something about not having a bass singer for the real low parts. Now I knew that I was decent, but I kept that under wraps because it was not something I never really saw myself doing. I wanted to be in control of the business end. We asked them to sing Swing Low Sweet Chariot just to have an idea of what all they could do, and before you knew it, I jumped my ass in there. Silky just about blew his top when he heard my voice. Drexler took my card and promised he would keep in touch, but the other guys still seemed resistant. We left them to enjoy the rest of their night. Once we were back outside, Carol-Anne had nodded off on the hood of the car. Anything could have happened to that crazy girl. Well, I was feeling so good that once Silky dropped us off to my car, I gave her a little taste of the good stuff. I just wanted to take the edge off because she was so sick. Man, I didn't think that girl would O.D. in my car."

"Say what?" Scott asked, moving the camera. His eyes were glistening as they pierced into mine.

"You heard me right. That ain't the worst part though. I took her back to her house and looked both ways before sitting her on the porch swing right there at her momma's house. Just left her right there like a piece of trash." I dabbed at my eyes with the tissue that was bawled up in my hand.

"What happened after that?"

"Well, her sisters found her that morning. They came 'round to my house cryin' and screamin' about how they had helped their sister kill herself. To take the guilt off myself, I offered to pay for the arrangements and thangs. They said they wanted to scatter her out here in St. Louis because this was where she was originally from. Trusted me with her ashes. I couldn't scatter 'em though. They been sittin' in a solid brass urn all these years. Couldn't bring myself to part wit' em." My shoulders heaved as I began to sob into my tissue.

"Uncle Benny, what's wrong?" Audrey asked, rushing over to us. I didn't realize she'd been paying attention.

"Oh, he umm, he was just telling me about some personal stuff," Scott covered for me. "We were about to join you all for dinner. I got it covered," he reassured her.

"Alright now. Y'all come on because we gotta make some headway tonight before we turn in." Audrey looked back at me suspiciously before going back inside the restaurant.

"So, we need to get her scattered, right?" Scott asked.

I shook my head yes.

"I'll tell you what. You give me a place, and I will make an excuse to stop. Just anywhere you want to go."

"Edith is still living, and I dug up an address for her. I wrote up a letter too. The urn is in my suitcase. All I wanna do is drop it off, and we keep on movin'. That way, I done my part."

“We’ll make it happen. I promise you. I just feel like there was something more you wanted to say.”

There was much more I wanted to say, especially about Red Rooster, but I would let somebody else handle that.

Chapter 20

Raymond 'Razor Mouth Slick' Hathaway

It was a relief to get back on the road after tearing them folks restroom up. Wasn't a damn thing golden about that corral. Folks didn't know a damn thing about seasoning no food. After sitting around for more than an hour swapping stories with the fellas, I was tired and ready to lie down. Audrey was picky about the hotels and refused to stop until she found one that met *her* standards. I picked up my satchel off the floor and pulled it open. The first thing I noticed, was my grandfather's old harmonica he used to play. I pulled it out, and the memories came spiraling back and slammed into my chest. I remember sitting at his feet when I was a youngin and praying that one day I would get us up outta that one-bedroom shack that had been passed down since slavery.

I remember being about seven years old. It was storming outside so bad that our house was swaying in the wind. It was only God himself keeping our house rooted to the foundation. My mother reached over to the wooden table that had seen better days and turned down the fire on the lantern. She pulled me into her lap and pressed my face to her breast. She rocked from side to side while humming something soft that soothed the fear knocking up against my ribcage.

There was a loud clap of thunder, and the house leaned in the wind. "Get under the table," my mother shouted as she jumped to her feet. I thought to myself, "Why the table?" If anything, she should've said a closet or better yet, under the bed. My eyes were glued to my mother's feet as they scurried around our 500 square feet of nothingness. I watched her from the silhouette of the lantern that was slowly flickering in the wind.

"Stay right there, sweetheart," my mother called out. Whatever she was looking for she couldn't find, and it made her panic. I stuck my head out from underneath the paper-thin tablecloth and watched her as she pulled on the front door.

"Momma?"

"Stay there, baby," she coaxed.

"Ma?"

"Just stay .... There," she snatched the door open, and it slammed up against the wall. Her hair blew wildly in the wind and her thin dress danced against her chestnut colored skin.

As she stepped out on the porch, the door slammed behind her. I ran full speed ahead. I was just a yanking and pulling on that door to no avail. Falling on my knees in defeat I leaned against the door pressing my knees into my chest. I don't know how long I was there but when I looked up I was cloaked in nothing but darkness. The rain had let up tremendously.

Standing to my feet, I brushed off my backside and pulled on the door once again. It slowly creaked open, and I stepped out onto the porch. I looked up in utter dismay. There were broken trees on the side of the road, cars overturned, and people in the street screaming and crying because their houses were reduced to piles of rubble. I walked down the four steps that cracked and splintered into the mushy red clay that clung to my toes; which soon crawled up my legs the more and more I walked. I was transfixed on something that glistened in the dying sunlight. I strolled over and kneeled down beside it. With my hands, I pulled the clay back little by little not knowing what I was witnessing. The more I revealed, the more I dug and the more my vision blurred. I don't know if I was crying or just drunk from the adrenaline coursing through my veins.

I called out for help as everyone began to crowd around me. I knew now, what that burning sensation was behind my eyelids. I felt someone grab my shoulder pulling me away from what was in front of me. I kicked and screamed, begging to be let go. I couldn't leave her, but she was already gone.

In the open fields of Mississippi, there was a tornado that blew my mother off course as she tried to save the few chickens we did have. Right by the chicken coop, was my mother, buried under a tree with her face pressed into the red clay the old folks called Mississippi Mud.

For three days, I sat on that porch waiting for my daddy to come home. After about the first week of not eating and not knowing, I got up off that porch and tried to figure out some stuff on my own. One of my mother's friends found me one night rummaging through the trash can and offered me a hot plate, a warm bath, and a place to rest my head.

After being with Ms. Montgomery for a little over two weeks, she finally packed up what little things I had and smiled in my direction. "We going on a trip, Raymond. Your daddy isn't coming back, and neither is yo' momma. Your sisters and brothers all been taken in by folks in the neighborhood, but everybody seems to think you is trouble. Now, I don't mean to sound callous, but I need you to understand this before we leave here tonight."

I nodded my head in understanding.

"Now, when Jackson goes to sleep. I'mma need you to help me push the car away, so we don't make a sound. After that, we gotta get that ole' jit started and get

up outta here, quick, fast, and in a hurry. Do you understand?"

I bounced my head up and down paying close attention because this woman was talking crazy, or so I thought.

That night when her husband came home, he was drunk. I could smell him clear across the room.

"What you in here doing, Rochelle?" he slurred.

"Nothing Jackson," she voiced timidly.

"Where my food at?" he asked as he kicked his boot up on the table. She placed his plate on the table and stood back twiddling her thumbs nervously. Jackson chuckled before reaching over to grab the flask of moonshine he kept in his jacket pocket. After taking a generous sip, he placed his foot on the floor and leaned forward.

"SPOON!" he bellowed.

Ms. Montgomery pulled a spoon from her apron pocket, blew on it, and then wiped it off before passing it to him.

He picked up a spoonful and shoved it into his mouth. It only took a few seconds before he spit it back into his plate. It was like watching a switch flip as his whole demeanor changed.

"BITCH!"

My eyes grew to the size of bo-dollars as I saw the fire ignite in his eyes. While I was worried about the curse words leaving his mouth at a rapid pace, I had no idea he had hit her until Ms. Montgomery landed on the floor.

I jumped to my feet, and the whole house shook, it seemed as I ran to her defense.

"Get off of her," I yelled, beating him in the back with my small fists. Jackson turned just enough and knocked me in the chest. I went sliding across the worn floorboards.

"Get up, lil nigga," Jackson growled at me. "You wanna hit a man when his back is turned?"

I shook my head no, still trying to catch my breath. He reached down and grabbed a fistful of my hair and began dragging me across the floor. I could feel my skin tearing as he drug me along the cracked floorboards.

I didn't hear her footsteps, but I heard her voice loud and clear.

"LET HIM GO YOU BASTARD!!!" Then there was a crack, and a loud thud as Jackson lay before me with his head split open. "Get up, baby. We gotta go." I scrambled to my feet, trying not to get blood on me.

"Razor!"

My thoughts snapped to as I turned and looked at Audrey. "Hey, suga."

"Don't hey suga me, Uncle Razor. I've been sitting here nearly ten minutes calling your name. Have you been taking yo' medicine?"

"Yes ma'am," I slowly laughed, glad to be in the present day. "So, what's up?"

"Y'all been acting strange all day. What's up with that?" she asked, eyeing me through the rearview mirror. The fellas were all in their own worlds with their phones and other electronics keeping them occupied. I leaned forward, speaking in a hushed tone.

"I don't know what you talkin about but since you're sitting here, you must wanna talk."

"Well, I wanted to know more about Red Rooster. Papa gets too emotional when it all boils down to it. Uncle Benny really didn't know him like that and my daddy is always trying to pretend like things don't bother him. Last but definitely not least, is Uncle Willie whom I love to death, but he can't seem to remember what year it is, so that leaves you."

"Now, I'mma tell you what I remember but you gone have to let ole' Papa cry through it. I wasn't around the nigga like that. His real name was Zaine Tsai. Said his mama was black and his daddy was a China-man. Anyway, the boy was always attracting trouble.

"Get back here with my stuff," the store owner yelled out as he chased the little boy out into the street. He couldn't have been much older than me. The little boy turned around quick enough to grab the crotch of his pants and stick out his tongue. The store owner waved his hand at him dismissively and turned and went back into the store.

I watched the lil boy stop a few blocks up and empty out his front pockets. With that being done, he reached into his back pocket and retrieved a brown paper bag, placing the items inside before standing to his feet.

"Aye," I called out, standing up so he could see me. He looked in my direction and turned back to what he was doing. I started across the gravel. "Aye," I called out again. "You dropped something." I pointed.

He looked over and picked up the orange that was beginning to roll. "I'm Raymond," I said, sticking out my hand.

"I'm none of yo' damn business," he said, snatching up the rest of his items.

I was a persistent lil cat so when he stepped off. I stepped off, "So why you stealing? You hungry or something?"

He completely ignored me.

"You don't hear me talkin' to you?" I followed him for the next block or so.

"Would you stop following me before you get me in trouble?" he gritted. "What do you want? You want me to give you an orange or something?" he asked with his face scrunched up.

Before I could open my mouth to respond, I heard, "Zaine, if you don't get yo' narrow black ass in here! Momma gone be home in a minute and if I don't have something on this table before she do, we all gone have to go find a switch." She looked up and cut her eyes in my direction. "And who is this? What I tell you about bringing strangers to this house, Rooster?" she asked, looking from me to Zaine. He just shrugged his shoulders and pushed past her into the house.

"The hell kinda name is Rooster?" I thought to myself.

For the next few days, I saw Rooster running through the neighborhood with somebody chasing behind him. It never failed. Then one day on my way home from school, I saw a group of white boys all in a huddle around something. There were a few blacks, but none of them wanted to get too close. I pushed through the crowd and soon noticed that right dab in the middle was none other than Rooster. He was swinging his little arms, but it was six boys to his one. I threw my coat off and my satchel down and got right in the mix of things. We got our asses kicked that day, but that was the day we bonded.

We went through what was left of grammar school together. But, when he went off to high school, his momma up and moved. I didn't see Rooster again until he was 15 years old. That was a year before he got killed. I was the one that put the Red in front of his Rooster, so his name didn't sound so goofy.

"Thank you for clearing that up for me. It seems that since you were the closest to him that you would be the most tore up about talking about him," Audrey stated, patting my hand. It was not something that came as a surprise to me. I always knew Red Rooster would get himself killed. Instead of saying anything, I wet my lips and began to play my harmonica. It was the only thing that kept tears from falling down my weathered, brown skin.

Chapter 21

Drexler 'Dick' Em Down' Davis

I was glad once everybody had taken their meds and fallen asleep, especially Razor. I was watching a movie on my electric tablet thingy when I caught him whispering to Audrey. No telling what he was lying about. Now that me, Audrey, and the two tired cameramen, Scott and Colin were the only ones awake, it was as good a time as any to sneak in a little bit of my own story without the fellas meddling. I tapped Audrey on the shoulder, startling her. I could tell she was tired, but my baby was too stubborn to go to a hotel. Something or another had gone on and we had stopped at a small, brown brick house, that sat on the outskirts of town. That cameraman, Scott, had whispered something to her before they helped Velvet out of the van to drop off something in a box. I had been craning my neck to see, but they were standing in the way. Velvet wouldn't say nothing about it once he got back in the van. He just took his meds without argument and conked out.

"Daddy, are you ok? I been asking you what you wanted." Audrey sounded a mixture of tired and irritated. Scott looked up from his phone to see what we were talking about. He thought he was slick, mashing all them buttons on that camera.

"Yeah baby. I'm okay. How you?"

"Daddy, I'm emotionally drained. This has been one hell of a day."

"What ole' Velvet have goin' on back there in St. Louis?" I questioned, looking back at him to make sure he was asleep.

"Can't really tell you that, daddy. It's his own personal business. He didn't even want me to know. Scott convinced him to tell me. It seems like all of you have some secrets. What's yours?" She had hit the nail on the head with that question. From birth, I had been hiding something from her. I just didn't want it to stain her view of her mother's family.

"This is something that might stir up some mess. You sure you wanna know?"

"Daddy, what could be messier than the things y'all done already said about each other? Whatever it is, lay it on me. It may help me stay awake."

"Alright baby girl. You asked for it. Scott, you backup a little bit. Camera so close it could kiss my lips like the women used to."

I took a deep breath knowing I was about to open a can of worms. She wanted the truth though.

"Hey baby, can I talk to you for a moment?" Audra asked before entering my hotel room.

"Yeah baby. Go on ahead. What you wanna talk to daddy about?" I smiled, reaching out my arms to hold her.

Audra's tiny arms crossed her chest as her right foot slid from under her long night gown, tapping the floor slowly. With her hair all done up in curlers, and not a lick of makeup on, she still looked as pretty as a picture.

"What's wrong with you? I mean what's really wrong with you?" Her face turned a shade of red that I had only see when she was feeling under the weather.

"What are you talkin' about, Audra?" I sat straight up in my bed. Now, I had an attitude.

"Can't take you nowhere. You are a low-down negro!" She reached in her pocket, pulling out not one or two, but six pair of women's underwear.

"Where you got them from?" I questioned. I recognized two of them, but the other four I had never seen.

"Don't you dare try to act all innocent. "Pop Rocks' and Bertha told me what happened last night at that after party. You had all the girls hanging off of you like a coat rack. You 'bout the sorriest thing I ever did see in my life. Got a good woman and you can't seem to stay away from all these whores running around here. You gonna mess around and catch somethin' you can't get rid of. I'm not gonna stick around for it. Give me some money so I can get me a bus home!"

"Hold on, baby; let me explain," I pleaded.

"My bags are already packed, and I called a cab. If you don't get me a bus ticket, I will call my daddy to come get me."

"Audra, you bein' unreasonable now. Them hens is clucking because they wanna get you all riled up. They know you the pretty one so they tryin' to get you gone so they can shine."

"Drexler Clydell Harris, I'm tired of your shit!"

"My momma cussed?" Audrey interrupted. "My momma never cussed a day in my life."

"She cussed me near 'bout all night, but I convinced her to stay. Told her I would stop foolin' around. I knew them panties was a set-up though, so I had a plan. While Silky Struthers was working on getting us a real deal, he had set up a bunch of concerts all over the country. We went to anywhere that would pay us a fair price. Our next show was in Tuskegee. That had to be the worst show of my life.

"You got a fine ass woman," Razor commented as Audra helped Willie get his hair together. Ronda sat there with a sour expression on her face. I could smell the Jack Daniels coming through her pores. This woman was gonna be drunk tonight. To make matters worse, once me and Audra made up, Papa and 'Pop Rocks' got into it. He sent her ass packing so quick, you would've thought she said she was pregnant.

"Your eyes don't need to be on my woman. You need to be keeping them on that sticky-fingered gal that belongs to you," I stated, cracking my knuckles.

"Sticky fingers or not, she gets the job done. We makin' pennies off these shows. If it wasn't for her fingers, we woulda been took our asses back to Detroit begging your daddy for a job," Razor asserted.

I couldn't argue with that. Ronda had picked many a white man's pockets during our shows. She wasn't even supposed to be in the audience, but they couldn't resist the ample hips and ass she had on her.

"All I'm saying is, you got the kind of woman that'll make a man wanna change his ways. Hell, we young and all, but you don't meet no woman like that, but once in a lifetime. If you ever fuck up too bad ... I'mma go after that." He pointed at Audra who was now shining my shoes.

"Nigga, I'll kill your first born about this one," I warned Razor before looking down at her.

"Aye, we got a full house out there," Velvet reported as he burst through the door with a tall, dark-

skinned, slim lady wearing a green chiffon dress that matched the color of our slacks. "Y'all meet 'Joanne' I mean Jumpstart," he corrected himself.

"Hey now. Come on in and have a seat with us girls," Audra greeted. Jumpstart followed her over to the corner where she was shining shoes while Bertha and Ronda stared her down.

"How you manage to find a woman in every city?" I whispered to Velvet, who was combing his hair in the mirror.

"The game is to be sold not to be told," he joked. "She was warming my bed last night, if you know what I mean. Plus, we go waaaay back." He spun around giving us a wink.

"Somebody is always warming your bed, nigga. You gon' have more kids than that lady that lived in that shoe," I joked.

"You got your nerve Dick'Em. You been dickin' down everything that got a nice wiggle in her walk. You got that high-yella thang out in Philly, had that redbone in Chicago, don't forget about that dark chocolate thang up in New York. Hell, ain't no tellin' how much pussy you been gettin' since we been in Tuskegee."

I waved my hands frantically trying to get him to shut up. It was of no use. He wasn't paying me no mind. He was too busy putting wave clips in his curls.

"That one girl you had the other night came by my room while me and Jumpstart was getting' it on, she liked to messed our groove up talkin' 'bout she needed some more of your lovin."

"Aye, what you doin fool?" Razor snatched the back of Velvet's pants causing him to turn around. It didn't take him, but a second to realize that Audra was in the room. There was dead silence as his mouth dropped open.

"I thought you said she was goin' home? I thought y'all had got into it," he finally managed to utter.

All of the women turned to me glaring as Audra calmly kept shining my shoes.

"Naw, that ain't right. That ain't right at all," Jumpstart spoke up. Audra rubbed her hand to comfort her.

"It's okay. I'm used to it."

That broke my heart to hear her say that. Razor just shook his head. Po-Man grabbed his things and left the room. Just that quick our whole morale had dropped down.

"Aye fellas, y'all wanna practice with a hymn?" Papa suggested.

I knew he was just trying to break the bad spirit in the room.

"Y'all need to sing Swing Low Sweet Chariot, because I cuts nigga like him," Jumpstart yelled as she leapt to her feet. All I saw was the glint of metal shining as she lunged toward me.

"Oh shit!" Velvet screamed as he ran out, colliding with her.

The next thing I knew I was on the floor lying under Velvet. Warm fluid trickled from my shirt as Audra screamed.

Papa snatched up Jumpstart and tossed her out of the room before helping Razor to get Velvet off of me.

"Oh my goodness, look at all that blood!" Ronda panicked. Audra kneeled next to me unbuttoning my shirt as Velvet sat down in a chair.

"How bad is it?" I questioned.

"Wait a minute. He ain't cut," Audra answered.

Our eyes all turned to Velvet who was panting for air. When Razor ripped his shirt open we saw the blood coming from his chest.

"Oh gotdamn! She stabbed him in the back. It went all the way through! Girls go get help now!" Razor commanded.

Willie was almost run over by the girls as he made his way back into the room. With no time to spare, I grabbed the towel draped over his shoulder and used it to wrap around Velvet as tightly as I could.

There wasn't a colored hospital for miles. We had no choice, but to take our chances and have Silky drive him since we couldn't afford to miss out on our money. You would think that would have taught him about that crazy bitch, but he went on to have kids with her. Meanwhile, Audra pulled me to the side after the show and told me that she had lost all respect for me. It hurt because she was my first and only girlfriend. I had many girls I used to be sweet on, but I loved her. She made me a vow that she would never give our child my last name, especially if we ever had a son. She said she didn't want him to be nothing like me."

"That's why I never had your last name? Why didn't you tell me before now? Y'all said it was because you weren't married at the time she got pregnant. You said it would have been inappropriate." Audrey dabbed at her eyes as I patted my pocket for a piece of tissue. "Wait. You both lied to me? I could understand you, but momma?"

"She wanted to protect me, baby. Her whole family turned against her because of me. Many of them didn't even care to lay eyes on you because they thought she was a fool to have my baby. We thought about getting your last name changed a few months after you were born. I messed up so many times, that Audra changed her mind about it. Then uh …," my hands shook so hard that I had to clasp them together. "I went on and gave her that son. She wanted two babies, ya know? I gave her that son, and I uh …"

"Son? Momma had another baby? Daddy, spit it out before I pull this van over!" Her shouting aroused everybody awake. That was what I was trying to avoid.

"She got pregnant 'bout five years after you were born. We were doin' real good by then and she was staying at home with you as much as she could. Every time she wasn't on the road I messed up."

"Wasn't no messin' up. You fucked up. Tell the damn truth about it," Razor instigated.

"You had your turn ole toothless muthafucka. I'm tellin' this."

"Get to the point, daddy."

By this time, Audrey had cried so bad that her makeup was running down the side of her face.

"Well, I had to tell her that I had gotten someone else pregnant. She was this little actress that was in a few little movies. See, our record company used to do movies and music, so they would have the actors and actresses ride with us on the tour bus to save money. Bastards was always cuttin' corners. Anyway, I got her pregnant and had to tell Audra. The studio made Janice abort her baby, and your momma just couldn't handle it. She lost our son. I'm so sorry."

I covered my face trying to hide my tears in the palm of my hands. The van was stark silent except for the humming of the medical equipment. I felt one hand, then two, then three, as Papa, Po-Man, and Velvet reached out to comfort me. The look in my daughter's eyes when I was finally able to hold my head up, was devastating. Instead of healing, this trip was hurting, and the pain would only get worse.

Chapter 22

The Cameraman (Scott)

&

Willie 'Po-Man' Jenkins

"Bertha, is that you?" Po-Man called out to no one in particular. "You need to come on over here and give the old man some suga."

"Nigga, ain't nobody finna kiss you," Dick'Em yelled out.

We all laughed because he knew Willie was a special case.

"I used to go up to the *'Suga Shack'* every Sunday and purchase a pack of squares and an orange drink. Bertha loved those orange drinks. They would cost me a whole nickel." Po-Man smiled and looked out the window at the passing scenery.

"When we going home, Bertha? I got a show to practice for and you … you gotta get them suits sewed up. Yup, and then we gone go to the zoo and see the animals." He looked around at all of us and pointed his finger.

"I remember you," he grimaced, pointing at Scott. "You was that white man that beat po' ole Rooster." He started to rock back and forth as the tears ran down his cheeks one after the other.

"They beat that po' boy so bad we couldn't even recognize his face. The Mayor just stood there wearing a smug look like he knew this day would come." Po-Man placed his hands over his ears. "The screaming, Diego screaming. I remember her beating her father in the chest.

Telling him that he was dead ass wrong for what he had done and that she would never forgive him. The cries of agony as she leaned over Rooster's battered body and held him close to her chest. I remember her looking up at Drexler and then …" Ole' Po-Man just froze and stopped talking. We were getting some good footage and then everything just stopped as if I had pressed pause.

"He didn't mean to kill that boy. That wench lied on him. She was screwing that boy all along and didn't want nobody to know. Her daddy was drunk that night he came to the show." We were all tuned into the story like we were watching channel 6 news. With Po-Man, he didn't talk much but when he did, it came out in code. It was like he was piecing the story together as it came to him.

"I don't think he saw me because if he did, he wouldn't have stabbed that boy. He smiled sinisterly and stabbed that man in his side repeatedly with what looked like an icepick. I remember watching in horror as he turned on his heels and walked out the door. Nobody understood what happened, but I understood." He turned in his seat and stared straight at Razor. "I understood." Po-Man nodded his head in confirmation. "I understood," he repeated. He looked around at all the shocked faces and turned back to the window.

"Bertha, bring me a sandwich. I'm hungry and you in there playing wit' yo'self. Wash yo' hands before you touch my bread'." Po-Man rubbed his hand across the top of his head and licked his lips before a wide grin spread across his lips. The next thing that came out his mouth was awe inspiring.

"Swing low, sweet chariot

Coming for to carry me home

Swing low, sweet chariot

Coming for to carry me home"

I panned the camera around as Dick'Em, Velvet, Razor, and Papa began to join in one by one. Their voices were still just as silky as they was back in the day. I caught a glimpse of Audrey wiping the tears away as she too listened. This was *Members Only* singing and to some, that was good enough; but to us, this was family. They sang as if tonight would be their last show and I'm glad that I was able to catch it all on film. Most of the documentaries I had been involved in were intent on making the celebrities look liked Gods. They dictated everything you could record and couldn't record. This was the first time in my career that I was involved in a completely unscripted project. You don't really know a person, unless you can truly walk in their shoes. Well guess what, I'm walking.

Chapter 23

Charlene 'Pop Rocks' Willow

Harmony Healthcare

That Mandala bitch thought she was nickel slick, but I had her penny change. How the hell you lose five old fools that don't know their left foot from their right? These niggas had planned this. Me, Bertha, and Ronda were convinced of it. Then Audrey disappeared too. That lil heffa had something to do with this shit.

"Aye, can we get some service?" Ronda shouted. Bertha was sitting on the bench looking like a statue of Jane Pittman or some damn body with her lips all poked out.

"Ma'am, can you please keep it down? It is after hours and residents are trying to sleep," the bag-of-bones, white manager said as he walked around the counter.

"If y'all would help us then we wouldn't be carryin' on, now would we?" Ronda shot back before taking a sip of her coffee.

I had a feeling that ole heffa had some Wild Turkey in that cup from the way she was swaying left to right with no music playing.

"We're doing everything that we can to locate them. The problem is that none of these men were placed here involuntarily which means that they were free to leave whenever they wanted to.

"Willie got problems with his mind. He won't take no medicine or nothing for it," Bertha finally spoke up.

"Muthafucka ain't gon' take nothing that costs more than fifty cents," Ronda whispered to me. She was sure right about that. Him and Bertha were tight as butt cheeks in the penitentiary. They mooched off all of us the whole time the group was together. Used to get on my damn nerves, but the fellas didn't seem to mind.

"Sometimes he says things that don't make no kinda sense. I just be wonderin' every day when he gonna forget about me." Bertha reached inside of the White Diamonds makeup bag that she was using for a purse and grabbed a McDonald's napkin to dab at her tears.

"Po-Man gon' be alright. If they all together, they gon' look out for each other. You better believe that," Ronda said as she took another sip. "They done been friends too long not to take care of each other, even if some of em' don't amount to the shit that comes out of their ass."

She had to be talking about her man Razor because he was the worst of the whole bunch. The only person I couldn't stand more than him was that slimy ass Silky Struthers. Even though Velvet was the one that introduced the guys to Silky, it was Razor who conspired with him to rob the other fellas blind. Ronda was in on it too which is why I made sure my purse stayed under my arm around her. I wouldn't trust that bitch with pocket lint.

"If you ladies would like to go lie down, you are more than welcome to do so in your respected mate's room. We're about to do shift change and it can get a bit hectic in this area," the manager explained.

"Look here pencil dick," Ronda stood up. "We want two things. We want to know where our husbands are, and we want that bitch Mandela, Mandoli, Madea, or whatever the hell her name is, fired. She had something to do with it."

"Ladies, I can assure you that we called Mandala after her shift ended. She is just as upset as you all are. When we have answers we will get them to you. It hasn't been 24 hours, so the police aren't even willing to listen at this point. Please rest and we can reconvene in the morning." He plastered that fake smile white folks always give when they didn't know what else to say.

"Girls, let's just do what the nice man said," Bertha insisted. "We all need to rest our nerves. Sittin' up here thinkin' the worst ain't gon' help matters."

I looked over at Ronda who winked at me. My girls were still as slick as wave pomade. These old heffas had a plan.

We shuffled off down the hallway until the manager could no longer see us. I had gotten his name off of his name tag for future reference. Sylvester was gonna have hell to pay if I didn't get Papa back in one piece. The door to Papa's room creaked open to an empty bed. It nearly broke my heart to think of all the things that could be happening to him right now. Bertha and Ronda slipped in behind me.

"Now, what us gon' do?" Bertha asked, settling into the recliner by the door.

"Don't look at me," Ronda chimed in, "Pop Rocks is the one that always does this type of thang."

I rolled my eyes at her. She knew I hated that name. It was well-earned though. Nobody in the history of the world knew how to pop up on somebody better than I did.

I was madder than all hell when Papa sent me home. The next day I got a call from Bertha that some crazy heffa had stabbed Velvet Rose. Quiet as kept, me and Velvet messed around a few times. It started with him walking in on me as I was getting dressed at one of our shows. Every now and then the fellas would let us come out on stage to be some eye candy for the men's. They didn't do it too often because the groupies got jealous.

"Oh shit! Girl you scared the hell outta me. I didn't know nobody was back here," Velvet exclaimed as he snatched the curtain close.

"That's okay. They shoulda' had us a proper dressing room so we didn't have to share with y'all."

I struggled getting the girdle pulled over my ample hips. For at least 15 minutes, I had been trying to get this thing on. I called out for Audra, Bertha, and Ronda, but none of them was nowhere to be found. That's when I realized they were probably next door at the dining hall still eating. I was always shamed to get dressed in front of the other ladies who had nicer bodies, so I usually slipped away to get ready alone. Today I had filled up on too much food and was bloated.

"Hey, Velvet you still there?"

"Yeah, I was looking for my tie," he answered from the other side of the curtain. The material was sheer enough for me to see the outline of him as he kneeled down at his suitcase.

"Can you help me right quick? It will only take a minute."

"Sure thing, baby." Velvet stood up dusting his hands off before he approached the curtain. I turned my back to him once he slid it aside.

"I can't pull my girdle up."

"Oh, you ain't said nothin' but a word woman. I used to do this for my momma every Sunday morning. The best thing to do is just bend over so the material can stretch out some.

I had never put my girdle on like that, but I took his word for it. As soon as I bent over, I felt the warmth of his fingertips as they grazed my waist.

"Okay now I'mma give this a pull. You hold on to that pipe in front of you."

That wasn't the pipe I wanted to hold on to. The first time I laid my eyes on the tall, dark, and handsome, piece of mahogany, I knew I had to have him. The man never looked at me twice though. He always had a different woman on his arm. That irritated me and Ronda because we both thought he was something sexy. Bertha even used to suck her teeth when he walked past. Audra was the only one that wasn't captivated by his magic.

"I can't seem to get it." Velvet struggled as his pelvis touched my hind parts. He was steadily pulling while I pushed my stomach out to keep it from coming up. The sensation of his hands around my waist reminded me of how gentle Papa used to feel when we we're making love. These days we'd rather argue than touch each other.

"How about if you do it like this?" I spun around yanking my girdle down with my panties going with it. His eyes bulged out like he had seen a ghost. "Come on and get this sweetness. She been waitin' on you." I stepped out of

the girdle kicking it to the side. Velvet licked his lips not knowing what to do with himself.

"Now, Charlene, you need to put ya clothes back on. Papa come up in here, he'll be ready to kill us both."

"At least I'll die with some good dick inside of me. Now pull that snake out or do you need my help?"

Before he could answer, I was down on my knees unzipping his pants. Just like I thought, he was packing like a horse. I pulled his pants around his ankles admiring the beauty of the biggest, blackest, thickest, prettiest, dick I had ever laid eyes on. I could feel myself dripping with excitement as I took him into my mouth. He may have felt bad at first, but pretty soon his hand was on the back of my head shoving inch by inch inside of my throat. When he thought I was choking, he eased up not realizing I didn't have a gag reflex. I sucked and slobbered all over that thang until it was as hard as a marble.

That negro bent me over and rammed off in me like he was packing gun powder into a musket. He was the only man to ever make me squirt. We kept that secret between us though. I never even told the girls. When I found out he had gotten stabbed, I knew I had to come see bout him. My daddy had a shiny red Ford truck that he was crazy about. For it to be a work truck, he made sure it stayed spotless at all times. While him and momma was sleeping, I snuck his keys off the top of the Frigidaire and stole that damn truck, filled that thang up, and got on the road. I drove to I near 'bout fell asleep behind the wheel thinking about not getting to say goodbye 'til Velvet gave me the strength to drive the rest of the way. I had to check four different hospitals until I found him.

"How did you get here?" Papa asked, folding up the newspaper he was reading. The tiny room was crowded with all of the fellas who had fallen asleep while holding vigil over Velvet.

"How you think I got here fool? I drove."

"You did what? You don't barely know how to drive."

"Well, I learned," I sassed, walking over to Velvet. Once he felt the touch of my hand it stirred him awake.

"Charlene?" He tried to sit up in the bed, but it was too painful.

Seeing the pitiful state he was in made me emotional. Papa came over hugging me from behind. He had no idea that I was crying because I thought I was going to lose my lover. After that night, I thought me and Velvet would be an item. He went back to his ways soon as he got to feeling better. Me and Papa went right back to fussin' too. He put me off of several tours and I always popped my ass right back up. That's how Razor came up with the name, 'Pop Rocks' for me.

"You over there talking to yourself. Maybe Po-Man ain't the only one losing his mind," Ronda suggested, twirling her finger around her ear to indicate that I was crazy.

"Nah, I was just thinkin' bout somethin,'" I laughed. "Remember, when Papa used to always kick my ass off the tour buses, I would always managed to find them in the next city. Ain't nothin' changed. I'm still 'Pop Rocks' got-dammit. Watch this." I grabbed my glasses from the chain around my neck before rummaging in my purse for my cell phone. I knew who could help us.

I tapped my foot impatiently as I listened to my daughters phone ring.

"Hello?" she asked, before clearing her throat.

"Rita, baby I know you gotta go to bed in the morning, but I need a quick favor. Is Walter still up?"

"Momma, it's late. You know I gotta get up at six," my daughter replied tiredly.

"I know, baby. It's just that your daddy lost his phone. You set up that thang on the computer for when we lost our phones last time, remember?"

"Y'all are too much. How he lose another phone? Let me see if I can log on real quick. I swear I should have let y'all get them flip phones," she fussed.

I gave Ronda and Bertha the thumbs up as they sat there smiling smugly. Once again 'Pop Rocks' was on the trail. This time she was bringing her girls with her.

Chapter 24

Sharonda 'Ronda' Hathaway

I couldn't wait for this old bird to find my husband. I had a few choice words for his ass. If he thought leaving like a thief in the night was okay, he had another coming. I didn't play that sneaking away shit. The only time I slinked and slid was when it was necessary and fucking with Razor it was always necessary.

After Razor saved my ass from stealing that souse meat, I used to sit back and watch him slink across the school grounds bopping his head to what, I didn't know. Razor was all of six-three with an athletic build. He had the brightest smile but the one thing that captured my heart was his skin tone. He was the color of close to midnight. It was something about his dark skin that drove my hormones into a crazed frenzy. I would watch him bopping his head to whatever song was dancing around in his head. He would look up and smile, nod his head in a way of speaking, and go back to whatever tune he had playing in his mind. The more I watched him, the more I wanted to get to know him. The block he lived on wasn't one I was allowed to go to. At the time, my daddy was so adamant about me not being a fast-tail girl that he didn't want me hanging around the hoodlums. Little did he know, I was one of the hoodlums. When I got the chance to go out to the stores, I would steal just about anything I could get my hands on. Whatever I didn't want to keep for myself, I sold to the very same hoodlums he didn't want me around.

One day, while sitting in the living room watching the black and white tv, Clara, the lady that my dad wanted me to call momma, pranced around in front of my program. She was on my nerve with all that carryin' on. The moment she disappeared into one of the back rooms, I knew it was about to be some trouble.

"What is this, Sharonda?" she asked, seeming to appear out of thin air.

I looked up and scowled in her direction. "Money. What it look like?"

"Where did you get it from?"

"Where did you get it from?" I asked, standing to my feet.

"Don't do that. Don't answer my question with a question. Just answer the question I asked you."

"What did you ask me because now I'm confused?"

"You know what. Go in your room and wait until your father gets here."

"Can I have my money back?"

"No," she stiffly said, placing my money in her brassiere. When my daddy got home he was too tired to argue and Clara was too drunk to care.

A few weeks went by and I was on my way home from my friend's house when I saw a lady sitting on the porch. "Excuse me, ma'am, are you lost?" She looked up from the thick book she was reading with the prettiest greenish-hazel eyes I ever did see.

"No, I'm waiting on James," she smiled.

"James who?" I asked with my eyebrows raised.

"James King. Do you know him?"

"Yeah, the bastard is my father," I replied, stepping around her and making my way up the stairs.

I could feel her on my heels as I jogged up the stairs to our modest apartment. I fished the keys out of my pocket as she gave chase. The door slammed right in her face as she made it to our doorstep. I didn't have a good feeling about whoever she was because women like that always meant trouble around our parts. I threw my items down on the coffee table and looked around. What my daddy didn't buy, I stole. When he didn't have enough money to make ends meet, I stole everything under the sun to turn a profit. I hated this shit, but it was my life and you know what they say ... you can only play the game with the cards you're dealt.

"Little girl, you better let me in!" the lady bellowed from the other side of the door.

It was no doubt in my mind that she was another one of daddy's scorned lovers. I knew if I didn't get outta here, I wasn't gone be shit but somebody's part-time lover myself or a permanent fixture to somebody's children. I wanted better than this two-bedroom bungalow. The more clothes I tossed into my suitcase the louder the woman beat on the door. Where the hell was Ms. Clara the one time I needed her?

Suddenly the knocking stopped just as abruptly as it had started. That's when I heard the jingling of keys before the front door popped open.

"Sharonda, you in here?" he asked, causing me to freeze in place. I didn't answer hoping he would just go away. No such luck. He waltzed right down the hall to my bedroom.

"Where you think you going?" he asked, sneering down his nose at me.

"Away," was my only response.

"Away? Away where?"

"Anywhere but here," I answered, closing my suitcase.

"We ain't got no family out here, Sharonda. Yo' momma been long gone and all her people down South. So, once again, where you going?"

"I'm going to find out what it's like to live. I wanna be somebody and all I do is cater to you. What is that gone get me? Huh daddy? Ever since momma left, I've had to fend for myself. You keep bringing these random women around here and they do nothing but suck up what little life we have in us. Don't you see it? Don't you see that these bitches ain't about shit? As long as you're giving them money and breakin' them off they're fine, but as soon as you're too tired or can't afford their lifestyle they up and leave. Ms. Clara stayed for all of six months before you told her no and she up and left. She left daddy, over ten dollars and a pack of Kool's," I yelled out, stomping my foot on the hardwood for emphasis.

"Now, some yella boned heffa is out there knocking the door down and for what? What she want because we ain't got nothin'. Just let me go, daddy. Just let me leave so I can live for once," I pleaded.

My dad put his head down and I could see the tears on his cheeks. "I didn't know you felt that way," was all he uttered. Sticking his hand in his back pocket, he pulled out his wallet. I folded my arms across my chest and waited and so did the young lady from the door. She had walked her ass up in our place just a skinnin' and grinnin'.

"Here," he thrust twenty-five dollars into the palm of my hand. Placing his finger under my chin, he raised my eyes to meet his. "Make this last as long as you can, because when you leave this house thinking you grown, you can't come back. Do I make myself clear?"

I couldn't believe his words were directed towards me.

With a smile on my face, I replied softly, "Crystal." That was the last time I saw him on this side of glory.

"Ronda, what the fuck you over there thinking about? We got shit to do and you over there in la-la land giving the munchkins a hand job."

I couldn't stand 'Pop Rocks' bad-body-having-ass but she was the Inspector Gadget out of all of us. She was always willing to kick ass and take names, but shit, we weren't in our twenties no more. Hell, sometimes my pimp hand ran outta gas.

"'Pop Rocks', don't start no shit. I'm tired and I wanna get some sleep. You done called yo' daughter already. What more do you want us to do?"

"I want you to pay the fuck attention. You know what, you've been a pain in my ass since I met you," she commented, twisting her wig around the right way.

"And you've been a pain in mine. So, what is yo' point?" I asked, standing up. This ole' kidney bean-shaped bitch wasn't gone keep talking to me like my name was Audra … God rest her soul.

"You know what-." She started across the room and Bertha shot to her feet. She could move fast for a big girl.

"Look, we're all tired." Bertha looked between us both. "Let's just get some rest and figure out everything in the morning."

I cut my eyes at 'Pop Rocks'. She knew I would bop her ass in a heartbeat, all while taking her keys, her money, and her car. I would jet out on these bitches so fast their lifespan would shorten. 'Pop Rocks' huffed, turned and walked away. Bertha cut her eyes at me before straightening her wig and making it out the door. I pulled my cell phone from my bra pocket and decided I needed to make a phone call of my own. Somebody was hiding some shit and I knew just who to call.

Chapter 25

Raymond 'Razor Mouth Slick' Hathaway

I was more than ready to get some rest when we got to the motel. What I was not prepared for was us to be bunking up in three rooms. Me, Po-Man, and Scott, the cameraman, got stuck together. In the next room, Dick'Em, Papa, and Velvet shared a room with the other cameraman, Colin. Audrey got her own room. Imagine that, getting your own room just because you got a kitty kat instead of a ding-a-ling. Didn't make any sense to me. I was willing to pay for my own room, but Audrey insisted that we kept a cameraman present just in case somebody wanted to talk in the middle of the night. Hell, I was all talked out. Right now, I wanted to wash my ass and hit the hay. The thought of having to sleep with Po-Man's ole gassy, snoring ass, was enough to make any man's dick permanently soft.

"You almost done in there? I gotta take a piss!" Po-Man yelled on the other side of the bathroom door. It was bad enough I had to have Audrey use her nursing skills to help me get in this shower. I was not about to rush for nobody, especially not that cheap bastard. He thought I didn't see him stick that bankroll in his sock after dinner. He had been doing that shit for years. If it wasn't him being cheap, it was his oversized, potato sack-built wife cutting corners. Cheap bitch damn near ruined several shows with her penny-pinching in our outfits.

"I don't think that looks right," Audra commented, standing upright. Silky had gotten us our first big show after Motown had passed on us. There we were in Cleveland, Ohio at a black-owned club called The Shot House. There were rumors that the owner, some cat named Billy Paisley, was affiliated with the mob. That explained why we were patted down so thoroughly by the biggest,

strongest, scariest looking Italian, I had ever seen in my life. I told him that he may as well have checked my prostate, the way he felt me up. That big spaghetti eatin' muthafucka didn't find that too funny. If it wasn't for Papa intervening, I would've had to put my razor on him.

"Yeah, tell me about it. Where Bertha at? She know this shit ain't right. I can't go out there with my ashy ankles showing," I commented sourly.

"What you want with Bertha?" Po-Man responded. His big ass always got defensive when somebody said something about that Jolly Green Giant he called a wife.

"Mane, look at my pants. Looks like I got my little brothers knickerbockers on."

"She worked hard on these threads and that's the way you talk?" Po-Man stopped combing the thick mass of naps he had been trying to part in the middle for an hour.

"Now fellas, we don't have to get hostile," Audra said, stepping between us.

"Fuck him. This is trash! I don't know what five and dime she got this fabric from, but it itches, it's ugly, and most of all it's too gotdamn little! I got a ball in each pocket!" I yelled indignantly.

"That sounds like fightin' words to me," Po-Man said puffing his chest out.

"No, y'all are not about to do this. This is the first time y'all going onstage, and you want to go out on a sour note?" Audra intervened.

"Fuck that! He think he can just bully people because he's built like Paul Bunyan. Ain't nobody scared of that big nigga. Come on and get them biceps carved up like

roast beef!" I swished my razor around in my mouth waiting for the right time to strike.

"This is just awful. I'm going to get the others. If y'all want to kill each other, I won't sit around and watch," Audra announced before bolting out of the dressing room door.

"Talk all that monkey junk you was sayin'. Don't get quiet now, Po-Man!"

"Razor, I could break your ass into a million pieces, but Audra is right. We got the biggest concert we done had so far and we out here ready to scratch each other's eyes out."

I knew he was right, but I was amped up. I didn't take too kindly to nobody trying to punk me.

"I don't want to hear that brotherhood shit. I'm tired of you always tryna' jump in somebody's face when they say something about these cheap ass outfits yo' woman be makin.' Look at my damn pants. All I need is a lamp and I could be a genie."

Willie shook his head, but I could tell he was trying not to laugh which softened me up a little.

"We ain't got no money. Hell, we ain't even got a name. Bertha be tryin' to do her best. She get the fabric from the scraps they throw away from that reupholster shop she work in."

"That explains why this shit is so itchy. This ain't made to put on nobody, this shit here belongs on a sofa."

"Yeah, I reckon so." Po-Man scratched the back of his head. "That would be one ugly ass sofa though."

We both got a good laugh as I stepped out of the hideous, lime green pants. We were still laughing when the fellas burst into the dressing room followed by Audra, Bertha, and Silky Struthers.

"What the hell goin' on in here?" Papa asked, looking at my bare legs.

"Lawd, don't tell me we walked in on no funny business," Bertha chimed in.

"The only thing funny is these clothes Bertha done put us in. What kinda material is this?"

"Some you didn't pay a dime for. Willie, what happened to your shirt?" Bertha ran over picking up the scraps at his feet,

"Baby, Razor is right," Po-Man admitted. "We can't wear this. I got a rash just from sitting in it. How we supposed to dance in this?"

Bertha's mouth dropped open in shock, as did all of ours. Po-Man had never checked her about the bullshit she made for us.

"That's how you feel? Fine. I can use my skills elsewhere." Po-Man followed Bertha as she stomped out the door bare chested and all.

"So, we don't got nothing to wear?" Velvet asked.

"You can always wear what y'all wore to the last show," Audra suggested.

"We haven't had a chance to get it cleaned. I ain't 'bout to go on stage smelling like a gym sock!" I replied.

"Maybe if we washed out our shirts right now and sat them in front of the fan, they could air dry," Papa suggested.

"Man please. We men. Everybody's arms gonna be musty as hell tryna' sing to these women's out here. Nobody ain't gonna wanna smell that," Dick'Em interjected.

"So, what y'all wanna do? You gonna just give up and go home? That's what it sounds like you're saying," Audra asserted, placing her hand on her hip. She rarely got angry, but when she did, it got all of our attention. "If we get in the van now, we might can make it to a thrift store or somethin."

"Audra, we ain't got enough money to cover that and get to our next town. We just gonna have to hand wash something," Dick'Em suggested. The door flew open as Ronda ran in with two bags in her hand. She tossed them on the floor before collapsing on a chair to catch her breath.

"I'm tired as hell. Thought them police was gonna bust me for sure. Look'a here," she opened the bags tossing the contents onto the floor. Our eyes lit up as heaps of fabric piled up in front of us.

"Gal, what you done did now? This sho is nice," Dick'Em said as he picked up some shiny gold fabric that changed colors in the light.

"They was having some kind of store closing sale up the road. I noticed it yesterday when we got here, but I ain't say nothin' cause' I know how y'all are. You can't be scary and broke though. I swiped them van keys from Velvet's room earlier and took off."

"What you was doin' in Velvet's room?" I questioned.

"Razor, that don't hardly matter. I wasn't about to let my man go out lookin' like no pickaninny. Where Bertha at? See, can't she do something with this. Audra, don't you sew?"

"I do a little by hand."

"Where Charlene at? She need to get her ass in gear and help out too."

"We got into it earlier," Papa admitted. "She said she was going to get some air."

"Ok, well let's get this together. We ain't got time to waste." Bertha came back into the room with swollen red eyes from where she had been crying. The moment her eyes saw that fabric, she dried those tears right on up and got to work. We had just enough of the gold material to make all of us a suit jacket. We washed out our shirts from the previous show, and luckily, we had clean underclothes. Once we were gettin dressed, we made the ladies leave, all but Audra, who was our unofficial stylist. She made sure all shoes were shined, heads were combed, and faces were shaved.

"Y'all look mighty fine," she remarked as she gave her final inspection. Since we didn't have full length mirrors, we had to trust her judgment. Not a single hair was out of place. She was the only person that could tame Willie's hair since he was too cheap to get a relaxer. I didn't trust no woman around my head with a straightening comb.

"There's just one thing," Dick'Em remarked after Audra left to join the other ladies. "We still ain't got no

name. We can't just keep going by Silky Struthers Singing Brothers, he ain't in this group."

"Maybe not, but he is booking us shows," I stuck up for my friend.

"Yeah, but he ain't on that stage," Papa co-signed. I looked over at Velvet and Po-Man who seemed to agree.

"What you suggest then?" I questioned. The room was dead silent. "That's what I thought."

A knock on the door caught all of our attention. "Come in," I answered.

"Hey, they got a few ladies out here want autographs before the show," Silky announced. "I know y'all don't normally do this, but the owner said there's a few more dollars in it, because these here ladies are VIP members."

"Members of what?" we asked in unison.

"Y'all ain't know, this here club is members only."

"Members only, huh?" Dick'Em repeated. We all looked around at each other nodding our heads.

A stagehand knocked on the door indicating it was time for us to go on. I led a quick prayer and we jogged out the door down the long corridor on the left. Once we were behind those velvet drapes it was show time. I silently prayed that Silky was able to make it to the lighting booth in time to instruct them to keep it dim.

"Ladies and gentlemen with no further ado ... hold up I got a message. You want me to say what?" the announcer asked.

"What the hell is happening out there?" Velvet whispered. I shrugged my shoulders. I was on the end, but I couldn't see no more than he could.

"Okay well, ladies and gentlemen, now is the time you've all been waiting for. Introducing Dick'Em Down, Velvet Rose, Po-Man, Razor-Mouth Slick, and Papa. Otherwise known as Members Only. Hearing our name announced like that made us realize how silly they sounded. It was no turning back now. I bumped fists with Papa right before the curtains began to go up. "Let's wreck the joint," I whispered. We rocked to the left then to the right before parting down the middle to allow Razor to slide up to the center mic in the front.

"If you jerkin' off you can just pull the curtain. I'm bout' to piss on myself," Po-Man screamed, beating on the door.

"Quit your whinin' and take a piss already. It ain't like I ain't seen that withered up garden hose you got anyway!" I yelled.

"It's still bigger than yours," Willie replied, opening the door.

"That ain't what your woman said last night."

"Razor, if you got that thang to work on my woman last night, then you would be in a wheelchair like Velvet and Papa. That heffa is heavy as hell." We both laughed as Po-Man used the bathroom. We were back to being brothers again, at least for now.

Chapter 26

Joanne 'Jumpstart' George

Meanwhile …

*Ring * Ring*

"Baby, can you answer the phone?"

"You answer the phone. It's probably for you anyway."

"Who gone be calling me at this time of night?"

*Ring * Ring*

"Ugh, you make me sick," I stated, reaching over to retrieve my ringing house phone.

"But, I see you answering the phone tho'."

"Hello," I answered, clearing my throat.

"Yes, may I speak to Jumpstart please?"

"This is she. May I ask who's calling?"

"Umm, my name is Sharonda Hathaway."

"Outlaw?" I asked, sitting up in bed.

"You would call me Outlaw," she softly chuckled. "You know you was the only one to give me a nickname," she sniffled.

I picked up my bedside clock and spied the time. "Umm, Sharonda. It's a little after two in the AM. What's wrong?"

"Are you sitting down?"

"More like laying down," I explained.

"How about we were asleep!" my husband yelled out, trying to get readjusted.

"I'm sorry to be calling so late but I really need you right now."

"What's going on?" I asked.

"You need to take that shit in the other room. I gotta get up in the morning and you talking like its two o'clock in the afternoon."

"Shut yo' ole' grumpy ass up," I yelled at my husband as I threw my legs over the side of the bed and slid my feet into my bedroom slippers. I placed my phone down on the bed, so I could stand and grab my bathrobe. "Okay, Sharonda?"

"I'm so sorry to be calling so late."

"No, tell me what happened and where are you?" I asked as I pulled the bedroom door open and stepped out in the hallway.

"Did you know that the fellas were in Chicago?"

"WHAT!!!"

"Yeah, they all decided to meet up in Chicago for one last hurrah."

"They too old for this mess."

"I agree," she softly chuckled.

"So, what's happened because I know you didn't call me to chit chat?"

"They're missing."

"MISSING?"

"Yeah, we came back to the facility and they were gone."

"Wait a minute, back up. Facility?"

"Yeah, they all decided to meet up at Harmony Healthcare and devise a plan."

"These ole' fools gone be the death of me," I replied as memories came flooding back.

"Jumpstart, when was the last time you talked to Benny?"

I sat down in the kitchen chair and sighed. The last time I talked to Velvet was about six or seven months ago. He was rambling on about something then, but I didn't pay it no never mind. "It's been a minute, Outlaw."

"How long will it take you to get to Chicago?"

"A couple of hours, why?"

"I need somebody I can trust to help me find my Razor."

"Somebody you can trust, huh?" I asked, pushing up from my seat. My bones cracked and popped as I forced my spine to straighten.

"Yeah, 'Pop Rocks' is on a power trip. Bertha's cheap ass is in there fiddling with the shower curtains and shit. If she steal these people shower curtains, I'm whoopin' her ass. I don't know why they just don't buy what they need instead of robbing Peter to pay Paul."

"Look, I'mma do this for you because my Velvet is out there somewhere but …" I trailed off, staring into the eyes of my husband who had wandered into the kitchen in his underwear. Wayne shook his head as to give me confirmation. "I'll be there in the morning."

"Thank you so much, Jumpstart."

"Don't thank me yet." I took a deep breath and hung up the phone. I made a pot of coffee and looked around my little square feet of happiness and thanked God that I've made it this far. There was a time where I didn't think I was gone make it. If it wasn't for my Auntie dragging me to church every Sunday, I probably wouldn't have.

Wayne pulled up a chair and kissed me on the cheek. "What's wrong, my love?"

"Why aren't you asleep? You have a busy day tomorrow."

"I know, but I was concerned. What did ole' Velvet do this time?"

"He disappeared," I replied honestly.

"At his age that couldn't be good. How can I help?" Wayne asked as he reached behind him to retrieve my old scrapbook from the junk drawer under the cabinet. I turned and made each of us a cup of coffee.

"Babe, who is this?"

I spun around on my slippered feet to acknowledge his question and before a word could slip out, a smile began to spread across my face. I placed our coffee mugs on the table and wiped my hands on my housecoat before reaching out to retrieve the photo he now held. Running my fingers across the faces, a tear slipped from my eye.

I sat on my husband's lap and pointed, “This here is Bertha. Bertha at one point in her life was and still is, in love with this man,” I pointed. “This is Willie, we called him Po-Man because he would wait right up until we finished eating to lick everyone’s fingers. It was terrible. He had all that money and wouldn’t spend it.” Smiling, I pointed to the next person in line.

“This, right here is Charlene, or as we often called her ‘Pop Rocks’. She would always pop up unexpected at the most inopportune times and start mess. I remember one day, we were all out with the fellas and we kept asking about her and Ronnie who we call Papa, which is her man,” I pointed at Papa.

He turned to us and said something like, *“I don’t know where that heffa is and I really don’t care. I’m trying to get next to that tall drink of water over there.”* We all shook our heads because we knew he could probably get to her, but it wouldn’t stay that way. Anywho, he walked over and licked his lips and whatnot and right when he was getting in good on the conversation, the clothes rack behind him began to move. We thought it was Sharonda,” I pointed to Outlaw.

“She was the groups booster, but we thought maybe she was in there stealing clothes. Naw, we were sadly mistaken when ‘Pop Rocks’ popped out and clocked that poor girl upside the head with her platform shoe,” I laughed.

“Y’all, was a handful,” Wayne voiced, rubbing my back soothingly.

"Yeah, we were, but we had so much fun. Just young and crazy kids that all came from nothing. We went from confused teenagers to even more confused adults, but we made due."

"So, who is this?" Wayne pointed.

I smiled, "That there is Razor," I chuckled.

"That nigga carried a blade under his tongue at all times. He said he wasn't gone allow the white folk to put they hands on him. I always thought he was a wild card. He didn't start nothing, but he damn sho' would finish it."

"And this?" Wayne asked pointing a gnarled finger at Audra.

My words tuck in the back of my throat for a moment. I rubbed the picture and smiled. "That's sweet Audra." My voice cracked, and I was glad that my husband was there to make the memories just a little bit easier. "She was about the sweetest woman that ever walked this earth. The girl deserved so much more than what she got."

"I can't believe him," I huffed out angrily. "I've been with that man for four years and he did this to me," I managed in between sobs.

"Come sit down, sweetie," Audra patted the empty space next to her.

"I don't wanna sit down. I wanna go up there and kill that nigga."

"Jumpstart, you ain't gone kill nobody. You just angry."

"Yeah, angry enough to stab him in his cold ass heart," I huffed and flopped down next to Audra.

"Come here, suga." She pulled my head to her shoulder and began to rub my back. "We all do some strange things for love. Look at me and Drexler. That man sleeps with anything in skirt," she lightly chuckled.

"How do you deal?" I asked perplexed.

"He's a man. You can't stop a man from being a man. They learn on their own accord. We can't change the lightbulb just because it's dim. We have to learn to shine through the dimness."

"Well, I don't wanna shine through a damn thing. I wanna go up there and watch Velvet and that bitch bleed out." I jumped to my feet and began to pace.

"I went up there and knocked on the door and he gone pull it open talking about he busy. When has he ever been too busy for me? I went to say something smart when I heard, "Who's at the door, daddy?" and I promise you, if I would've had my pistol, I would've shot the bastard dead."

"You don't mean that."

"The hell I don't, Audra."

"You're just angry right now."

"Why don't you get angry? Why don't you leave? What is it about Dick'Em that keeps you rooted?"

Audra stood to her feet and walked over to the window and sat on top of the air conditioner. She smiled revealing deep dimples that almost appeared as slits in her face.

"The thing is that you all see Dick'Em. I see Drexler. I remember sitting on the porch one afternoon, watching all the neighborhood boys playing touch football

out in the street. Drexler was sitting off to the side with his back pressed up against the fence. Every once in a while, he would give a head nod to his friends in passing. My father came home from work that day drunk and pissed off about something. He walked up to me and began yelling incoherently, "Michelle, get yo' black ass in the house. I don't know why you out here fuckin off with these hoodlums." Of course, he called me by my middle name when he was sloshed. Naturally, I jumped right on up to go into the house so he wouldn't make an example out of me.

"What is that on your dress?" daddy asked, slurring his words.

I didn't know what he was talking about, so I spun my dress around the best I could and that's when I noticed the blood. My period had started, and I was terrified.

"I think it's my period," I responded.

"Yo' period?" he asked, dropping his lunch pail. "You out here wit' yo' ass bleeding!"

By this time, I was too shamed because I knew everybody had heard him. When I looked up, Drexler was making his way across the street towards us.

"Daddy, I didn't-." He grabbed my arm and snatched me around to face him.

"You didn't what? Huh, you lil tramp?" he yelled in my face.

"I didn't know," was all I could manage to say as he squeezed my arm so hard it was starting to bruise.

Drexler told daddy to get his damn hands off of me. You can imagine how scared I was knowing that my daddy could beat Drexler down with his eyes closed.

"I ain't gotta do a damn thang, lil nigga. This is my child," daddy said.

Daddy turned back towards me and bent at the waist, so we were eye level. "Get yo' narrow ass upstairs and wash yo' monkey."

My eyes widened in shock because he had never talked to me quite that bad.

"Don't stand there catching flies. Get on upstairs now." He shoved me forward, causing me to trip over my feet and fall.

Drexler knocked the wind out of daddy that day. He just pounced on him and went to work. When he was done, daddy needed stitches above his left eye."

I know some may ask, why would I wanna be with a man that disrespected my father in such a way and my answer is always and forever will be ... because he saved me from a life of turmoil." She turned to me and smiled. "Baby, you only get what you allow, and I've allowed Drexler to be Drexler. There's no need in teaching a dog new tricks when he's been a dog since the age of fifteen. You just go with the flow and wait in the rain for the sun to shine and eventually ... It does. You just have to be patient." Audra patted my hand and walked away.

I wiped my tears away and handed the picture to my husband. "I'm sorry, my love. I didn't mean to stir up old memories."

"It's okay, we learn, and we grow," Wayne said reassuringly.

“That’s a fact.” I got off of his lap and stretched my old bones before grabbing our coffee mugs to place in the sink.

“Whatever happened to ole’ Velvet?” Wayne asked. “You mentioned everybody but him.”

“He got old,” I smiled and continued on. I needed to pack a bag. I had just a few short hours before I was reunited with the women of *Member’s Only.*

Chapter 27

Drexler 'Dick 'Em Down' Davis

I couldn't understand how everybody could sleep so comfortably. My mind was a mixture of different emotions. Audrey was not ever going to forgive me. I had hidden so much from her because I didn't want her to be disappointed about the man her father really was. She was likely to be mad at Audra too, because she helped me to hide a lot of it. She thought the sun rose and set on me, no matter how much I had put her through. Even when she lay on her death-bed, she told me that she would not have changed anything. I couldn't say the same. I would have changed the day she chose me.

"Now, don't think I didn't see you eyeballing the pastor's son. That boy is bad news. You hear what I'm tellin' you, gal?" Audra nodded her head yes as her Aunt Clodine proceeded to the 'amen corner' with the church mothers. Audra lowered her head as she walked toward her post at the front door. In her usher uniform, a pleated black skirt that fell right below the knees, and a long-sleeved white dress shirt, she managed to outshine every woman in the church. Even though I was just 14 at the time, I knew I was gonna marry that girl.

"Y'all settle down now, you're in the house of the Lord," my Nana chastised as she sat one of her fruit-inspired hats on top of the piano. She patted her perfectly plaited bun into place before taking her seat behind the organ.

"I hate when she plays. That means we got to sing hymns all service," my cousin, Pee-Wee, complained. I jabbed him in the ribs just as she turned around to silence us with those big bug eyes of hers. I smiled at her

innocently, but Pee-Wee's disrespectful self gave her a frown. That got him yanked out of the choir stand by his ear as she led him to the basement where he was sure to get that switch put on him.

"Hey young fella', you wouldn't happen to know where Pastor Davis is, would ya'?" I couldn't hardly speak for staring at the man talking to me. He was at least 6'2, dark skinned almost the color of my momma's leather purse, with big white teeth that looked like chiclets in his mouth. His eyes were hidden behind some dark sunglasses which was peculiar because it was the dead of winter.

"He in the office prayin', I think," I finally managed to answer.

"Thank ya kindly." It wasn't until the man turned, that I realized there was a short, stout, woman, with long auburn curls behind him. She had her hand in the small of his back as if she was helping him walk. Me and the rest of the junior choir watched in amazement as my momma walked over to direct them to the pastor's study.

"What you think that's all about?" Michaela asked. She was a nosey, plump, buck-toothed beaver looking girl with long, stringy hair that she wore in two plaits. Her momma thought she was the bees knees because she was a beige color with freckles all over her face. None of us could stand her though.

"Any fool can see that man blind. You 'bout as dumb as a box of rocks," I grumbled. One thing about having a high-pitch voice was I got stuck sitting in the alto section away from all of the boys. They tried to pick at me about it, but soon learned that my hands could put something on them that their momma's switch couldn't. We sat around whispering until the bell rang in the back of the

church. That signaled that it was praying time. The whole church got quiet as everyone silently prayed to themselves with closed eyes. Any child caught whispering, laughing, with their eyes opened, or even flipping through a hymnal, would be in deep trouble. This was the only time I could steal an uninterrupted glance at Audra, so I pressed my hands over my face peeping between my fingers. She smiled knowing exactly what I was doing.

"Lawd, I know I'm gonna be with you one of these old days"

My eyes popped open at the sound of a smooth, male, tenor singing during prayer time. The blind man was sitting at the organ adjusting the microphone as the whole church looked at him like he was crazy. At any moment now, my Nana was gonna get him for sure. Plus, he had knocked her hat off of the bench onto the floor.

"I say Lawd, I know I'm gonna be with you

One of these old days.... Oh yeah

Early in the mawnin'

Before the day starts

I hear the wind blow

And the birds talk

Lawd I'm gonna be with you

I know ... one of these old days"

The way that man's fingers tickled the keys on that organ was something I had never heard. I stood to my feet clapping before I realized what I was doing. Momma gave me a disapproving look, but the entire church was on its feet in a matter of seconds joining me. Even those old hens from the 'amen corner' had to stand to their feet. My father strutted through those double doors like he was somebody that day. His chest was puffed up, his hair was gleaming, and his smile lit up the place. That was when I realized that music was my true calling. After every line the man sang, I added a run right behind it that won me a huge grin from momma. After his sermon, daddy announced that Stormy Blue was our new organist. Nana stormed out of that church so fast I thought she would break a heel. She had been the organist since before I was born. It was Stormy who really whipped our choir into shape and also taught me about secular music.

Up until that time, I only heard music when I was going to the store with momma or when a group was singing for dollars out on the corner. After that Sunday, Audra joined the Junior choir. I had no idea how much something so small would impact my life.

"A'ight now, since you pretty good at keeping a note, I want you to switch places with Mallory," Stormy advised. Mallory stomped past me in a huff. She had a nice, strong, voice and loved to out sing all of the altos. Audra switched places with her happily because that placed her next to me.

"I can hold a note too ya' know," Mallory grumbled under her breath,

"I also know you like to eat sardines before practice and I'm tired of smelling it," Stormy replied. We all snickered as Mallory folded her arms across her chest.

"Now, where's my boy?"

"Here I am, Mr. Stormy," I answered.

"What I done told you 'bout that? You make me feel like an old man and I'm in my prime. I want you to get up there and direct that song we was practicin' before everybody got here."

I pointed to myself as if he could see me.

"Go on now. Let these folks know what you can do. That boy was in here singing all parts. Start with sopranos and work your way down."

Nana had always directed us from the organ. Her warbling, operatic voice led every song so that none of us ever got too "full of ourselves." I didn't even know what to do standing there with 32 sets of eyes on me, not counting Stormy's.

"Go head now," he encouraged. I cleared my throat and began to sing This little light of mine in the soprano key. Audra's mouth fell open. I think I saw her cheeks blush a little too. Mallory's teeth were clinched together so tightly, I thought she would break them. Our rehearsal went so smooth that night that we got out a full 30 minutes earlier which gave me the perfect opportunity to walk Audra home. After I locked up the church, we both said goodnight to Stormy, and his wife, Rosewater. I later found out she got that name as a lounge singer.

"It sure is chilly out here," Audra complained. The fact that it was at least 10 degrees outside, made me wonder why her aunt insisted that she wear skirts all the time. Her bony legs trembled with each step; although, I knew her top half was warm in the sheepskin coat she wore.

"Take these." I stopped to give her the thick gloves Nana had knitted for me. All of her grandchildren had a pair. Audra thanked me before slipping them onto her hands.

"That was a real nice rehearsal. You got a voice that's like the birds in the sky, Drexler."

"You think so? I think it's just that jazzy arrangement that Stormy came up with."

"No, it's you." Audra laced her fingers through mine.

"If I could really sing, I would want to be just like Mahalia Jackson. You got the voice that could get you there. I just do enough to get by. I only got in the choir to be closer to you anyway," Audra admitted shyly.

"Say what now?"

"Drexler, don't put on like you ain't seen me lookin' at you. My aunt even seen it. She got on me because you got a reputation."

I lowered my head, "Yeah, but nobody don't understand what it's like being a preacher's son. All kind of girls be throwin' it my way."

"That don't mean you got to catch it," Audra replied.

"You right. I mean, I like you, but I didn't wanna say so. You got a few boys looking at you. Tommy Lee is crazy about you."

"I ain't hardly thinkin' about Tommy Lee, Dexter, or Charles; I just like you. Now, can you say the same?"

Audra stopped in her tracks taking both hands in mine. We were just a block away from her building. If her daddy came out there and saw us, he would shoot me first and tell my daddy later.

"You know I'm crazy bout' you, Audra. But I ..." Audra stood on her tiptoes pressing her lips against mine. It wasn't my first kiss, but it was the first one that made me feel something more than a hardness in my pants. I walked her the rest of the way and that was that.

If she had let me finish, I would have told her that I was not the committed type. I knew that back then. If I had told her that, she surely wouldn't have died the horrible death that she did. I only prayed she would forgive me on the other side.

Chapter 28

Benny 'Velvet Rose' Pryor

"What you over there doing, Dick'Em?" I asked, watching him pace back and forth.

"Nothing old man," he gritted.

"Well, why you pacing and shit?"

"What, I can't pace now, nigga?"

"You can do whatever you wanna do as long as you do it far away from me," I challenged.

"Nigga, this room so damn small if you ran around in a circle fast enough you'll knock everything down."

"Well, we ain't gotta worry about that happening with yo' peg leg having ass," Papa grumbled under his breath.

"Keep talking shit, Papa, and I'mma take this leg off and kick yo' skull in."

Colin spit his soda out in a poor attempt to keep from laughing out loud.

"Nigga, fix yo' face," I snapped.

Colin snapped his lips shut and went back to fiddling with that damn camera. I hope he was done recording us because I was tired of looking at that damn thing.

"Velvet," Papa called out.

I snapped my head in his direction. "What's up?"

"Whatever happened to that one girl we met in Tallahassee?" Papa asked.

"Wait, before y'all start traveling down memory lane and shit. Let me go hop in the shower," Dick'Em interrupted.

"Why you telling us?" Papa replied sourly.

"You know what," Dick'Em started across the floor as Papa swung his legs around to hop out of the bed.

Colin shot to his feet right in the nick of time. "Aye, maybe you need to go take that shower," Colin suggested.

Dick'Em slapped Colin's hand away and glared at Papa. "I got you, nigga." He pointed in his direction before storming off.

"What was all that about?" Colin asked, plopping back down in his seat.

"Old nigga shit," I said, lighting the joint I pulled from my breast pocket.

"You can't smoke that in here.," Colin panicked like I had pulled out a gun.

"Who gone check me? Ain't that what they say?"

"Yeah but-."

"But nothing." I toked my joint and passed it to Papa.

"You know I don't smoke that shit no mo'." He fanned his hand in front of his face trying to eliminate the smoke.

"Well, more for me then." I placed the joint to my lips, inhaled, and blew out smoke rings.

"So, back to Tallahassee," Papa reminded me.

"That should've been that bitches name," I laughed. "That chick was straight niggarish."

"Niggarish?" Colin asked confused.

"Let me tell you how it went down youngin" I placed the joint back to my lips and folded my hands behind my head.

"Excuse me sweet thang, can I borrow some of yo' time?" I asked the cute lil redbone standing at the bar.

"How may I help you, sir?" She spun around and stared into my chest. Her eyes traveled up the length of me before meeting my eyes.

"You can help me by giving me your name."

"Now, why would I do something like that?" she asked, placing her hand on her hip.

"Cause I'm a beautiful nigga and a beautiful nigga like myself deserves something exotic on his arm."

"Okay Billie Dee," she blushed.

"Oh no baby girl, that's not my name and being that Billie Dee is a cool cat and all, it ain't shit like having a Velvet Rose."

She looked up at me and smiled, "You smooth."

"Am I smooth enough to get yo' name?"

Her dimples showed up as she stuck out her hand, "Sunrise."

"You trying to run game, baby girl?" I chuckled.

"Not at all." I hit her with the head nod and turned and walked away. I didn't have time for bull-shitters. I could hear her behind me calling my name, but I paid her no never mind.

"So, you just left her standing there?" Colin asked, leaning forward, elbows pressed into his knees.

"Hell yeah, I wasn't at the booty bar."

"Booty Bar?" Colin asked, scratching his head.

Papa chuckled and jutted his thumb in Colin's direction. "The boy still wet behind the ears, Velvet." He slapped at his knee. He turned to Colin and very slowly said, "The booty bar … Is a strip club, if that makes sense."

Colin shook his head in understanding and turned back in my direction.

"Coming to the stage … Member's Onnnnllllyyyyy..."

The crowd erupted in a chorus of screams. We strutted out on that stage in lime green suits that Bertha had done sewed together. This was the first time in a while that she got it right. We stood in place and the lights dimmed. We all looked at each other and then the bass to our song dropped. We were up there popping and snapping our fingers getting the crowd riled up when Papa belted out the first verse …

"You got to roll your hips

Then let me do my dip

Tell that man of yours

Ain't no need to trip

See I wanna love you

Just for a night

Let that fool buy you a ring

I already know you ain't right"

We all stood beside him as we danced in unison. I could see Sunrise standing out in the crowd frozen in place as she watched my hips move. Papa smiled into the crowd and offered up a wink and the women swooned.

The spotlight panned, and it was my turn at mic ...

"I wanna make you feel

That this love is real

If I only have one night

Then let's make this love thang real

I wanna kiss you from your head to your toes

Just give me the green light baby

And I'll show you what's it's like to be with a Velvet Rose"

After we got off the stage that night, the backstage was flooding with women. I pushed through the crowd and bumped into Sunrise.

"Let's get outta here," she smiled.

"Follow me." I grabbed her hand and led her through the crowd. We ended up back at my hotel where we took a shower together. One thing led to the other and I ended up branding her with this rod.

"So, what happened next?" Colin asked, rubbing his hands together.

"She left, like a thief in the night," Dick'Em responded, stepping out of the bathroom, wiping the water from his head.

"Damn, that's rude." Colin sat back in his chair pouting as if it was him.

"Naw, what was messed up was … she dissed this nigga in every state. We almost thought the broad was related to 'Pop Rocks' the way she used to pop up at different shows and shit. The only difference is … she always popped out right before the sun would rise," Dick'Em chuckled.

We all looked at each other and in unison we said, "Niggarish,"

"I'm still not getting it." Colin scratched his head.

"Boy, she would suck and fuck this man into a coma and then leave before sunrise. What broad you know gone get dicked down and pick up and leave?" Dick'Em waited and when Colin couldn't respond, he smiled. "Exactly, not a one. A bitch always wanna cuddle and steal all the covers and shit but not Sunrise. The worst part is she would always get this fool drunk first. That's why we named her ass, 'Tequila Sunrise'."

Dick'Em pulled a pair of boxers from his duffle bag and slid them on underneath his towel. "Any more questions?"

Colin shook his head no.

"Aye Velvet, what made her finally stop coming around?" Papa asked, scratching his patchy beard.

"She got pregnant," I answered, lowering my head.

"And kept getting pregnant," Dick'Em threw in his two cents as he tossed his towel on the bed. "How many kids did you bless her with?"

"Three," I responded through clenched teeth. He knew I hated talking about my children.

"Damn, but didn't Jumpstart get pregnant too?" Dick'Em continued.

I nodded my head in confirmation. "And before you ask, she also had three."

"But wait a damn minute, because I remember that one chick screaming at the concert that night that she was pregnant as well," Papa pieced together.

"I remember that shit," Dick'Em chuckled.

"Get yo' long ass out here, Velvet. I don't give a fuck about that black-ass gal hanging offa' you." Jumpstart hopped up racing for the door, but I grabbed her just before she turned the knob.

"Naw baby, let me handle this," I whispered against her lips.

Jumpstart had been hanging around Razor too damn long because she started rolling her tongue around in her mouth like she had a razor in her mouth.

"You better handle it, Benny. I ain't afraid to go to jail up in this muthafucka."

BOOM! BOOM! BOOM!

"You better open this damn door before I kick it down," the female voice yelled out, still beating and kicking on the door.

I straightened my blazer and ran my hands across my fresh finger waves before placing my hand on the knob. The scowl on my face did nothing to change the mood of the short, wiry, dark-skinned girl leaning against the door frame. Her lips were poked out just like a duck's beak.

"You think I'm playing with you, nigga?" she asked.

All I could do was stand there and try to think of something to say that wouldn't get us both killed.

"So, you just gone stand there on mute now? You wasn't on mute last night.," she snapped.

The look of anguish in her eyes was all my fault. This woman had every right to be pissed off. "Baltimore, can you please calm yourself for a moment, so we can talk?"

"BALTIMORE!" the fellas all yelled in unison.

Grabbing her by the waist, I took a deep breath before looking over my shoulder. "Meet Baltimore Brenda, fellas."

They all gave her dry hellos and turned back to what they were doing.

She sucked her teeth and tried to push away from me the moment she laid eyes on Jumpstart.

"Tell me what's wrong," I pleaded as her expression hardened. "Look at me, Baltimore." She looked up at me as one lone tear slid from her eye and her lips trembled.

"I'm pregnant," she announced sullenly.

"Oh, hell to the no," Jumpstart uttered as she lunged toward us.

Baltimore Brenda slid behind me gripping my waist for dear life. All of that fighting energy she had earlier was now gone.

"If I wasn't pregnant I would kill you right where you stand you tall, lanky, slanky son-of-a-bitch! But instead, I'mma be the bigger person and walk away. You ain't worth the air I breathe!" Jumpstart tried to get around me to walk out of the door, but I couldn't let her leave like that, so I grabbed her wrist.

"Where you think you going Jump-."

Before her name could leave my lips, she sliced me across my arm in one swift motion.

"Don't you ever put yo' filthy hands on me. I ain't like these other bitches you lay up with." she huffed, pushing me and Baltimore Brenda over as she stormed out of the room.

Dick'Em felt so good about himself to be telling my business but he was the worst out of all of us. I couldn't wait for the time to come for him to reveal his true self because this nigga in front of me was acting like his shit didn't stink. Not only did it stink, but it made the rest of ours smell like roses.

Chapter 29

Willie 'Po-Man' Jenkins & Razor

"You don't say." I rubbed my chin thoughtfully as I gazed at the other fellas sleeping. Even Scott had laid the camera down for some shut eye. The first bursts of the morning sun were just beginning to come up over the clouds. I hadn't been in Knoxville, Tennessee since I was a young boy picking beans in the field with my Uncle Floyd. Grabbing my glasses, I picked up the piece of paper with the names of the doctors I had written down before the trip started. My son, Wallace, didn't understand why I needed so many different ones when I had called him for his help. As spotty as my mind was these days, he was probably just glad that I recognized him. This decision wasn't one that was easy to come to, but I refused to be a burden on my family by losing all my marbles.

I couldn't seem to get Bertha out of my face. I told her I would treat her to a two-for-one at the Red Check Lounge, thinking that would cause her to get up out of my face. Instead, she sat right there in her rocking chair smiling at me as I tried to make my phone call. I had gotten so flustered I dialed the number four times and messed it up.

"Bertha, that's what you wearin? You know Audra is gonna say somethin' 'bout that. You can't go on stage with me lookin' like a ragamuffin. Gone get that new dress I bought ya."

"You ain't bought me a new dress since 1976. Here you go with that fool talk. This why you need to get your meds."

"Look here, I ain't takin' no medicine to help me remember what I wanna forget. Keep playin' I'mma have Jumpstart come in here and get on your ass."

That was enough to send Bertha flying into the bedroom. That was a mean tactic, but she was all in my business. Sometimes I had to make her think my mind was already gone so I could get some privacy. She had been clinging to me like flies to shit ever since that doctor told her I had dementia. Some days I did wake up screaming because I didn't recognize my surroundings. I may have called her the wrong name a few times, but I'm old. Ain't I entitled to a few mistakes? Once I heard her rummaging through her closet, I took a deep breath before calling Henry Parnell. I hadn't said nothing to the man since the night his sister Harriet had died.

There was so much guilt on my heart for leaving her behind. That had been over fifty years or so ago. He couldn't possibly be mad at me still.

"Who dis here calling me from Flint Michigan? I don't know nobody up North," Henry's raspy voice answered.

"Hey Henry, this here is Willie... Willie Jenkins."

"Willie Jenkins... Po-Man?" he laughed into the phone.

"Yeah, it's me, Henry. How you been feelin?"

"Well, I been up and down. How you been? Long time no hear. Boy, I thought you was dead. What happened to your music?"

"Hell, we old now. We all broke down. Niggas in wheelchairs, my mind leavin' me, all kinds of thangs, man.

How ya momma been?" She was the real reason for my call. I didn't mind shooting the breeze with Henry, but I wanted to get this over with.

"Funny you should ask. Momma passed in her sleep. We found her a few days ago. Probably gonna funeralize her this weekend." I sank back in my chair. The news had completely caught me off guard. I knew she was up in age, almost 90, but I didn't have any idea that she had passed. My plan was ruined.

"You still there?" Henry asked.

"Yeah, I'm here. I'm just so sorry to hear that."

"Yeah, me too. Momma would have loved to see you. All she talked about was you and Members Only. She had all your records."

"She did?" That caught me by surprise. I had assumed that Ms. Crowder didn't like me.

"Yeah, she thought highly of you. Said you was a mighty fine boy."

"What about what happened to Harriet? That was my fault."

"Nah, that wasn't your fault, Po-Man. Shit just happened," Henry sniffled. "Them peckerwoods killed my damn sister and got clean away with it. Wasn't nothin' nobody coulda did."

"You don't understand, Henry. I coulda stopped it. If I had stayed it never woulda happened."

"How you figure that? What you coulda did? Them crackas woulda killed you too."

"Maybe so, but I knew that Harriet had been messing with one of the Chesney boys; that blonde-headed one with the blue eyes."

"You talkin' 'bout Byron Chesney?"

"I reckon that's his name. The one used to always hang out with the colored kids. She called herself takin' a likin' to him. I knowed it, but I loved her so I ain't say nothing," I admitted,

"Now, let me stop you right there. Don't you tell me nothin' bad about my sister. Harriet dead and gone now. She can't defend herself."

"I promise you this the honest truth. I got to get it off my heart."

"Gone ahead." I could hear Henry begin to sob lightly.

What I was about to tell him would break his heart, but it been held in mine for so long.

"Well, I knowed she liked him like I said. We went on courtin' but I got word she was sneakin' over to the Chesney house after she left Ms. Mae's house from washing and cleanin.' The little brother told me. He say they daddy saw her sneak out Byron's window one night. She had been doing it the whole time we were together. My dumb ass thought I was her only one. That girl could have told me the sky was silver and I woulda' believed her. Well, for long she got pregnant. Me and her had been messin' round so I was ready to take care of my business, only she lost the baby. Never knew who the baby's pappy was; me or Byron."

"Baby? Harriet lost a baby? What you say?"

"Found out through the grapevine that Mr. Chesney made her drink a concoction, some shit this witch woman from New Orleans had gave him. I never told her I knowed what she done, but I couldn't face her, and I wanted to kill Byron and his daddy so I got from round there and went up North to take care of my momma. She musta' told somebody 'bout it that night I left and got herself killed."

"Oh, Lawd Harriet," he cried.

"All this time we never knew the whole story. You know them Chesney boys all ended up getting' killed. Byron was the last one. Shot himself in they daddy's pick-up. Now it all makes sense."

"I'm sorry, Henry. I wanted to tell y'all, but my heart couldn't take it. I thought Ms. Crowder wouldn't never forgive me.

"Momma loved you Po-Man. She was right proud of you. We all was. You turned out to be somebody. We still in the same place we was when you left. I got me a small farm, but not nothin' to write home about. Claude, and Aaron married and done had a mess of kids. We all settled here, and you really did it up for yourself. You ever come back down home, you come see me. I got to take my heart pills. This done did me in. Thanks for calling. I know it was hard."

I couldn't do nothing but mumble a quick bye before I broke down.

"Baby, what's wrong with you?" Bertha asked, stepping out of the bedroom.

"My momma done died on me." It was time to play crazy again. I had never told Bertha the whole story about Harriet.

"Aw suga, she been dead for twenty-somethin' years."

Just like that I played everything off.

After dinner that night, I called my son and got the names of several doctors.

I had been researching several ones that could help me without trying to talk me out of what I wanted to do. The time to go was now before everybody woke up.

I scrawled down the name *Members Only*, on an envelope before calling a Taxi. If everything went well, I would be long gone by the time the fellas found it. Then I crept out of the hotel as quietly as I could. The Smoky Mountains greeted me as my foot tapped the pavement nervously. I looked back at the hotel room every five minutes. If they woke up now, they would try to stop me. I had made my mind up though. I was leaving.

Razor:

I woke up stretching my arms out as if I was in the bed alone.

"Oh, shit, Po-Man'; I apologize," I said groggily. When I didn't get a reply my eyes fluttered open. Po-Man was nowhere to be seen. Scott was snoozing in his bed soundly. Turning over, I looked at the bathroom door which sat open. Po-Man wasn't in there either. My first thought was maybe this fool done called his woman and ratted us out. However, I sat up noticing that his phone was on the table right next to the hotel phone. That's when I saw a curious white envelope. Leaning over as hard as I could, I reached for it.

“Shit,” I muttered. My arms weren’t long enough. The only thing I could think to do was throw my pillow at Scott.

“Cut it out you guys, please. We barely got any sleep last night.”

“Scott, wake your pasty ass up. Po-Man gone.”

“Seriously?’ Scott fumbled around in his blanket nearly falling off the bed.

“See for yourself.” Scott looked around the room before getting up to check the bathroom and closet.

“Okay, maybe he stepped out to get coffee. Maybe he’s with the others in the next room.”

“What that is right there?” Scott pointed.

“It’s a letter. Here’s his phone though. He probably didn’t go far without his phone.”

Scott looked relieved, but I knew something was wrong.

“Who that letter addressed to?” Scott reached over picking it up. He looked up at me with a grim expression. “This is addressed to *Members Only;* should I go get the others?”

“Yeah, you do that. Let me see it first though.”

Scott handed me the letter before tossing on some clothes and a pair of shoes. As soon as the door closed, I nervously unsealed the envelope.

Hey fellas,

I knew y'all would make a big fuss, but I had to do this my way. Please send my best to Bertha. Tell her I love her and this ain't have nothin' to do with her.

I swept a tear from my eye as the room door flew open.

"What's it say, Razor? What done happened?" Papa ran over to me in his underwear and a t-shirt. Benny rolled in behind him, and Dick'Em brought up the rear. Audrey was standing outside of the room with the door open talking to Scott who was visibly upset. I cleared my throat and began to read aloud.

Members Only saved me from a life of working in the fields like the rest of my family. All of them near 'bout died in that sun from sharecropping, working on other folks land until they were too old to do anything else. I know I never talked much about Harriet to y'all, but that gal haunted me in my dreams. I knew how much she loved me and I left her behind. That shit ate at me for years. With all the money and success I had, I was never able to shake how I felt about her. It was always my mission in life to make it up to her. I decided that I wanted to buy her a headstone. I didn't want nothin' raggedy, but something right nice for her remains to be placed under. I went out and priced a slab and headstone and paid for it with Marsh Monument Company up in Lansing. Y'all always talked about how cheap I was and that's true, but I put 10,000 on her headstone and a slab to get it shipped and placed in Mississippi. See y'all spent y'all money all crazy, but I invested. Me and Bertha lived like regular folks, so we had something to leave behind for our kids. I already got my will set up and squared away, but I needed to leave y'all with something.

Papa, you was always a good friend to me. You had the most level-head out of all of us. I'm sorry to say that I was not as good a friend. I was slippin' around with 'Pop Rocks' behind your back. Any time I could get some lovin', I took it because Bertha was stingy with that kitty kat. I apologize.

"I don't think a dick in this room hasn't been inside of that woman in some kinda' way," Papa commented lightheartedly. We all laughed knowing he was telling nothing, but the truth.

Razor, I know you and Ronda were robbing us blind after Silky got killed. I never wanted her to be involved with our business, but you insisted on it. All those times your pockets came up light, was because I was running up in them after you started drinking. You was too much of a show-off to put your money in the bank, so I helped myself.

"Son-of-bitch," I muttered through clenched teeth. Me and Ronda had been fighting about that for years because I assumed it was her.

Dick'Em, I think I owe you the biggest apology. I was the one ratting you out to Audra. You ain't do her right and I felt sorry. She deserved better than you, so I kept letting the cat out the bag, hoping she would leave you. Lastly, Velvet, I think you were about the coolest one of us, but I hated how you would spread these kids all around the country and never did shit for 'em. I'm the one that gave Tequila Sunrise your information, so she could find you every time we had a show. Just wanted you to get a taste of your own medicine. If all goes right, I will be resting in heavenly peace by the time y'all read this. Now, I done squared all my business away, I can now join Harriet. I found me a doctor down here willing to make a concoction that will have me sleeping with the angels in no time. Don't worry 'bout trying to look for him. I decided this was my choice. Y'all don't know what it's like to live with your mind going in and out. I rather leave this world while I still can remember who I am. Y'all take care of Bertha emotionally, I got the money part handled. What I'm doing ain't legal, so I couldn't risk telling y'all about it because I don't want no trouble. Just know that ole Po-Man went out on his own terms.

Signing off,

The Cheapest Member of Members Only

P.S. Go ahead and laugh because y'all all talked about my penny pinching.

A somber tone filled the room as all of us looked around at each other. Not a dry eye was present. I didn't even notice that Scott and Colin had been filming. I didn't really care.

"Ole Willie," Papa commented, sitting down on the bed. "He went out with a bang. Who woulda' thought?

"If I had known he was gonna do this last night … I'd stayed up with him," I managed to get out before my body began to tremble as the grief slowly made its way from the pit of my stomach.

"Razor, you didn't know. None of us coulda known. We got to honor him by doin' what he asked … even if he was a rotten muthafucka," Velvet said, laughing.

We all chimed in with him as we wiped our eyes. Something told me that these tears would reappear real soon. The question was … for who?

Chapter 30

Joanne 'Jumpstart' George

Meanwhile …

I followed my GPS to Harmony Healthcare and I was quite impressed. Pulling into a vacant slot, I pulled my sun visor down to check my lipstick. I hadn't seen these women in years and I'll be damned if I pulled up looking any ole' kinda way.

After checking to make sure my appearance was up to par, I snatched the key out the ignition and pushed the door open. One stiletto heel at a time, my feet kissed the pavement. It was more than chilly out here in old Chicago, so I pulled my faux fur a little bit closer to my neck. My Chanel eyeglasses protected my eyes as the wind whipped my hair about my head. *I didn't dress right for this occasion,* I thought to myself as I popped my trunk and retrieved my duffle bag, throwing it over my shoulder.

The front desk was empty when I entered. I squinted my eyes to see if I could locate anyone when my eyes landed on 'Pop Rocks'. Lawd, she done aged like a worn welcome mat. I started in her direction when she turned and waved at me.

"What are you doing here?" she asked, out of breath.

"I received a phone call," I responded, adjusting my duffle.

"Did Audrey call you?" she asked with a little bit of hope.

"I don't know if I remember an Audrey."

"Dick'Em's daughter he had with Audra."

"I never met her. Audra was pregnant with her when I decided to leave."

"How are your children? I bet'cha they all grown up and successful."

"Yeah, they're doing pretty well."

"My goodness! Look at this rock," she gasped, checking out my wedding ring. "When did you get married?"

"About 10 years ago."

"10 YEARS! Did Velvet know?"

"Yes, he did." She was starting to get on my damn nerves.

"Wow, I can't believe you're standing here."

"Me either, where is everybody?" I questioned.

"Oh, I'm sorry. Follow me." She turned on her heels and started up the hallway. "It's been crazy all morning. We been trying to track the fellas phones. That nurse that was taking care of them got reprimanded because one the company's vans is missing. The same van we believe they driving around in. If I can get my hands on the plate number I can locate their whereabouts. Bertha's okay, even though she's worried about her husband and all. Did you know he was losing his mind? Anyway, Ronda is in there trying to play like she innocent. I know why her man left her, because she probably done stole all his savings just waiting for him to keel over. You never know with a thief. But, we'll get caught up sometime later because I'm still on the trail. Here's the room right here. Nice seeing you again, Jumpstart."

When she finally shut up, I had to take a breath. I watched her in disgust as she sashayed down the hall. I vowed to tell her to never do that again because there was nothing sexy about it.

"Hello," I called out as I pushed the door open.

Bertha's head snapped up and her eyes squinted. Scratching her head, her wig tilted before she started towards me, "Jumpstart? Jumpstart!" she screamed and ran over and hugged me.

"I haven't seen you since that night everything went haywire at the club."

"Yeah, that was it for me. I couldn't …" I paused and shook my head trying to escape the memories.

The bathroom door pulled open, "Bertha, what you out here screaming fo' now? These damn people gone put our old asses outta here," Ronda said, fixing her belt.

"Well, I don't know about y'all but I ain't old," I responded.

Her head snapped up and she adjusted her glasses on her face.

"No, it ain't who I think it is."

"It's me," I squealed.

Sharonda ran across the slick linoleum and gave me a hug. "Look at you," she pulled away from me to give me a look over. "We have so much to discuss."

“If you start rambling on like ‘Pop Rocks’ then I’m leaving.”

They all laughed as Ronda offered me a seat while Bertha started across the room to sit on the bed.

“Let me freshen up first,” I required while adjusting my bag on my shoulder.

“You better hurry up, because I got the license plate number from this cute lil Mexican guy at the DMV,” ‘Pop Rocks’ said, busting up into the room.

I went into the bathroom and closed the door. I knew this was a bad idea when I agreed to it. Whipping my phone out, I called my husband.

“Hello, Wayne George speaking.”

“Hey love. I just wanted to call you to let you know I’ve made it safely.”

“That’s good to hear. I was waiting on your call. How’s it going?”

“It’s going. I’m starting to regret this,” I sighed into the phone.

“Why? Talk to your man.”

I smiled for the first time today, “I just feel like there’s gonna be a lot of demons that I’ll have to face. I didn’t realize it until now that some of those demons where never expelled. I don’t wanna do this,” I fake pouted.

“Babe, listen to me. I didn’t tell you this at first, but sometimes you wake up in the middle of the night in a cold sweat. I didn’t tell you this because with one touch of my hand you would roll back over and fall asleep. Whatever is chasing you down in those dreams that you don't wanna talk about, you have to face head-on. We can't always get closure, and this is why I allowed you to do this. You need this for you. Maybe after this trip you can get a good night's rest."

Taking a deep breath, I exhaled. "Okay babe and thank you so much for always being there when I need you most. Let me get back to the girls. I'll text you when I know where I'm going."

"Okay babe, I love you and be careful," Wayne added thoughtfully.

"I love you too and I will." I disconnected the call and unzipped my duffle bag. It was time for Joanne to go sit down somewhere and let Jumpstart come out to play one last time.

When the door opened, I was dressed down in a wife beater, pair of jeans, and my favorite pair of Jordan's. I had my hoodie tied around my waist and my hair pulled up into a messy bun.

"So, what's the tea?" They all looked at me confused. I had to remember I was younger than them by at least ten years.

"The tea? Who ordered tea?" Bertha asked, looking between us.

"Nobody Bertha, I was asking what do we have so far?"

"So far, I can't find my husband," Bertha sniffled.

"Okay, so we don't know shit," I shrugged, throwing my hands up.

"My friend said it'll probably be an hour before he can get that information so let's chit chat," 'Pop Rocks' suggested.

"What you wanna know?" I asked, ready to face the firing squad.

"What happened that night in *Satin's Closet*?" 'Pop Rocks' asked, folding one flappy thigh over the other.

Well, the show had just ended, and I was trying to get Velvet to take me home because I was shit-faced. I recall him passing me some money and telling me to call a cab. He strutted away and I remained on the dance floor. A few minutes later, Razor walked up on me with this angry look in his eyes, his tongue was rolling around in his mouth. It's a wonder he didn't cut his tongue off.

"Hey lil sister, I'mma need you to bust a move," he said, gripping my forearm.

"I'm not leaving without Velvet," I slurred

"Look, it's some shit going down and we don't need you in the way."

I looked up into his eyes and they were stormy grey.

"Like I said, I'm not leaving here without Velvet." I snatched my arm from him and sat down on an open bar stool.

"Fine, sit'cho dumbass right there if you want to but you better not move."

I just looked up at him when he closed in on me.

"Do you hear me, Jumpstart? Because I ain't none of Velvet."

I nodded my head letting him know that I heard him loud and clear.

When he turned his back, I stuck my tongue out at him. I was gone tell Velvet about this because nobody talks to me any ole' kinda way. Razor turned and disappeared into the back room. I knew what went on in the back room even though we women folk weren't allowed.

"What can I get you sweet thang?" the bartender asked.

"Some coffee." My head was spinning but Razor had made me nervous and I needed to sober up some.

A few minutes turned into a few hours and I was getting antsy. I rose up off the bar stool and started towards the back. The bouncer stretched his hand out to stop me when there was a loud commotion behind him.

"Nigga, you cut me," I heard someone yell out.

"And I'll cut yo' ass again, nigga," Razor said smoothly.

"Is that right?" the man challenged.

"So, you gone shoot me, nigga?" I heard Razor ask and the fire inside me was steadily starting to boil as I listened on.

"There's no need for all that," I heard Velvet say. "We just all need to calm down and think this through."

"Fuck thinking shit through. Them dice was loaded. You niggas think you can come up in here and con us up

outta our money. Naw, nigga, that ain't how it work around here."

By this time, the bouncer had done ran off to get help and I eased on down the hall. I had the small 380 that Velvet had gotten me as a birthday present tucked away carefully in my garter belt.

"Move Velvet," Razor spat angrily.

"What you gone do with that? That nigga got a gun pointed at us, Razor. Think!"

"Yeah, ain't nobody taught you that you shouldn't bring a knife to a gun fight or in your case, a razor," the man spoke. Everyone in the room began to laugh.

I soon heard, "Razor, Noooo ..." and then a shot rang out. I was terrified even with my gun in my hand. I closed my eyes and prayed that we made it out of this alive.

"You muthafucka, you shot my brother. You shot him," I heard Velvet say but it still wasn't registering. Who was shot? What brother was he talking about?

I came around the corner like Velvet taught me. Legs spread apart, shoulders squared, and pistol aimed. The dude with the gun spun around in my direction and smiled at me, "I see you brought yo' bitch, to fight yo' battles," he chuckled.

"Ain't nothing bitch about me playboy," I offered him a smile just as wicked. I could see Velvet out my peripheral shaking his head to stop me, but I was already in survival mode. I took my eyes off my opponent for one second and he squeezed the trigger missing me by an inch. I steadied my breathing and caressed the trigger the way I

was taught and let it rip. I heard a total of five shots before everything else began to fade out.

I remember my hearing going in and out.

"We gotta go! Get up, Jumpstart! Please baby get up!"

When I snapped to reality. Velvet was on one side of me and Razor was on the other. I was confused. I thought Razor was gone.

"Who got shot?" I asked, scared to hear the answer.

"Silky Struthers." Velvet shook his head sorrowfully.

"Who did I shoot?"

"It doesn't matter," they both said.

I learned by watching the news that the night of the shooting. There was a nineteen-year-old boy killed. His name was Raynathan Carmichael. When they flashed his picture across the screen I was no more good. I think I cried for about two weeks. I decided right then and there, that even though I loved Benny past logical thinking, that my life and my dreams, mattered more than his.

"Damn," 'Pop Rocks' said as she slid to the edge of her seat before getting up. "Where were we?" she asked, pulling a cigarette from her pocket book.

"The fellas had already sent y'all home. I showed up late as usual," I shrugged.

"Well, I'm glad that you were there, or I would've lost my Razor that night," Ronda chimed in.

"Yeah well, I need to go call this boy back to see if he has any info," 'Pop Rocks' said with a cigarette dangling from her lip.

We all shook our heads to let her know we heard her.

"Aye," she spun around. "Whatever happened to-."

She was silenced at the ringing coming from someone's cell phone.

"Whose phone is that?" I asked, checking my purse.

Bertha jumped up and dashed across the room. "Who is this calling me from a private number. Hello?" Bertha pulled the phone away from her ear and placed the call on speaker. "I'm sorry, baby. What's that?"

"Is this Ms. Bertha Jenkins?"

"Yes, this is she."

*BEEP * BEEP*

"Hold on, suga; I got another call coming in. Hello?"

"Auntie Bertha?"

"Who is this?" Bertha asked confused.

"This is Audrey."

"Oh, thank God. I'm so glad you called, baby. I was so worried. How is your Uncle doing, and where y'all at because y'all just up and left in the wee hours of the morning without a peep?"

"Auntie."

"Yes baby."

"I have a little bit of bad news," Audrey spoke solemnly.

"Uh-Uh, what done happened? See that's what y'all get for trying to creep up outta here," 'Pop Rocks' yelled over my shoulder.

"Would you shut up, so this girl can say what she called to say," I uttered, shooing her away.

"Aunt Bertha?"

"I'm here, Audrey. Now, what's happening? Is my Willie okay? You know he gets antsy sometimes."

"That's what I called you about, Auntie."

"Well, spit it out, baby. I ain't got all day now," Bertha replied anxiously.

"Uncle Willie is gone."

"What you mean by gone, baby?" I could see Bertha's eyes instantly moisten.

"He's gone, Auntie; he slipped away in his sleep."

"No, not my Willie. He promised he would never leave me," she sniffled.

Calming down just enough, she wiped her eyes. "Baby, do me a favor. Go over there and shake him one good time. You know he's a tough sleeper."

"Auntie, I need you to listen to me," Audrey sniffled. "There's no need in shaking him. He's gone. He ain't coming back."

“NO, LAWD NO!!! NOT MY WILLIE, JESUS!!! BRING HIM BACK, LAWD!!!” The phone fell to the floor before Bertha’s knees buckled. “BRING HIM BACK, LAWD!!!! WHAT I’SE GONE DO?!?” Bertha laid out on the floor and wailed.

“I’m sorry, Auntie,” Audrey softly spoke before the line was disconnected.

Chapter 31

Ronnie 'Papa' Willow

It didn't hardly feel real. We sat around swapping stories about Po-Man with the cameramen in the van while Audrey walked away to call Bertha. We couldn't bear being in her presence when she made the announcement.

"Remember that time we were at that greasy spoon out in Bama?" I asked.

"How could I forget?" Razor chimed in.

"Po-Man damn near got us lynched out there," Velvet laughed.

"What happened exactly?" Scott asked.

"For Willie to be from the South like me, he had no sense when it came down to dealing with these crackas. Alabama had to be the most racist state in the country at the time, but ole Willie didn't give a damn. All he saw was a sign that said, "cheap eats," I explained.

"What y'all grumblin' 'bout? I guess I'm the only one hungry," Po-Man complained, twirling the toothpick in the corner of his mouth.

"All I am sayin' is that them folks had good food in Athens. Why you ain't eat while we was there?" Razor snapped.

"Man, they wanted three dollars a plate!" Po-Man complained.

"Gotdamn Po-Man, they was nice enough to let us do an integrated show so we didn't have to do twice the work. You can't spend three dollars? Nigga, you sucked

that leftover meat off my chicken bones so good I almost put you on the corner," Razor stated, rolling his eyes.

Me, Velvet, and Dick'Em burst out laughing. Po-Man had this crazy look in his eyes.

"Razor, I done told you about that sassy ass mouth of yours. I don't give a damn 'bout you bein' a Chicago nigga. I'mma give you a down South ass whoopin. Keep on talkin' shit, and I'mma fly you to the moon with ole Blue Eyes.

"Oh yeah. Step over here and I'mma slice you up like a Thanksgiving ham. You want spiral or regular cut?"

"Will y'all cut it out? Po-Man you cheap as hell, we all know it. Your woman knows it too. We don't need to stop if we tryin' to get back up to Nashville tonight."

"You just gon' agree with him, huh? Y'all wanna always gang up on me. Call me cheap all you wanna. Bet you I be sittin' on a million when I retire while y'all out here wastin' money on hoes and corn liquor. Some of y'all might be into the harder stuff, but I ain't gon' call nobody out." He rolled his eyes over in Razor's direction.

"Oh, I know you not tryin' to say I'm a junkie. The only drug you ever saw me take was some reefer and we all hit that."

Po-Man ignored him stomping to the back of the bus where he plopped down on the last seat.

"He gets on my nerves. If he couldn't sing I would say vote him out."

"Razor, how you sound? Vote the man out because he's cheap? Him and Bertha done saved us a whole lot of

money. Let his ass be cheap and not enjoy his life. That's his business," Dick'Em defended

We all nodded our agreement and disbanded to get some rest. It was times like this I was glad we weren't in that cramped van anymore. The musicians all chose to take turns driving it which left us the entire bus. We had more than earned it though. Silky Struthers had us booked in a different city damn near every night. Because it was so far South, we kept the ladies at home just in case it got too rowdy. If a white man said a word to my 'Pop Rocks', I would get myself killed because I would be on his ass. One by one, we drifted off to sleep. I was the last one to go. The sound of rubber screeching woke all of us up as the bus jerked to a stop.

"Dean, what's goin' on?" I asked the driver, rubbing my eyes. When they fluttered open I could see Po-Man standing over him

"Po-Man said he got to use the bathroom."

"Go piss in a bottle. We ain't got time to be stopping," Razor complained.

"For your information, I ain't gotta piss," Po-Man replied with his lips curled back.

"He think he slick," I replied, noticing the faint lights of an old country store. It had seen better days with its screen door barely hanging onto the hinges. An elderly white woman peered out from behind a curtain as me and the rest of the fellas exited the bus. From the sneer on her face, I knew we were in for a rude awakening. Po-Man walked up to the door all happy-go-lucky. Once he disappeared inside, we all looked at each other.

"I don't feel like havin' to cut a muthafucka today," Razor said, shaking his head.

Dick'Em patted his back, letting us know he had his pistol tucked into his waistband. I hadn't even thought to grab mine off of the bus. Velvet nodded his head letting me know he had his piece on him too. Dean's scared ass stayed on the bus. I was sure if anything went down that nigga would leave all of us out here in bumfuck Egypt. Velvet held the door open allowing us to walk in ahead of him.

"How y'all fellas doin' this evening?" the elderly lady asked from behind the counter. The store had fared much better on the inside than it had on the outside. Four tables sat in the corner covered in Confederate flag tablecloths. Rows of homemade goodies graced every shelf as far as the eyes could see. This old biddy had probably cooked everything in the store.

"We doin' pretty fine. Just stopped to use the restroom. You got it smellin' mighty good up in here though," I answered.

"Oh, that's them collards and thangs I got goin' in the kitchen. We call ourselves makin' Sunday dinner. Got some fried chicken and watermelon too." She smiled a toothless grin. This old bitch was tryna' be funny.

"Where your bathroom? I'm needing to relieve myself," Velvet said as he eyed the place suspiciously. We saw no trace of Po-Man.

"Now, y'all boys know that don't no coloreds use bathrooms in the South. Y'all got an outhouse out back. Got to be careful cause this is snake country. Would hate to get your privates bit off." She reared her head back

laughing, revealing toothless gums that were almost black. We all cringed looking down her gullet.

"Let me go get this fool," Razor whispered, walking back out the front door.

"What brings y'all fellers round' this way? We don't get too many coloreds here."

"We're on the road performing. That's our tour bus," Dick'Em replied as he inspected a jar of pickled pigs feet.

"Is that right? Well I be doggone. Wait 'til my boys get here. Y'all gon' have to sign a few autographs. What y'all go by? Let me guess. Y'all must be the Niglets, or better yet, the Coons." She let out a loud screeching laugh patting her leg this time. She had amused herself so, that her eyes were tearing up.

"No need for the name calling," Velvet remarked, causing her to shut her pie-hole.

"You must be from up North. You sound like an uppity nigger. Only a Yankee would sass a fine, young, white woman such as myself."

"Bitch, you ain't fine or young, but you're right about one thing." Velvet walked over to the counter, leaning over in her face. "I'm from Chicago, the Southside to be exact. See, we don't take kindly to no toothless-old bitches flappin' their gums. Now, you might wanna swallow your words, rang up whatever we decide to buy out this raggedy muthafucka, and maybe I won't make you swallow that tobacco you chewin' on."

I could hear her swallow the lump in her throat before she reached under the counter.

"I wouldn't do that if I was you." Velvet patted his hip. "Fellas, y'all get what ya gon' get and let's get out of this shack before I light it up like the Fourth of July."

The smell coming from the small kitchen had my mouth watering.

"You 'bout the biggest fool I ever did see," Razor complained as he opened the door pushing Po-Man inside.

"Let's get outta here," I remarked, leering at Po-Man.

"Not til I get what I came here for. I done took my leak, now I'm ready to eat. Any of y'all got a dollar I can borrow?"

"You got paid just like we did. Naw, we ain't got no dollar." Dick'Em stated furiously as he grabbed a few snacks off the shelves.

"So that's how y'all gon' do me? My wife makes all our costumes and y'all gonna do me like that?"

"Man please. My woman steals all the gotdamn material," Razor declared. "You got us out here near 'bout ready to be lynched over a damn plate of what I'm sure is some unseasoned ass food."

As we all began to argue, nobody witnessed that old cracka reach from under that counter.

BOOM!

A warning shot from a shotgun rang out as pieces of the ceiling crumbled to the floor.

"Oh shit," I whispered under my breath as she turned the double barrel shotgun on Velvet.

"I tried to play nice but y'all won't allow that. Now, tell me why I shouldn't blow this disrespectful nigger's head right off his shoulders."

BEEP!! BEEEP!!

The sound of Dean blowing the horn turned all of our attention to the set of headlights approaching outside.

"Fuck, I ain't got my pistol," I whispered to myself.

"Looks like my sons done showed up. Y'all in for a treat now," she laughed, never once lowering that shotgun.

"Well fellas, you know what we gotta do," Velvet said as he turned his attention back to the old lady. A piece of silver hair had fallen from her sweaty forehead and lingered just above her eye. From the way she was blowing it out of her face, I could tell it was irritating her.

"You the biggest fool I ever did see," I whispered to Po-Man who was posted behind Razor even though he was the biggest one of us.

"Y'all shoulda' let me stop a while back; this wouldn't have happened."

"Whoa now. What we got here?" a tall, slim, white man asked as he opened the door. Two more tall, brawny men followed him inside. Judging from the overalls, bowl haircuts, and run over work boots, I could tell these men farmed.

"Son, these here niggers don't know their place. This big apish one done sassed me sumthin' terrible." She used the rifle to point at Velvet.

"Is that right?" He paused to look around at us. "My name is Randy-Paul and I don't take kindly to no

uppity niggers sassin' my mother," he stated, walking up on Velvet who was oddly calm.

"Hold on big fella," Dick'Em stated, pulling out his pistol as one of the other guys tried to approach Velvet from the other side.

"Well, look'a dere. This nigger got a pea shooter. Darnell go get my nigger blaster out the truck."

The youngest of the guys took one step toward the door. His buck teeth, too-close-together-eyes, and odd walk, indicated he was probably the victim of incest. There was no doubt his mother and father were brother in sister.

"Naw, ain't nobody goin nowhere," I spoke up, shutting the door. "We gonna have a shootout like the OK Corral up in this bitch."

"Oh, that's how you want it?" Buck-tooth asked, reaching into his pocket, whipping out a pocket knife. Razor's face lit up. It was show time. I winked at him, giving him the signal. Without thinking, Razor tossed his pistol over to me before ripping his blade out of his mouth.

"Shit!!!!" Buck-tooth yelped in pain causing the old lady to lower her rifle. Velvet grabbed it by the barrel, conking her over the head with the butt of it while Po-Man jumped in tackling the biggest brother. The last one tried to put his hands up in defeat, but it was no use. We were ready to go in for the kill. I kicked him right in the groin waiting until he doubled over to pistol whip his ass. Blood was coming from every direction.

"Po-Man, what you doin?" I asked as he ran to the back. A few seconds later that fool ran past me with a greasy paper bag in his hands.

"Let's get the fuck outta here!" he yelled, jumping over the battered bodies in front of the door. Razor looked at me for reassurance. He was thinking the same thing I was. As Po-Man ran out to the truck, we grabbed everything we could get our hands on. The boy Razor had cut was bleeding out something terrible causing me to slip in his blood. I quickly collected myself and we hopped our asses back on that bus.

"Everybody accounted for?" Dean asked excitedly.

"Yeah," Dick'Em answered, trying to catch his breath.

That short run had me so winded that I had to unbutton my shirt and stick my head out a window. I smoked too many gotdamn cigars to be running like that. As Dean mashed that gas, we all tossed our take on an empty seat.

"We took every damn thang," Razor laughed as he shifted through the pile of shoe polish, canned oil sausages, chewing tobacco, soda, pickles, and an assortment of other things that would come in handy on the road. The smell of chicken wafted to the back of the bus as Po-Man tried to slump down in his seat.

"Hell naw, nigga. You sharin' that shit!" Velvet demanded. Po-Man scowled as he made his way to the back of the bus with the greasy paper bag. There had to be at least 15 pieces of chicken in there. We all took a piece or two before giving Dean the breast.

"That is some story," Colin remarked from behind his camera.

"You all could have been killed," Scott remarked.

"Yeah, we coulda' been killed, but we wasn't no damn punks," Velvet responded. "We were men and we always handle ourselves just like that. The generation y'all from don't know nothin' bout that. I used to get paid to whoop ass and take names. Didn't have nothing but these." He kissed his knuckles. "Ole Po-Man got us in a bind that night, but there were other times when he saved our asses. I'm sho' nuff gonna miss him."

Audrey stepped onto the van. We could tell she had been crying her eyes out.

"What I miss guys?"

"Only the most amazing story ever," Colin answered. "Did you know these guys were all bad asses?"

"Where you think I get it from?" Audrey answered as she settled herself in the driver's seat. She turned the ignition before adjusting the rear-view mirror to look back at us.

"Next stop, Alabama. Uncle Ronnie, I hope you're ready."

"Suga, I was born ready," I winked.

Chapter 32

Velvet Rose

Back Down Memory Lane

We were on our way to Alabama and I'm taking it, everybody was inside their heads. We had been driving for more than an hour and all we could hear was the sniffle of Audrey every other second. Colin was now in the passenger seat twiddling his thumbs and I, Velvet Rose, was sitting back here with the medical equipment buzzing and snapping in my ear.

"Ahem, why don't we turn on some music fellas," Audrey suggested. With a snap of the finger, everyone's mood shifted.

"Welcome back to hot 96.5 where we play nothing but the oldies. This is your DJ Frankie Maze and it's a beautiful day out today at a brisk 61 degrees. The traffic is light and the jamz is spinning. So, this next song I hope you enjoy. HOT 96.5 OLDIES CONNECTION!!!"

"Never thought I would have to say

Goodbye to my friend who's gone away

As I stare at the sky

I wonder can you hear me

What I wouldn't give to have you once more near me"

We all hung our heads and listened to the lyrics play out … It was a hell of a time for this song to play by one of our biggest rival groups, The Diamondbacks. They made a whole lot of sappy shit that would keep you crying.

Probably why their star ended up fading out years before ours did. I tried everything to keep my eyes from misting, but it was no use. All I could think about was Po-Man and the times we all had shared.

Velvet

"Aye man, look," I jumped to my feet and headed for the window. It was a nice night out tonight and the breeze from the summer's night was blowing just the right amount of summer's breeze.

"Is that .... Is that Po-Man?" I asked my friend, Rico, who stayed on the floor beneath me.

Rico was laughing so hard he rolled off the arm of the couch. "Yeah, that's that nigga," he continued to chuckle.

I stuck my head out the window to get Po-Man's attention. "Po-Man, why the hell you running down the street like a chicken wit' yo' head cut off?" He bent at the waist and placed his hands on his knees trying to catch his breath. "And where yo' shoes at?" I continued to question.

"Man, they got ..." he panted, "Dick'Em down there ..." he stopped to catch his breath. "Held up in front of Mean Lady's."

"What you talkin, Slick?' I asked him, slipping on my shoes.

"Just come on." He took off running in the direction he just came from. I had no idea what was going on, but I made my way down the stairs and out the door. I ran in the direction I seen Po-Man run. By the time I made it to Mean Lady's, there were a total of seven niggas surrounding Dick'Em.

"We gotta problem?" I asked, walking up from behind.

"This problem ain't yours, playboy," the man answered never bothering to turn around.

"This problem is mine, Slick. You see that's my brother you got surrounded."

The dude turned around to address me and before he could, I hit him dead in the mouth. There was fists flying and feet stomping.

"Alright, that's enough!" We all heard it but paid it no never mind.

"I said, that's enough!" We all heard again.

POW!

We heard the gunshot so we all stopped instantly. It was like everything slowed down. We turned just the slightest and instantly broke out in laughter

"This shit ain't funny," he grunted.

There on the ground was Po-Man like a turtle on its back feigning to be flipped over.

"Y'all gone help me up or just stand there?" he asked, still kicking his legs.

"Gimmie this," I hollered, snatching the .357 magnum from his grasp. "What you got this big ass gun for wit' yo' non-shooting ass?"

"I was trying to help you niggas," he said with a straight face as I stuck out my hand to help him up.

"Take yo' ass home Po-Man," Dick'Em and I said in unison.

"Don't call me no mo' when yo' ass in a jam." Po-Man stomped off.

"I didn't call yo' ass the first time, but aye, I appreciate' ya, bruh." Dick'Em could barely keep a straight face.

Po-Man waved his hand at us dismissively as he crossed the street. "Fuck y'all," he tossed over his shoulder.

"Nobody understand but me

Maybe nobody else can

To the world you weren't nothing special

To me you were my only friend

We used to skip rocks in the pond

Ride our bikes in the rain

Courted girls on opposite sides of town

Fought off thugs on the train"

Dick'Em

"Get yo' ass outta my house acting crazy, Po-Man."

"I ain't acting crazy. I'm just trying to teach you the steps."

"I don't need to learn the steps as long as my hips work."

"See, that's yo' problem right there."

"What's my problem, Po-Man?"

"You more worried about these females than you are the group. I'm starting to think that's the only reason why you sing."

"Is there any other reason?"

"Yeah, because it feels good to ya. You know, for some, it's a release of emotions. "

"Yeah, you right because I be having her releasing all her emotions all over this dick," I said, thrusting my hips forward.

"You know what ... One day yo' dick gone fall in the toilet bowl," Po-Man chuckled.

"Don't be wishing that bullshit on me? I'm Dick'Em Down. What good would I ever be without it?"

"Can we just do the dance steps and stop talking about ... You know?"

"What, Po-Man?" I grabbed my dick. "Say it, nigga; it's okay to say dick. We all grown."

"Dance steps man, dance steps." Po-Man mopped his brow with his sleeve. I loved making his country-fried ass nervous.

"I be dancing all night, sometimes till early in the morning if she can hang," I winked.

"You know what, I'm going home since you can't take this seriously." Po-Man snatched up his coat and stomped towards the door like a struck white girl.

"Bring yo' ass back over here so I can learn these damn dance step."

Po-Man huffed and threw his coat down on the sofa. "Alright, so follow my lead ..."

"We all need somebody

Somebody we can call

You listened to every word I said

When needed you never said naw

This pain is so deep

My wife can't even soothe me

Preacher tried to hit me with the word

That didn't even move me"

Razor

"Look, we finna go in this sto' and I'mma get us something to eat. All you have to do is watch my back."

"Watch yo' back? What you mean watch yo' back?" Po-Man looked as nervous as a white man in the projects.

"Just what I said. Watch my back. You want something to eat, don't you?"

"Yeah, but-."

"Ain't no buts, Po-Man. We ain't got no money. So, I need you to watch my back."

"Alright, come on, Razor. But if Old Lady Betty come down 'nem stairs, you own yo' own."

"So, you just gone leave me?"

"Old Lady Betty," he whispered between his thick lips pointing at me as I pushed the door open to enter the store. I had a bad habit of rolling my tongue around in my mouth when I was either nervous or felt threatened and at this point ... I was nervous.

"Would you hurry up," Po-Man asked, half-panicking. I could hear his knees knocking together he was so nervous as we walked down the aisles scanning them for something easy to grab.

"Go back up-front Po-Man. Shit, you making me antsy."

"Making you antsy?" he questioned.

I shoved him up off me, so I could move freely. A couple of candy bars were calling my name as well as a Coca-Cola. After filling up my pockets I backed into Po-Man who was supposed to be the look out. Instead, he was staring over my shoulder.

I spun up and Old Lady Betty was coming down the backstairs wielding her signature baseball bat.

"Thieving bastards!"

I backed up right into Po-Man. Cautiously, I murmured, "Back up slowly."

"Why? What happened?" he asked as if he didn't hear her voice just like I did.

I wanted to slap his ass upside the head.

"Back up, Po-Man, and do it now," I ordered.

Po-Man stood there stuck on stupid as Old Lady Betty came down those stairs grimacing with her one good eye squinting at us. Before she could utter a word, Po-Man screamed so loud it was damn near a screech. Before either one of us could react, he bolted, leaving me standing there with a pocket full of goodies that I eventually had to work off.

"Ease the pain

Oh, Lawd I need you to ease the pain

Sunshine and rain

Oh, Lawd I need you to ease the pain

My friend is gone

Oh, Lawd and now I'm all alone"

Papa Willow

"I'm not going down there with you tonight, Po-Man. I'se tied."

"You always tied. Just leave 'Pop Rocks' a note and tell her you gone be with me."

"What good is that gone do anybody? You know how that woman is."

"Yeah, you right, but it's Diana Ross. Do you know how long we been chasing Miss Ross?"

"Yes, Po-Man I know," I huffed.

"Come on, she right in our city. I already have the tickets. We just gotta make it downtown," he stated excitedly.

"A'ight, let me go put on something dapper. You know I gotta look my best for when I meet Miss. Ross."

"Well do yo' thang," Po Man chuckled.

We made it down to the theater and the house was packed. Po-Man had got us VIP passes so we didn't have to stand with the crowd. We wasn't known like Miss Ross just yet but we was getting there.

After the Supremes did their thing then exited stage left, I smiled as she passed me.

"Hi Miss Ross," I greeted, catching up to her.

"My name is Papa Willow. You sho' was lovely out there tonight."

She smiled in my direction but whatever she was saying to me was lost in the noise of the other people clamoring around to get her autograph. Not trying to seem too anxious, I stood back as she signed a few pictures. Then something miraculous happened. She reached out and pinched my cheek, turned on her heels, and went on about her way.

"Man, did you see that?" Po-Man asked me looking like a kid on Christmas morning.

"Did I see what?" I asked, still in shock.

"Man, she gave me her number," Po-Man announced proudly.

My head snapped in his direction, "Who?"

"Mary Wilson."

"What you say? Mary Wilson? I bet ya that's a fake number. Gotta be."

As security ushered us toward the exit, I snatched the piece of paper from Po-Man, holding it up to the light. It was definitely a female's handwriting. We started out the back door and through the alley.

"Do you think we'll ever get that famous, Papa?"

"If we keep at it. We can out do them damn Temptations," I smiled, poppin' my collar.

"I like the sound of that." Po-Man's eyes filled with dreams never mentioned.

"(Shower me with love)

(And strength from above)

(But most of all)

(Tell my friend I miss his calls)"

As the song began to fade out, we all wiped our tears and snot away. It was time to move on not that it would be easy, but we all carried Po-Man with us in spirit.

Audrey turned the radio down and took a deep breath before adjusting her rearview mirror.

"We just entered Birmingham, but we still have a little ways to go," she announced.

We all nodded our heads as Papa prepared himself for what was coming next.

Chapter 33

Ronnie 'Papa' Willow

Down Home Blues

"We gotta do something to lighten the mood," Colin whispered to Audrey.

I had started having a coughing fit, but I was able to make out what he said clearly. How the hell he expected the mood to be lightened when we had just lost our brother? He began to rummage through a bag on the floorboard as Razor patted my shoulder.

"Papa, you okay? I think you need this."

He handed me my portable oxygen tank carefully slipping the tubes over my ears. Instantly, I felt a little bit better. The dry coughing slacked up just long enough for me to catch something shiny glaring in Colin's hand.

"What he got there?" Razor asked. I shrugged my shoulders. We all craned our heads forward trying to see what was going on when a funky guitar riff came out of the speakers.

"Oh, shit now. That's some real music right there," Dick'Em squealed as he clapped his hands.

Velvet's face even lit up. I swayed from side-to-side in my seat as Razor whipped a comb out of his overnight bag and held it up to his lips like a microphone.

"You thought you had the best of me

But girl you had the rest of me

See I knew about Peter and Paul

And Jerry, and Tim, I knew it all

Thought that you were breakin' my heart

But oh I knew right from the start

Then you tried to pin that baby on me

She got Tim's eyes and Paul's nose and teeth ……………. Oh yeah"

We all rocked to the music waiting for the beat to drop back in. Razor was in his element gyrating in his seat like he did the first time we performed this song at the Apollo Theatre in Harlem.

"You musta thought that I was a fool

The way you played me now you know that ain't cool

You musta thought that I wasn't smart

But girl you never ever had all my heart

Well let me tell you what I'm gonna do

I'm gonna feed ya' with a long-handed spoon"

Hands were clapping, and bodies were moving all throughout the van. I saw Audrey even snapping her fingers as she drifted down the highway. We sung four more tunes before it was time to take a piss break. As we pulled into the rest stop, I got Scott to help me grab my meds and a bottle of water. Everybody else got out of the van to use the restroom and stretch. My eyes panned the back of the van. We had enough medical equipment in here to open a damn hospital. Each of us had a monogrammed bag with our prescriptions. Dick'Em had two bags. I wondered what in the world he needed with all that medicine. We had become the old farts we said we would never be. Speaking of old farts, I was surprised that my wife hadn't popped up on us yet. That woman had worked my nerves since the day I laid eyes on her, but over the years, she had been worth the trouble. Unlike the other fellas, it was hard for me to leave my woman behind.

It would have been too painful for me to carry her along with me knowing what I had to do. The thought of pulling up to that old country house in the middle of a field in Verbena, Alabama, gave me the chills. It was the one place I swore I would never set foot in again. That place held secrets that nobody ever knew, and I hoped they never would find out. I flicked a tear from my eye as Scott stuck his head in.

"Papa, you okay?" he questioned, noticing my somber expression.

"Yeah, son. I was just thinking. Going down home always gets my mind to goin.' Saw thangs no child should ever have to see. Done thangs no child should ever have to do. How much time we got?"

Scott looked down at his watch then over his shoulder.

"We have a little while. Dick'Em, I mean, Mr. Drexler had some pain in the bathroom so Audrey had to go in and check on him. I actually came back to grab his bag. Do you need me?"

"When you get done with him, come on back with your camera. I got something to say." Scott nodded before reaching in the back to grab Dick'Em's bag. I wondered what was wrong with him that would make him have a problem in the bathroom. His bowels were probably giving him hell. None of us were exactly known for eating healthy. I personally had eaten every part of the pig except the toenails, and hell, they may have even been mixed in there too. Momma didn't waste nothing. We didn't have nothing to waste. Lulu Willow was a nice, sophisticated, sweet, young thang … at least that's what most people thought. I on the other hand, knew better.

"Ok Papa, give me one second to get ready," Scott said as he hopped into the van. I was thankful when he reached up and turned the air on because it was hotter than a fat woman's panties in this here van. Audrey had that heat blasting to comfort our old bones in the Winter's air, but she must have turned the damn thermostat to hell. Scott counted me off with his fingers. I wasn't ready when he reached one, but it was now or never.

"Ooh Papa, that feels so good. Now, put your tongue inside of it just like I taught ya'. Hurry on up now before your sister gets home."

The tangy, fishy, aroma that was coming from her sticky bush made me want to throw up. I knew what was in store for me if I didn't comply. My backside seemed to have permanent scars from being whipped with that thorny switch from the rose bushes.

"Do what I say and make me feel good before I tell your daddy you been sassin' again," Lulu demanded. I pinched my nose as best as I could before disappearing back between her generous thighs. She wrapped her legs around my head like a bandana threatening to squeeze the life out of me.

"Oh yes, Papa! Eat that pussy, baby! Come on, baby I'm almost there!"

"What the hell is goin' on in here?" my sister Penny yelled, running into the room.

She dropped the clothes basket in her hand before snatching me up. "Run Papa!"

I stood there in utter shock as Lulu tried to scramble to her feet from the feather bed she shared with my father.

"Get outta here now!" Penny repeated.

I shot out the front door not knowing where to run to or what to do. Tears intermingled with the other liquids on my face as I raced over to the water pump. No matter how much water I tossed onto my face, the stench of Lulu seemed to still be in my nostrils. My dog Gnarls ran over, lapping up the water that had fallen on the ground as I kneeled down to pick up the pail I used to get water for the pigs. I jumped when I heard what sounded like glass breaking coming from the house. Armed with the pail as a weapon, I sprinted back to the house as fast as I could.

"You is a sick bitch! I don't know how my pappy ever came to marry you! I knowed you was trouble the day you came around here all hot in the ass with them little ole short pants on! What good can come from a man marrying a woman young enough to be his own child? Tell me that!" From the way Penny was standing, all I could see was blood slowly begin to seep around her feet.

It wasn't until I was fully inside the kitchen that I saw the broken piece of mirror in her hand. It dripped blood down onto the floor in neat drops.

"What you done did, Penny?" I whispered, tiptoeing closer.

"Gone on now, Papa. I told you to go down the road. You don't need to see this." The curiosity of what was only a few hundred feet in front of me would not allow my feet to go in reverse; I just had to know. I cautiously held my hands out just in case Penny turned on me. Once I was close enough, I cupped my hand over my mouth to silence the scream. Lulu laid splayed on the floor butt naked with water gurgling from her throat like a fountain. Her eyes fluttered up and down rapidly as she desperately attempted to catch her breath. Penny spun around pushing me with a maniacal look on her face.

"Why you ain't told me this woman was touchin' you wrong? I ought to beat your tail! How long it been goin' on?"

"I-I - don't know," I stammered, backing up. I didn't want to tell her that Lulu had been making me perform various sex acts on her for the whole three years she was married to my father. I was scared she might kill me. I felt my head hit the screen door as Penny dropped the piece of glass and closed in, grabbing my shoulders.

"Get you a bag packed and get outta here. I'ma go next door and get Guinea and Pete to help me clean this mess up. Gone now!"

I followed her request, jumping over Lulu's lifeless body. Her eyes stared straight up at the heavens knowing good and well she was destined for hell. Since my momma had decided she didn't want me and sent me and Penny to the country, my life had been a nightmare. My pappy had more than a few women come around. Penny never liked any of 'em and tended to run them off. The last straw was putting hair remover in his girlfriend's shampoo bottle. Pappy tanned her hide pretty good that day. He was so embarrassed when Missy broke up with him that he moved us to a whole 'nother town where he met Lulu and fell in love. All she ever did was sit on her ass and order us around all day. Pappy was always working in somebody's field, so he never cared what was going on at his own home as long as she was okay. Oftentimes, when I told her I didn't feel right touching her, she would tell him that I sassed her, and I got my ass whooped right outdoors with my pants pulled down. Pappy didn't know how to show love to nobody, but her.

After I gathered my things, I crept back into the kitchen where Guinea and Pete were being directed by Penny to wrap Lulu up in a sheet. She turned to me holding out her arms. As I embraced my sister, I could hear her heart beating rapidly. She held my head to her chest when I tried to move away.

"You don't never be nothing like him. You hear me, Papa? You may look like him, talk like him, even walk like him, but don't you never be like that no-good nigga. He rather choose pussy over his own family. You prolly not gon' see me no more because I gots to get way from 'round here now. You take this and see how far it'll take ya." My sister pressed a ten-dollar bill into my palm. I had never seen that much money in all of my 13 years.

"We gotta get movin', Pete just pulled the truck up," Guinea said. Penny released me from her grip, planting a kiss on my forehead. I snatched the one picture of both of us off of the mantelpiece in the living room before running out of the house. With all the clothes I owned and ten-dollars in my pocket I trekked three hours until I got to town. Trains had always enthused me, but I had never ridden one. What I did know was a few miles down from the station was where all the hobos jumped on to take a ride. Since I only had that money, I knew I had to make it last, so I trudged through the field wishing I had

brought along a snack. After about 20 minutes, I came across a group of at least 15 people that were waiting on the train. A woman and 3 children caught my eye. They were eating fried chicken that smelled like heaven to me.

"Where your momma?" the woman asked, tossing a drumstick bone over her shoulder. I shrugged my shoulders.

"She sent me and my sister with our pappy and I ain't heard from her, ma'am."

"Damn shame. You a fine boy. Come get you a piece of this chicken. Julius, save him some of that clabber milk. This boy here prolly thirsty."

A snotty nose little boy rolled his eyes angrily as she snatched the mason jar from his hand handing it to me. By the time the whistle of the train sounded off I was full as a tick.

"Now, look here fella, you gotta be quick. Normally I would help, but I got to help my sister get her chillun' on here. It's just like this." A tall man dressed in tattered overalls demonstrated how I should leap to make it onto the train. I practiced a few times trying to catch my rhythm.

"Get down child fo' you get us caught!" the woman yelled out. I sank to the ground like the rest of them watching as the train chugged by. To my dismay, ever car seemed to be closed. I had counted over 30 cars when I heard, "A'ight now boy! Run!"

To my amazement the woman was the first one aboard. She caught one child as her brother leapt on carrying the little boy Julius. One of the other men grabbed a third child and before I knew it I was left alone. They called for me to come on, but the speed of the train terrified me. I could see the woman's face as she teared up. My moment had passed. I stood there feeling defeated when in the distance I saw another open car. This time I just went for it, I leapt onto the train with such force I thought I had broken a rib. I sat up doubling over in pain as the car jerked me back and forth.

"Well, I be gotdamn. Manny wake up. We got company," a voice shouted from the darkness.

A filthy, barefoot, toothless, white man stumbled over to me with a bottle in his hand. "You okay lil' feller?' Must be your first time. This will take the edge off."

He handed me a bottle of what I immediately recognized as being corn liquor. I took a short swig to keep from offending him, but I was not about to get drunk and get robbed. I later found out his name was Schwartz and Manny was his brother. They had busted out of jail and were on their way up North.

"That was the last time I ever stepped foot in Verbena although we came to Alabama for many shows over the years."

"I'm sorry you had to go through that. It's a horrific thing," Scott replied.

"That ain't hardly the worst part. My sister got all the way to Texas before she got caught. My daddy was intent on making her pay for what she did to his wife. Penny ended up killing herself in jail right before the trial. She left a note sayin' that if she had to die she was gonna die free. I never got over that part really."

"So, that's why you're going back home? "

"Yeah. Got to put flowers on her grave. All this time I never could do it. Now I know I got to. They tore down the old house, but we still own the land. When my pappy passed, I never did nothing with it. Figure I will go look around and see if it's something my own children may want."

"I totally understand that. Oh, the others are coming. Here."

Scott handed me his nice, clean, handkerchief to wipe my eyes.

"You ain't piss on yourself did ya'?" Razor joked as the fellas were loaded back on the van.

"I know how to hold my liquids. Y'all fools the ones with weak bladders. Can't even laugh at a joke without squirting something out," I laughed.

"Hell, you can't laugh either. Nigga bound to cough up a lung every time." Dick'Em shot back.

After stopping at a little soul food joint to eat, I was finally on my way home. The dirt roads looked just the way I had left them minus a good amount of trees.

"Uncle Ronnie, are you sure this is the right way?" Audrey asked, looking at her phone.

"Gal, these roads ain't gonna be marked on that map you lookin' at. These here is man-made roads. I told you to make a right, I mean make a right."

Audrey gave me a warning look as she turned onto County Road 65.

"Now, see that there church on the right? That's my old church. Used to be the only place black folks could gather for anything."

A silence filled the air as the cemetery came into view.

"These places give me the willies," Velvet commented.

"As they should. At our age this the last place we should wanna see," I remarked as Audrey came to a stop near the front entrance.

"Hang tight y'all. I'mma keep the air on. We'll only be a minute," Audrey explained as Colin jumped out to help me down.

"Here you go," Velvet said, handing me the bouquet of silk flowers I had gotten Penny. I knew fresh ones wouldn't make the trip.

"I'm gonna film from here and let you have your moment," Scott assured as I walked passed. I nodded my head back to the fellas who all understood what I was going through. We had all lost brothers and sisters along the way. In fact, I think each of us had outlived all of our siblings.

"Let me help you, Uncle Ronnie," Audrey offered.

"Nah, I done made it this far. I'll call you if I need you."

According to the directions my daughter had printed off for me, Penny was somewhere in the back. I reached in my breast-pocket grabbing the paper.

"Okay, in the left corner by a tree. Damn there's more than one. Oh shit," I mumbled to myself.

After walking down several rows my breathing started to become ragged with each step. Finally, a familiar headstone of an angel on a swing came into view.

"Hot dog, I found it!" I yelled over my shoulder.

I could hear laughter as I approached Penny's grave. I will never forget having the stone commissioned when I was on tour. It was the first expensive thing I had ever paid for and I was proud of it even though I knew I didn't have the guts to come see her grave. This made it all too real. As best I could I stooped down dropping the bouquet onto her slab.

"Penny, if nobody ever cared about me, I had you and ole 'Pop Rocks'. My own momma didn't think enough about me to stick around. You know what's funny though?"

A gust of wind blew up causing my lapel to hit me in the mouth.

"You tryna' still make me be quiet ain't you?" I joked. "Seemed like that lady that gave me that chicken and clabber milk the day I left, sho' resembled you. Had a son Julius that looked like me at his age. I always thought that may have been our momma. Don't matter none now. Oh, I almost forgot. Look'a' here."

I reached into my other pocket pulling out the picture I took from the house the day I left. I was 6 and she was 11. We were smiling on our grandmother's porch holding plates of sweet potato pie. I could still smell it. My knees creaked wearily as I bent all the way down. I curled the picture up placing it inside of the flower holder before placing the flowers in the middle. "Now, you can rest sweet gal. I came back for ya."

A lone teardrop zig-zagged down my face as I turned to the right. What I saw almost knocked me over. They had buried Pappy right next to her.

"Those sons-of-bitches."

I peered back at the church. I had explicitly instructed them not to bury him nowhere near my sister. Even though I didn't attend his funeral, I still made the arrangements and paid for everything. I was overcome with fury as I rose to my feet. Accounting for the wind, I turned my back to Penny's grave and whipped out my johnson taking a long, hard, piss on his grave. I could hear Audrey gasp as she looked away.

"Hope y'all get this on film!" I yelled over my shoulder. As soon as I was done, I zipped up my pants and wiped my hands on the sides of my pants.

"That's something you been waiting on a long time ain't it sis?" I chuckled spinning back around to face Penny's grave.

"Gave that old fool just what he deserved. I wish I knew where Lulu was buried. I would piss on her too."

"Uncle Ronnie, are you ready to go now?" Audrey yelled from behind me.

"Just a second, chile. Can't you see I'm tryna' do somethin'?"

With my head towards the heavens I looked up to find the sun resting right on top of the clouds. The warmth of its rays caressed my body as I begin to feel a tightness in my chest. The chilly wind didn't feel so chilly no more. I knew it was coming and as much as I wanted to give in, I was frightened. My chest pumped up and down furiously as

I tried to take in another breath. If I had wanted to utter a sound I wouldn't have been able to. It was too late to turn back as my body began falling in slow motion. By the time my head hit the ground behind me, I was already gone. I didn't feel a thing. My whole life, I wondered what it would feel like to die and it was less painful than living.

Chapter 34

Benny 'Velvet Rose' Pryor

"Welcome back to HOT! 96.5 where we play nothing but the oldies. This next song, is one of my favorites. I give you My Dearest Friend by the Commotions …"

"We were more kin

Than blood cover ever make us

Shared our hopes and dreams as kids

Never knowing where it'd take us"

"Uncle Roonniee!!!!" Audrey screeched as she ran toward his fallen body.

"Uncle Ronnie, please, get up. You can't do this to us." Audrey's shoes kept sliding on the red clay dirt as she tried climbing up the incline.

Dick'Em went running behind her.

"Audrey!" He grabbed her, pulling her close to his chest. "Let Scott go check."

"No daddy please," she cried, punching her tiny fists in his chest.

Dick'Em turned to Scott who was still standing in the same place with his mouth held open.

"SCOTT!!!!" he bellowed.

Scott jumped before placing his camera down and running up the incline with me hobbling not too far behind him. My prosthetic was thrown on in a rush and not secured properly enough to ensure I wouldn't fall.

Scott kneeled down and placed his fingers at Papa's neck. Not feeling what he was looking for he looked up at us with solemn eyes and shook his head.

"Let me go." Audrey pushed at her daddy's chest. "LET ME GO!" she yelled and slapped at his face.

"Calm down, Audrey. You only gonna make yourself sick with grief," Dick'Em stated before relaxing his grasp on her.

She shook her head repeatedly as her knees buckled and crumbled underneath her.

I held onto anything I could find to keep from breaking my neck over all the scattered twigs and pine cones. Once I reached the back of the cemetery, I fell down besides Papa, placing his head in my lap.

"Damn niggah, how you gone wait until you get all the way to cracka-ville USA to die on me?" I chuckled as his lifeless eyes looked up at the sky. I had to press a few times to keep them closed.

"Aye, you remember that night we picked up them girls from the juke joint? Man, that night was crazy. I remember that girl holding on to you like a lost memory. She was all into you until you heard that rattling going on in the trash can. I thought honestly it was a big ass rat and decided to pay it no never mind. Ole' girl that was hanging offa' my hip looked at me like I had done dipped off in the good drugs." I paused to rub the snot away with my sleeve before I continued. "Man, you stopped me in the middle of my mack talking about, "Velvet, you hear that man?

“Then my ass just brushed you off telling you that yo’ woman had you paranoid. Soon as you could whisper in ole girl’s ear good. What happened?” I chuckled softly. “You remember, because all we heard was, *“Papa Dirty Dick Willow!!”* We all turned around and there was yo’ crazy ass woman crawling outta the damn dumpster. She had dirty diapers clinging to her, old bananas peelings hanging from her head and was wearing the meanest scowl I ever did see. All you could so was stand there and be shamed.

“Then ‘Pop Rocks’ holler, so you just gone stand there, nigga? We rushed over there to help her dumb ass out the dumpster while our fillies broke the fuck out on us. Guess they figured since old ‘Pop Rocks’ was crazy enough to crawl out of a dumpster, ain’t no telling what she would do next.”

Papa suddenly felt much heavier than before. Now, I understand what the term, ‘dead weight’ meant. “I’mma miss you, old man. There sho ’nuff will never be another like you.” At that moment, Papa’s eyes fluttered back open. A part of me hoped he had just been funnin’ but another part of me new that he was gone. I closed them for the last time before rocking him in my arms.

When I looked up, the EMTs were wiping their eyes as they moved forward. They lifted Papa off of me to help me to my feet. I had to take one last look before turning and walking away.

“Washed in the same old basin

In the middle of the field

To your wife you was a knight

But to me you were a shield”

As we waited around for the coroner, we watched as the EMTs worked on Papa Willow to no avail. We knew he was gone way before they even arrived. They got him adjusted on the gurney and started towards the coroner's van once it pulled up. Dick'Em turned and stuck his hand out to stop them.

"Unzip the bag," he stated calmly.

"Sir, we can't -"

"Unzip the bag," he repeated indignantly.

"Sir-"

"UNZIP IT, NIGGA!!!"

The tall, lanky white guy looked to his boss who gave him a head nod to unzip the bag.

"Looked after me more than my own brothers and sisters

I always knew we brothers from other misters

Thought we had forever

To go on our adventures

Sippin shine out of mason jars

While sitting next to us was our dentures"

"What you leave me here with these fools for, huh? You could've told a nigga you had a change in plans. You never did play fair. You know, I think you was the one shaving the dice for Velvet," he laughed.

"I'm gone miss you, old man. We all started from the slums. We always said that would make it out together and we did. But you leaving me like this, I understand. I'll see you soon, make sure you leave a spot for ole Dick'Em Down." He bent down kissing Papa on the forehead before making the sign of the cross over his chest.

"How can I go on (Go on)

Now that I know (I know)

The world without you is so cold"

Audrey walked up next while clinging on to her father's hand.

"I hope that my dad doesn't take this the wrong way but, you were my best friend. When daddy was always out on the road you filled his shoes nicely. You were the one who taught me how to Chicago two-step," she chuckled, wiping her tears away. "I remember the first boy that asked me to the school dance. You ran him off momma's porch so fast he didn't talk to me ever again," she laughed. "You were good for chasing away all the bad apples. You reminded me every chance you got that I was a queen deserving of a king. I always kept that in mind up until the day you and daddy walked me down the aisle. You were my best friend, Uncle Ronnie, and I'mma miss the talks we used to have." She leaned over and kissed his cheek and took his hand in hers.

"When you see my momma, give her a hug for me and tell her that I love her still. Goodbye for now, old man," she finished, turning her head into her dad's awaiting embrace.

The coroner pushed the gurney down a little further in Razor's direction.

"I can't .... I just can't ... I just, I don't understand," he belted out as his tears fell.

"Yo' wife gone kick our ass," he laughed, licking his dry lips.

"Now, what we gone tell her when she pops up? If I wasn't in this here chair I would be the first one running," he coughed. "I oughta whoop yo' ass for this shit here but I get it. Sometimes, God do work in the mysterious of ways. At least you got to make your peace before you left while pissing on the devil's head. You're our guardian angel now, you and ole' Po-Man. Continue to watch over us." He put his head down covering his face with his hands.

I nodded my head giving the EMTs the go ahead. They zipped the bag up, pushed Papa into the back of the van, and closed the double doors. We all huddled around Razor's wheelchair as they climbed inside the cab. We watched them as they backed up and turned around. Without turning on the lights, they started down the road. Without notice, Audrey took off after the van, "You can't leave me! WAIT!" she cried out as she fell to her knees in the middle of the road. Scott and Colin were about to give chase, but Dick'Em told them to leave her be. She deserved her grief just as much as we deserved ours.

Chapter 35

Ronda & The Ladies of Members Only

"Thank you, baby. I sho appreciate the call. Where are y'all at? Hello? Hello?" I hung up the phone with a cramp building in the pit of my stomach. My eyes landed on 'Pop Rocks' who was applying lipstick in the visor mirror.

"Ronda, what's that look about?" she asked, eyeing me out of her peripheral.

"That was Audrey. Papa is gone."

"Hold the fuck up! You must have heard her wrong! Call that gal back right now!" 'Pop Rocks' demanded.

"I am telling you what she told me. She was crying. He is gone, suga." I tried to reach for her but 'Pop Rocks' dodged my embrace.

"So, these fools left from 'round us so they could die? First Po-Man and now Papa? This don't make no sense. It don't hardly make no sense," 'Pop Rocks' managed between sniffles.

Jumpstart reached back handing her a tissue.

"I'm at a loss for words myself. Makes me wonder who's next. Jumpstart why you so quiet?" I asked turning to her. Ever since we hit the road she'd been in her own world.

"Ronda, I'm just thinkin'. I sho' would like to see Velvet one more time. I need him to hang on in there."

"This just ain't fair. Papa was 'bout the most decent one in the whole group." We all whipped our heads in 'Pop

Rock's' direction. Even Jumpstart looked up in the rearview mirror.

"I ain't one to speak ill of the dead, but let's not get ahead of ourselves. That nigga was a trip just like all the rest of 'em. I don't mean no harm, but I saw him go across your jaw one time. Nigga tried to punch you out like a timeclock," Bertha remarked.

"What you talkin'?" 'Pop Rocks' asked, dabbing at her eyes.

Bertha looked at me, but she was the one that opened the can of worms. I had never mentioned the incident and here she was blabbing at the mouth after the man just took a dirt nap. I looked down at my hands as Bertha searched my eyes for reassurance to keep speaking. This was one-time Ronda was gonna stay in her own lane.

"You remember that time we went all the way to Nevada? We got all the way out there and them janky promoters ain't wanna pay the fellas?"

"I remember that," Jumpstart chimed in. "Razor 'bout scalped that white man out there at that casino."

Bertha rolled her eyes at the interruption before continuing.

"Like I was sayin', I saw him put his hands on you that night, that's all. Now, my Po-Man was really 'bout the best one. Y'all all know it. He didn't keep no mess goin' and he didn't run through no money. Y'all will be surprised how much he left me and the kids in his will. Soon as I get home, I know I got to a nice lump sum waitin' on me. Just gotta figure out where his body is."

“You got to be out your rabbit-ass mind. Po-Man almost got the fellas lynched. Plus, that nigga would squeeze a dollar so tight that George Washington could catch a migraine. You think you tellin’ somethin’, but you don’t know what you talkin’ about,” ‘Pop Rocks’ snapped.

As hard as I tried to keep my mouth shut, I couldn’t help, but laugh. “Plus, you wasn’t no better Bertha. Takin’ yo’ ass in them thrift stores buying all them musty ass drapes to make outfits with. This ain’t *Gone With the Wind*, and you damn sho’ wasn’t no Scarlett O’Hara. Y’all was just some tightwads.”

By this time, I was dabbing at the corners of my eyes laughing at ‘Pop Rock’s as she went on her tirade. Jumpstart managed to hold it in, but I knew she was bursting at the seams too.

“Ronda, am I lying? If it wasn’t for you with your ole thievin’ ass, the fellas would have been hospitalized with staph infections from all the hand-me-down shit this heffa was bringin’ in.”

“‘Pop Rocks’, I ain’t got a dog in this fight,” I replied, raising my hands. “Now, ain’t the time for all this anyway. Hell, all of ‘em were dogs in their own way. Even if Papa did pop you in the eye, we know he ain’t did it for no reason. Can we please change the subject?” I pleaded.

“Naw Ronda, we ‘bout to set this here straight,” ‘Pop Rocks’ responded before clearing her throat. Bertha turned towards the window like she hadn’t started all this mess. I just shook my head as she gave us the full rundown of that night.

“So, here you go again. How the hell you manage to pop up in Vegas? You supposed to be at home with the kids. Who you got watchin’ my babies?” Papa’s nostrils

flared as he cornered me in the dressing room. The one time I needed my girls to stay around and they all left me. "Woman you betta' tell me somethin'."

"Papa, you need to calm down and get out my face. I got as much a right to be here as the other girls. You done threw me off every tour. I ain't leavin' this time. Nobody here treats their women like you treat me. Soon as I piss you off I gotta go home. Fuck you, ya' yella-pink dick-bastard. I ain't goin' nowhere. My sister got the kids and they just fine. I left her with enough money to care for em' for a week or so."

Papa took a step back looking me up and down.

"You left my babies with a junkie? I know I ain't hear that one right. Come again," he cupped his ear. I looked down at my feet wondering if I should take the chance and repeat myself.

"She don't do that no more, Papa. You know she done been clean. Why you always gotta bring that up. Nobody ain't said nothin' about your sister bein' a jailbird."

POW!

It took me a second before I realized that Papa had struck me. He had never raised a hand to me. I always had a warning to get the hell away before he exploded into full-blown anger. I knew his sister was a touchy subject, but I never thought in a million years it would cause him to strike me. He never told me the full story about why she had killed herself, but it hurt him something terrible.

"You hit me," I gasped, grabbing the right side of my face. A nice-sized welt was already beginning to form. It

wasn't nothing that my make-up couldn't cover, but my heart towards him would never be the same.

"I'm sorry, baby. I asked you not to ever bring Penny's name up. You just don't know that ... I asked you to just leave it alone. I didn't mean to put my hands on you. Let me see." I held him off at arms-length as he approached me

"Your best bet would be to get the hell away from me before I go ask Raymond for his Razor. Move outta my way."

I pushed Papa aside as I ran over to the vanity. My face was a complete mess. If I changed into my long wig I would be able to play it off. I raced over to my suitcase to look for it when the door popped open. Bertha, and Ronda walked in wearing deep frowns on their faces. I silently prayed they hadn't seen anything.

"Excuse me, ladies," Papa said as he squeezed past them and slithered away like the coward he was.

"Hey girl, we was coming to see if you wanted to go grab some food from the buffet. You know I got my freezer bags ready." Bertha patted her huge macramé purse. I hated that ugly bag and the thrift store she bought it from.

"You okay?" Ronda asked, leaning close to me.

"Yeah, I just feel a little queasy. Y'all go ahead without me." Everybody knew I wasn't one to miss a meal, so they exchanged troubled glances. Finally, Ronda patted me on my shoulder, before turning to leave. When they were gone I got all the way down on my knees clasping my hands together just like momma had taught me.

"You know I wouldn't trouble you if I didn't have to Father, but I need your help. I don't know what done got into that man of mine. We've always fought and fussed, but he ain't never struck me. That's unacceptable. My momma didn't let no man whoop on her, and I sho' ain't gonna let no man whoop on me. I done gave this man the best years of my life and three children to go along with it. I've cooked, cleaned, prayed, traveled, and suffered embarrassment all on account of this man. Not for him to go and hit me like a man in the streets; I can't hardly forgive that. You may forgive him, but I never will, and I hope you understand that."

"'Pop Rocks', I mean Charlene, I don't mean to interrupt," Velvet said peeping his head inside. I gestured for him to come and kneel next to me. He looked both ways before stepping inside.

"Now, if these knees get stuck down here, you gotta call the fellas for some help," he joked. "So, that's what he's talkin' about. Look at that." Velvet ran his hand gently across my face.

"I wanna kill him. You understand me. I'm up here prayin' to the good Lord that I don't just cut him in his sleep tonight."

"No, please don't do that. We need this money. I just found out I might have another mouth to feed."

"Say what? That thang is dangerous." I looked down at Velvet's crotch."

"Tell me about it. Jumpstart gone kick my ass when she finds out. I just ain't like other men though. This one-woman thing ain't for me. I got to get it in where I fit in."

"You shoulda' had enough of that by now," we both laughed.

"Maybe so. I just ain't no got-damn good. Now, Papa on the other hand, he' bout the best one out of all of us."

Bertha snorted loudly. I just gave her a warning look knowing that 'Pop Rocks' was liable to knock the hell out of her at any moment.

"You got something to say, Bertha?" she paused and listened intently. "Oh, that's what I thought," she snapped. "So, like I was sayin' before this heffa started throat-boxin' over here."

"He just hit me across my face so excuse me if I don't agree." Velvet took my hand in his as he helped me to my feet. "What I tell you is between us two, because he don't even know I know it. You understand me?" I nodded my head yes.

"He say that you mentioned his sister and he lost his cool. That girl walked in on something that never shoulda' happen to no young child."

"*Velvet went on to tell me the whole story. I had no idea my baby had went through all that, but it began to make perfect sense to me why he was so protective of our children. Velvet had read Papa's journal. It got mixed in with his luggage one time. He said once he realized what it was, he wanted to see if Papa had bad-mouthed him. Turns out, he read the whole thing. I went back and apologized to Papa, but I never did forgive him for hitting me. Now it's too late,"* Pop Rocks sniffled."

"Hold on now. What happened to him? You got us all wonderin'," Jumpstart asked.

"Some thangs are sacred. Even though he's gone, I wouldn't feel right telling his story. Just know that he had a whole lot of guilt attached to him. That's why I still say, he is the best out of all of em'. Velvet said so himself."

"That don't mean much coming from him." I commented. Jumpstart looked up at the rear-view mirror giving me the evil eye. "Aye, I'm just tellin' the truth. Razor got his demons too. The main demon hunting him down is the one I caused." I began to fumble with my fingers. "That's a story for another day though. Point is, ain't none of 'em perfect. Now, let's just change the subject."

"Amen to that, Ronda," Bertha agreed. We rode the next few miles listening to music, but a funny feeling was beginning to form in the pit of my stomach. Razor had better hold on tight because I had a confession to give before he could leave this world.

Chapter 36

Raymond 'Razor-Mouth Slick' Hathaway

Confessions of The Heart

We had about eleven hours before we were headed back in the direction we just came from. I swear this whole trip was ass backwards. It was like bad karma across the entire highway. Everywhere we stopped, some shit was happening. First it was Po-Man with his Houdini Act and then Papa Willow. I hung my head and let the sound of the road soothe me some. I looked up at the sound of the hum of Audrey's voice. It wasn't too loud or too soft.

"I was born by the river in a little tent

Oh, and just like the river I've been running ev'r since"

I closed my eyes and thought about my childhood. I've been running barefoot through this life of mines since my momma died in that tornado. My real brothers and sister were long gone by now and had never reached out to me until I became famous. I looked around me and these were my brothers. Well, what was left of them. I came in the world alone and I knew for damn sure, I was gonna go out that way.

I wondered what my Ronda was doing right about now? She worked my nerves most days, but I would never forget the day we committed our lives to one another. Velvet had thrown me one helluva bachelor party. I mean, there were women everywhere. We had a few friends scattered here and there but the only thing that mattered, was I had my brothers to share this moment with. That next day, we were all sick as a dog. It took us forever getting dressed, being we kept running back and forth to the bathroom.

"Man, hurry up, I gotta take a shit," Velvet yelled, beating on the bathroom door.

"Nigga, wait yo' turn. My stomach to' up. What y'all put in that sausage thing y'all brought to the party?" I asked, straining. My face was red as hell and my asshole was on fire. I was done fucking with that Mexican food.

"Look Slick, you ain't gone have no best man if I fuck up this here tuxedo," Velvet fussed.

"A'ight man, damn," I said, wiping my ass and flushing the toilet. I fixed my slacks and washed my hands before throwing some water on my face.

Pulling the door open, Velvet rushed in, "GOT-DAMN!!!!!!" he exclaimed with his face balled up. "Aye Slick, is yo' insides alright?" he asked with his lips curled up in a snarl.

"Nigga, my insides cool. You the one need to be concerned about yo' insides after all the swine you ate last night," I chuckled.

"You know I don't fuck wit' that shit. What you talking, playboy?" Velvet glared at me offended.

Papa walked past and patted Velvet on the shoulder. "Do you remember ole' girl from last night?" he asked.

"Naw, what girl?" Velvet asked, confused and still doubled over rubbing his stomach.

"That fat bitch I told you not to fuck," Dick'Em yelled from where he stood in front of the mirror fixin' his tie. "That fat bitch kept making pig noises as she laughed, and you thought that was the cutest shit," he chuckled.

"Nigga, yo' ass was slapped. Po-Man tell 'em what you said when you came out the back room," Dick'Em laughed.

"I told 'em that you had made me hungry enough to buy my own meal the way you was munching down on that thing. You was moaning and smacking and shit. I didn't know whether to call Bertha up or get me one of nem' Johnny Girls ole' Ray Charles used to sing about." Po-Man slapped at his knee and doubled over in laughter.

"I can't stand y'all niggas," Velvet grunted as he unzipped his pants and snatched them down.

"The fuck is you doing? Close the door, ole nasty muthafucka." I gritted, pinching my nose in disgust. Velvet let out a loud fart before he closed the door.

"Nigga, if you don't-." Dick'Em gagged and ran for the trash can.

Ten minutes later, we were standing in front of the pastor. My knees were trembling like a shake dancer. As I looked around at the almost empty church. I noticed Sharonda's family but nobody important. Her daddy didn't want her marrying a man like me, so he didn't bother to show up.

When I looked to the left of me, my side of the church was practically empty as well. I knew my mother would be proud of the man I had become with a few added flaws. I had no idea who my daddy was so that thought was up in the air, and poor Ms. Montgomery; she died three years before I was able to say, 'I do'.

The pastor cleared his throat before the double doors pushed open. The pastor's wife stood to her feet to serenade us. In her heavily-beaded chiffon gown with a hat that rivaled anything Dick'Em's nana ever wore, she cleared her voice and began to yowl like an alley cat. Not one gotdamn note was on key. Just as she raised her index finger preparing for a high note, Dick' Em walked over, snatched the mic from her hand, and dared her to say something.

He leaned over and told the pianist what he needed and cleared his throat. I looked up at Ronda who gestured for everybody to start over.

"Y'all ready? We ain't got all day the way my stomach bubbling," Dick'Em yelled into the microphone.

"Yeah, because I don't think I'm gone make it," Velvet announced.

Ronda nodded her head in my direction and I pointed to Drexler and he opened his mouth to sing and the ladies began to glide as they came down the aisle. He was singing so hard I just knew Audra's po' panties were soaked from the way she was smiling. The ladies walking in behind her were looking at Velvet, Papa and Po-Man. The ladies in the pews was just a giggling. We couldn't help it, we were some sexy ass niggas.

"Keep yo' eyes up front whoever you are because that one," I saw 'Pop Rock's' point and say, "Is mine. Don't get Pop-Rocked in this muthafucka."

The woman, whoever she was, clamped her mouth shut and didn't say shit else. I tried not to laugh but this was far from a normal wedding.

"I love you in a place

Where there's no space or time

I love you for my life

You're a friend of mine"

Ronda reached for my hand as I helped her up the steps of the altar.

"Who gives this woman to be married to this man?" the pastor asked, looking around.

"Do you see anybody, sir?" Drexler stopped singing to ask the pastor.

The pastor shook his head, "No."

"Well, can you come on before I shit on myself?"

Ronda's cheeks turned beet red before she glared at Drexler in embarrassment.

"Ahem, repeat after me," He looked at Sharonda first. "I Sharonda, take you Raymond, to be my husband, to have and to hold from this day forward,"

"Excuse me, umm, Pastor ..." Velvet called, raising his hand.

The pastor rolled his eyes, "Yes young man?"

"Can we skip to the end?" he asked, hopping from foot to foot.

The pastor looked at me and before I could speak Ronda belted out, "I do, Damn!"

"And he does too," Drexler commented.

"By the power vested in me by the state of Illinois, I now pronounce you husband and wife. You may now kiss your bride."

I grabbed Ronda by her waist and kissed her like the day I first walked her home in the rain.

"Ahem," the pastor cleared his throat and we pulled apart. She was giving me that look that always made my dick hard.

"Girl, look," I heard someone whisper.

Ronda looked down and noticed my erection and snapped her head in ole' girl's direction. She tossed her bouquet to 'Pop Rocks' and hiked her dress up as she marched down the steps. "Get yo disrespectful ass up and get the fuck up outta her before I go upside yo' head!"

"It ain't even that serio-." Before she could get her words out, Ronda popped her in the mouth. 'Pop Rocks' jumped down off the altar when she saw some girl trying to help her friend. Before you knew it, the whole church was in an uproar. By the time we made it to the reception we were all bone tired.

"Razor."

My head snapped up at the mention of my name.

"Come here."

Ronda had to be up to something. I stood to my feet and followed her through a long dark corridor.

"What's up?" I asked worried.

"Look what I got," she said, raising her dress and pulling out a small Crown Royal bag. She turned her back to me and poured it out on the table behind us. She emptied out watches, necklaces, rings, pendants, earrings and about two hundred dollars in cash.

"What did you do?" I asked, looking at her strangely.

"When I was whoopin' that bitches ass, I took her money and her jewelry," she laughed, placing everything back in the bag. "Here, stick this in yo' pocket." I shook my head at her but did as she asked.

"Come here." She pulled me close and stuck her tongue in my mouth. That night in that dark corridor, I hiked my wife's' dress up and fucked her to So Amazing by Luther Vandross, that was playing softly in our background.

A few months later she called me while I was on tour and told me she was pregnant with my heir.

"Alright fellas, my eyes is getting heavy. So I'mma pull over in a minute and grab us some rooms for tonight," Audrey voiced as she turned on her blinker.

Looking at the time, I noticed we had been rolling for a little over five hours. "Is it cool if we get our own rooms this time? I think I just wanna be alone with my thoughts tonight."

"It's cool with me as long as you're paying for it, Uncle Razor."

She drove a few more minutes and turned into what looked like the Bates Motel.

"Umm Audrey?"

"Yes, Uncle Razor,"

"The hell, are we?"

"Effingham, Uncle Razor."

I sat back and closed my eyes, she was trying to get us killed. Audrey parked and went inside the building and came out a few minutes later with room keys. "Uncle Razor, if you gone get yo' own room you better do it now or you'll be sharing a room with Uncle Benny."

"Hell, to the naw. That nigga loves a good midnight shittin' session," I grumbled.

"Nigga, you married a piece of shit," Velvet shot back.

"Man, Scott help me outta here before I have to body the ole' pirate-leg-ass-nigga."

After purchasing my key, I made it to my room. Scott knocked a few minutes later with my bags.

"Audrey said to make sure you take your medicine and if you need anything we're in the room two doors down."

I nodded my head while watching him walk away before I closed my door and rolled over to the bed.

I sat down and rummaged through my bag until I located my cell phone. Powering it on, I went to relieve my bladder. After washing my hands, I threw some water on my face. After washing myself as best as I could at the sink I picked my phone up. Ronda had filled up my voicemail with messages.

Before I could locate my glasses to call her back it vibrated in my hand. Pushing the necessary button. I answered, "Hello."

"Oh, thank God. Hey baby, how are you?"

"I'm fine, Ronda. What's up? Is something wrong?"

"No, nothing's wrong," she sighed.

"You called me over thirty times. So, something has gotta be wrong."

"Razor," she sighed.

"Ronda, just say what you need to say."

"You know I love you, right?"

"Aw shit. What you want?"

"I don't want nothing, but I do need to tell you something. It's been weighing heavily on my heart and I need to unburden myself."

"Okay fine."

"I just ask that you let me finish saying what I need to say before you say anything,"

"Okay Ronda. Damn."

"Okay, umm, hold on ..." I could hear static on her end like she was moving around. "I'm on the phone, can y'all give me a minute? What does it matter to you who I'm talking to? I ain't gotta tell y'all shit." Then the line disconnected.

I laid the phone down on the bed ready to rest my weary eyes when the phone rang again.

"Hello?"

"Sorry baby! Now, where was I?"

"Say what you gotta say, Ronda. I'm tired," I grouched.

"Oh yeah, Raymond Jr-," she paused.

"What about, Ray J? Is he okay?"

"He's fine, Razor."

"So why did you bring him up?"

"You remember that night I told you I was raped?"

"Yeah. How could I forget? Caught my first body that night. You know I don't like thinking about that. Why you brought that up?"

"Can you just let me explain, old man? Told you to let me talk."

"Fine Ronda. Spill the tea or whatever y'all women be saying these days."

"Well, that night I went out with some friends and ran into my old boyfriend. We all went back to his place and had a few drinks and one thing led to another. I didn't mean to cheat on you and the only reason I lied was because well … Velvet saw me leaving Donnie's house that night. I thought maybe he would tell you, so I rushed home and told you I was raped."

"What the fuck is wrong wit' you?"

"That's not all," she sniffled. "The day we got married, I was already pregnant, and the baby wasn't yours, it was Donnie's. I hate that I lied because if I hadn't of lied, then Donnie would still be here and well … if I hadn't of lied, then you wouldn't be carrying this guilt."

I couldn't even speak. This whole time this dirty bitch had been playing me for a fool. Wait, did this heffa just say the baby wasn't mine.?

"You tellin' me that Jr. ain't mine? Raymond Jr. who I nicknamed, Ray J., the day he crawled out of your sorry ass pussy, ain't mine?" I asked slowly, just to make sure I got the correct answer.

"No, Jr. isn't yours?"

"Are the other two mine?"

"Now, you wait a damn minute, Raymond Debonair Hathaway. I know I fucked up, but you will not make it sound like I'mma two-timing hoe."

"That's exactly what you are wit' yo' smut ass! Forty plus years, Ronda, and this is what you do! I loved you! You was the only family I had and you betrayed me. I killed for you and you lied to me! Now, you wanna tell me that my first born ain't mine! Bitch, I could slit your throat right muthafuckin' now!"

"Baby, please … just hear me out," Ronda pleaded.

"FUCK YOU, RONDA!!!! FUCK YOU AND THIS HOAX OF A MARR -."

Uuuuggg, Uuuuggg!

"Raymond, baby what's wrong?"

"Uuuuggg Uuuuggg!

"Raymond please …" I could hear her crying but there was nothing I could do.

I couldn't breathe. I fell back on the bed kicking as hard as I could, knocking the alarm clock to the floor. I clawed at my neck for some much-needed oxygen but to no avail. The gurgling never ceased as my mouth filled with blood. This was some bullshit here.

"Razor! Now, stop all that foolin'! Razor!" Ronda continued to scream. It was too late. There was nothing she or nobody else on earth could do. An excruciating pain filled my throat as my vocal cords were being sliced open. My hands still clawed at my neck thinking I could somehow spit it out. There was no use in fighting when I couldn't even scream for help. As I felt myself slowly dying, all I could think about was how I played the cards I was dealt.

"Coming to the stage all the way from Chicago Illinois...

(MEMBERS ONLY!!!! MEMBERS ONLY!!!!!)"

The crowd's energy kissed our hearts as we looked at one another. "You ready?" I asked, sticking my hand out.

"I was born ready," Velvet spoke. His hand joining mine.

"You already know I am," Dick'Em responded as he threw his hand on top of Velvet's.

"Let's do this," Papa chimed in. His hand fell on top of Dick'Em's.

"On three," Lastly, was Po-Man's hand as he took up the rear.

"1 .... 2 ... 3..."

"MEMMMMBBBBER'S OOOOONLLLLLY !!!!!"

We all rushed out on the stage and the lights dimmed. The band started to play the beginning of a song I had wrote for Ronda. It was at a time when our marriage was at its lowest point. I spun around and grabbed the mic ...

I thought I had enuff time to love you

I thought I had enuff time to care

I thought I had an eternity to hold you in my arms

And now your longer here"

I could hear my wife, crying and screaming in the background for me to say something, but I couldn't. As I stared up at the ceiling, I thought about the question Audrey asked me at the beginning of this journey. She wanted to know what I was afraid of and at that point in time, it was nothing. But now, at this moment, I was afraid of dying alone.

"I thought I had an eternity to love you

I thought that every day would be a new beginning

I thought that our love would endure

I thought we had forever"

I felt a tear slip from the corner of my eye as I slowly began to realize. The one thing that I've learned to wield like Thor's Hammer was the very thing that took me out. I guess what they say is true, if you live by the blade, you die by the blade.

Chapter 37

Drexler 'Dick' Em Down' Davis

That Razor was a smooth operator to the very end. Whoever thought that razor blade in his mouth would spell out his end? He had done so much damage to other folks with it. Now, it was only me and Velvet, the two that probably were the least close in the whole group. For some reason, we had been rather distant from each other for a while. I never knew why to be honest, and now it hardly even mattered. All we had left was each other. Sitting here waiting on the coroner to pick up Razor's body made me realize just how unpredictable this whole trip had been. We all were supposed to have one last hurrah, all of us had something important to do. We were dropping like flies though, like got-damn flies. There was a time that we thought we would live forever. We were at the prime of our lives.

"Now, y'all know I can go on and on about these fellas. We got Michigan, Alabama, Mississippi, and Chicago all rolled up into one. Y'all heard of The Temptations, The Delfonics, The Manhattans, The O'Jays, and The Miracles, but what y'all know about MEMBERS ONLY!!!"

Razor shot past all of us to make sure he hit the stage first. The rest of us exchanged chuckles as we sprinted out behind him. My johnson felt like it was on fire, but I attributed it to the aluminum foil-like material that we had on. We looked like we were about to get in somebody's oven with this bullshit on.

"You say you wanna lover

One like no other

You say you like it slow

But girl I gotta go

You see my woman is waiting at home

She is ready to get it on

So you see I gotta be quick

Now turn around and let me hit it like this"

We all thrust our hips at the audience causing the women to go crazy. There was a redbone in the first row that caught my eye. She grabbed her nipples through the thin fabric of her jumpsuit. Even though I was married with a child, there was always somethin' that nagged at me when I saw a nice set of hips. She winked at me, prompting me to unbutton my shirt. Our eyes interlocked as I moved in front of the rest of the fellas, walking to the edge of the stage. The screams of the crowd made it impossible to hear what she said to me as I kneeled down in front of her. Several hands roamed all over my body as me and that redbone gravitated towards each other. She puckered out her brightly painted pink lips as I leaned forward. Then the unthinkable happened. Those groupies pulled me right down into the crowd. Security couldn't get to me fast enough as fabric was being torn from my body, somebody had straddled me, and I could feel my dick being tugged at as if somebody was trying to take it home with them.

"Get 'em off me!" I yelled.

The music was so loud, the women so vicious, and I was sure I was about to be trampled to death. Redbone was nowhere to be seen and the woman straddling me had to have been twice her size. I felt my throat burning as I continued to scream. Just when I thought I couldn't take anymore, I felt my body being hoisted up. One of our bodyguards, Hurricane, threw me over his shoulder as he mowed down every woman in his path. We had nicknamed him 'Hurricane' because of the way he knocked down everything around him. The fellas were still onstage putting on one helluva show as Hurricane burst out the side exit where he stood me gently on my feet.

"Got-damn Dick'Em, them heffas tried to kill you."

I felt the breeze as I looked down at my body. My underwear and waistband was all that was left of the bottom half of my outfit. I was surprised I still had my damn shoes on. "Oh shit! My ring! Somebody got my ring!" I panicked.

"Audra gonna kill you. How you keep gettin' yourself in all these situations? That woman is good as gold to you and you wanna keep on playin'. These women gonna be the death of you."

"Tell me 'bout it. I saw a pretty face and went crazy. I don't know where I get this shit from. My daddy was good to my momma. He didn't never step out on her, at least not far as I know. Something is just fucked up about me. Maybe I never shoulda got hitched to begin with." Hurricane crossed his beefy arms tightly across his broad chest as he looked down at me.

"Your problem is that you're sorry as hell. All y'all niggas sorry. Out here on the road making all the money you ever dreamed of, and all of y'all still sorry. Razor wanna be a damn thug, Velvet wanna populate the earth, Po-Man' wanna bum off everybody, Papa can't control his woman, and you can't keep your pants zipped. I've done security for The Temptations, The Supremes, The Marvelettes, and a few others, and I don't understand none

of y'all. Money does something to niggas. Makes you feel like you can do whatever the hell you want to without no repercussions. You gonna pay a heavy price behind the way you handling that woman. If I was ten years younger, I would take her from you."

"You would do what?" I challenged. Hurricane was built like a brick wall, but I was ready to take him on if I needed to. "Keep talkin' like that and you gone need a job. Don't think I won't whoop your big, burly ass out here."

"You think I'm worried about you? Y'all fellas don't have the best reputation. You fire me, and nobody is gonna work for y'all asses again. Believe that. Now what you need to do is go grab some clothes and get on that stage before these folks start rioting. They paid to see five of y'all, not four."

He walked back inside, leaving me out there with my thoughts. I was mad as hell about what he said, but it all made sense.

"Thought I might find you out here."

I turn around to find redbone walking from around the back of the building. She approached me smackin' a pack of Kool's in her hand. She must have sprayed the hell out of her wig because it didn't even move as the wind swirled around us. The red dress she wore stopped just above the top of her thighs. It looked more like a shirt than anything else.

"You disappeared on me. What happened?" I questioned.

"I wasn't about to ruin a new outfit messing with those heffas. You gonna need this though." She reached down into her breasts handing me something shiny.

"You had my ring?"

"I figured it was my way of making sure we met up. Surely you wasn't 'bout to dismiss this concert without lookin' for it. What would your wife think?"

"Damn, what would my wife think?" I thought silently. "I appreciate you returning it to me. What I owe you?" Her eyes roamed down to my crotch. I had forgotten I was basically standing there in my draws.

"That right? Come on then." I followed her around the back of the building where I wasted no time hoisting up her dress. Her kitty was warm and ready as I tested it with my finger. She passed the sniff test too. With her bracing the brick wall as best as she could, I whipped out my snake and proceeded to put it on her.

"That's right, baby. Oooh right there, honey. You in my spot. Oh shit."

All of her moaning was music to my ears because Audra was somewhat quiet. I could never tell if I was pleasing her until I felt her begin to tighten around me. This woman was bucking her hips and gyrating so that I could hardly keep myself from cummin inside of her. It took everything I had to slide out of her and let loose on the ground. She pulled down her dress, thanked me for the good time and disappeared into the night without even so much as giving me her phone number. A few days later I would regret it all.

"Why you so quiet?" Velvet asked.

“Just over here thinkin about the past. That’s ‘bout all we have left now.”

“That’s a fact,” Velvet agreed. “Damn shame about how this all went down. We so busy resolving all these issues we had with everybody else that we ain’t handle what was going on between us. Nobody ain’t said nothing ‘bout how we broke up.”

“That’s because don’t nobody wanna admit they was wrong. We all had a part in it. I know I did. Let me ask you something though. Why you always seemed like you had a problem with me?”

Velvet placed his chin in his hand as he gave it some thought. “You was always a cocky muthafucka. Thought you sang the best and looked better than everybody. You and Papa looked down on everybody else because we was darker than y’all. I heard all the slick shit you said about me having all these kids. How about how you let that bitch give you the clap? You ain’t so innocent either. Audrey wouldn’t have her chest stuck all out about you if she knew you were the reason Sweet Audra was dead.”

“You keep that shit down to a whisper. You think I ain’t been workin’ on a way to tell her about that? I been confessin’ to a whole lotta shit if you been payin’ attention. She don’t look at me like no hero no damn more after all the shit I done told her. What about all your kids you don’t even fool with? They just waitin’ for you to drop dead so they can collect them some money. You ain’t no better than me.”

“That’s what I been tryin’ to tell you all these years. Not one of us can call the other one out but that’s all the fuck we ever did. Got a few nickels to rub together and lost our got-damn minds. You probably still don't even remember why me, and you fell out, do you?" I shrugged my shoulders. I had gotten into it with all the fellas time and time again. I had lost count.

"See what I'm talkin' about? You and Papa was ready to have my neck and neither one of y'all could remember why. We were playing in Dallas, Texas. It was at that crazy steakhouse with them big ass T-bones. Remember they had that contest to see who could eat the biggest steak?" Velvet laughed.

Now Po-Man might not be good for nothin', but beggin', but that muthafucka stripped that steak like it was a car left in the projects overnight."

Razor laughed patting Po-Man on the back.

"I'll eat another one too, long as somebody else is paying."

I didn't know how he could possibly be ready for a show in two hours with that full stomach of his bulging out. Everybody laughed as he struggled to get out of his chair. After settling the bill, the rest of the fellas all went in their own direction before it was time to start worrying about wardrobe. This was the first time we had traveled without Bertha to make alterations. In fact, all the ladies had stayed home this go around except for Audra. She was always trying to make sure she was by her man's side, but I knew in reality she wanted to make sure that Dick'Em didn't step out on her like he was prone to do. He seemed annoyed about her tagging along because she stayed up under him the whole time.

"I'm gonna go have me a cigar. Audra, please go find something to do with yourself. You been hangin' over me like an extra shadow since we got here. Ain't there

somethin' you could be doin?" Instead of answering him, Audra grabbed her purse and marched back over to the motel next door.

"Damn, that was rough," I commented as Dick'Em reached down to grab his hat off the table.

"Man please, she gets on my got-damn nerves sometimes. She's worried about me slippin' out, like I can't just disappear if I wanted to. There's a waitress here that's been eye-ballin' me the whole time. What she gon' do if I just slip off with her?"

"Come on now. You ain't gotta fuck somethin' in every city we go to," I snapped.

Dick'Em shrugged his shoulders.

"Some folks collect valuables and souvenirs, I collect panties. That's what I like to do. If she don't like it, she can run back to Detroit and take care of our baby like she should be doin' anyway. No need on travelin' around the world chasing me when she could be a kept woman in a nice, big house. Plus, you really got some nerve, Velvet. How many kids you got runnin' around now? Worry about that, why don't ya?"

"Whatever you say. I'm gonna check on the pants for this suit. You know Bertha has a tendency to fuck up the length on my pants."

"Hell, she always have my inseam so tight my balls be screamin," Dick'Em chuckled. My eyes rolled as I watched him walk over to the front counter flirting with the waitress he had told me about. When I saw him reach in his pocket, I already knew what he was up to. I just shook my head and ventured back over to the hotel. It wasn't like I could say too much. He was right about all my children,

but I didn't have no ring on my finger. Jumpstart would like to think she was my wife because she was around the most, but there was also Tequila Sunrise, Baltimore Brenda, and Flexi Lexi. Not one of them had any damn sense.

"Sorry Audra. I didn't know you were in here," I commented, averting my eyes.

"That's okay. I didn't mean to intrude, but there's somebody going at it in the room next to me and Drexler's, so I just wanted to come in here and use the phone."

"Go ahead. I'm just trying to see if my pants are fitting right."

I grabbed my garment bag and went in the bathroom. I quickly pulled my clothes off, crossing my fingers before I pulled out the burgundy and gold tuxedo pants. The outfit had been designed to look like a bellhop from a hotel, to go along with our new single, "Hotel Honey." I was shocked that my pants fit like a dream. Bertha had really outdone herself. I admired myself as best as I could in the mirror, but it wasn't long enough, so I stepped out to look in the bigger mirror by the closet.

"Oh, those look really nice, Velvet."

"Thanks. Ole Bertha really did a good job. I might have to stop talking about her now," I laughed. I stepped back in the bathroom to take the pants down. As soon as I tugged on the zipper, it went flying across the bathroom floor.

"Got-damn!" I yelled, looking down at the gaping hole in my pants.

"Are you alright in there?" Audra asked, running to the door.

"Gotdamn zipper went flying. That cheap bitch got me again."

"Oh Lordy. Let me go grab my sewing kit. I'm not as good as Bertha, but I should be able to rig it enough to work." While Audra slid next door to get the kit, I walked into the room observing myself in the big mirror. If I hadn't been wearing draws, my whole damn dick would be on display. Audra rushed back in with a cookie tin in her hands.

"My momma used to keep her sewing things in one of those too," I commented.

"I think they all did. This one used to be my momma's. The only thing I got of hers. I don't go anywhere without it. Now, come on and let's get this fixed."

"You want me to take 'em off or what?"

"Nah, it will be easier if you keep them on, so I can make sure they fit right." Audra gestured for me to stand in front of her while she sat on the bed. Once she started, I tried to keep a conversation going so it wouldn't be awkward. About 20 minutes later, she was on the last seam.

"Now, where are my scissors? I bet Drexler took them to cut his cigars with. I done told him about doing that," she complained.

"I think I got some nail clippers in my overnight bag," I offered.

"That's okay, I'm gonna just try to break it." Audra pulled and pulled, but the stubborn thread wouldn't give. When she leaned forward I didn't know what to expect, she pulled the thread tight in her fingers and bit down to break it. Just as she lifted her head up the door burst open.

"What the fuck is going on in here?" Dick'Em yelled. His face was a shade of red I had never seen before. I could tell he had just got done fucking from the way his shirt hung out of his pants.

"I was just fixing Velvet's pants," Audra answered, holding up the thread for him to see.

"Yeah, I bet you were. Get your stuff and get on in the room," Audra paused and looked at me. "Audra don't make me tell you again."

"I told you what was going on. The nerve of you walking in here smelling like dime shop perfume and questioning me about what I'm doing. How dare you?" Audra tossed her supplies in her tin and pushed past Dick'Em who stood there fuming.

"I had forgotten all about that," I laughed. "Yeah, it did look crazy though. You gotta admit that."

"Maybe so, but you knew what kind of woman you had. You and Po-Man did good in that department. The rest of us just settled if you ask me. The thing is, you never really was the same with me after that. Never wanted to hear what really happened. You just needed a reason to be mad at her to justify what you was doing wit' ya dog ass. Now, it's down to the two of us, so we better make this shit count."

Chapter 38

Joanne 'Jump Start' George

Switching Lanes

Meanwhile …

"Did he tell you where they was at?" 'Pop Rocks' asked Ronda who was bawling her eyes out.

"I don't know what happened," she cried.

"I'mma need you to calm down and tell me what happened."

"What?" she asked, looking over the seat at 'Pop Rock's'. "Didn't I just say I don't know what happened?" she repeated.

"Look, I know you're upset and all, but you ain't gotta get all snappy."

"Can you just give her minute, damn?" I spoke up.

"I don't know who you think you talking to," 'Pop Rocks" snapped her head in my direction.

"How about I just do one better and pullover and whoop yo' ass," I belted out.

"You ain't gone whoop shit," 'Pop Rocks' replied, rolling her eyes.

"Aye, we ain't got time for this shit. I need to find out what happened to my husband," Ronda interjected, pulling her phone from her bra. She stabbed them buttons so hard and fast, it's a wonder she didn't break a nail.

"If he answer let me talk to him." 'Pop Rocks' leaned over the seat and stuck out her hand.

"Why would Razor wanna talk to you?" I asked, looking in the review.

"Because," she said, bucking her eyes. "I know how to get through to him," she smirked.

"You a triflin' bitch. What you do? Fuck and suck him like you did the rest of 'em?" I questioned snidely.

"Now, look here bitch-." 'Pop Rocks' was suddenly cut off.

"HE'S NOT ANSWERING!!!!" Ronda yelled out, throwing her phone into the dashboard.

"Well, that ain't gone get him to answer. You know what, I have an idea."

"And what's that?"

"I can call, Papa …" 'Pop Rocks' pulled out her phone and dialed out. We all looked at her like she was crazy because we knew Papa Willow wasn't finna answer no phone unless, she had a direct line to heaven. As she placed the phone to the side of her face, reality began to set in.

"What am I doing?" she sniffled. She pulled the phone away from her face and looked at Ronda first and then me.

"Ronda?" Her head snapped in my direction. "Can you grab my phone outta my purse for me?" I waited as the tears clung to her cheeks like lost icicles.

"Press … 4 … I think it's 4 and put it on speaker."

Sharonda looked at me strangely but didn't ask any questions.

"Hello?"

I breathe a sigh of relief as I heard Velvet's voice. "Hey Velvet," I smiled.

"Jumpstart?"

"Yeah, it's me, ole' Jumpstart," I chuckled.

"How are the kids?" he asked.

"They're not kids anymore, Velvet."

"I know that, Joannee. Just figured I'd ask."

"Oh, so you do know my given name?" He laughed and began to cough, which made me worry.

"Velvet, are you okay?"

"I just lost another one of my brother's. How do you think I'm doing?"

Ronda cried silently as Velvet continued to talk.

"You don't have to get smart. I was just making sure you were alright health-wise."

"My health is the least of my concern." Velvet coughed.

"Where are you?" I asked, scared outside of my mind that I wouldn't see him before he left me. There was so much I needed to say beforehand.

"I'm not supposed to say but the way we're all dropping off, I feel like you should know in case I'm next in line."

"Don't talk like that, Velvet. You're starting to scare me."

My eyes watered up in fear. It made me remember a conversation I once had with my grandmother before she past. She told me that when a person said it was their time to believe 'em. I knew I was married but a part of my heart still belonged to the slick talking Chicagoan.

"I'm not scared anymore, Joanne. If my time comes before I see you again, just know that I love you and I left something for the kids. I know I didn't always say or do the right things, but I meant well."

By this time, I was cryin like Ronda. "Where are you?"

"We're on our way back up North. We should be in Chicago in a day or so."

"Shit! I'm turning around. I'll meet you back at Harmony Healthcare."

"Okay," I went to hang up when I heard my name being called. "Joanne?"

"Yes, Velvet?" I replied, wiping away the waterworks because my vision was becoming blurred.

"I always did love you. If you don't remember anything else, remember that. If I could've done things differently, then you know I would've."

"I know," I whimpered.

"Take care of yourself, Joanne."

Just like that, the phone disconnected. I had to pull over to the shoulder. I couldn't stop my heart from beating erratically. I just knew Velvet wouldn't make it back home. The children would be devastated being they never really knew their father. I done told them more than enough stories, but nothing is like sitting down and receiving those same stories from the source.

I placed my hand on the gearshift and Ronda placed her hand on top of mines. I guess this was her way of giving some of the comfort back that she received from me. I could sho' use it as I put on my blinker to merge back into traffic.

"Hey, y'all remember this song?" Bertha asked as she took off her ear buds. We thought she was sleep, but she had been drowning us out the whole time.

"What song?" I asked, voice cracking.

"Ronda, pass me that there aux cord."

Ronda rolled her eyes before passing Bertha the aux cord.

"Turn it up, Jumpstart."

Glad to be lightening the mood, I turned the volume up loud enough to make the speakers thump.

"What's up ladies?

My name is Papa

I need one luck lady

Is it you sweet thang?

(CHEERS)

I just wanna spend a little time

Spend a little cash

And get to know you better

Is that alright?

(CHEERS)

Can I kiss you right there?

Yeah, you like that don't you

Can I touch you like this?

(CHEERS)

If you don't mind,

I wanna know if you can be my Hotel Honey"

(CHEERS)

Ronda chuckled, bopping her head. "I remember that night. That was the night Papa chased 'Pop Rocks' down the street. She was screaming for about three blocks, *"He crazy,"* at the top of her lungs," she laughed, holding her side.

"I was there that night because I remember Velvet running out of the room in his bathrobe. He didn't have no draws on," I giggled. "Po' Velvet was outside trying to stop Papa Willow from killing you with his dick swingin'."

"Wow, those were the days. We had so much fun traveling the world. Doing it with the one person you couldn't seem to live without was more than enough. I could've done without the constant women always screaming and yanking on my man, but it was the life," Ronda beamed.

"Jumpstart, do you remember when we was all in Seattle and Ronda walked in the Woolworth and tried to steal that fabric for Bertha?" 'Pop Rocks' asked.

"Giiiirrrrlllll, that was the funniest shit. We were standing outside at the food vendor when Ronda here," she pointed, "came flying pass us wrapped in the reddest material she could find. I think it was Dick'Em who started calling her fire breather."

Sharonda wiped her tears from crying, she was laughing so hard.

"That's not the only thing," Bertha laughed. "She had fabric come from the hem of her knickerbockers. Did you stuff fabric in yo' britches?" Bertha questioned, laughing.

"Bitch, I had fabric coming from everywhere. I was tired of my man being up on that stage in aluminum foil pants suits and thrift store drapes," she chuckled. "And then Po-Man, with his broke ass didn't mind the rash and the constant scratching. He looked like a full-blown junkie up on that stage trying to keep up with the dance moves."

"Not to mention, every time Velvet came back from doing a show, his neck would be a different shade of red. For the longest, I thought he was cheating on me until I seen the outfit he had to wear the night before," I laughed. "Can one of y'all tell me where she got that one material from that was lime green and sparkly because Velvet had glitter on his balls for weeks," I continued despite the unamused expression on Bertha's face.

“Wait, I know which outfit you’re talking about because I asked the same question. I just knew Papa had been sleeping with one of those disco ball bitches and it was Po-Man who told me that Bertha, of all people, had a chest of clothes she’d found in the back-dressing room at the Apollo. Apparently, one of The Shirelles or The Pointer Sisters had left behind their garment bag and Bertha snagged it.”

“No, so Velvet had on a dress the whole time?” I hollered.

“That’s fucked up. If Razor knew he was prancing around in women’s clothes he would’ve had a fit.” Ronda kicked her feet laughing.

“We gotta hurry up, we gotta get back to Chicago. How long we got Jumpstart?” Bertha inquired.

Looking at my watch, I sighed in frustration. “We have about five and half hours.”

Turning the music down I said a silent prayer. I needed to hurry up and get my black ass back to Chicago and quick.

Chapter 39

Benny 'Velvet Rose' Pryor

"You sleep over there?" I asked Dick'Em who was slumped over in the seat across from me.

"Naw, just thinking. This trip sho' ain't what I thought it was gone be. We been doing mo' crying 'den laughing seem like."

"Hell, that's because these old fools done took the short road without us. Whoever thought we would be the last ones standing? Well, not me on account of my leg, but you know what I mean."

"I knew you would be the first one fucked up. Used to stay doing all them splits and carryin' on. It's a wonder you ain't rip open a ball sack a long time ago," Dick'Em joked.

I had to laugh with him because it was true. I practiced my dance moves more than the others because I didn't have the ability to hit the high notes that the ladies went crazy over.

"Hey, whatever happened to ole girl?" Dick'Em snapped his fingers. "The chick that could put both her legs behind her head." A smile slithered across my face.

"Flexi-Lexi, what they called her. The first black contortionist to work for Ringling Brothers. She moved to London after having the baby. Never really heard too much since."

"I'mma ask you something and forgive me if it sounds mean-spirited, but don't you ever feel bad about the way you left all them chillun? I mean damn, Velvet. You got a lot of lil ones runnin' round here that don't know you."

"Of course, I feel bad. Every time I popped my cork it seemed like somebody was gettin' pregnant. It was either stay on the road and do what I knew could provide for all of em' or go work in somebody's factory for peanuts. I never really had a choice."

"You could have visited them more though. We had down time to go on vacations."

"It's more complicated than that. Hell, they moved on and had boyfriends and husbands and shit. I didn't want to interfere. I knew all my kids were cared for, so I left well enough alone. Next subject."

"Fair enough. Back to Flexi-Lexi. That was the foxiest thang you ever had on your arm. Remember that night we went to the premiere of Mahogany?" Dick'Em reminded.

"How could I forget? I got embarrassed on national television?"

"I'm gonna tell you one thing now. If 'Pop Rocks' shows up acting crazy tonight, I'm liable to slap that bitch my damn self," Razor warned as he took another shot of Tequila.

"First of all, you not gon' do a damn thing to my wife. Let's get that straight right now. Secondly, she at home with the kids. I done already checked. Everybody else got they women with them, but y'all always got to say something about my wife. Ain't that a bitch?"

That's because she don't know how to act. Always got to be loud and carryin' on," Dick'Em chimed in.

"Y'all be nice. Charlene is sweet. She's just a little misguided at times," Audra defended. She saw the best in everybody, but we all knew 'Pop Rocks' was trouble. That's why we specifically didn't tell her we were going to this premiere. She loved Diana Ross and probably would have made a fool of herself in front of the woman.

The limo stopped. "It's about to be show time y'all," I remarked, adjusting my bow-tie in the mirror. Lexi finger combed her platinum blond curls that made her cinnamon skin tone look like it was glowing. Her juicy, red-coated lips, were the perfect foil for sparkling white teeth with a slight gap in the middle. She couldn't have been no bigger than a size 4, in her royal blue mermaid evening gown that was transparent down both sides. My girl didn't mind showing the whole world what she was blessed with. I couldn't wait to hit the red carpet.

"Okay gentlemen, right this way," the chauffeur said as he opened the limousine door. Audra and Dick'Em were the first to step out welcomed by a chorus of cheers. Next, Razor and Ronda stepped out followed by Papa. I shook my head as Po-Man' and Bertha exited, wearing some shit that looked like it came from a Motown swap meet. I don't know why that woman was so stuck on shiny fabrics. They looked like two bottles of ketchup in their matching red jumpsuits. Po-Man's was so tight that he had to take down his suspenders just to sit comfortably.

"You ready, baby?" I turned to Lexi.

"Of course. Let's class up the joint."

The chauffeur helped Lexi out of the limo then reached back to help me.

"Oh, I know the fuck he didn't," a female voice said.

"Not tonight Lawd, please not tonight," I prayed, recognizing the female's voice. Before I could get all the way out the car, Jumpstart was heading straight toward Lexi on the red carpet.

"Get your hands off of me, pig!" she yelled to the police officer holding her behind the barricade.

"Just smile for the cameras and ignore her," I instructed Lexi as I took her arm, leading her down the carpet.

"You son-of-a-bitch! You raggedy mouth cock-sucka! I'mma fuck you up! How you out here with this bitch when you got children that ain't even seen you?"

"Is that true?" Lexi asked through her teeth as she continued to smile for the cameras.

"Baby, just keep it moving. She's crazy."

I smiled and waved at the crowd while posing for pictures before leaning down to kiss Lexi's cheek to reassure her.

"Always have been crazy."

By this time, the fellas were all turning around, making it more obvious that something was going on. A television correspondent made her way over to talk to us. I just wanted to get inside of the theatre.

"Well, well, well, who do we have here? None other than the fifth member of the legendary R&B group, Members Only. How are you doing tonight Velvet, or should I call you Benny?"'

"You should call him deadbeat because that's what he is. Only a bum would run off on his own flesh and blood!" Jumpstart yelled at the top of her lungs.

"Benny is fine, and this is my date-."

"That's his date to the clinic! Pencil dick bastard! Dick feel like a coffee stirrer when it's up in you!"

I whipped my head around gesturing for the officer to take her away. He was too busy laughing just like everybody else in the crowd.

"Hi, I'm Lexianna Fischer."

"Nice to meet you, dear. I love your dress. Who are you wearing?"

"Actually, I'm wearing-."

"She better be wearing a bulletproof vest!" Jumpstart hollered.

That was enough to make the policeman finally drag her away from the scene. My head hung low as Lexi finished talking to the correspondent. I didn't even want to pose in front of the movie posters at the entrance of the theatre. All I wanted to do was get inside and away from flash bulbs popping in my face.

"Diana!!!!!! Where is Diana?" another voice yelled over the noisy crowd.

No no, no. Not her. Anybody, but this bitch, I thought to myself.

"Get your hands off me. My husband is in the group!" 'Pop Rocks' yelled.

She had popped up on us again. I wouldn't have put it past her to have rode with Jumpstart. The question was who even told them about the event.

"Ma'am, if you want to take pictures, you'll have to step behind the press."

"Damn that. I didn't get dressed up for nothin.' Velvet, tell them who I am!" 'Pop Rocks' demanded.

I grabbed Lexi's arm as she attempted to spin around.

"Keep moving," I whispered.

"Velvet, what is going on? You got two women out her calling your name. I thought you said we were exclusive. I don't have no time to be fighting. You see how tiny I am? I get in a fight with somebody and they will tear me apart."

"Relax, suga', that ain't gone happen."

We both breathed easier once we were inside of the theatre.

"Get in this picture!" Razor shouted over the noise and commotion. I instructed Lexi to stay put while I ran over to join in a few group pictures.

"You know 'Pop Rocks' is outside," I whispered to Papa through clenched teeth.

"I heard. She gonna stay her ass out there too. She done got all dolled up and everything. I ain't never seen that wig or that dress she had on," Papa whispered.

After we finished with pictures, I ran back over to grab Lexi, who was nowhere to be seen.

"Shit. I told her to stay right here." I had Audra check the ladies' room and I checked the men's bathroom. There was no sign of her. I began thinking the worst when the ushers corralled us toward the main screening room.

"Maybe she ran back to the limo," Po-Man suggested.

"I told her ass to stay right damn here. She will just have to be left outside. My night is already fucked. I'm not about to worry about it."

We took our seats that were placed directly behind our biggest rivals, The Temptations. David Ruffin turned around speaking to Papa and Dick'Em, but me, Po-Man, and Razor just mean-mugged their whole crew. The lights dimmed as Diana and Billy Dee took the stage. Ms. Ross wore a floor length silver gown with a matching mink stole around her shoulders. She flicked a stray hair from her face before walking up to the microphone.

"Where he at? Velvet, were you at so I can whoop your ass?"

The lights immediately brightened as Jumpstart trotted down the aisle looking in both directions. An usher tried to grab her, but she flung him off. "Now, I know you in here! Don't make me call you out. Your little girlfriend gave me her VIP pass! When was you gone tell me y'all was expecting?"

The whole theatre erupted in whispers and laughter as security ran in whisking her out. I was too embarrassed to stay after that, so I took my black ass out to the limousine where I remained for the entire movie.

"Ain't really heard from Lexi since she had the baby. Don't even know what she named him."

"That was some funny shit looking back on it. They lit our asses up in the newspapers and tabloids after that night," Dick'Em laughed. "We sure did put these women through some craziness. Even though Audra never caught me with my dick out, she always managed to find out. I can't believe Po-Man was rattin' me out."

"You gotta think about it though, he was all about dedication. His woman stayed up under his nuts. That heffa know she made us some ugly ass outfits. Remember them potholders she made our pants out of for the Christmas album cover? They looked good on the cover, but them jokas had my chestnuts roasting on an open fire," I laughed, slapping my knee. Even Scott and Colin were chuckling.

"I kinda feel like we would have done better, a whole lot better if we had spent more money on ourselves and got a personal stylist like the other groups had. We just used what we had, but man we could've really shot to the top if we hadn't been so cheap."

"Velvet, I look at it like this, and correct me if I'm wrong. Not one of us ever had a drug problem. None of us never stayed locked up more than few days and we all took care of our families, even if we weren't physically with them. How many other groups can say that?"

"I never thought about it like that," I responded, rubbing my chin.

"I know you didn't. That's why I'm telling you. Not one of us died without something to leave behind for the next generation. We may have tricked off a good bit of money, but we all had sense enough to put something away for a rainy day. Not to mention, we owned our publishing rights. We were some fools, but we wasn't no got-damn fools; there's a difference. Success ain't always about money."

"Amen to that daddy,' Audrey co-signed. This was the most sense I had ever heard this man make and I had been knowing him since I was 19 years old. All it took was 50 years to understand him.

Chapter 40

Mandala

Harmony Healthcare

I was nervous as hell. I had been pacing back and forth for a little over thirty minutes. Where could everybody be? If I didn't get this van back, my ass was gone be without a job. I pulled my phone from my pocket and called my mom and she didn't answer. I then tried calling 'Pop Rocks' and still no one bothered to pick up.

I hadn't heard from Audrey since she called me and told me that Mr. Po-Man had passed away and that was 2 days ago.

"Have y'all seen, Mandala?" I heard my boss asking as he walked past the storage closet.

"Naw, she was down there in room 236 when I last saw her," someone answered.

"A'ight, if you see her before I do, can you tell her she needs to report to my office?" I could see the shadow off his footsteps as he continued on. What the fuck, man? I was about to lose my job and for why? I was just trying to help out. They could've at least called to let me know there moves so I could be ahead of the game. I had already turned off the GPS tracker and if I turned it back on, then we would all be in trouble.

I reached for the door knob when my phone vibrated. I ripped it from my pocket and pressed the phone icon. "Hello," I rushed out.

"Hey baby, you okay? You sound a little flustered."

"I am flustered. Where in the hell are you?" I harshly whispered.

"Watch your tongue, young lady."

"Cut the shit, momma. I'mma 'bout to lose my job thanks to you and yo' friends. So once again, where *in the fuck* are you?"

"For one, you will respect me at all times. I am *still* your mother at the end of the day. For two, you better check yo' neck before it gets knock off. Just because I go to church every Sunday don't mean I won't fuck you up. For three, I should be back in Chicago in a few hours. Now, did I answer all of your questions, Mandala?"

"Yes ma'am."

"Now, that's better," she said before she started rambling.

"G*one have me put my Jesus on the shelf because you wanna be mad. Hell, I'm mad too. I'm the one out here driving up and down the highway," she scoffed. "Then you gone have the audacity to talk to me any ole' kinda way. Me, outta all people. She got me fucked up."*

I didn't have time for this, so I hung up, took a deep breath and pulled the door open.

"Mandala," I bucked my eyes at the sound of Chandler's voice.

"I've been looking all over for you." I rolled my eyes up in my head before turning around to face him. "Why don't you follow me," he suggested, walking past me, headed to his office. Like a well whooped child, I shuffled my feet to my next destination.

"Have a seat, Mandala,"

"I would rather stand."

"Okay, that's fine," he responded, sitting behind his desk. "You've been working here how long?" he asked, picking up a discarded file.

"Four years," I responded.

"So, you've been here four years and outta those four-," he paused. "I've never had a van come up missing." He stopped and stared up at me. "You care to explain, why one of my vans is missing and before you lie," he turned to his computer and clicked some buttons. "I have it all on camera."

He didn't have shit on camera because the cameras didn't work in this facility. All this money they was charging folks to come and die and they couldn't even fix the security cameras. I looked at him and called his bluff.

"I don't know what happened to the van."

"So, who is this?" he asked, spinning his computer around. I could see myself at the loading dock ordering Audrey's cameramen around as they loaded up the medical equipment and the cameras.

"That's me," wasn't no need in lying. Hell, I was caught red-handed and what made the shit so sad, I was caught by one of these snitching ass muthafuckas' I work with. Somebody had recorded me from their cell phone.

"So once again, what happened to my van? You can either tell me the truth or you can tell it to the police," he threatened.

I snatched off my badge and placed it on his desk.

"You know what, Chandler, I ain't gotta tell you shit."

I turned to walk out when he called my name.

"Mandala," I paused with my hand on the knob as he stood to his feet. "I know that *Members Only* was in my facility. I know somehow your connected to them. Now, I don't really know what's going on but-," he shook his head and groaned in frustration. "Here," he said, picking up my badge and handing it to me. "I don't want you to quit. Your one of my best workers and the patients love you. I don't know what's going on, but can you promise me that the van will be returned by the end of the day?"

I reached out for my badge and nodded my head. "I'll call my mother and inform her of your request."

He smiled, and his cheeks turned a bright red color.

"Thank you," I smiled and pulled the door open.

"Aye Mandy," I turned and glared at him. I hated when anybody called me Mandy. "Do you think you can get me an autograph?"

"I'll try," I said, walking out of his office and into the hallway. If my momma and her friends didn't get back in a timely fashion, I was gonna need a whole lot more than an autograph.

Chapter 41

Drexler 'Dick 'Em Down' Davis

"Audrey, can you stop for a minute? I need to take a leak."

My face grimaced and contorted as I tried to hold my water. Even though I had been taking my medicine faithfully, I was growing more and more tired.

"You a'ight?" Velvet asked with a worried expression on his face.

"I'm fine. Just gotta piss. If this girl don't hurry up and pull this got-damn thang over, I'mma piss myself."

"I'm in the middle of the highway, daddy. What do you want me to do?" Audrey asked angrily.

She looked up in the rearview mirror waiting for a response, but I didn't have time to deal with her smart-ass mouth right now. Colin whispered something in her ear, the next thing I knew, she swerved over into the emergency lane sending me, Velvet, and Scott flying towards the van doors.

She exited the van looking very frustrated as she walked around to the side door. Colin jumped out behind her.

"Their asses should have been strapped in!" I heard her yell at him. "I been babysitting them all this time! They act like they don't know what the hell is going on here! This shit has been so stressful. They got me out here wanting a cigarette and you know I gave up smoking at least 10 years ago. I just didn't think it would be this hard." Her voice began to crack up as if she was crying. Scott held up one finger before sitting his camera down to exit the vehicle.

"Audrey, you just need to take a breather. I'll find somewhere for him to use the bathroom," Scott directed.

"Colin, you grab Velvet and walk in the opposite direction."

Scott reached inside of the van to help me down. Audrey didn't even look at me when I stepped out. I knew we had been a little hard to deal with, but I had no idea that she was this upset.

"Hell naw. Y'all leave me in here with the heat," Velvet said to Colin as Scott lead me towards a wooded area. The cars were so close that the van was shaking each time one passed.

"There goes a spot down there by the tree. You wanna go on down there?"

"Yeah, that's fine," I answered.

Scott latched onto my arm being careful to keep me away from the thistles and thorns poking out at every angle.

"I ain't had to piss outside since that one time in ole cracka'-ass Mississippi. I don't mean to say that round you, but that's what it was. They talked bad about Alabama, but Mississippi was the real bitch if you ask me." As soon as we got to the tree, Scott let me go to do my thing. I whipped out the snake relieving myself with both relief and pain shooting out of my dick. It always felt like I was pissing out glass or razor blades.

"Good got-damn," I mumbled, shaking my head.

"You alright over there? I-." Scott's words caught in his throat as he looked down at my crotch.

What I held in my hands no longer resembled the penis I was born with. All of the knots and lumps in it, made it look more like a rotten cucumber. I was used to looking at the chancre sores, because I had lived with them for so long. They always shocked other people even though they didn't hurt a bit. That's why I made Audrey walk out when she was trying to help me go to the bathroom at the rest stop. I just wasn't ready for her to have to deal with that.

"Does Audrey know?" Scott asked before turning away from me.

"No, she doesn't, and I would like to keep it that way. When the time's right, I'll explain everything. Now, help me up out of here please," I replied, zipping up.

I noticed he was careful not to touch my hand as he assisted me, but I didn't feel too bad about it. After all, I had just pissed with no sink in sight. Music was pumping in the van when Scott slid the door back. Audrey and Colin were nowhere to be seen, so I just took my seat.

"Here you go," I handed Scott a bottle of hand sanitizer out of my overnight bag.

"Thank you. What you listening too, Velvet? That has a nice beat." Scott remarked to Velvet who was snapping his fingers and lip-syncing.

"Lawd hammercy. How you got *Members Only* in the van with you and don't know their music?" I replied. "Let me show you how it's done."

I grabbed a small mustache comb from my bag and a disposable razor that I handed to Velvet. He smiled knowing that it was show time.

"Back door Brenda thick as she can be

Back door Brenda keep the light on for me

Back door Brenda a true rump shaker

Lovin' so good she'll send you to your maker

Big red lips that know just what to do

Back door Brenda I'm in love with you

Make a man leave his family for a taste of her candy

Back door Brenda got me feeling fine and dandy"

Scott snapped his fingers as he filmed us.

"Man, oh man, that was a good one. I had almost forgot about that one. What radio station that is?" I asked Velvet.

"Hell, if I know? I just punched it on my phone. It look like a Pandora or somethin' or another. Ronda the one put me on to all this new shit. You know I don't give a damn 'bout no phone. *The Way You Do the Things You Do* started up next prompting Velvet to turn it off.

"Why do you all dislike The Temptations so much? I mean, I know you were from the same era and all?" Scott inquired curiously.

"Shit, you wanna tell the story or you want me to tell it?" Velvet asked.

I nodded my head at him. "Well, it was all about the way they did us at Motown. The Temptations had just got signed and Berry Gordy was looking for another boy band. Well Silky Struthers had gotten us an audition. We went in there and sung our souls out. They didn't even bat an eye before telling us no. Now, me being me, I had been in the industry moving around a little while before I met the fellas. I asked a few of the artists there and they said Berry told them we were too much like the Temps. Man called us a damn knock-off. Now, you know we was hot about that," Velvet stated gruffly.

"That ain't the worst part," I chimed in. "When we left that day, they was all standing around outside having a cookout on the front lawn. Eddie Kendricks started laughing as we were walking out of the building with our heads down. Hell, we felt bad enough without him rubbing it in. Now, he was talking to Martha Reeves, so it could have been some flirtin' goin' on, but then they both looked over there at me. The next thing you know, a few more had joined in on the joke. I asked what the hell was so funny. Somebody bust out and said, *"Your chances of getting signed."* That's when all hell broke loose. I ran over and started swinging on the first person I saw. If Smokey would ever tell the truth, he would say it's a miracle he got his ass out of there without a blacked-eye because I was throwin' haymakers," I voiced proudly.

Scott's eyes bugged out of his head like everybody else we told that story to.

"From that day forward, Velvet, Willie, and Razor didn't have nothing to say to them. Me and Papa kept it cool because we ran in the same circles, but it was always tension there."

“I would love to have a rematch with Otis,” Velvet snarled, balling up his fists. “One thing about it was we wasn’t no punks. The whole label ganged up on us, but we hung in there though.”

“This is fascinating stuff,” Scott remarked.

The sounds of laughter could be heard from outside as we looked up to see Audrey and Colin walking toward the van. She was smiling a little too hard like that white boy had just gave her the pink meat.

“Whew! Are y’all ready? Is everybody good to go?” Audrey asked, collapsing into the driver’s seat. Colin started messing around with his camera as Scott began to sniff the air.

“Yeah, that’s what you think it is. Somebody been out there passing the peace pipe,” I whispered, jabbing him in his knee. “Look at ‘em, sittin’ up there high as Mount Rushmore.” We all snickered as Audrey turned around peering at us through red-rimmed eyes.

“Daddy, what y’all laughing at? Who got some snacks back there? Scott, I know you love to keep them nasty ole granola bars with the peanut butter in ‘em. Let me have one please.”

“What’s so funny though? I want in on the joke?” Audrey asked, eye-balling me.

“Nothing baby. I got some diabetic prune snacks in my bag,” I offered.

“I got some unsalted nuts.” Velvet presented an unopened bag from his belongings. Audrey burst out laughing so hard that we all had to join in. I mean that girl slapped her knee and everything.

“Unsalted nuts? Those don’t sound too good. I like a good, salty nut. They got more seasoning.”

Everybody else thought that was hysterical but wasn’t a damn thing funny to me. She quickly realized that from my look, so she flipped that ignition and got us the hell out of there. Damn girl was gonna get enough of playing with me.

Chapter 42

Benny 'Velvet Rose' Pryor

(The Studio)

Audrey jumped her ass in the van talking about salty nuts and Dick'Em was about to take her head off, he was so mad. I couldn't help but laugh, but I knew if it was my daughter, I would feel the exact same way. Audrey merged back into traffic after Colin handed over his Snickers bar.

"Aye Velvet, you remember umm," Dick'Em snapped his fingers. "What was that nigga's name?" He scrunched his face up like that would help him remember. "Damn, it's right there on the tip of my tongue too," he scratched his head and looked up at the ceiling. "I got it, it was Struthers older brother, Switchblade," he chuckled.

"Yeah, I remember that janky ass nigga," I snarled.

"You ever wondered why they called that nigga, Switchblade? He couldn't cut a main vein if you showed it to him."

"Yeah, but he was sharp when it came down to that music shit. Even though we recorded at the oddest of places," I laughed.

"Switchblade?" Colin asked, turning down the music more.

"Y'all knew somebody named Switchblade?" Audrey laughed as if her soul was tickled.

"Yeah baby girl," Dick'Em glared at her and then Colin. "We knew somebody by that name. He couldn't cut shit but that's what he had us for." He breathed down Colin's neck.

You could see Colin go through three different shades of red before he cleared his throat.

"Scott, do you have your camera booted up?" Dick'Em asked, voice shaking.

"Yeah, I got it booted up," he chuckled.

"Maybe we can get some footage on this, Switchblade," he swallowed. "Since ole Colin here got the giggles like my daughter. Y'all woulda got killed back in the day for not takin' a nigga's nickname seriously."

Scott chuckled to himself as he placed the camera up on his shoulder. "So, Benny-."

I cut my eyes at Scott because he knew better. "I'm sorry, umm, Velvet. Can you tell us more about this, Switchblade?"

"Yeah, and you better keep up because I don't know how long I'mma be able to talk before my condition kick in."

Scott nodded his head and then counted down with his fingers before pointing in my direction.

The door slammed up against the wall as it flew open. "Aye, I got some good news," Silky Struthers said as he ran up in the house.

"You better have some good news the way you just slammed up in here," I said, inspecting the wall.

"Y'all remember when I said I can get y'all signed if we can record a demo?"

"Yeah, and?" Dick'Em finally looked up.

"My brother has a recording studio and he said that he can help us out."

"Yo brother?" Razor asked, coming from the kitchen and biting into a ham sandwich.

"Yeah, my brother," Silky confirmed.

"Nigga, when you get a brother? We ain't never seen this nigga. Velvet you seen this nigga's brother before?" Razor asked.

"Yeah, I know the nigga, but his reputation precedes him."

"Is that a good thing or bad thing nigga, speak English." Razor glared dramatically, chomping on his sandwich.

"Naw, it ain't a good thing," I responded, still glaring at Silky.

"Look, we need this if y'all plan on making it big. Y'all forgettin' how many people I know in the industry. I can probably slip in, talk to some of the fellas and slip 'em yo' demo. Y'all could possibly be singing with the greats."

"Nigga, we already great," I remarked cracking my knuckles.

"Just one demo and if it doesn't work I'll let y'all do things y'all way. Just give him a shot."

"You get one shot, nigga, and that's it," I replied.

"Man, we followed that nigga over to these row houses and all hell broke loose," Dick'Em laughed and sat back so I could finish the story.

So, we follow Silky over to the row houses on the lower east side. There was kids running around, drug dealers posted up and girls vying for our attention.

"Hey Silky, when you gone let me come over and give you a taste of this medicine?" some girl yelled from across the street at us.

"Who's your friend, Silky?" some strange- looking girl called out. She had some ample hips on here though.

"He fine with his tall self."

I looked around and realized she was talking about me. When she returned my smile, I noticed she had three missing teeth.

"Hey Roe, leave my friends alone you know how you like to do," Silky laughed right in her face. She sucked her teeth in frustration and went back to her conversation.

"A'ight fellas, this is it," Silky said, stepping up on the porch.

I looked at him and then around at the fellas. I had to hold in my laughter at the scared look on Po-Man's face.

"You alright Po-Man?" He nodded his head so fast, I thought it would fall off.

"A'ight let's go," Silky directed.

We all piled into Switchblade's disgusting house. There were used baby diapers on the floor, dishes in the sink and food splattered on the walls.

"The fuck is this?" Razor asked.

"Just come on," Silky replied nonchalantly, stepping over trash and whatever else.

He pushed open a basement door and started down the stairs.

"Yo' Switchblade, I brought the fellas," he yelled down.

We all walked around the wall that divided the stairs from the sitting area and caught that nigga Switchblade with his pants down literally.

"Ohhh, right there, Switchblade. Stab that thang, nigga! Make this pussy bleed!"

The girl screamed. I could've thrown up in my mouth from the tart, sardine smell emanating from her.

"Aye Nigga!!" Switchblade jumped and uncorked himself.

"I'm sorry y'all had to see that," he chuckled, fixing himself up.

"Hey Slim!" He slapped the girl on the ass. "Get yo' clothes on. I got shit to do."

She stood up smiling in my face and licking her lips. "Damn you fine," she voiced in a hushed tone.

"My dick long too," I replied, winking. She blushed while biting her bottom lip.

"You care to show me?" she asked, reaching for my crotch.

I slapped her hand away. "I don't mess around with smuts."

She jerked her head back and threw her arms into her dress, snatching it down over her head.

"Well, fuck you too 'den," she said, stomping away.

"Aye fellas, if you must know, I'm Switchblade. The sharpest nigga in the jects." He stuck out his hand in greeting.

"Man, ain't nobody finna shake that shit," Razor responded. "Go wash yo' hands so we can get this demo done. I got people to do and shit to see." Switchblade ran off to the back bathroom to wash his hands.

"A'ight, I got y'all set up back here," he said, stepping out of the bathroom. We followed him to a room he had turned into a makeshift studio. There were mics and some hand-me-down equipment that had seen better days.

"This shit work?" I asked, walking around about 60 square feet of nothing. The keyboard off in the corner was missing a few key pieces. Some of the mics were missing the covering. Not to mention, only one of the turntables worked.

"What is this shit man? We was better off going at this shit ourselves," I huffed.

"Stop looking at what don't work and watch this," Switchblade responded as he flicked on some buttons. The harmony coming from the few speakers that weren't busted was soulful. "What can y'all do with that?"

We all huddled together and started to harmonize.

"Velvet, I need you to go lower before we get on this mic," Papa yelled, correcting me.

"Nigga, if I go any lower I'mma be serenading the Devil himself."

"Just do it, damn. This place gives me the heebie-jeebies," Razor cut in.

"A'ight y'all ready?" Switchblade asked, pressing some buttons, starting the song over. We all rolled our eyes at him.

"Let's get it," he exclaimed excitedly as we turned around and grabbed our mic's.

"SHIT!!!" Dick'Em jumped.

"What's wrong with you?" I asked confused.

"I just got shocked. Ole janky ass mic." He glared at Switchblade who was so close to getting an ass whoopin.

"Come on, let's just get this over with," Po-Man voiced impatiently.

"1 ... 2 ... 3 ...." Switchblade pointed and started the music. We were all swaying to the beat and right when my mouth fell open it happened.

"Carlos, I'mma need you to come get this baby while I put the groceries up!" some girl screamed into the room.

"CARLOS??" We all said in unison.

"Don't you see me working?" Switchblade answered.

"I see five ain't shit niggas, one wanna-be manager, and yo' broke ass. So, no, I don't see you working. Working requires you to leave the house, not stay in the basement playing with yo' friends."

"Bresha, care yo' monkey ass upstairs and take CJ wit you," Switchblade replied, embarrassed.

"BRESHA? Lawd, this sound likes somebody straight from Brewster," I joked.

"Fuck you, you broke down pimp wanna-be," she snapped. "Now, back to you, here," she snarled as she shoved the baby in this nigga's lap.

We started grabbing our things when Switchblade was like, "Hold up, let me lay him down real quick."

When he came back in the room, he rubbed his hands together like he was up to something. "Y'all ready?" We nodded our heads and waited for the music.

Papa grabbed his mic and stepped forward. "I was down on my luck," he started and then ....

POP! - POP! - POP!

We all dropped down and waited for the gun shots to stop.

"Man, I'm getting the fuck up outta here." I hopped to my feet brushing the dust from my pants.

"Come on, man; third time's the charm," Switchblade convinced.

I looked over at Silky, he knew after this he was gone get his just due. I was gone fuck him up just because I believed in this scandalous bullshit he called a studio. The music started, and Papa stepped back to the mic.

"I've been down on my luck sweet thang (Umph)

I've been so down on my luck (Yeah)

See if I had you darling, you could be my lucky charm"

He was crooning along nicely when the music stopped abruptly.

"Y'all hear that?" Silky asked.

"Hear what?" we answered.

"Listen." He crept past me and paused before placing his finger up to the ceiling.

"That, y'all hear that?"

We all stopped and stood still for a few seconds before we heard ...

"Oh yeah daddy, beat that thang up!"

"Like this?" some nigga asked.

"Oh yeah, just like that!"

"You like how that feel, huh?"

"Umm-hmm, I love how it feels!"

"What's my name, baby?"

"Ohhh, Big Daddy!"

"I love it when you call me, Big Daddy!"

"Damn Pearline, you poppin' that coochie just like ya' mama used to! Right there! Don't stop. Oh Shit. I'm about to!"

"Aww, hell naw. Nigga, I'mma bout to beat yo' ass," Dick'Em voiced, pointing at Silky.

"Naw man, let's just go," Po-Man suggested.

We turned to leave and there Po-Man stood, pointing a shaky finger at a big ass cockroach on the door.

"You scared of a damn roach? You ain't no real country boy. Move out the way," Papa declared, snatching up a magazine. "All you gotta do is smack it." He raised his hand to smack at the roach and it took flight.

"Where it go?" Po-Man asked, looking around panic stricken.

"Hold still, Po-Man," Razor replied, creeping up on him.

"Yeah, it's on yo' shoulder," Papa said, stiflin' his laughter as he walked towards Po-Man slowly. Po-Man looked down and screamed. He went to slapping at his head and running around in a circle tearing up what was left of Switchblade's makeshift studio.

We got the hell up outta there so fast it's a wonder I didn't leave my shoes in the spot I skirted from. Po' Willie was traumatized for weeks it seemed. After Silky was killed, it wasn't even a month later before Switchblade was found beaten, with his tongue missing. He never was the same after that but who could blame him? They say he used to sit in the dark and mumble and when they asked who he was talking to, he would write on a piece of paper, Silky.

They had his ass admitted. Rumor has it, that's where he eventually took his last breath," I explained.

"Well," Dick'Em cleared his throat. "Let's not talk about death for a change. We done lost too much as is. Say Colin..."

"Yes sir?" Colin answered, turning around.

"Pass me that there peace pipe."

Colin glanced over at Audrey for confirmation.

"I don't know what you looking at her fo'. She came outta' my sac. Not the other way around." Colin handed Dick'Em the pipe and some baggie full of brightly colored weed that looked like breakfast cereal.

"Be careful, Mr. Drexler; that ain't no regular weed. That's gas," he cared to explain.

"Nigga, you wouldn't know gas if it blew in yo' face," I chuckled. Even though I wasn't much on smoking these days, I took a few hits off of the pipe to ease my mind. We had a cool minute before we made it back to Chicago, so I was gone relax while I still could.

Chapter 43

Benny 'Velvet Rose' Pryor

Looking Back

"Damn!" Another one bites the dust!"

"What you over there fussin' about, Velvet?" Po-Man asked.

"Just called one of my partners I grew up with. He said that one of our other friends named Smokey Joe got killed last night outside the Marmalade Palace in Boston. Seems like everybody I came up with is falling off the map."

"Smokey Joe? That nigga owed me twelve dollars. Guess it would be a little petty to ask his ole lady for it now," Razor asserted as he checked himself in the mirror.

"Not only would it be petty, but it might get your ass whooped and I'm not helping you out. My hands already messed up from all this scrappin' I been doin' over the years," I stated for the record.

"You got that right. Your shit looks like pig knuckles," Po-Man laughed.

"You would know witcha' country ass. You done had your greasy lips around every part of the pig. Never seen a nigga so glad to eat a chitlin' in my life."

Po-Man shot me a dirty look before flipping me off.

"Hey fellas!" Audra yelled, knocking on the door.

"Come on in, Sweetie," I responded nonchalantly.

Dick'Em cut his eyes over at me sharp enough to slice bread.

"Hey, I was just checking to see if you all needed anything. The ladies and I were about to go grab some lunch before the show. We might even do a little shopping."

That made Po-Man drop the shoes he was shining.

"I know Bertha better not go spendin' my money. We ain't got no money to be blowing on no foolishness."

"Man, would you calm your thrifty nickel ass down? Let that woman live a little. Bad enough you got her living in a house your grandmother's, grandmother lived in. Y'all still got that outhouse 'round back?" Razor joked.

Po-Man stood, balled up his fist and shook it in Razor's face.

"Calm down, big fella. I'd hate to have to dice you up like an onion." Razor swished his mouth around for his blade.

"That's a sin and a got-damn shame how cheap he is. Last night he went through all of our leftovers and made him and Bertha plates. Mind you, I cleaned my chicken bone like nobody's business. Man, he picked up the gristle," Papa remarked as he ironed his pants.

"If you all don't need our help, I'll be moving along," Audra commented.

Something about the way Audra stood in that doorway appealed to my senses. There was a sadness in her eyes. Dick'Em wouldn't even look at her. Something was brewing, and I was about to get to the bottom of it.

"I'll be back in time for rehearsal. I'm about to go take me a smoke break and try to walk down some of this food."

As I made it to the doorway, I discreetly took Audra's hand, leading her down a dark corridor. I kept looking back to make sure we weren't being watched because I knew Dick'Em liked to pack a pistol. I silently prayed that the alarm wouldn't sound when I opened the side door marked exit. Thankfully nothing happened.

"What's the matter, Velvet?" Audra asked once we were safely outside.

"That's what I wanna know. Why y'all not talking? I noticed it on the bus, at dinner last night, and this morning at breakfast. Plus, I know y'all stayed in separate rooms. What's going on, Audra, and don't lie to me because I'll go confront him right damn now."

Audra's faced slowly lowered to the ground as a fat tear dropped, rolling down the front of her leather heels.

"It's just that .... I don't want to start no problems."

"Audra, if you don't tell me what's going on, it's gone be a problem. What that fool done did now?"

"I think he may have given me something. I'm not no dirty woman. I never been with another man."

"You mean V.D.? Lawd, I told that boy to strap up. We all told him."

"Velvet, I've been feeling so sick to my stomach. I'm tired, I got little bumps all over. I'm scared to know what it is. To top it all off, he said I can't sleep in the bed with him until we find out. The crazy thing is he don't have

a bump or sore on him. He accused me of two-timing. Can you believe that? Me of all people."

My hand landed on the back of my neck as I scratched thoughtfully. This was not hard to believe for one minute, but that didn't keep it from pissing me off.

"Please promise me you won't say nothing," Audra pleaded.

"Audra, I-."

"Please. I have a reputation and a child to think about. I just want this to stay between us. At least till I find out what this is. Maybe it's something else."

She knew just like I knew, that this was something bad. I just nodded my head yes as I reached into my jacket pocket for my handkerchief. It had a phone number written on it, but I offered it to her anyway.

"You got my word. What you really need to do is leave that nigga though. He may be like a brother to me, but he ain't no good. No damn good at all. I got all the kids, but he's the one with all the women."

"Where would I go? What would I do? All I know how to do is be a roadie. My daughter has a good life, better than both of ours was. Plus, I know he would fight me for custody of her just to be spiteful. He may not love me, but he loves his baby-girl. The road is no place to raise a child."

"You gone just let this man drag you down though? He don't even have the decency to hide what he's doing. He let a bitch slide out of the hotel with your diamond necklace. He has a problem that just can't be fixed."

Audra dabbed at her eyes careful not to ruin her makeup.

"That may not be his fault. His mother told me something before we got married. I just didn't want to take heed to it." My ears were wide open.

I needed some kind of way to understand Dick'Em as we were never all that close to begin with. We didn't exactly clash, but it seemed we had the least in common.

"She said that his father used to be a real cat-daddy when they were courting. He had this woman and that woman and never really thought much of her because she was chaste and said she wanted to wait for marriage to have sex. Well, he didn't take too kindly to that, so he went out just messing around with everybody. Once they got married, everything stopped because he was called to the ministry. She finally had the man she dreamed of. What she didn't know was that he had trunks of girly magazines that he didn't part with. They were in the attic at his parent's house. Drexler used to always go over there for singing lessons with his granny. She would have him at the piano singing and then to reward him, she would let him get candy and explore in the attic."

"He got ahold of the magazines, didn't he?" I concluded.

"Yes, he did. Then before they knew it he was going over there more and more often. His granny caught him up there playing with himself one day. He had messed over the magazines so, that the pages were stuck together. She say there had to be at least 60 magazines up there and all of them were sticky. Well, his granddaddy made him confess in front of the church. Can you imagine that? As a child,

having to get up there and admit something so embarrassing?"

"Naw, I can't say I can imagine that. It had to be hard for him," I remarked thoughtfully.

"All it did was drove him to start doing worse things. He slept with a prostitute a few months later. Not too long before I met him. The girls at church tried to tell me about him, but I thought they were just jealous. Then the older ladies at the church started telling me to watch out for him. He went through every last girl in that choir and even the junior choir director. They told me that her mother had her moved out to New York with her grandparents. He just can't help the way he is. I just can't help that I love him."

"I don't really know what to say about that. I guess we all have our struggles. Just promise me that you're going to get yourself taken care of. You're the only woman that makes sense in our lives. Why do you think we call you, Sweet Audra?" She just gave me a weak little smile.

I kissed her forehead and walked back in to get ready with the fellas. Before I opened the dressing room door, I had to put my game face on.

"So, you mean to tell me that you wouldn't knock off Sophia Loren? Man please. I would fuck the accent out of her ass," Dick'Em was saying as I walked in. I kept my head down and went over to the corner where I grabbed my shoes to polish.

"You can keep that pink pussy. Give me Pam Grier. You know that's my woman right there," Razor chimed in before taking a swig of something in a brown bag. Knowing him, it was probably some cheap corn liquor.

"Po-Man who you got? Don't you say Bertha's big draws wearing ass. We know you like 'em big, but who would you get if you had a choice?" Papa asked.

Po-Man looked up at the ceiling for a second. "I think Chaka Kahn looks good."

"My nigga!" Dick'Em high-fived him. "I knew deep down you had some good taste hidden in there somewhere."

"Who you got, Velvet?" Dick'Em questioned me. I clenched my jaws for a few seconds fighting the urge to say Audra just to piss him off.

"I got time to rehearse that's what I got. Come on fellas because Razor was a little bit slow on them moves last show."

"That's probably because I was drunk. You ain't have to call me out like that." Razor slammed his bag down on the vanity in front of him. I could feel Dick'Em's eyes on me as I walked over to the center of the room stretching. Tonight, was the debut of our new single 'Baby Gone Bye'. When I wrote it, I was feeling bad about Jumpstart leaving me for the millionth time. She said she was tired of my shit and I was too but settling down was just not an option. I said a few things I didn't mean, and she left right in the middle of our show. Left with some pretty-faced motherfucker with crazy colored eyes. It wasn't long before she was having his baby. I held onto the song until I felt like the time was right. If it hadn't been for Po-Man finding it on the tour bus, I never would have released it.

"What y'all waiting on? Get right." I snapped my fingers.

The fellas lined up on either side of me. Dick'Em was grilling me hard now. It always felt like he was a little upset when he didn't get to lead a song. Tonight, was my night and I knew just who I was sending it out to. After a few run-throughs, we took a break to eat and then showered before the ladies got back. Bertha checked our clothes for any last-minute mends while Ronda was out pick-pocketing the hell out of the farmers in the convention center. I noticed how Dick'Em was being soft and careful with Audra. It was a complete 360 from earlier. Maybe he had heard us talking outside. It didn't matter to me because it wouldn't be no shit unless he started some. I sprayed my afro down before handing the oil sheen to Po-Man with his bad hair having ass. Nigga's hair was so nappy you could rub it against a tree and start a brush fire.

"Alright now. Y'all look real nice. Last looks fellas," Audra warned, looking at her tiny wristwatch. We all checked ourselves in the mirror before walking out to the backstage area. My nerves settled in as soon as I peered from behind the curtain. The theatre was so crowded that you couldn't see the aisles. This had to be against the fire code.

"I know this is your first-time leading, but you'll do just fine. I believe in you," Audra whispered from behind me.

"I sho' appreciate it, sweetie."

It was a hell of a waiting game as the announcer, a stand-up comedian, made at least fifteen bad jokes.

"Muthafucka, you cuttin' into our time slot," I muttered. Maybe I was louder than I thought because he whipped his head around so fast that his afro wig flew right off of his head. That won him more laughs than his whole

set. He promptly put down the mic and stormed right toward me.

"We got a problem, playa?" Razor asked, sliding up next to me.

"Man, this jive ass turkey gon' talk shit while I'm out there doin' my thang."

"The only thang you need to be doin' is movin' out the way before you get tossed up like that cheap ass wig," Papa snapped.

"Oh, so y'all gone gang up on ole' Billy Ray?"

"You got-damn right," I answered, imitating Isaac Hayes.

"If you take one of us, you take all of us. How you wanna do it?" Po-Man stepped up. He took one look at Po-Man's Bigfoot- looking- ass and got out of dodge. The crowd began to chant as our music began to play.

"Come on fellas before we have another riot on our hands," I said, leading the way. The lights dimmed in the audience, placing the spotlight on us. I could hear my heart beating it was so loud. As the stagehands ran out placing the mics in front of the other fellas I knew there was no turning back.

"This song is dedicated to every woman that's ever loved the wrong man

See we mess up sometimes not knowing when we have a good thing

That good thing I had was you girl and I will never forget the times we shared

I love you wherever you are

(Cheers)

Some blame it on choices of youth

But girl to tell you the truth

I didn't deserve the love you gave

Some say it was the circumstance

Damn babe, you gave me so many chances

And I wasted them all away

Come on fellas help me

Baby gone bye

Didn't even leave a letter

Made my heart cry

But I'm glad she's doin better"

I sang my heart out on that song, but it had an effect that I didn't expect. So many ladies in the audience were crying that we had to change it up real fast. Dick'Em was quick to slide to the front to sing Whip That Thang Out. I thought Audra would pass out when he ripped his shirt off, tossing it into the audience. Some chick caught it and got mauled by at least five other chicks trying to snatch it from her. They had to end up being escorted out. A few fights broke out after that causing us to have to end the show early. I was pissed off as security escorted us backstage.

"This don't make no sense. He knew that shit was gone happen. Now we got all these folks goin' off because they want their money back!" Razor shouted, stomping

down the hallway. "He just mad because Velvet outshined his ass! Light-skinned niggas are always mad when they get showed up. That's what I call bein' a bitch!"

"You got somethin' on your mind, Razor? We can take this outside," Dick'Em shouted, pushing past me and Po-Man.

"Come on out here pretty boy so I can slice some of that ego out ya," Razor spat.

"You ain't said nothing! Let's go!" Dick'Em countered.

"Naw, y'all not about to do that. You need to check yourself, Dick'Em." Papa chimed in.

I had never really seen him check Dick'Em; it surprised the hell out of all of us.

"Check myself? Velvet out here making these women cry and I go in and try to get everything going and now y'all mad? You taking these nigga's side?"

"I'm not taking sides with nobody. Right is right. You know you can't through shit in that audience. Remember that incident in Cleveland?" Papa reminded.

"Ok, I see we got a mutiny on our hands. Y'all wanna come down on me because I turned it out. That's fine. Y'all think I'm the problem then I can just go home with my woman and y'all finish this shit without me."

"Fine with me," I spoke up.

"Velvet, you speakin' for everybody now? You got one got-damn lead and now you speakin' for everybody?" Dick'Em responded.

"If it wasn't for Velvet, we would be still doing chitlin circuit ass shows. You can come up off him," Po-Man intervened.

"Man, to hell with all y'all. Where Audra at? Audra!" Dick'Em backpedaled to the dressing room while we stood out in the hallway trying to get our thoughts together.

"He got a huge ego. That's gonna be the ruin of him," Papa said.

"Sho nuff. He's letting these women blow his head up. Speaking of women, let's get the ladies and get out of here." Razor suggested.

"I'll go rustle them up," Po-Man offered. As he ran off we just stood there. Nobody wanted to go in the room with Dick'Em. The sirens got closer and closer making me nervous about the weed I had stashed in a Crown Royal bag.

"Drexler!!!!" Po-Man's voice could be heard as he ran around the corner past us. We followed him inside of the dressing room where Dick'Em was sliding a t-shirt over his head.

"What you want?" Dick'Em replied sourly.

"It's Audra. They got Audra in the ambulance!" Po-Man answered.

"You jiving?" Without giving Po-Man time to answer, he shot past with us hot on his trail. Once we got outside we could hear Bertha wailing.

"Aye, what's going on? That's my wife!" Dick'Em tried to run through the barricade of officers surrounding

the ambulance. It wasn't until she was placed inside that they let him past.

"Bertha, what happened?" Papa questioned. She was sobbing too hard to say anything.

"We had come out here to get some air because she started feeling hot. Next thing we know, she just passed out. If it hadn't been for 'Pop Rocks' she would've hit her head."

"Passed out? She ain't never passed out before when she got hot. Maybe she's pregnant," Razor suggested.

"Naw, you know Audra is teeny tiny. She woulda' been showing by now," 'Pop Rocks' responded.

I stood there helpless knowing exactly what was wrong and not being able to say. We went down to the hospital that night and held Vigil around Audra. She got checked for everything imaginable. The only person outside of Dick'Em that knew her diagnosis was me. Poor sweet Audra. That was the last tour she was well enough to go on with us. Her mind started leaving far before her body did. I knew in my heart that Dick'Em never would be able to forgive himself.

Chapter 44

Joanne 'Jumpstart' George

Groove With You

"Oh, damn baby," I called out with my legs wrapped around Velvet's waist. "I love you so much," I voiced, breathlessly.

"Damn," he groaned as he slowly wound his hips.

"Velvet," I pressed my breast into his chest and allowed my head to roll back in ecstasy.

"Yeah baby," he whispered up against my sweaty neck.

"Tell me, you love me." I needed to know that he loved me, if just for a moment. I needed to feel loved because everybody around me always wanted or needed something. Well, now I needed something and that was love.

"Mmmmm ..." He pressed deeper.

I arched my back deeper and let the tears go. "Please baby, tell me you love me." I tightened my Kegel muscles around his girth and held on to his stroke.

"SHIT!" he yelped and bit into my shoulder.

"Tell me," I begged as I pinched my nipples while winding my hips. I was 20 years of age and Velvet made me feel things that I shouldn't have. I shouldn't love him as much as I did. I knew he was a junkyard dog, but his dog was a bit more tamed than his brother's.

"Jumpstart, damn!" He pushed up on his hands and looked down at me. "Open your eyes beautiful." My eyes fluttered open and I stared into his light brown irises. I could feel the love leaking from his pores, but I knew he was afraid. I could feel the fear as he kissed me. I could smell it on his breath as he said my name in the throes of passion. He was afraid, and his fear matched my unknowing.

"Tell me," I continued to beg as I wound my hips.

He bit his bottom lip and followed my hips. "I love you," he smiled.

I smiled up at him as I surrendered. I knew, at that moment he was no longer afraid. He was taking the plunge with me. So I surrendered, yet not understanding, that I was falling, falling into a never-ending spiral of heartbreak.

I held onto him that night as he laid on my chest. I could feel his heartbeat thumping up against his chest before it began to slow. I could still feel his fear. We had just made love for the very first time and we were both afraid of the outcome. I loved Velvet more than I loved myself and that was scary in itself.

"What you over there thinking about?" Ronda nudged me. She had been driving for a minute now. The car was quiet for once and we were all left with our thoughts.

"Oh nothing," I responded, turning back to the scenery.

"It didn't look like nothing," 'Pop Rocks' remarked.

I choose to ignore her, and she smacked her teeth. I just knew she was rolling her eyes. I wish they would pop out and roll up under the backseat.

"So, Jumpstart," 'Pop Rocks' called out.

"What you want?" I sighed in response.

"Did you and Velvet ever hook up after you stopped being a roadie?"

I turned around in my seat slightly. "Why is that any of your business?"

"I was just asking, being that I used to see him all the time. Once me and Papa moved closer to him. I think we was down there in Carbondale, Illinois."

"Naw girl, we didn't hook up," I responded, turning around in my seat.

"The last time I saw ole' Velvet, giiirl," she exaggerated.

Ronda looked at me out the corner of her eye and gave me the look. I didn't wanna beat this woman's ass, but I would if I had to.

"You know, Papa had just went to the store to get us some beers," she continued laughing. "I put on some ole' Al Green," she snapped her fingers. "You know what type of mood Al put you in," she paused as she danced around in her seat. "Anyway, Velvet was up dancing you know. He was drunk off that cherry moonshine we had brewed up. So, he reached over and stuck out his hand, so we could dance. I fanned his hand away, but he insisted," she said, placing her hand on my headrest.

"So, we standing in the middle of the floor dancing and giiirl, Velvet leaned in and kissed me. Chiillle, my knees buc -," and that was the last word she said before I reached over and punched her in her shit.

"Velvet, would never sleep with yo' tied ass." I swung again and connected with her chin knocking her partials out. Ronda swerved, before pulling over on the shoulder.

I went in for a third punch and Ronda grabbed my arm. "Jumpstart?"

"WHAT!!!" I was pissed at this triflin, bad-body built, wig on sideways, ass bitch.

"We in the middle of lunch hour traffic and you wanna fight? What if I would've crashed trying not to get punched in the head. What then?" she questioned seriously.

"Shut yo' ass up. That don't even make sense," I smirked.

"Look what you did to poor 'Pop Rocks'. Bitch, you done knocked out her teeth!"

Ronda was laughing so hard she was slapping at the steering wheel. "Whoo, I needed that." She looked back at 'Pop Rocks' and chuckled. "You alright, girl?"

"I'm cool," she responded, snapping her teeth in place and finally securing her wig. I turned around and sat back and allowed Ronda to pull out into traffic.

"Can I ask a hard question?" Sharonda asked, looking at me. "Why don't you like Charlene? It's like nobody likes her but me," she giggled.

"I forgot you were the blonde one outta the group. We all knew Audra was the naive one but you, I knew you was dingy when you stood in the middle of the floor and told Velvet that even though the sky was blue, didn't mean he had to look at it," 'Pop Rocks' chuckled from the backseat. "That was your way of saying, just because she pretty don't mean you have to fuck."

"Oh my," Ronda replied looking at me.

"Anyway, this heffa here," I pointed over my shoulder at Charlene. "She know why I don't like her."

"You ain't gotta like me. Velvet liked me just fine," she said snidely.

I turned around in my seat so fast, I was about to close her left eye.

"What I miss?" Bertha asked, wiping the sleep slob from her mouth. I swear that woman could've slept through the Civil War. Hell, she was old enough to remember it.

"Jumpstart?" Ronda called. "Tell me the story."

I gave 'Pop Rocks' a dirty look before turning around in my seat and took a much-needed breath.

It was my 25th birthday. The fellas had decided to splurge on us a little and take us to the mountains out in Wyoming. We had spent the first few days in the area just laid up and enjoying one another's company.

"Audra, what you in there burning?" I ran into the kitchen and she was standing over the stove zoned out. "AUDRA!!!" I yelled, and she gave me no response. I pulled the pan off the stove and threw it in the sink. I turned around and Audra was wearing a scowl on her face.

"Audra, baby, it's me Jumpstart."

"I know who you are, bitch," she snapped, jabbing the knife she was holding at me. "You probably fucked him to," she laughed hysterically. "Everybody's fucking my husband except me." She dropped the knife and fell to her knees. I reached out for her and she slapped my hand away.

"I'mma go and get Dick'Em," I said, turning to run out the kitchen to get her husband.

"FUCK HIM! FUCK EVERYBODY! NOBODY FUCKIN UNDERSTANDS!!!!" She jumped up and ran out. I was concerned for her mindset because one minute she was happy and the next she was angry. I was starting to think she was bipolar.

That night, Dick'Em decided that he would take her out on the town so we all agreed to go with them because we had been locked in that house for days. We all got dressed and met the fellas at the limo they splurged on. We ended up at this big fancy restaurant and we were soon escorted to our seats.

"You remember how we all sat around and laughed and joked with one another? It felt so good to have someone that I could call family. I had a small sense of stability. I had my man and his friends and also their wives who had accepted me with open arms. I felt safe within that small circle of friendship. Then I was betrayed …." I snarled but continued the story.

I remember Velvet getting up and kissing my cheek, telling me he was going to the restroom. I remember kissing his lips before he walked off. No more than five minutes passed before 'Pop Rocks' said she had to use the restroom, kissing Papa's lips and sauntering away.

It had been almost fifteen minutes before I realized that Velvet wasn't back yet. I excused myself, praying that he wasn't sick because if he was, we were leaving ASAP. Then I walked through the long hallway to the bathroom where I pushed the door open and called his name. I didn't receive a response so then I pushed open the women's bathroom door and called out 'Pop Rock's' name because she hadn't returned either. There was no answer. That's when my mind started going. Where the hell would two people be who are supposed to be in the bathroom? After checking my makeup in the mirror, I walked further down the hall towards the payphones when I heard moaning. The noise led to a door that was well-hidden because it matched the paint and décor of the wall. The only reason why I found it was because the door was slightly cracked.

"Damn Velvet, now I know why that young thang hang off you," I heard 'Pop Rock's' say as I peered inside.

"Stop playing damn, before we get caught," Velvet said, trying to pull away from her.

"We ain't gon' get caught. Who gone come way back here?"

"Move now," Velvet insisted.

"Nope. We done been down this road before. Why you gotta act brand new now?" was the last thing she said before she wrapped her lips around Velvet's girth. She must've been doing a damn good job for him to throw his head back and close his eyes.

I turned to walk away and bumped into the trash can.

"What the fuck was that?" I heard Velvet say as I sprinted through the hall and towards the dining area.

"I ran past y'all and straight out the door. That made me look at everybody differently. I just knew everybody was out to see me fail, even the person I loved more than anything.

"Damn," Ronda whispered. She looked up in the rearview mirror and glared at 'Pop Rocks'.

"What?" she asked.

"Did you ever apologize?" Bertha asked.

"The past is the past. Why live in it? Me and Velvet had messed around before."

"So, you ain't gone apologize?" Bertha asked getting visibly upset.

"Nope," 'Pop Rocks' said popping her lips.

"You know what, if she was to reach over this seat and whoop yo' ass. I'mma laugh at yo' stupid ass," Bertha asserted folding her arms.

"Too late for that," Ronda giggled. "You missed all that when you were back there snoring."

She didn't have to apologize to me. I already asked God for the forgiveness I needed for falling in love with a man He didn't send.

Chapter 45

Benny 'Velvet Rose' Pryor

Signs of the Times

"Okay, now I want one with all the fellas. Come on now. Y'all scoot together. Don't be shy. I need to get y'all all into one shot," the photographer directed. Razor was the only one not complying as he stood off on his own with his hands in his pockets. It was ridiculously hot inside of the diner with all the lights beating down on us. Everybody wanted to get it over with, but he had an attitude for some reason.

"I'm over here frying like bacon grease. What is the fool doin?" Po-Man asked between clenched teeth.

"Not really sure, but he's about to make me kick off into his ass," Papa co-signed.

"Raymond, can you please scoot in for the shot?" the photographer directed.

"Not until they fix that." Razor pointed toward the window where about 30 models were posed with their faces close to the window as if they were trying to get inside of the diner.

"What's the problem?" Dick'Em asked.

"The problem is I ain't about to pose for no picture that ain't got no brown girls in it. Now y'all know we couldn't even get close to no white girls at a real show. Why they hell should they be on our album cover? Y'all can be chumps if you want to. But I ain't doin it."

"This nigga always gotta mess somethin' up!" Dick'Em yelled, jumping up from his position on the floor. I

grabbed his shoulder just as he attempted to lunge at Razor.

"He actually got a point." I even surprised myself by saying that, but it was true.

"Velvet, you defending this shit? We just now getting our foot all the way through the door and putting a name for ourselves out there. How we look arguin' with folks about a damn album cover?"

"Fellas, I don't have all day. The record company has only paid me for an allotted amount of time. We need to make a decision."

"Arthur, give us a minute please." I held up two fingers. He sat his camera down on a booth and walked off.

"Now look here, Razor is right. We were told that we were gonna have women down here for the shoot, but they ain't told us nothing about them being no white gals. What kind of message this gonna send on our first record? I'm with Razor. We got our own women that's way prettier than these gals out there. Why they can't be here? Instead, they holed up in a cheap motel next door. That ain't right," Po-Man huffed. He never had any opinion on anything outside of spending money, so it was surprising to hear him have a stance on this.

"So, what y'all wanna do? You wanna call it off?" Dick'Em asked angrily.

"We ain't got to do that. I got an idea," Razor remarked.

He walked out of the side entrance around to the front of the diner where Arthur had sat down to light a cigarette. The models were all talking amongst themselves, so we didn't know what was going on. From the looks of it, Arthur and Razor were having a very intense conversation.

"Ain't no tellin' what that fool out there sayin.' He liable to piss the man off," Papa complained.

"Give him a minute. We can't always count him out," I defended.

We watched from the counter as Arthur stood up stubbing out his cigarette under his foot. He directed the girls back over to the window where they were to lean almost close enough to press their faces against it. Then he walked back around, but Razor went in the opposite direction. Everybody looked over at me like it was my fault.

"Okay fellas change of plans. It seems to me that Raymond had some ideas about the way this was going. I was given instructions on how this was supposed to look by the record executives. However, I do understand the issue that is being had. Razor is gone next door to get your lady friends. We are going to take pictures both with them in the crowd and with them out of the crowd. It is the record labels choice as they are the ones paying me. Is that understood?" We all couldn't help but bust into a grin.

"We got it," Dick'Em answered. We talked among ourselves for a few minutes before Razor came back in with a scowl on his face. He walked back over to the counter in the same position he was in earlier.

"Well, what they say?" we asked.

"They said it was fine," Razor answered.

"Well, what you mad at?" I questioned.

"Ronda in there talkin' bout it's gonna take her at least a half hour to put her face on. I told her to put some

damn body else's on then." We all burst out laughing as Razor tried his best to hold a straight face.

The next few hours were grueling, but we had faith that Arthur had some good shots to choose from. Once we were getting ready to leave, the owners of the diner showed up to lock everything up for the night. The biggest, tallest, redneck I had ever seen in my whole life climbed out of a rusty, blue Chevrolet truck. The passenger side door popped open next with a man only an inch or so shorter. When two more climbed out of the bed of the truck a familiar feeling of unease coursed through all of us. Arthur didn't seem to mind as he continued packing up his equipment.

"I'ma go get the girls and walk over to the motel. I'll be right back though," Po-Man commented, breaking the tension.

"They come in here with that bullshit and I'ma cut the bacon off one of them big muthafuckas," Razor said as Po-Man stepped outside gathering the girls. They all looked back inside at us scared. We gestured for them to go with Po-Man.

"Well, looks like we bout' to get dirty. Might as well take off these jackets so they don't get blood," I remarked.

As we all disrobed, the four men walked inside speaking to Arthur. He shook hands and was out of the door with his first load of equipment. Something about how fast he was moving made me nervous.

"Well, well, well, look'a here," the driver said, folding his arms. "We got us some celebrities out here on route 66. You know a whole lot of 'em come through this way. We don't really get a whole lot of colored ones though. At least not on this stretch of road."

"What that mean? We paid for our time being here and we really don't want no trouble," Papa insisted. The man held his hands up.

"I didn't say nothing about what ya' paid. I said we don't get many colored folks 'round this stretch of road. Ain't that right boys?" The other three men nodded their heads in agreement.

"We ain't got time for all this here talkin.' We got things to do. You see that ole bus out there? That belongs to us and we got a ways to go in it so we need to be turnin' in pretty soon," Papa explained.

"Y'all not bout' to go nowhere."

I watched out the corner of my eye as Razor pretended to cough and spit his blade into his fist. It was about to be show time.

"David, go fire up the grill. Anthony, you get on the shake machine, and Charlie, you hit the fries." The boys disbursed walking around the other side of the counter where they began firing up appliances.

"My name is Dale Wesley, and this here is my diner. Passed down from my grandpa, Stoney Wesley. He's the one on that picture just above your head."

"I wanna show you all my appreciation for choosing my place for your album picture. Have a seat and I'll get ya' some menus."

"You shittin' me?" Razor asked.

"Not at all. I saw a fella going outside with some ladies. You tell them to come on too. Everybody in your crew eats for free." We all looked at each other speechless.

"A'ight now let's dance," Po-Man said rushing through the door with Arthur on his heels.

"Man, go get the girls and the driver. They feedin' us," I explained.

"For free!" Dick'Em chimed in. I thought Po-Man would peel the rubber off of his shoes from running so fast. We settled into a few of the booths closest to the road as Dale handed us menus.

"We're not all bad people. Some of us come from bad seeds, but it's up to us what we wanna grow into."

"That's alright with me." Papa extended his hand which Dale shook eagerly. We had more than we could ever imagine eating that night. Po-Man and Bertha made sure to take a doggy bag so that nothing got wasted. It was the first time that we had ever been treated so well by a white person. On our trek we ran into quite a few that didn't give a damn about us having a hit single on the radio. They would even turn off their neon signs when we pulled up. Through the tire blowouts, overheating of the engine, and arguing with our women, we finally made it to California for the first time of many. We were well on our way.

Chapter 46

Drexler 'Dick' Em Down' Davis

The cold air tore through my bones as the weather changed causing my eyes to flutter open. My heart grew weary looking at the way my old neighborhood had went to the dogs. The corner store where I used to get fried pies and ice cream sat empty with the glass busted out. Broken liquor bottles and other debris sat discarded outside of it. The beauty parlor where my mother used to get her hair done was hollowed out as if a hurricane had been through it. Graffiti covered the pink walls that Ms. Pearlie, the owner used to be so proud of.

"Times sho' have changed," Velvet commented. He shook his head as we passed Ms. Grace's house where we would sing outside for one of her famous chicken plates. She never got her restaurant license, but people came from miles around to eat at her house. A bunch of thugs covered the porch smoking weed and drinking out of red cups. I saw one of them pour what looked like some cough syrup into one of them.

"You ain't never lied, Velvet. They used to take pride in their neighborhoods. Now look at this mess." I mentally prepared myself to see my father's old church. I purposely avoided this place whenever I came to Detroit because of the guilt I felt behind it.

"Daddy, isn't that it just ahead?" Audrey asked from the front seat. I craned my head forward squinting.

"Well, I'll be damned," I mumbled under my breath. "That's it. That's what's left of Fresh Anointing." The van slowed up in front of the abandoned storefront, the wrought iron doors swung open with a gust of wind as if welcoming us. The front windows were bullet-ridden but hadn't completely shattered yet. I shuddered to think what the inside may look like.

"Are you sure this is safe?" Scott asked Audrey.

"It's pretty early so this is about as safe as it's gonna get. Just in case, I'll grab my 38. I ain't got time for no thugs running up on us. Let's get in and out of here as quickly as possible because we are technically trespassing. The city owns this place now."

Scott and Colin got out first. Colin cautiously looked both ways before placing his shirt tail over the door knob to open it. "The door is locked," he said, looking back at us.

"Well daddy, I'm not for breaking and entering. Sorry." Velvet cut his eyes over to me laughing. "What's so funny?" Audrey questioned.

"Girl, ain't I ever taught you there's more than one way to skin a cat? I'm a Detroit nigga born and raised. I'll show you how to get in here." Scott reached for my arm helping me down while Colin helped Velvet.

"Now, it was right around here." I pointed as I approached the building. With my hand I felt along the siding on the left side of the door.

"Daddy, what are you doing?" Audrey whispered nervously.

"Girl, back up off me and let me get some light please."

Audrey stood back as I peered under the crevice. Just like I remembered there was a shiny silver key taped under the siding. I don't know how it had survived there so many years. I snatched it free from the tape handing it to Audrey.

"Your great-grandmother was the worst about keeping up with keys. Every choir rehearsal we had to deal with her looking for her keys forever in those big ass purses she used to like to wear. So, me and daddy came up with the idea to tape a key right here where she could easily find it. Go ahead and try it."

Audrey looked at me apprehensively before placing the key inside the door. When she turned it, the lock popped with a loud click. A loud creaking sound followed as she pushed it open.

"Look what they done did. Lawd hammercy," I commented as I walked inside.

Several pews were turned over, the podium was missing, and the place reeked of piss. The side windows that had been stained were all busted out with their glass littering the floor. Even the carpet had been pulled up exposing the concrete underneath. I could barely contain myself.

"This don't make no sense. They done tore up everything. Look at the choir loft. Folks don't got no respect for the house of the Lord," Velvet commented, feeling just as overwhelmed as I did. His chair rolled over crushed glass everywhere he moved.

"Aw daddy, I'm so sorry. I didn't know this place would be in this bad of condition. Online they only showed what it used to look like."

"That's okay, baby. Things happen. If it had stayed in my family's hands it would've never got like this. Give us a second or two will ya?"

“Velvet, come on let’s check out the dining hall.” Scott handed me my cane which I hadn’t used the whole trip.

“Daddy, be careful. We don’t know who or what's in here.”

“You’re right about that. Just follow behind us with the camera.” I shuffled around the broken-down pews to the side hall of the church.

“Now, this used to be where they held Sunday school,” I explained, pushing a door open with the tip of my cane. All of the tables and chairs were still there, but the room smelled heavily of piss, so I shut that door quickly. “Now right here, was the bathrooms. I used to get in trouble because I walked in on the ladies in there.”

“Yeah and tried to say you thought it was empty,” Velvet laughed.

“Sho’ did. I don’t know how many times I got my butt whooped for lyin’ about that. Now straight ahead is the kitchen.” The scent of sewage combined with trash filled my nostrils before I step foot over the threshold. The old wood-burning stove had been taken out. The sinks were filled with a mixture of trash and dishes. Not a single table or chair was left intact. Whoever had come through here had torn up everything.

“We used to sell plates back her to raise money for the building fund. Never did get quite enough to move out of here. Velvet, remember that time ‘Pop Rocks’ was helping with the bake sale and ate that whole sweet potato pie?”

“Mannnnn, she still won’t admit it til this day. Talkin’ bout she sat it outside to cool and a racoon ate it.”

We all joined in laughing.

"Aunt Charlene was a mess. She tried it," Audrey remarked.

"Don't get me wrong, we had a coon problem over here, but she know she ain't 'bout to sit no pie anywhere that ain't near her lips. That girl could eat," I commented.

"Hell, she still can. Wait a minute now, I know you remember that." My eyes followed Velvet's as he crept toward the pantry door.

"Now wait a minute, it's probably all kinds of rats in there," I warned.

Velvet ignored me reaching for the door knob. We all stood back. The stench of rotten food poured out making all of us gag. The can goods were so rusted that they were stuck together in a permanent display. Velvet reached inside feeling along the wall as we stood there cringing. The sound of Velcro being pulled brought a smile to my face.

"Now, I know you remember this," Velvet smiled as he pulled out a heavy, wooden, paddle.

"The brown bomber. I don't know how many times I got my hind quarters tore up with that thing. Now you lucky you wasn't round here as a little child. Granny sho nuff woulda' tore you up."

"You ain't gotta tell me. I already know. Hell, she was mean to me as a grown man. Every time we came around she was fussing about my clothes not being ironed enough, my hair was too nappy, or shoes weren't shined to her standards. I didn't mind it though because she felt like a mother to me. Now, I can't hardly see that, but it looks like there's some carving on there. What that say, Scott?" Scott took the paddle from him holding it up to the light filtering in through the window.

"Let's see here. It looks like *'property of Mrs. Annie Mae Davis'*."

"That's great grandmother Annie," Audrey exclaimed as she reached for the paddle.

"Well daddy, at least some history has been preserved here. Let's see what's in these cabinets."

"Now, I wouldn't-."

"Agh rats!" Audrey yelled, slamming the cabinet door shut. "Oh hell no. I'm done. We're outta here. This place is gross. Watch your step too because I saw some holes in the floor." I took one look back before exiting the kitchen. It was gonna be hard to keep my heart from breaking once we left here. I grabbed Audrey's arm as everybody headed toward the front door

"Just one last thing I gotta see." I led her over to the other side of the choir loft where a lone door barely hung onto the hinges.

"Pastor E.L. Davis," she read the nameplate over the door.

"This was the pastor's study. I got called in here many a days. My daddy said to hell with that paddle. He would wear you out with a leather strap. Go on in." A few roaches scattered out as Audrey nudged the door open with her foot. The wood grain was the first thing I noticed. It had been chipped away exposing layers of insulation.

"Daddy, that could be asbestos." Audrey covered her nose.

"Nah, that's regular old insulation. When daddy lost the church, they came in here and redid everything."

The huge desk he had bought from a white lady's rummage sale was now splintered and warped from water damage and destruction. The padding in his chair was ripped out with shreds of cotton stuck to the floor from where the rain had seeped in. Bird shit covered almost everything in the room.

"You okay, daddy?" Audrey rubbed my back softly.

"It wasn't supposed to be like this. This was our legacy. I messed it up. I messed it all up," I cried.

"What did you mess up?" she asked somberly.

"I messed up everything. I coulda saved this place. My pride … my pride just got in the way."

"Daddy, let's go because you're getting worked up."

"No, I gotta tell you something. We in a church, I might not get another chance to confess it."

"Naw, we can talk about it later. It's not safe being in this place. There's bird poop everywhere."

"I come from shit! I come from the Brewster Housing Projects. You think I'm worried about some birds. Now, you listen to what I gots' to say and let this be a lesson to you. You hear me?" I wagged a gnarled finger in her face.

"Yes sir. I hear you."

"Okay then." I leaned on my cane for support.

"When I left this place, I was sho' nuff mad at my daddy. He never let me do what I wanted to do for real because he was worried about the old biddies that used to sit on the mourner's bench. See, a bunch of em' had dead husbands they was collecting pensions for. They were the ones that tithed the most, so they had the most say-so. Well, they never liked the way I did the choir. They wanted hymns, said I was too jazzy with my arrangements. Just used to fuss like nobody's business. He didn't stand up to them, so I left. I knew I was wrong for putting him in that position, but I was young."

"But you and granddaddy always seemed to get along so well."

"That's because we were both pretenders. He pretended not to mind being henpecked by these women in here. He pretended that he didn't miss me when I left. I pretended like I didn't want to call him every time something bad happened."

I reached in my breast pocket for my handkerchief to dab at my eyes.

"Well anyway, my momma called me all the way out in Las Vegas when we were on tour for our successful album. She told me that the church was losing money because some of the older members had died off and they weren't taking in too much. Everybody was struggling at the time. She asked me if I could pay the mortgage up a few months." I gripped the wall behind me as Audrey rushed over to my side.

"I'm okay, baby. Just lost my footin.' So anyway, she asked me, and I said no. I flat out said no to my momma."

"Why though?"

"I told you I was young and dumb. I was also prideful. I wanted daddy to call and say he needed it. Thought he had put momma up to it. Well, I later found out he didn't know about the call, but it was too late. They foreclosed on the church. Didn't even let him come in and get what belonged to him. They just chained the doors."

"Oh, my goodness. I never knew, daddy. I'm sorry."

"He never told nobody about it far as I know. My momma didn't neither. Folks speculated how they could lose a church when their son had a number four record on the charts. They never would speak on it though. I avoided the question in interviews too. You are the first person I done told."

"I don't really know what to say. Did you ever make amends with him?"

"I offered to buy him a bigger, better church. He told me that his time had passed though. He was about to go home. That's just what he did too. He went on home. Man sacrificed everything he had for his family and community and died from a broken heart caused by me."

"That's really something else. I can't imagine how you feel carrying that guilt all these years. We need to get on out of her though."

"There's just one more thing. I'll be quick about it though."

"Okay. Lay it on me," Audrey said as she rubbed my arm.

"Well, this ain't something I ever wanted to tell you. I thought about writing it in a letter. I even thought about taking it to the grave with me. I have a feeling I will feel better if I just spill it out though."

"Go ahead, daddy. I'm here for you."

"I know you were young when you lost your mother."

"Yeah, I was just turning twenty; happy to be in college and on my own, but I was always worried about her."

"I will never forget that look on your face when I told you she passed. It was almost like you were at peace."

"Well, she suffered a lot. The sores all over, the crazy babbling, the constant crying. I hated to see her like that. It's one of the reasons why I run the cancer marathons. I do it in her honor." My knees began to buckle slightly under the weight of what I was about to reveal. A single bead of sweat dripped down my left temple.

"She ain't had no cancer, baby."

"Say what?"

"I say she ain't have no cancer."

"That's what you told me it was. That's what everybody told me. You lied to me?" Audrey's eyes pleaded for explanations as she let go of my arm.

"That's the way she wanted it."

"She wanted it, or you wanted it?" Audrey tightly folded her arms across her chest. "What happened to my momma?" I looked up to the ceiling through the holes.

"I gave her syphilis. I had been catting around for years on her and I didn't know I had it because I didn't have no symptoms. By the time they caught it she was pretty bad off. They say something about it lays dormant in women longer than men. She hadn't been feeling good for a long time, but we brushed it off. Then she started getting the sores all over. I wouldn't allow her in the bed with me. I even accused her of messing around." My voice cracked as I covered my face with my hands.

"You did this to her? You did that to my momma? How could you? You was supposed to love her? Then y'all both lied to me about it? Do you have any idea how much it hurt me to be without her? Do you even care?"

"Audrey, are you okay?" Scott asked from the sanctuary. I didn't realize he had been standing there the whole time.

"No, I'm not! I need a moment."

"Audrey, please just-."

"I don't have anything to say to you right now." She cut me off. I was almost knocked down as she rushed past me and out the front of the church.

"Now, she gonna hate me forever. I knew I shouldn't have said nothing."

"Just give her a second. In the meantime, let's get out of here. There are some people walking around outside now. They're probably going to call the cops on us."

"Go ahead, Scott. I'm coming right behind you, I promise. I just need one more look at the place before I go. I'll never get a chance to come back." Scott obliged me by taking a few steps backward into the sanctuary. I walked over to daddy's desk. So many names had been scratched on it over the years. So much destruction and disrespect that could have been avoided. I ran my hand over the splintered middle of the desk. Something hard and plastic was wedged right there. I bent down closer to find a hypodermic needle. It looked like somebody had just had a good fix and jammed it right down in there. This was not the place for things like this. My father had labored his whole life to clean up these streets and look how he had been remembered.

A flood of memories came over me. It was common place to find junkies, pool hustlers, and prostitutes eating in the dining hall because he felt like the kingdom belonged to everybody. Momma would give away some of her nice dresses to women who needed something nice to wear to job interviews. We had lock-ins right there in the sanctuary during the winter time, so the poor kids would have a warm place to sleep. Everything he had done, and it came down to this. My chest heaved up and down as I felt the sobs trying to erupt from my gut. I held them in as best as I could, but then a tingling sensation began to run through my whole body like electricity. The heaving in my chest got stronger. I tried to stand up straight but found I couldn't even move my body. Something was happening. The room began to circle around me into a dizzying blur. The last sensation I felt was that of me collapsing onto the desk. Then brightness. Nothing, but brightness.

Chapter 47

Audrey

I was inconsolable as the stretcher holding my father's lifeless body was pulled out of the abandoned building. It felt as if the wind had been knocked out of me, not once but several times. The thought of no longer having either one of my parents was something I never imagined having to go through. I thought Daddy would live forever.

"I'm so sorry, Audrey," Scott commented as he leaned against the side of the van next to me.

"Not your fault. We all knew this was a possibility. Out of all the things my daddy went through in his life, a damn stroke took him out. Then to top it off, I stormed out of there mad at him. I said it was his fault momma was dead. How can I ever move past that knowing those were the last things I felt about him?" Scott pulled me into his arms as he gently rubbed the back of my head.

"Audrey, we're here for you," Colin whispered. "If you want I can call your husband," he offered. I nodded my head "yes".

"Oh no, Uncle Benny." I yanked my head up racing to the van door. It was empty. "Uncle Benny! Uncle Benny!" I ran to the back of the van where the ambulance was parked. Rigged there between both vehicles sat Uncle Benny. He shook violently in his chair with tears streaming down his face. All I could do was wrap my hands around his neck. Although not a sound was emanating from his lips, I could tell that he was grieving in his own way. His shaking subsided somewhat before I was tapped on my shoulder by one of the paramedics. I listened intently as she gave me instructions. As much as I wanted to jump on the back of the ambulance and shake him, I knew it wouldn't do any good. It was painful watching them work on him to try to regain a pulse that was not coming back. He was gone. The man, the myth, the legend, had officially left the building.

"Hey Audrey, I got Earnest on the phone here." My hand shook as I took the phone from Colin.

"Hello," I answered weakly.

"Hi baby," his smooth baritone voice instantly soothed me.

"Earnest, he's gone. My daddy is just..."

"I know, love. I know. I'm gassing up the truck as we speak. I should be to you in about an hour or so. Colin gave me the address. I don't want you on that road, so y'all grab a room and we'll go from there. Okay?" I was so busy sobbing that I couldn't speak.

"Hey Earnest this is Colin. We'll take care of her until you get here. Just let me know what you want us to do. Okay, that's fine let me grab a pen." Colin walked away with my phone as Scott approached me followed by a heavy-set officer with a wig so dry it looked like straw. That was enough to make me crack a small laugh.

"You okay, sweetie? I'm Officer Frye and I was a really big fan of your father and all. They were a little before my time. But my parents always played them."

"That's really nice of you to say. Thank you." She shook my hand before going back to her cruiser. I didn't even realize how clogged traffic had gotten. Everybody was rubbernecking trying to see what all the fuss was about. "Did you want to go up to the hospital? I can drive," Scott offered.

"Nah, They can't bring him back. No need of me going up there getting in the way. I just want a hot shower and a bed."

"That's understandable. What are we going to do about Velvet? He seems a little worse for the wear."

"I'm old, but I ain't deaf. Nothing wrong with me. Give me one of them there oxygen tubes. I ain't leavin' my niece. We can go back to Chicago once she get his business squared away."

"Yes sir," Scott replied, red-faced with embarrassment. He wheeled Uncle Benny over to the chairlift as I took one last look at the scene around me. Several officers were ushering the onlookers to move around so that they could get enough room to let the ambulance out. I swallowed back a scream as Colin took my hand leading me back to the van. He helped me up into Uncle Benny's awaiting arms. He felt frailer than I remembered as I laid my head on his lap.

"I know a thang or two about losing a parent. A child never gets over that type of loss. Your daddy was flawed like all of us, but he loved you. I don't think he ever loved nobody else, but you."

"What about momma?"

"He tried to love her. He just wasn't wired right for romantic love. He would shower her with gifts and money, but he never could give her his heart. Me and him were the same that way. I had this woman and that, never did settle down and find somebody to grow old with. The one that I should've had all along belongs to somebody else now. I probably wouldn't be much fun now anyway with all my problems."

"Don't say that, Uncle Benny. Somebody somewhere loves you. I know my momma did. She even said one time that if she had her pick out of any of the others, it would have been you."

"What you say? Audra said that about me? Don't that beat all? I wish she had told me that to my face. I mighta' messed around and gave you a brother or sister."

"I don't need that visual," I laughed.

"Time is filled with swift transition, like the old song say. We just gotta hold to his hand," Velvet responded emotionally.

"Hold to his hand

God's unchanging hand

Build your hopes on things eternal

Hold to God's unchanging hand"

"Wait a damn minute. You been hiding that voice all this time?" he gasped.

"I never wanted to be a singer. After nursing for a few years, I got the notion to start doing these films. Music was daddy's calling, but filmmaking was mine. I wanted to write and direct; do anything but be in front of the camera." I finally sat up beginning to feel slightly better.

"Colin, where are we going?"

"Earnest left specific instructions to take you to Crowne Plaza."

"Oh hell no. That place is pricey. Let me call him because he must have lost his mind."

“Audrey, he said it’s already being booked. He wants you to go there to relax. He got a room for us and Velvet as well.” That sounded just like Earnest; always thinking of others. Nobody would allow me to lift a finger once we reached the hotel. I took a long, steamy shower, wondering what was taking my husband so long. As I laid on the bed with my towel wrapped around me, I scrolled through my photo albums on my phone. There were so many pictures of my parents. They had managed to meet Kennedy, Nixon, Obama, Oprah, Michael Jackson and so many more important people. The magazine covers were what I loved the most. Seeing the transitions in their style always made me laugh. Poor Uncle Willie always had the worst looking hair. They should have just made him wear a wig. A slight knock on the door startled me.

“Who is it?” I answered, not really wanting to be bothered.

“It’s Uncle Benny. If you got a moment, I need to talk to you.”

Chapter 48

Benny 'Velvet Rose' Pryor

The Break-Up

"Uncle Benny?" Audrey answered, dabbing at her eyes. I held out the bottle of *Crown Royal* that I had just purchased. Even though I was not much of a drinker, I knew I would have to take a sip in memory of Dick' Em since it was his favorite.

"Thanks." She hugged me. "Come on in."

I shuffled in as a best as I could taking a seat on the chair nearest the door.

This is a nice room. Your husband sho' know how to put you away right," I remarked, looking around.

"He better. He's had more than enough time to learn me and what I like. Besides, we spoil each other. I do have a question though since you are here."

She poured us both drinks before settling in the bed across from me. I wasted no time draining my glass. It burned like hell hitting the back of my throat, but that was the least of my worries. Audrey tucked a stray curl behind her ear.

"We done traveled from state to state and I still haven't heard how you guys broke up. I thought I would hear the story from daddy, but you see how that turned out."

"Audrey, that's opening a can of worms. I really rather he had told you about that."

"Please Uncle Benny, I need somewhere else to place my thoughts."

I closed my eyes and allowed the thoughts to dance in my head before they left my lips. If I was gone tell this story I needed to make sure all angles were indeed covered.

We had just finished our last show and we were all excited to get backstage. All the ladies of Members Only minus one, was waiting with hand towels and bottles of water.

"Damn, that was awesome. You see the way the crowd reacted tonight?" Dick'Em yelled in excitement.

"Naw, but I see the way you reacted," Papa voiced as he reached for the towel 'Pop Rocks' was holding in her outstretched hand.

"What you talkin 'bout, nigga?" Dick'Em asked defensively.

"I'm talkin bout ever since Audra got sick and can't come on the road with us no more, the more reckless yo' tired ass dick gets."

"Man, fuck you," Dick'Em responded, snatching his towel from the high-yella girl he now had hanging off his arm.

"Fuck you, nigga. Did you call to check up on yo' wife today?" Papa asked angrily.

"Yo' bitch gone be checkin' on yo' ass in a minute, muthafucka." Dick'Em spat as he dabbed the beads of sweat from his forehead.

"That's Enough!" Bertha yelled. "We're not doing this tonight. Y'all just had a good turn out and now y'all wanna turn on each other?" she asked perplexed.

Dick'Em glared at Papa as he brushed past Bertha to our dressing room.

"What was all that about?" Jumpstart inquired.

"Leave it alone," I warned as I took her hand in mine, draping the towel over my shoulder.

"Bertha, I'mma need you to go get our things ready." I heard Po-Man say when he joined myself and Razor as we ventured down the long corridor.

"Damn, you sexy." I heard one of the random women say in the crowd as we pushed through. I held onto Jumpstart's hand just a little tighter.

"Look, I'mma need you to go with the ladies and get our things together," I informed her.

"I'm not leaving your side tonight, suga," Jumpstart said with a smile. There was no need to argue if I could avoid it. I pushed the door open to the dressing room where Dick'Em and Papa were still glaring at one another.

"The fuck you keep lookin over here for?" Dick'Em asked, pulling off his shirt.

"I'm lookin at yo' monkey-mouth ass," Papa responded, standing up and removing his own shirt.

"Aye, can we just hash this out and move forward?" I tried reasoning with them.

"So, you gone condone his bullshit?" Papa asked me.

"That's not what I'm saying, Papa." I was trying to be the voice of reason being that the voice of reason was pissed off right now.

"What the fuck is you saying then? This nigga got a brand-new bitch hanging off his dick and his wife is laid up in the hospital probably because he can't keep his dick to himself. Ain't you learned shit, nigga?" he asked, now lookin at Dick'Em.

How the hell did he know? I wondered to myself. Surely, he didn't just come up with that all by himself. Audra must have told someone else besides me. It was probably 'Pop Rocks' no-good ass.

Before my long legs could move. Dick'Em was across the floor in a flash. He hit Papa so hard he fell on his ass.

Papa spit blood from his mouth and pushed himself to stand up. "That's how you feel, nigga?" he laughed maniacally. "You know what, fuck you and this tired ass group!"

"Alright, that's enough got-dammit," I voiced, standing between the two.

"Fuck you, Velvet! Matter fact, you can pack up yo' shit and leave with this nigga," Dick'Em suggested. I was stunned stupid.

"Hol' on now, Dick'Em. I know you pissed off, but you can't start firing niggas and shit. We did all this shit together," Razor finally spoke up. "It's been what, fifteen

years almost and you wanna get pissed off behind the truth of this man's word?"

"Fuck you too, Razor." Dick'Em stood in front of his mirror as if nothing had transpired. "Sheryl, go grab my bag for me, would you?" High Yella ran off wide eyed.

"Dick'Em, maybe we all just need to calm down and talk about this another time," I insisted.

"Fuck yo' reasonin'," he yelled out.

The door swung open and the ladies walked into the room with their bags packed and ready to go. "Po-Man, why you standing over here by the door?" Bertha asked him before lookin around the room. "What's going on in here, Velvet?"

"Dick'Em's stubborn ass having a fuckin tantrum," Razor responded.

"I'll show you a tantrum, nigga," Dick'Em said, throwing down his hair comb.

"Bring yo' goat mouth ass on over here and watch me make a believer outta yo' ass," Razor voiced, spitting his razor into his hand.

"Y'all stop this shit," Ronda yelled, stomping her small foot. "Ever since Audra been sick and in the hospital y'all been acting crazy."

"Leave my wife's name out yo', you thieving bitch!"

"Bitch? Nigga, I know you ain't just call me a bitch," Ronda cried out, voice cracking. "You just gone let him disrespect me like that Razor?" she asked looking to her husband. Razor was focused and beyond pissed as he

raised his arm slightly. I lunged in the way and he caught me instead.

"Son-of-a-bitch," I hissed.

We heard the click of a switchblade and we all turned to see Jumpstart standing there seething. "Don't nobody cut my nigga but me," she said through clenched teeth as she lunged at Razor who jumped back in the nick of time.

Papa still laughing grabbed 'Pop Rocks' hand and tried to walk past us all. "The fuck you find so fuckin comical?" Dick'Em asked.

Papa turned around wearing a mug like that of a prize fighter and cracked Dick'Em in his jaw knocking him on his ass.

"Ay, Dios Mîo," High yella said under her breath, which made all the ladies snap their necks in her direction. "Look, I don't know what's going on, but I don't want any part of it."

I nodded my head and asked her to leave. High Yella grabbed her things and headed towards the door.

Dick'Em stood to his feet, "She ain't gotta go nowhere, but you niggas," he pointed. "Get the fuck out!

"I'm leaving," Papa agreed. "Because if I don't, I'mma end up in the penitentiary. Come on Charlene."

"Wait a damn minute, ain't nobody going any damn where," I wheezed out. I was tired of fighting and shit. "Dick'Em, you my brother and I love you but this shit," I pointed at High Yella who was still standing by his side, "has got to stop. You have a brand-new bitch every show my nigga. I understand you're hurting but that ain't gone

make the shit no better or any different. We all miss Audra but that don't mean to take yo' shit out on us. You fucked up and now you mad. Nigga, we didn't do the shit." I flopped down in the chair still holding my side where I had been slashed.

"Baby, we need to get you to Sinai," Jumpstart said, lifting my shirt and wincing. "You might need some stitches."

"I'm good," I grunted. "Papa," I called out making him turn to face me. "You gone leave?"

He looked around the room before focusing back on me. "Yeah, I'm done. I've had a good run, but I can't sit here and watch my brother destroy not only himself but these women. Audra didn't deserve the fate she was lead to. She definitely didn't deserve this nigga, but she loved his fraudulent ass. We all sat back and watched this nigga destroy her and we did nothing about it. We didn't even offer a warning and now look. So yeah, I'm so done with this shit because if I don't leave, I'mma hurt that nigga," he pointed and with that, he grabbed his wife's hand and walked towards the door.

"Papa! Papa!" I yelled out, but he kept walking. I shook my head as I winced in pain. I applied pressure to my wound and I could feel the blood seeping through my shirt.

"Excuse me, but can I say something?" Our necks snapped in High Yella's direction. "I met Drexler or Dick'Em as y'all so eloquently put it, a few years ago. I don't know who this Audra person is, let alone, did I know he was marr-," she couldn't even finish her sentence before Ronda was all over ass.

"Bitch," ***WHAP!*** *"How dare you?"* ***WHAP! WHAP!***

"Ronda, get yo' ass up. You not supposed to be fighting and you pregnant," Bertha intervened, trying to get Sharonda off High Yella. High Yella was getting her ass whooped.

"You," ***WHAP!*** *"Are not ..."* ***WHAP! WHAP!*** *"Allowed,"* ***WHAP!*** *"To have a fuckin opinion. You hear me, bitch?" she cried out as she was being pulled off by Razor.*

"You pregnant?" Razor asked her questionably. Instead of answering, she just placed her face in his chest and cried.

High Yella laid on the floor dizzy with her mouth and nose bloody as Bertha dragged her out into the hallway by her ankles.

"Po-Man?" I whispered.

He wiped away his tears. It was hard to see Po-Man show emotion because he rarely did. "I'mma get a cab back to the hotel. This has been a trying day. We don't know what's gone happen as far as Audra is concerned but I sho' do miss her," he smiled. "One thang for certain and two things for sure, we had a great run. We've been places that we could only dream of. I thank you fellas for making me feel like I was 'part of something special. I know my wife sometimes overdone it with the costumes, but we made it work. I know my cheap ass didn't help matters either but hey, we made due. I hate to see all that we've worked so hard for falling apart at the seams. The saying goes, that all good things must come to an end." He wiped away his tears and looked over at Dick'Em. "You have a daughter to raise and I'm not telling you how to do your job but, riddle me this. Would you want your daughter to date a man like you?"

Taking a deep breath, he paused to look around the room before turning to his wife. "Come on, Bertha." Bertha wiped her tears away before offering me a smile. Taking her husband's hand in her own, they made their exit.

I looked at Razor who was still holding onto a distraught Ronda. "Don't even ask," he said as he stood to his feet and helped his wife stand. "That's a sorry muthafucka right there. I know I ain't shit, but you a sorry muthafucka," Razor asserted, pushing Ronda gently toward the door.

Jumpstart' stared down at me as my eyes became heavy in my head.

"I'm going to call the ambulance." She rushed out the room.

I turned to Dick'Em.

"You happy now?" I asked weakly.

"Very," he smirked as I blacked out.

When I woke up in the hospital, Jumpstart was beside me. She had explained to me all that had taken place while I was resting. *Members Only* was no more. Razor and his wife had moved to California for a short while. Po-Man and his wife had moved back down South. Papa and 'Pop Rocks' was in Canada some damn where. The first time we all saw one another again was when your mother passed away.

“So, after momma's funeral you went your separate ways for good?” Audrey asked, already knowing the answer to her question.

“Yeah, it had been almost twenty years before you came along with this here project,” I silently chuckled.

“I'm glad I did though because there were so many unanswered questions.”

“Well, I hope I was able to help,” I remarked, sliding to the edge of my chair.

“Yeah, you did a good job, Uncle Benny.” Audrey rose from the bed offering me her untouched drink. I politely declined before letting myself out. Now that she had the full truth, maybe her healing could begin.

Chapter 49

Audrey

Once Uncle Benny left, I turned up that damn bottle. I needed something to get my mind off of my issues. My daddy had really been something else. It was so infuriating that so many people saw him as a hero and some grand person that he wasn't. I would always love him but my view of him would be forever changed. The sound of light rapping on the door made me sit up in bed.

"Who is it?" I asked, reaching for the hotel robe to slide on.

"It's me, baby," Earnest answered. I don't think my feet touched the ground as I raced towards the door. I jumped into his arms nearly knocking the food containers out of his hand.

"I missed you. I'm sorry to see you under these circumstances, but I missed you so much," he whispered. "Now, close your robe woman before the whole place see your goods." I snatched it across my body before reaching for his suitcase. "Now, you know better than that. Get on in there and let me get this." I backpedaled into the room as he wheeled in his suitcase. Once the door was safely closed behind him I let my robe fall slack as I wrapped my arms around his waist. He walked me over to the table so that he could put down the food before whisking me into his arms as he took a seat in one of the chairs.

"I won't ask you if you're okay. I know you aren't. You loved both of your parents very much. I can't say I know how you feel either, because I still have mine. What I can say is that I love you and I'm grieving right along with you because they were good to me too. Remember how scared I was to meet them?"

"How could I forget? Momma had really started losing her faculties by then. She came on to you. I just thought I would die."

"She wasn't doing nothing but showing that she had good taste," Earnest joked. "On her good days she would tell me all kinds of stories about Mr. Drexler. On her bad days she would go to a real dark place. I wish I had met her before she got sick, but I was glad to know what little of her that I knew."

"Daddy thought very highly of you. He used to say that he didn't understand why you had these strings in your hair." I fingered his dreads. "But, he understood that you loved me and that was all that mattered. Every guy who I ever thought about before then, he turned down without thinking about it. You came in the house and got drilled by the whole crew and just took it in stride. He said that meant you weren't a bitch." We both chuckled at that. Daddy was never one to pull punches.

"Do you ever wish we had given them grandbabies?" Earnest asked. I looked at him funny.

"What made you ask that?"

"I just wondered. That was the only thing we never gave them."

"To be honest, once momma died and daddy was still on the road, I figured he would never have time for a grandchild. You gotta understand, they were on the road my whole life just about until momma got real sick. By that time, I was going to school. My grandparents basically raised me. I think that my grandfather was both proud of daddy and disappointed in him because he didn't spend as much time with me as he could've. They're just some people that have things that they're destined to do. My daddy was destined to sing all over the world. He wasn't destined to be tied down. I get it now."

"I'm glad you can look at it that way. I think that's one of the things that my mother loves so much about you. She always wanted a daughter. That was all she ever talked about. Then when I brought you home, it was over. She was not about to let me marry anybody else. The good thing about you is that you have the sweetness of your mother with the determination of your father. You don't take shit from nobody. I wasn't worried about those old guys being with you. I said my baby is rough. They have no idea what they are in for. At the end of the day, I hope you had some needed conversations with him."

"Baby, I learned a lifetime of things. Some of them I wish I had never found out. What you got smelling so good?"

"I thought you would never ask. It just so happens that momma made a big dinner last night. When I told her what happened, she told me that she didn't want you eating any greasy restaurant food, so she sent some baked chicken, yellow rice, peas, cornbread, pinto beans, all kinds of stuff. She still overdoes the meals sometimes even though me, Emma, and Erin have been out of the house for years." He didn't have to tell me twice. I hopped off of his lap to wash my hands. Earnest was always gentle with me, but that night he was angelic. That night as I laid in his arms listening to him snore softly, a realization came over me. This whole trip had been just as much about saying goodbye as it was about making amends. It finally resonated with me. In his own clever way, daddy was trying to explain his whole life over the course of just a few days. He wanted me to know that I was always loved. He wanted me to know that he made a lot of mistakes. I get the memo, daddy. Kiss my momma for me.

Chapter 50

Joanne 'Jumpstart' George

End of The Road

"Ronda? How far are we away from Detroit?" I asked in a panic.

"About a half an hour, why? What's wrong?" she asked, turning on her right blinker. I put my head down and cried into my hands. I can't believe Dick'Em is gone. I thought he would live the longest out of the five. I felt the car come to a stop and then a hand touched my shoulder. "Jumpstart, what's wrong? Who was that on the phone?"

I looked up with fresh tears on my face, "It was Audrey. She just lost her daddy. He had a stroke in his father's old church. The paramedics couldn't revive him."

"Damn, I can't believe ole' Drexler went out like that," Charlene barely whispered. "I remember when he told us he had the sugar. I thought that would take him out before anything else but a stroke?" She shook her head before covering her face.

"That's crazy," Ronda whispered. "I remember when I met ole' Dick'Em," she chuckled. "He was all posted up against the wall outside of Mean Lady's one day I walked past. He reached out and caught my arm before I crossed the threshold," she smiled. "I remember looking up at him and thinking, damn he's tall. I recall him staring down at me licking his lips. As soon as he opened his mouth to speak, Razor walked up and slapped his hand down. They had a stare down right there in the middle of the sidewalk. I thought they were gone come to blows and of course I was scared for him because Raymond always carried a razor in his mouth," she chuckled.

"I went to diffuse the situation when they both laughed and slapped hands. I was still confused until Raymond introduced us and I found out it was his brother. They never acknowledged one another without saying the word brother. It was like they needed that semblance to fit in and they found it one another. When one person came for them it was always five against one," she laughed.

"They never fought a battle alone. Not even this last one." She wiped her tears away and closed her eyes.

"Well, looks like we can either go to Detroit or head back to Chicago," Bertha spoke.

"We're going to Detroit, Charlene. Audrey needs us," I voiced.

"Yeah, whatever," 'Pop Rocks' tried to mumble under her breath.

"You got one more time, Charlene. Just one more time and you ain't gotta worry about Jumpstart," Ronda spit out angrily.

"Here it is this baby needs us, and you sitting back there with your face bawled up. Let me hurry up and get away from you," she continued, while putting the blinker on to get back out in traffic.

"Can y'all turn some music on?" Bertha asked from the backseat.

"I ain't turning on shit," I huffed as Ronda completely ignored her.

"Fine. I'm not the one to be mad at. Hell, I lost my damn husband too ya know," Bertha snapped.

“We are all on edge right now, Bertha. Music is not gonna help. If anything, it will bring back more bad memories.

“Well that’s all you had to say. No need on going off on me when I am just trying to lighten the mood up a little bit. There’s just too much sadness in here. What we need to do is get these tears out, so we can carry on the rest of this journey,” Bertha suggested.

I closed my eyes as Bertha began to hum the lyrics to an old church hymn that I recognized.

“Swing low, sweet chariot

Coming for to carry me home,

Swing low, sweet chariot,

Coming for to carry me home.”

I laid back and closed my eyes and let sleep consume me. When I woke up, we were riding through downtown Detroit.

“Where we going?” I asked, sitting up.

“Colin, one of the cameramen said that they were at the Crowne Plaza,” Ronda responded, shrugging her shoulders. “I hope you don’t mind, but I had answered your phone since you were sleeping so peacefully

“I know where that is, it’s kinda pricey but I got us this time around.”

I needed a hot shower and a comfy bed. I had been on the road for hours and I was bone tired.

After getting our rooms and going our separate ways I was finally able to relax. I had to call my husband and let him know what was going on. I knew he was worried about me because I hadn't talked to him in two days it seemed.

Throwing my duffle up on the bed. I gathered the things I would need for my shower and headed in that direction. I sat under the spray of the water for more than ten minutes before I washed my body, threw on my underwear and crashed.

Knock * Knock

"Ugh," I grumbled as I threw the covers back. I picked up my phone and the time read 1:20 AM. *Who in the hell?* I asked myself, throwing my legs over the side of the bed and making my way to the door. Peeking through the peephole I didn't see anyone.

Knock * Knock

"Who is it?" I yelled.

"It's me, Velvet."

I stood there stark still.

"Open the door, woman. I know you in there now," he coughed.

"Let me go throw something on," I reasoned.

"Well hurry up. I'm not finna be out here all night."

I ran across my room to my duffle bag where I snatched on a pair of yoga shorts and a wife beater. Rushing back to the door, I pulled it open.

“So, you just gone stand there and look at me all crazy, Jumpstart, or are you gone let a nigga in?”

“I’m sorry,” I said, stepping to the side so he could roll himself in. The last time I saw Velvet, he was 6 feet 5 inches of athletic muscle. He had the whitest smile and the most beautiful brown eyes. He was bold, beautiful, and bullheaded. This man sitting in front of me was not the man I fell in love with. This man was aged, frail, but yet and still, bullheaded.

“So, I guess you heard about ole’ Drexler, huh?”

I nodded my. “Yeah, I did. How is Audrey holding up?” I asked concerned.

“How in the hell you think she holding up?”

“I just asked yo’ strong neck ass a question. You ain’t gotta talk to me like that.”

“Well, stop actin’ like you ain’t got the God given sense He gave you.”

“You know what, I ain’t got time for yo’ shit. So, you can just roll yo’ ass on up outta here,” I voiced, stomping over towards the door.

“You still feisty I see,” he smiled. “You remember when we had that backyard barbeque and you shot the backyard up?” he chuckled.

“I remember that. That was the day that Baltimore chick showed up at my house talking about she was pregnant by you,” I responded with my eyes squinted.

“You was always the wild card.”

“And you made me that way,” I responded.

"Girl, you was crazy way before I met you though."

"I might've been, but you enhanced it."

Velvet laughed that silky laugh that used to get him anything he wanted.

"Come here, Jumpstart." I waltzed across the floor in his direction.

"Sit down, I wanna talk to you about something important."

"Ugh," I groaned.

"Groan one more time, Jumpstart. Just one more time, you hear."

"And what you gone do?" I wanted to know.

"Can you just sit yo' *'always gotta have the last word'* ass down somewhere, damn," he said angrily and soon began to cough.

"Fine," I said, handing him a bottle of water.

"Now, what I gotta say, I need you to be quiet to receive it."

I nodded my head. "I mean it, Jumpstart."

"Okay, damn," I huffed.

"Now look, I gave Audrey some papers to give to you and the kids in case something happens to me. I need you to know that even though I wasn't a good man to you, that I was the best man I knew how to be. This trip has taught me a lot and even though I still have some bad ways about myself, I've learned how to forgive," he sniveled.

"I thought when I got to a certain age that I would wanna settle down and be that man for that special lady, but it just wasn't in me. I looked at Dick'Em today and before he died he had the world on his shoulders. The moment they rolled him past me to the coroner van, I knew he was at peace. I know it may be frightening for some to die, especially with not knowing that this could possibly be the last breath you'll ever take. I wasn't afraid to die until I realized that I was the last one standing. Then it hit me, where will I go when all this is over? Then I thought about my kids. I have about nine kids out there, if not more, and they don't even know me. I didn't take up the time I needed to step up to the plate and handle my responsibilities like a man. But in death, they shall be taken care of.

"I want you to know, that I'm sorry." He leaned forward and took my hands into his shaky ones. "I'm sorry for hurting you. I'm sorry for not believing in what we could've been. I'm sorry for not being the man you needed me to be and for not being the father that my dad was to me. Before I walk outta this room, Joanne, I must know that you forgive me." The tears coated his chocolate, sand-colored cheeks as he waited for my response.

I cleared my throat and held on to Velvet's shaking hands. "I forgave you a long time ago. It was right after the night we made love for the last time. You held me and told me you would never love me the same way I loved you. I cried into your chest that night because I knew that I had to let you go and also, I was getting married a few short weeks after it happened. I couldn't carry you with me throughout my marriage. I knew I had to love you at a distance. I knew you wasn't meant for me because God didn't send you when I needed you the most; he sent my husband. I will always love you and yes, I do forgive you."

I rose to my feet and kissed his lips one final time before watching him turn his back and leave my room. I sighed and laid back on the bed and allowed my thoughts and once again sleep, consumed me.

Chapter 51

Jumpstart

Standing Still

It had been two days since Dick'Em's passing and since we were in his hometown, Audrey decided to have a small gathering with just his close friends and family. I called Bertha and she agreed to fly in, so she could pay her final respects. Since she had Po-Man cremated, we hadn't gotten a chance to honor him the way I would've liked. We waited outside Detroit Metropolitan waiting for her to get off the plane.

"I wonder how she's holding up? I haven't talked to her since she caught the Amtrak back home," I asked, looking around at all the pedestrians.

"Well, I talked to her a few days before Drexler's passing. She was getting the house together. She's talking about selling it," Ronda barely whispered.

"She can't do that. That house holds the most memories."

"Which is probably why she's selling it," 'Pop Rocks' said, looking out the window.

"It's just wrong, you know," I responded.

"Jumpstart, why is it wrong? Would you wanna sit in the house that produced and shattered your dreams? That woman went through hell. She sewed all of the fellas' clothes. That wasn't always appreciated. She looked out for us when Audra passed away and we treated her like she was second best. Then she had to deal with Po-Man's cheap ass 24/7 and not to mention the countless miscarriages. The house of laughter and tears is what she should call it. If those walls could talk they'll probably tell her to pack her shit up and what she don't pack, she needs to burn to the ground," Ronda reasoned.

"We can't let her sell the house. Even if she does wanna sell. I can just buy it."

"Jumpstart, why would you wanna buy that two-bedroom shack?" 'Pop Rock's asked.

"Because, it's a part of our history. Bertha's is where it all started," I chuckled.

"There she is," Ronda pointed excitedly as she pushed the door open.

Bertha looked around and when she noticed us she smiled before opening her wide arms and pulling us into a hug.

"Dry them tears, ladies. Let's go say goodbye to our brother."

We rode back to the hotel in silence. Audrey hadn't stopped by since I'd been here, but she kept sending that Colin boy down there to check on me. 'Pop Rocks' was a pain in everyone's ass, so they stayed clear of her and poor Ronda was off in her head more than anybody else. I was starting to think her mind was slipping. She would be crying one minute and laughing the next.

"Bertha, come on in here and make yourself comfortable. We going down to the cemetery in a few hours so I'mma need you to pull it together," I stated as I tossed my keycard on the desk and my purse in the chair.

"I got something real fancy," she said, throwing her bag on the bed.

"Bertha, now I know what fancy is but what's your kinda fancy?"

"Let me show you," she smiled, unzipping her patched up suitcase. "Ta-da," she said wearing a smile.

"Nope, you not finna do this today, Bertha." I shook my head.

"Do what? What's wrong with it?"

"It's all wrong. What is this?" I asked, pointing at the strange material.

"That's one of Willie's old suits, and this one-," she pointed, turning the material around, "Is one of Raymond's," she smiled. "Oh, and right here," she stretched the material out. "This here, this is for Razor, the last patch on the elbow I added from Audra's night gown and Dick'Em's pajama pants," she chuckled. I couldn't believe my eyes. She had to have stolen a smock from a barber shop because she had razor patches all over this patched-work dress she done made clearly out of boredom.

"You can't wear that, Bertha."

"Well, what am I supposed to wear? This the only thang I brought besides my mu-mu's."

I slapped my hand across my forehead and picked up my phone.

"Give me your size, Bertha."

"My size?"

"Yes," I said, holding my phone to my ear.

"My size is whatever I throw together. Now this dress, is my size," she confirmed.

"It's cool, Bertha, I got you. Why don't you go and get washed up." She nodded her head and walked away.

We had about a little over two hours to meet up and head over to the cemetery. Bertha was getting her hair and nails done. I quickly whisked her off to the nearest department store and since I didn't know her size, she tried them all on until we found the perfect one.

"Y'all ready?" 'Pop Rocks' asked as she busted up in the room with a cigarette dangling from her lip.

"Yeah, just waiting on Bertha," I said, fixing the collar on my shirt.

"Why you got on a suit? You look like that one girl, what's her name," she asked. flicking her ashes on the carpet. "She played in that one Tyler Perry movie. What was her name? Umph, I got it," she snapped her fingers. "Janet Jackson," 'Pop Rocks' chuckled.

"Bertha, come on," I called out.

"Here I come."

I could hear her heels as they clacked across the floor.

"Damn, if I was one of them dyke things, I would try to talk to you," Ronda smiled.

Bertha stood before us in a black off the shoulder dress, nothing too fancy. I had them sweep her hair up in a bun, while also lightly beating her face to the God's. I had no idea that ole Bertha was built like a brickhouse being that she wore all them damn mu-mu's. "

"Let's go ladies," I ordered. We all climbed in my car and headed over to the cemetery. I looked up at the sky and I could see the storm clouds rolling in. I said a small prayer as I followed the GPS to Woodlawn Cemetery.

After driving around for a few minutes, Bertha pointed to the small crowd gathered on the grass. "There they are."

I pulled the car in behind Audrey's husband's car and we all piled out.

"Who is that fine drink of water?" 'Pop Rock's whispered, hoisting up her skirt.

"That's Audrey's husband, Ernest," I whispered back.

"Bitch, don't start acting like you ain't got no home training," Ronda spoke from behind us.

"Have y'all been like this since I left?" Bertha asked.

"Yup," I huffed as I walked over to Audrey giving her a hug. "I'm sorry, baby," I said, rubbing her back soothingly. "Your daddy was a good man." She nodded her head in my chest and continued to cry.

"Come here, baby," Bertha stuck her arms out. "I know you don't wanna hear this right now, but your daddy is in a better place."

"AMEN!" 'Pop Rocks' co-signed, lighting a cigarette.

Bertha cut her eyes at her before she continued, "I know you have your husband for times like these, but if you ever need me, I'm only a phone call away. You hear me, baby?"

"Yes ma'am," Audrey mumbled as she looked up.

"Are we ready?" the pastor questioned impatiently like we was wasting his time.

"Yeah, we ready; you got somewhere to be Pastor?" 'Pop Rocks' asked, flicking her cigarette in an empty grave.

"Umm no," he said, clearing his throat.

"That's what I thought," she responded while flickin' her wrist back and forth signaling for him to carry on.

"We meet here today to honor and pay tribute to the life of Drexler Davis and to express our love and admiration. We're also here to bring some comfort to those of his family and friends who are here and have been deeply hurt by his sudden demise. Today is also a day for memories, today will be remembered for many reasons, but mainly I hope it will be remembered by you all; as a very special day, even though we've come to say a sad and fond farewell to a wonderful man. A man whom we were all so very privileged to have known. We've come together from different places, and we're all at different stages on our journey throughout life. Our paths are varied, and we look at life in different ways. But there is one thing we all have in common, at one point or another, and to some degree, our lives, have also touched the life of Drexler's. I know today is a sad day, but I hope at the end of this farewell ceremony that you will feel glad that you took the opportunity to do some of your grieving in the presence of others who have known and loved him."

There wasn't a dry eye in attendance. We was all a blubbering mess. I tried being strong for Audrey, but she was being a pillar of salt for us.

"I heard that there was a song someone wanted to sing," The pastor looked up closing his Bible.

Myself, Bertha, 'Pop Rocks', and Sharonda stood to our feet. We wrapped our arms around one another and smiled. We all took a deep breath and hummed the harmony. Bertha closed her eyes and the most angelic of notes left her lips in a whisper.

"Not a second

Not a moment

Since you came into my life

Have I ever had to worry

About life's pain and strife's

You carried me over dangers

Both seen and unseen

You knew what was best for me

When I thought you were being mean

You made a way

Always made a way"

We finished the song as the pastor walked over. Standing at the foot of Dick'Em's casket, he bowed his head.

"In sure and certain hope of the resurrection to eternal life through our Lord Jesus Christ, we commend to Almighty God our brother, Drexler Davis, and we commit his body to the ground; earth to earth; ashes to ashes; dust to dust."

Audrey nodded her head at the gravediggers and we watched as they lowered Dick'Em into the ground. I walked over and picked up a fist full of dirt and threw it on top of his casket. "I love you, man. Keep me a spot open." I kissed my fingers and held them up to the sky before turning on my heels and heading back in the direction of my vehicle. It was time to go home.

Chapter 52

Audrey

The applause was so loud as the closing credits began to roll that I plugged my ears with my fingers for a second. Ernest had tears in his eyes as he mouthed, "I love you, babe."

I mouthed it back as a camera flashed in my face. For at least ten minutes, I stood there on stage transfixed by the response. Blair, who was supposed to have taken his seat already, walked behind me gently placing a hand on the small of my back for support. I glanced down at his initials before dabbing at my own eyes. He just didn't know that he was not getting this back.

"Please, if you'll please take your seats. There's something else that I must do."

I lowered my hands gesturing for everyone to take a seat. It still took a while to get complete silence.

"As you all know, composing any type of film can take such a long time. In that time, so many things can transpire. You got a glimpse into the lives of these men that I loved and admired, and you saw all of them go on to their reward. All of them except for my Uncle Benny or as you know him, 'Velvet Rose'. It has been a year and a half since we wrapped up filming and released the documentary and, in that time, his health has taken a dip. As the last remaining member of *Member's Only*, I think it's only right that we pay homage to him. Parkinson's may have taken away his speech and limited his movements, but he's still among us and what many would consider a national treasure. As he comes, I would like for you all to direct your attention to the monitors as we have one last scene that was not included."

Using my hand to shield my eyes from the bright stage lights, I glanced out into the sea of people until I located four rows from the front, my aunts Bertha, Charlene, and Sharonda, but Joannee was missing. It was when I heard the round of applause that I turned to my left where she was dressed in a beautiful gold evening gown, pushing Uncle Benny who was smiling as hard as he could muster in his matching gold blazer. I began to clap myself as she stopped center stage where she kissed him on his cheek before locking his wheelchair. Her husband joined her at the stairs where he helped her offstage and to her seat. It touched me how selfless he had to have been to allow her to do this one thing for a man she was in love with for many years.

"Keep it together, Audrey," I whispered to myself as the sound of Uncle Benny's voice began to boom through the speakers. I took a seat next to Blair as we turned our attention to the screen.

"Hey now. If you're watching this, then it means that I've finally lost my ability to speak. For a while now, I've been struggling to talk and everything, but I been trying to play it off. If you see me sitting here shaking it ain't because I'm doing a new dance," the audience laughed.

"It's because this damn Parkinson's done got me down. That's okay though because y'all got this damn camera in my face so I can say what I wanna."

Uncle Benny reached inside of his breast pocket grabbing a pair of reading glasses that Colin had to help him put on.

“Reach over there in that bag and hand me that there letter. Don’t be tryna’ be nosey either,” he directed Colin. The audience chuckled again.

“Alright now, y’all don’t mind the wording. I had a little bit to smoke the night I wrote this. Anyway, here it goes. Out of all of the things that y’all know about me, I think that one thing was kept hidden. I was not the best father to my nine or ten kids. Hell, I say ten because I lost count myself.” I couldn’t help but grin at that. “All the time on the road I was thinking about my brothers. I was thinking about my women, and I was thinking that I could use my money as a way to take care of my business. What I didn’t realize was, that my kids needed to see my face. They needed to be able to know about where they came from. I thought the occasional phone calls would suffice. Turns out, I was wrong. I got two sons in prison. Some of my girls got pregnant as teenagers. I got a daughter that sings and produces, and I even got two doctors out of the bunch. Sad to say, I’ve never been to any of their weddings. I haven’t met my grandchildren, and I have to die knowing that they may feel like I didn’t love them. I was the only one in *Members Only* that never got married. Being a playboy was what I was known to do. At any given moment I would have Jumpstart, Baltimore Brenda, Tahiti Sunrise, Flexi-Lexi, or that other one, her name slips my mind, but they was always on my arm.” The crowd for some reason cheered at that.

“Now, that's what I call a real playa,” Blair remarked, laughing.

“Tell me about it.”

“So anyhow, I was always with this woman or that one, searching for something I never really found. Well I did, but it was too late because I had already watched her walk into another man's arms. Somebody once told me that we can start our day over at any time. I believed that then and I still do now. With that being said I want to do this." He pointed weakly at something off screen. Colin walked over sitting a suitcase on his lap.

"This here is all the money I have in the world. Also, my insurance, my rights to my music, and a few personal items that I've sat aside for my children and their children. I'm not gonna say the amount, but I know it's enough to make sure that they don't want for nothing. One thing I always was in this business was a shark. Silky Struthers taught me everything I knew. Why you think none of us died broke? We did what everybody else said was impossible. Sam Cooke told me about the importance in owning our music and we took it to heart. We may not have been as well-known as some of these groups, but we had way more damn sense. Anyway, I want to give this to my children and their children. Not as an apology because it's too late, but as an investment in their future. On one last note, I want to say this. It was hard seeing my brothers all leave me. We fussed and fought like cats and dogs, but at the end of the day, blood couldn't have made us any closer. I felt cheated when they started going off to glory leaving me behind. When you've lost as many people as I have, you begin to feel that way. I will always remember the times we had. There was shit we actually couldn't put in this damn film because my black ass would be under the jail somewhere." He clapped his hands together chuckling.

"We were some fools. Razor had a hell of a body count. Dick'Em had more women than King Solomon. Po-Man was the only man I knew that would buy his draws from the thrift store. That Papa was a smooth one, but that thang was mean. He threw his wife off of more tours and vacations than we could count. Then there was me; I had more children than Saint Jude's Hospital. We was all fucked up in some kind of way but that's what made us so real. That's what made our music so different. We wrote what we lived. Now let me see if I can remember this little piece of song I been humming." Uncle Benny closed his eyes and tilted his head up toward the heavens.

"I'm thankful for what I've done

Thankful for what I've had

Thankful for all the good

Thankful for all the bad

The good Lord up in Heaven

Knew Just what I needed

Sending me my brother

Came from nothin' then succeeded

I know we made mistakes

Were human that's what we do

Can't wait to see them again

When we all come back to you"

There wasn't a dry eye in the house as the screen faded to black. Slowly, the lights on the stage came back on. Uncle Benny's shoulders heaved as the tears ran down his face. His hands shook so violently that I walked to the front of his chair placing his hands in mine. I knew he would not want cameras picking up on him being so emotional. He was all I had left, so I had a duty to protect him. I looked over my shoulder gesturing for Scott and Colin to join me on stage. Without having to be told, Colin grabbed the suitcase taking it down to Joannee and her husband. All of the other baby-mommas side-eyed that, but I didn't know them enough to entrust them with anything. All that was left to do was take a final bow. Since Uncle Benny couldn't, I spun around as elegantly as I knew how and curtsied before unlocking his breaks. He raised his left hand in a feeble attempt to say bye as I pushed him across the stage toward the wings. Scott looked puzzled as he ran over to me.

"Where are you going?"

"I'm done. That award is for you and Colin. It's because of you all that I was finally able to understand my parents and forgive them. That's something that money can't buy. Now if you'll excuse me. I have to leave while the crowd is still cheering, gotta keep them wanting more ... Daddy taught me that," I smiled, while turning on my heels and making my exit.

Made in the USA
Columbia, SC
27 July 2024

39435814R00240